Micah Steel
Dolan enjoye
rush of the
But now, fin
any room for love?

SHE NEEDS
A HERO

Two compelling, satisfying romances
by two fabulous, international
bestselling authors.

SHE NEEDS
A HERO

The Last Mercenary
DIANA PALMER

A Man Apart
GINNA GRAY

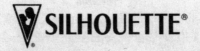 SILHOUETTE®

This collection is first published in Great Britain 2006
Silhouette Books, Eton House, 18-24 Paradise Road,
Richmond, Surrey TW9 1SR

SHE NEEDS A HERO © Harlequin Books S.A. 2006

The publisher acknowledges the copyright holders of the
individual works, which have already been published in the UK in
single, separate volumes, as follows:

The Last Mercenary © Diana Palmer 2001
A Man Apart © Virginia Gray 2000

ISBN-13: 978 0 373 60380 0
ISBN-10: 0 373 60380 0

064-0806

Printed and bound in Spain
by Litografía Rosés S.A., Barcelona

The Last Mercenary
DIANA PALMER

Dear Reader,

I do hope you enjoy reading this book. Callie Kirby helps Micah Steele lure the drug lord, Lopez, into a trap. In the process, Callie and Micah discover that the danger Lopez presents is equal to the danger of giving in to temptation. Can an independent woman settle for a man who has never known compromise—and can a mercenary give up the adrenalin rush of his lifestyle for the serenity of a small town?

Micah Steele has appeared in several books, and I thought he needed a longer book because of his complicated personal life—so he gets a Special Edition novel. I also like the chance to have an exotic location or two, particularly the Bahamas, where I have spent some of the loveliest days of my life. Nassau is such a beautiful blend of past and present, and I have a very special memories of watching the little tugboats turn the big passenger ships in the harbour, and walking through the straw market at Prince George Wharf.

Not that Texas has any less impact in my memories! I have seen the cattle market at Fort Worth, and I have stood where Bowie and Travis and Crockett stood and died. I have seen vast ranches and majestic cities. And I have loved even the smallest of the small Texas towns.

I have tried to show these wonderful places as I first saw them, with the same awe and sense of delight and wonder that I felt.

I hope you enjoy *The Last Mercenary*, and the surroundings where the story unfolds. As always, thank you so much for all your kindness and caring over the years. When you have a minute, stop by and visit me at www.dianapalmer.com or write to me care of Silhouette Books. I am slow to answer mail, but, oh, how I love to get it!

Love,

Diana Palmer

In memoriam, Brenda Lou Lilly Rogers.
My friend.

Chapter One

It had been a jarring encounter.

Callie Kirby felt chilled, and it wasn't just because it was November in south Texas. She watched the stepbrother she worshiped walk away from her as casually as if he'd moved around an obstacle in his path. In many ways, that was what Callie was to Micah Steele. He hated her. Of course, he hated her mother more. The two Kirby women had alienated him from the father he adored. Jack Steele had found his only son wrapped up in the arms of his young wife—Callie's mother—and an ugly scene had followed. Callie's mother, Anna, was sent packing. So was Micah, living mostly at his father's home while he finished his last year of residency.

That had been six years ago, and the breach still hadn't healed. Jack Steele rarely spoke of his son. That suited Callie. The very sound of his name was painful to her. Speaking to him took nerve, too. He'd once called her a gold digger like her mother, among other insults. Words could hurt. His always had. But she was twenty-two now, and she could hold her own with him. That didn't mean that her knees didn't shake and her heartbeat didn't do a tango while she was holding her own.

She stood beside her little second-hand yellow VW and watched Micah bend his formidable height to open the door of the black convertible Porsche he drove. His thick, short blond hair caught the sunlight and gleamed like gold. He had eyes so dark they looked black, and he rarely smiled. She didn't understand why he'd come home to Jacobsville, Texas, in the first place. He lived somewhere in the Bahamas. Jack had said that Micah inherited a trust fund from his late mother, but he'd sounded curious about his son's luxurious lifestyle. The trust, he told Callie privately, wasn't nearly enough to keep Micah in the Armani suits he wore and the exotic sports cars he bought new every year.

Perhaps Micah had finished his residency somewhere else and was in private practice somewhere. He'd gone to medical school, but she remembered that there had been some trouble in his last year of his residency over a lawsuit, stemming from a surgical procedure he refused to do. Neither she nor his father knew the details. Even when he'd been living with his father, Micah was a clam. After he left, the silence about his life was complete.

He glanced back at Callie. Even at a distance he looked worried. Her heart jumped in spite of her best efforts to control it. He'd had that effect on her from the beginning, from the first time she'd ever seen him. She'd only been in his arms once, from too much alcohol. He'd been furious, throwing her away from him before she could drag his beautiful, hard mouth down onto hers. The aftermath of her uncharacteristic boldness had been humiliating and painful. It wasn't a pleasant memory. She wondered why he was so concerned about her. It was probably that he was concerned for his father, and she was his primary caretaker. That had to be it. She turned her attention back to her own car.

With a jerk of his hand, he opened the door of the Porsche, climbed in and shot off like a teenager with his first car. The police would get him for that, she thought, if they saw it. For a few seconds, she smiled at the image of big, tall, sexy Micah being put in a jail cell with a man twice his size who liked blondes. Micah was so immaculate, so sophisticated, that she couldn't imagine him ruffled nor intimidated. For all his size, he didn't seem to be a physical man. But he was highly intelligent. He spoke five languages fluently and was a gourmet cook.

She sighed sadly and got into her own little car and started the engine. She didn't know why Micah was worried that she and his father might be in danger from that drug lord everyone locally was talking about. She knew that Cy Parks and Eb Scott had been instrumental in closing down a big drug distribution center, and that the drug lord, Manuel Lopez, had reputedly targeted them for revenge. But that didn't explain Micah's connection. He'd told her that he tipped law enforcement officials to a big drug cargo of Lopez's that had subsequently been captured, and Lopez was out for blood. She couldn't picture her so-straitlaced stepbrother doing something so dangerous. Micah wasn't the sort of man who got involved in violence of any sort. Certainly, he was a far cry from the two mercenaries who'd shut down Lopez's operation. Maybe he'd given the information to the feds for Cy and Eb. Yes, that could have happened, somehow. She remembered what he'd said about the danger to his family and she felt chilled all over again. She'd load that shotgun when she and Jack got home, she told herself firmly, and she'd shoot it if she had to. She would protect her stepfather with her last breath.

As she turned down the street and drove out of town, toward the adult day care center where Jack Steele stayed following his stroke, she wondered where Micah was going in such a hurry. He didn't spend a lot of time in the States. He hadn't for years. He must have been visiting Eb Scott or Cy Parks. She knew they were friends. Odd friends for a tame man like Micah, she pondered. Even if they ran cattle now, they'd been professional mercenaries in the past. She wondered what Micah could possibly have in common with such men.

She was so lost in thought that she didn't notice that she was being followed by a dark, late model car. It didn't really occur to her that anyone would think of harming her, despite her brief argument with Micah just now. She was a nonentity. She had short, dark hair and pale blue eyes, and a nice but unremarkable figure. She was simply ordinary. She never attracted attention from men, and Micah had found her totally resistible from the day they met. Why not? He could have any woman he wanted. She'd seen him with really beautiful women when she and her mother had first come to live with Jack Steele. Besides, there was the age thing. Callie was barely twenty-two. Micah was thirty-six. He didn't like adolescents. He'd said that to Callie, just after that disastrous encounter—among other things. Some of the things he'd said still made her blush. He'd compared her to her mother, and he hadn't been kind. Afterward, she'd been convinced that he was having an affair with her mother, who didn't deny it when Callie asked. It had tarnished him in her eyes and made her hostile. She still was. It was something she couldn't help. She'd idolized Micah until she saw him kissing her mother. It had killed something inside her, made her cold. She wondered if he'd been telling the truth when he said he hadn't seen her mother recently. It hurt to think of him with Anna.

She stopped at a crossroads, her eyes darting from one stop sign to another, looking for oncoming traffic. While she was engrossed in that activity, the car following her on the deserted road suddenly shot ahead and cut across in front of her, narrowly missing her front bumper.

She gasped and hit the brake, forgetting to depress the clutch at the same time. The engine died. She reached over frantically to lock the passenger door, and at the same time, three slim, dark, formidable-looking men surrounded her car. The taller of the three jerked open the driver's door and pulled her roughly out of the car.

She fought, but a hand with a handkerchief was clapped over her nose and mouth and she moaned as the chloroform hit her nostrils and knocked her out flat. As she was placed quickly into the back seat of the other car, another man climbed into her little car and moved it onto the side of the road. He joined his colleagues. The dark car turned around and accelerated back the way it had come, with Callie unconscious in the back seat.

Micah Steele roared away from the scene of his latest disagreement with Callie, his chiseled mouth a thin line above his square jaw. His big hands gripped the steering wheel with cold precision as he cursed his own lack of communication skills. He'd put her back up almost at once by being disparaging about the neat beige suit she was wearing with a plain white blouse. She never dressed to be noticed, only to be efficient. She was that, he had to admit. She was so unlike him. He seemed conservative in his dress and manner. It was a deception. He was unconventional to the core, while Callie could have written the book on proper behavior.

She hadn't believed him, about the danger she and her stepfather—his father—could find themselves in. Manuel Lopez wasn't the man to cross, and he wanted blood. He was going to go to the easiest target for that. He grimaced, thinking how vulnerable Callie would be in a desperate situation. She hated snakes, but he'd seen her go out of her way not to injure one. She was like that about everything. She was a sucker for a hard-luck story, an easy mark for a con artist. Her heart was as soft as wool, and she was sensitive; overly sensitive. He didn't like remembering how he'd hurt her in the past.

He did remember that he hadn't eaten anything since breakfast. He stopped to have a sandwich at a local fast-food joint. Then he drove himself back to the motel he was staying at. He'd been helping Eb Scott and Cy Parks get rid of Lopez's fledgling drug

distribution center. Just nights ago, they'd shut down
the whole operation and sent most of Lopez's people
to jail. Lopez's high-tech equipment, all his vehicles,
even the expensive tract of land they sat on, had been
confiscated under the Rico statutes. And that didn't
even include the massive shipment of marijuana that
had also been taken away. Micah himself had tipped
off the authorities to the largest shipment of cocaine
in the history of south Texas, which the Coast Guard,
with DEA support, had appropriated before it even
got to the Mexican coast. Lopez wouldn't have to
dig too deeply to know that Micah had cost him not
only the multimillion-dollar shipment, but the respect
of the cartel in Colombia as well. Lopez was in big
trouble with his bosses. Micah Steele was the reason
for that. Lopez couldn't get to Micah, but he could
get to Micah's family because they were vulnerable.
The knowledge of that scared him to death.

He took a shower and stretched out on the bed in
a towel, his hands under his damp blond hair while
he stared at the ceiling and wondered how he could
keep an eye on Callie Kirby and Jack Steele without
their knowing. A private bodyguard would stick out
like a sore thumb in a small Texas community like
Jacobsville. On the other hand, Micah couldn't do it
himself without drawing Lopez's immediate retalia-
tion. It was a difficult determination. He couldn't
make himself go back to the Bahamas while he knew
his father and Callie were in danger. On the other
hand, he couldn't stay here. Living in a small town
would drive him nuts, even if he had done it in the
past, before he went off to medical school.

While he was worrying about what to do next, the
telephone rang.

"Steele," he said on a yawn. He was tired.

"It's Eb," came the reply. "I just had a phone call from Rodrigo," he added, mentioning a Mexican national who'd gone undercover for them in Lopez's organization. He'd since been discovered and was now hiding out in Aruba.

"What's happened?" Micah asked with a feeling of dread knotting his stomach.

"He had some news from a friend of his cousin, a woman who knows Lopez. Have you seen Callie Kirby today?" Eb asked hesitantly.

"Yes," Micah said. "About two hours ago, just as she was leaving her office. Why?"

"Rodrigo said Lopez was going to snatch her. He sounded as if they meant to do it pretty soon. You might want to check on her."

"I went to see her. I warned her…!"

"You know Lopez," Eb reminded him somberly. "It won't do her any good even if she's armed. Lopez's men are professionals."

"I'll do some telephoning and get back to you," Micah said quickly, cursing his own lack of haste about safeguarding Callie. He hung up and phoned the adult day care center. Callie would surely be there by now. He could warn her…

But the woman who answered the phone said that Callie hadn't arrived yet. She was two hours late, and her stepfather was becoming anxious. Did Micah know where she was?

He avoided a direct answer and promised to phone her back. Then, with a feeling of utter dread, he climbed into the Porsche and drove past Kemp's law office, taking the route Callie would have taken to the adult day care center.

His heart skipped a beat when he reached the first intersection outside the city. At this time of day, there was very little traffic. But there, on the side of the road, was Callie's yellow VW, parked on the grass with the driver's door wide-open.

He pulled in behind it and got out, cursing as he noted that the keys were still in the ignition, and her purse was lying on the passenger seat. There was no note, no anything.

He stood there, shell-shocked and cold. Lopez had Callie. Lopez had Callie!

After a minute, he phoned Eb on his car phone.

"What do you want me to do?" Eb asked at once, after Micah had finished speaking.

Micah's head was spinning. He couldn't think. He ran a hand through his thick hair. "Nothing. You're newly married, like Cy. I can't put any more women in the firing line. Let me handle this."

"What will you do?" Eb asked.

"Bojo's in Atlanta visiting his brother, but I'll have him meet me in Belize tomorrow. If you have a number for Rodrigo, call it, and tell him to meet me in Belize, too, at the Seasurfer's Bar. Meanwhile, I'll call in the rest of my team." He was remembering phone numbers and jotting them down even as he spoke. "They're taking a holiday, but I can round them up. I'll go in after her."

Eb suggested calling the chief of police, Chet Blake, because he had contacts everywhere, including relatives in positions of power—one was even a Texas Ranger. Micah couldn't argue. If Eb wanted to tell the man, let him. He was going to get to Callie while she was still alive.

"Just remember that somebody in law enforcement is feeding information to Lopez, and act accordingly. I've got to make arrangements about Dad before I leave.''

"I'm sorry, Micah.''

"It's my fault,'' Micah ground out furiously. "I shouldn't have left her alone for a minute! I warned her, but what good did that do?''

"Stop that,'' Eb said at once. "You're no good to Callie unless you can think straight. If you need any sort of help, logistical or otherwise, I have contacts of my own in Mexico.''

"I'll need ordinance,'' Micah said at once. "Can you set it up with your man in Belize and arrange to have him meet us at that border café we used to use for a staging ground?''

"I can. Tell me what you want.''

Micah outlined the equipment he wanted, including an old DC-3 to get them into the Yucatán, from which his men would drop with parachutes at night.

"You can fly in under the radar in that,'' Eb cautioned, "but the DEA will assume you're trying to bring in drugs if they spot you. It'll be tricky.''

"Damn!'' Micah was remembering that someone in federal authority was on Lopez's payroll. "I had a contact near Lopez, but he left the country. Rodrigo's cousin might help, but he'd be risking his life after this latest tip he fed Rodrigo. So, basically, we've got nobody in Lopez's organization. And if I use my regular contacts, I risk alerting the DEA. Who can I trust?''

"I know someone,'' Eb said after a minute. "I'll take care of that. Phone me when you're on the ground in Cancún and make sure you've got global positioning equipment with you.''

"Will do. Thanks, Eb."

"What are friends for? I'll be in touch. Good luck."

"Thanks."

"Want me to call Cy?"

"No. I'll go by his place on my way out of town and catch him up." He hung up.

He didn't want to leave Callie's car with the door open and her purse in it, but he didn't want to be accused of tampering with evidence later. He compromised by locking it and closing the door. The police would find it eventually, because they patrolled this way. They'd take it from there, but he didn't want anyone in authority to know he was going after Callie. Someone had warned Lopez about the recent devastating DEA raid on his property. That person was still around, and Micah didn't want anyone to guess that he knew about Callie's kidnapping.

It was hard to think clearly, but he had to. He knew that Callie had a cell phone. He didn't know if she had it with her. Kemp, her boss, had let that slip to Eb Scott during a casual conversation. If Callie had the phone, and Lopez's people didn't know, she might be able to get a call out. He didn't flatter himself that she'd call him. But she might try to call the adult day care center, if she could. It wasn't much, but it gave him hope.

He drove to the center. For one mad instant he thought about speaking to his father in person. But that would only complicate matters and upset the old man; they hadn't spoken in years. He couldn't risk causing his father to have another stroke or a second

heart attack by telling him that Callie had been kidnapped.

He went to the office of the nursing director of the
center instead and took her into his confidence. She
agreed with him that it might be best if they kept the
news from his father, and they formulated a cover
story that was convincing. It was easy enough for
him to arrange for a nurse to go home with his father
to Callie's apartment every night and to drive him to
the center each day. They decided to tell Jack Steele
that one of Callie's elderly aunts had been hurt in a
car wreck and she had to go to Houston to see about
her. Callie had no elderly aunts, but Jack wouldn't
know that. It would placate him and keep him from
worrying. Then Micah would have to arrange for
someone to protect him from any attempts by Lopez
on his life.

He went back to his motel and spent the rest of
the night and part of the next day making international phone calls. He knew that Chet Blake, the police chief, would call in the FBI once Callie's disappearance was noted, and that wasn't a bad idea.
They would, of course, try to notify Micah, but they
wouldn't be able to find him. That meant that Lopez's man in law enforcement would think Micah
didn't know that his stepsister had been kidnapped.
And that would work to his benefit.

But if Lopez's men carried Callie down to the Yucatán, near Cancún, which was where the drug lord
lived these days, it was going to become a nightmare
of diplomacy for any U.S. agency that tried to get
her out of his clutches, despite international law enforcement cooperation. Micah didn't have that problem. He had Bojo, one of his best mercenaries, with

him in the States. It took time to track down the rest
of his team, but by dawn he'd managed it and arranged to meet them in Belize that night. He hated
waiting that long, and he worried about what Callie
was going to endure in the meantime. But any sort
of assault took planning, especially on a fortress like
Lopez's home. To approach it by sea was impossible.
Lopez had several fast boats and guards patrolling
the sea wall night and day. It would have to be a
land-based attack, which was where the DC-3 came
in. The trusty old planes were practically indestruc-
tible.

He couldn't get Callie's ordeal out of his mind.
He'd kept tabs on her for years without her knowledge. She'd dated one out-of-town auditor and a
young deputy sheriff, but nothing came of either relationship. She seemed to balk at close contact with
men. That was disturbing to him, because he'd made
some nasty allegations about her morals being as
loose as her mother's after she'd come on to him
under the mistletoe four years ago.

He didn't think words would be damaging, but
perhaps they were. Callie had a reputation locally for
being as pure as fresh snow. In a small town, where
everybody knew everything about their neighbors,
you couldn't hide a scandal. That made him feel even
more guilty, because Callie had been sweet and uninhibited until he'd gone to work on her. It was a
shame that he'd taken out his rage on her, when it
was her mother who'd caused all the problems in his
family. Callie's innocence was going to cost her
dearly, in Lopez's grasp. Micah groaned aloud as he
began to imagine what might happen to her now.
And it would be his fault.

He packed his suitcase and checked out of the motel. On the way to the airport, he went by Cy Parks's place, to tell him what was going on. Eb was doing enough already; Micah hated the thought of putting more on him. Besides, Cy would have been miffed if he was left out of this. He had his own reasons for wanting Lopez brought down. The vengeful drug lord had endangered the life of Cy's bride, Lisa, and the taciturn rancher wouldn't rest easy until Lopez got what was coming to him. He sympathized with Micah about Callie's kidnapping and Jack Steele's danger. To Micah's relief, he also volunteered to have one of his men, a former law enforcement officer, keep a covert eye on his father, just in case. That relieved Micah's troubled mind. He drove to the airport, left the rented Porsche in the parking lot with the attendant, and boarded the plane to Belize. Then he went to work.

Callie came to in a limousine. She was trussed up like a calf in a bulldogging competition, wrists and ankles bound, and a gag in her mouth. The three men who'd kidnapped her were conversing.

They weren't speaking Spanish. She heard at least one Arabic word that she understood. At once, she knew that they were Manuel Lopez's men, and that Micah had told the truth about the danger she and Jack were in. It was too late now, though. She'd been careless and she'd been snatched.

She lowered her eyelids when one of the men glanced toward her, pretending to still be groggy, hoping for a chance to escape. Bound as she was, that seemed impossible. She shifted a little, noticing with comfort the feel of the tiny cell phone she'd slipped into her slacks' pocket before leaving the office. If they didn't frisk her, she might get a call out. She remembered what she'd heard about Lopez, and her blood ran cold.

She couldn't drag her wrists out of the bonds. They felt like ropes, not handcuffs. Her arm was sore—she wondered if perhaps they'd given her a shot, a sedative of some sort. She must have been out a very long time. It had been late afternoon when she'd been kidnapped. Now it was almost dawn. She wished she had a drink of water....

The big limousine ate up the miles. She had some vague sensation that she'd been on an airplane. Perhaps they'd flown to an airport and the car had picked them up. If only she could see out the window. There were undefined shadows out there. They looked like trees, a lot of trees. Her vision was slightly blurred and she felt as if her limbs were made of iron. It was difficult to concentrate, and more difficult to try to move. What had they given her?

One man spoke urgently to the other and indicated Callie. He smiled and replied with a low, deep chuckle.

Callie noticed then that her blouse had come apart in the struggle. Her bra was visible, and those men were staring at her as if they had every right. She felt sick to her soul. It didn't take knowing the language to figure out what they were saying. She was completely innocent, but before this ordeal was over, she knew she never would be again. She felt a wave of grief wash over her. If only Micah hadn't pushed her away that Christmas. Now it was too late. Her first and last experience of men was going to be a nightmarish one, if she even lived through it. That seemed doubtful. Once the drug lord discovered that Micah had no affection for his stepsister, that he actually hated her and wouldn't soil his hands paying her ransom, she was going to be killed. She knew what happened in kidnappings. Most people knew. It had never occurred to her that she would ever figure in one. How ironic, that she was poor and unattractive, and that hadn't spared her this experience.

She wondered dimly what Micah would say when he knew she was missing. He'd probably feel well rid of her, but he might pay the ransom for her father's sake. Someone had to look after Jack Steele, something his only child couldn't apparently be bothered to do. Callie loved the old man and would have gladly sacrificed her life for him. That made her valuable in at least one way.

The one bright spot in all this was that once word of Callie's kidnapping got out, Micah would hire a bodyguard for Jack whether he wanted one or not. Jack would be safe.

She wished she knew some sort of self-defense, some way of protecting herself, of getting loose from the ropes and the gag that was slowly strangling her. She hadn't had time for lunch the day before and she'd been drugged for the whole night and into the next morning. She was sick and weak from hunger and thirst, and she really had to go to the bathroom. It was a bad day all around.

She closed her eyes and wished she'd locked her car doors and sped out of reach of her assailants. If there was a next time, if she lived to repeat her mistakes, she'd never repeat that one.

She shifted because her legs were cramping and she felt even sicker.

Listening to the men converse in Arabic, she realized her abductors weren't from Mexico. But as she looked out the window now, she could see the long narrow paved ribbon of road running through what looked like rain forest. She'd never been to the Yucatán, but she knew what it looked like from volumes of books she'd collected on Maya relics. Her heart sank. She knew that Manuel Lopez lived near Cancún, and she knew she was in the Yucatán. Her worst fears were realized.

Only minutes later, the car pulled into a long paved driveway through tall steel gates. The gates closed behind them. They sped up to an impressive whitewashed beach house overlooking a rocky bay. It had red ceramic tiles and the grounds were immaculate and full of blooming flowers. Hibiscus in November. She could have laughed hysterically. Back home the trees were bare, and here everything was blooming. She wondered what sort of fertilizer they used to grow those hibiscus flowers so big, and then she remembered Lopez's recent body count. She wondered if she might end up planted in his garden...

The car stopped. The door was opened by a suited dark man holding an automatic rifle of some sort, one of those little snub-nosed machine guns that crooks on television always seemed to carry.

She winced as the men dragged her out of the car and frog-marched her, bonds and all, into the ceramic tile floored lobby. The tile was black and white, like a chessboard. There was a long, graceful staircase and, overhead, a crystal chandelier that looked like

Waterford crystal. It probably cost two or three times the price of her car.

As she searched her surroundings, a small middle-aged man strolled out of the living room with his hands in his pockets. He didn't smile. He walked around Callie as if she were some sort of curiosity, his full lips pursed, his small dark eyes narrow and smugly gleaming. He jerked her gag down.

"Miss Kirby," he murmured in accented English. "Welcome to my home. I am Manuel Lopez. You will be my guest until your interfering stepbrother tries to rescue you," he added, hesitating in front of her. "And when he arrives, I will give him what my men have left of you, before I kill him, too!"

Callie thought that she'd never seen such cruelty in a human being's eyes in her life. The man made her knees shake. He was looking at her with contempt and possession. He reached out a stubby hand and ripped her blouse down in front, baring her small breasts in their cotton bra.

"I had expected a more attractive woman," he said. "Sadly you have no attractions with which to bargain, have you? Small breasts and a body that would afford little satisfaction. But Kalid likes women," he mused, glancing at the small, dark man who'd been sitting across from Callie. "When I need information, he is the man who obtains it for me. And although I need no information from you, Miss Kirby," he murmured, "it will please Kalid to practice his skills."

A rapid-fire burst of a guttural language met the statement.

"Español!" Lopez snapped. "You know I do not understand Arabic!"

"The woman," one of the other men replied in Spanish. "Before you give her to Kalid, let us have her."

Lopez glanced at the two thin, unshaven men who'd delivered Callie to him and smiled. "Why not? I make you a present of her. It should arouse even more guilt in her stepbrother to find her...used. But not until I tell you," he added coldly. "For now, take her to the empty servant's room upstairs. And put the gag back in place," he added. "I have important guests arriving. I would not want them to be disturbed by any unexpected noise."

"My stepbrother won't come to rescue me," she said hoarsely, shocked. "He isn't a physical sort of man. Aren't you going to ask him to pay ransom?"

Lopez looked at her as if she were nuts. "Why do you think Steele will not come after you?"

"He's a doctor. Or he was studying to be one. He wouldn't know the first thing about rescuing somebody!"

Lopez seemed to find that amusing.

"Besides that," she added harshly, "he hates me. He'll probably laugh his head off when he knows you've got me. He can't stand the sight of me."

That seemed to disturb Lopez, but after a minute he shrugged. *"No importa,"* he said lightly. "If he comes, that will be good. If not, it will make him even more concerned for his father. Who will be," he added with a cold smile, "next to feel my wrath."

Callie had her mouth open to ask another question, but at a signal from Lopez she was half dragged out of the room, her pale blue eyes as wide as saucers as she shivered with fear.

Chapter Two

Callie had never been in such danger in her life, although she certainly knew what it was to be manhandled. She'd been in and out of foster care since the age of six. On a rare visit home, one of her mother's lovers had broken her arm when she was thirteen, after trying to fondle her. She'd run from him in horror, and he'd caught up with her at the staircase. A rough scuffle with the man had sent her tumbling down the steps to lie sprawled at the foot of the staircase.

Her mother had been furious, but not at her boyfriend, who said that Callie had called him names and threatened to tell her mother lies about him. After her broken arm had been set in a cast, Anna had taken Callie right back to her foster home, making her out to be incorrigible and washing her hands of responsibility for her.

Oddly, it had been Jack Steele's insistence that he wanted the child that had pushed a reluctant Anna into taking her back, at the age of fifteen. Jack had won her over, a day at a time. When Micah was home for holidays, he'd taunted her, made his disapproval of her so noticeable that her first lesson in the Steele home was learning how to avoid Jack's grown son. She'd had a lot of practice at avoiding men by then, and a lot of emotional scars. Anna had found that amusing. Never much of a mother, she'd ignored Callie to such an extent that the only affection Callie ever got was from Jack.

She closed her eyes. Her own father had ripped her out of his arms when she was six and pushed her away when she begged to stay with him. She was some other man's bastard, he'd raged, and he wanted no part of her. She could get out with her tramp of a mother—whom he'd just caught in bed with a rich friend—and he never wanted to see either of them again. She'd loved her father. She never understood why he couldn't love her back. Well, he thought she wasn't his. She couldn't really blame him for feeling that way.

She was still sitting in a small bedroom that night, having been given nothing to eat or drink. She was weak with hunger and pain, because the bonds that held her wrists and ankles had chafed and all but cut off the circulation. She heard noise downstairs from time to time. Obviously Lopez's visitors had stayed a long time, and been quite entertained, from the sound of things. She could hear the soft whisper of the ocean teasing the shore outside the window. She wondered what they would do with her body, after they killed her. Perhaps they'd throw her out there, to be eaten by sharks.

While she was agonizing over her fate, the sky had darkened. Hours more passed, during which she dozed a little. Then suddenly, she was alone no longer. The door opened and closed. She opened her tired eyes and saw the three men who'd kidnapped her, gathered around her like a pack of dogs with a helpless cat. One of them started stripping her while the others watched. Her cell phone fell out of the pocket of her slacks as they were pulled off her long legs. One of the men tossed it up and laughed, speaking to another man in yet a different foreign language.

Callie closed her eyes, shivering with fear, and prayed for strength to bear what was coming. She wished with all her heart that Micah hadn't pushed her away that last Christmas they'd spent together. Better him than any one of these cold, cruel, mocking strangers.

She heard one of them speaking in rough Spanish, discussing her body, making fun of her small breasts. It was like a playback from one foster home when she was fifteen, where an older son of the family had almost raped her before he was interrupted by the return of his parents. She'd run away afterward, and been sent to another foster home. She'd been saved that time, but she could expect no help now. Micah wouldn't begin to know how to rescue her, even if he was inclined to save her. He probably wouldn't consider ransom, either. She was alone in the world, with no one who would care about her fate. Her mother probably wouldn't even be bothered if she died. Like Micah, she'd blamed Callie for what had happened.

Desperate for some way to endure the ordeal, to block it out, Callie pictured the last time she'd seen her grandmother before she passed away, standing in an arbor of little pink fairy roses, waving. Callie had often stayed with her father's widowed mother when he and Anna were traveling. It was a haven of love. It hadn't lasted. Her grandmother had died suddenly when she was five. Everyone she'd ever loved had left her, in one way or the other. Nobody would even miss her. Maybe Jack would. She spared one last thought for the poor old man who was as alone as she was. But with her out of the way, perhaps Micah would go home again...

There was a loud, harsh shout. She heard the door open, and the men leave. With a shivery sigh, she moved backward until she could ease down into a worn wing chair by the fireplace. It wasn't going to be a long reprieve, she knew. If only she could free herself! But the bonds were cutting into her wrists and ankles. She was left in only a pair of aged white briefs and a tattered white bra, worn for comfort and not for appearance. No one had seen her in her underwear since she was a small child. She felt tears sting her eyes as she sat there, vulnerable and sick and ashamed. Any minute now, those men would be back. They would untie her before they used her. She knew that. She had to try to catch them off guard the instant she was free and run. If she could get into the jungle, she might have a chance. She was a fast sprinter, and she knew woodcraft. It was the last desperate hope she had.

One of the men, the one who'd asked Lopez for

her, came back inside for a minute, staring at her. He pulled out a wicked looking little knife and flicked it at one shoulder strap of her bra, cutting right through it.

She called him a foul name in Spanish, making herself understood despite the gag. Her mind raced along. If she could make him angry enough to free her, which he'd have to do if he had rape in mind... She repeated the foul name, with more fervor.

He cursed. But instead of pulling her up to untie her, he caught her by the shoulder and pressed her hard back into the chair, easing the point of the knife against the soft, delicate upper part of her breast.

She moaned hoarsely as the knife lightly grazed her flesh.

"You will learn manners before we finish with you," he drawled icily, in rough Spanish. "You will do what I tell you!"

He made no move to free her. Instead, he jerked down the side of her bra that had been cut, and stared mockingly at her breast.

The prick from the knife stung. She ground her teeth together. What had she been thinking? He wasn't going to free her. He was going to torture her! She felt sick unto death with fear as she looked up into his eyes and realized that he was enjoying both her shame and her fear.

In fact, he laughed. He went back and locked the door. "We don't need to be disturbed, do we?" he purred as he walked back toward her, brandishing the sharp knife. "I have looked forward to this all the way from Texas..."

Her eyes closed. She said a last, silent prayer. She

thought of Micah, and of Jack. Her chin lifted as she waited bravely for the impact of the blade.

There was a commotion downstairs and a commotion outside. She'd hoped it might divert the man standing over her with that knife, but he was too intent on her vulnerable state to care what was going on elsewhere. He put one hand on the back of the chair, beside her head, and placed the point of the knife right against her breast.

"Beg me not to do it," he chuckled. "Come on. Beg me."

Her terrified eyes met his and she knew that he was going to violate her. It was in his face. He was almost drooling with pleasure. She was cold all over, sick, resigned. She would die, eventually. But in the meantime, she was going to suffer a fate that would make death welcome.

"Beg me!" he demanded, his eyes flashing angrily, and the blade pushed harder.

There was a sudden burst of gunfire from somewhere toward the front of the house. Simultaneously, there was shattering glass behind the man threatening her, and the sudden audible sound of bullets hitting flesh. The man with the knife groaned once and fell into a silent, red-stained heap at her feet.

Wide-eyed, terrified, shaking, Callie cried out as she looked up into a face completely covered with a black mask, except for slits that bared a little of his eyes and mouth. He was dressed all in black with a wicked looking little machine gun in one hand and a huge knife suddenly in the other. His eyes went to her nicked breast. He made a rough sound and kicked the man on the floor aside as he pulled Callie up out of the chair and cut the bonds at her ankles and wrists.

Her hands and feet were asleep. She almost fell. He didn't even stop to unfasten the gag. Without a word, he bent and lifted her over his shoulder in the classic fireman's carry, and walked straight toward the window. Apparently, he was going out it, with her.

He finished clearing away the broken glass around the window frame and pulled a long black cord toward him. It seemed to be hanging from the roof.

He was huge and very strong. Callie, still in shock from her most recent ordeal, her feet and hands almost numb, didn't try to talk. She didn't even protest. If this was a turf war, and she was being stolen by another drug lord, perhaps he'd just hold her for ransom and not let his men torture her. She had little to say about her own fate. She closed her eyes and noticed that there was a familiar smell about the man who was abducting her. Odd. He must be wearing some cologne that reminded her of Jack, or even Mr. Kemp. At least he'd saved her from the knife.

Her wounded breast hurt, where it was pressed against the ribbed fabric of his long-sleeved shirt, and the small cut was bleeding slightly, but that didn't seem to matter. As long as he got her out of Lopez's clutches, she didn't really care what happened to her anymore. She was exhausted.

With her still over his shoulder, he stepped out onto the ledge, grasped a thick black cord in a gloved hand and, with his rifle leveled and facing forward, he rappelled right out the second-story window and down to the ground with Callie on his shoulder. She gasped as she felt the first seconds of free fall, and her hands clung to his shirt, but he didn't drop her. He seemed quite adept at rappelling.

She'd read about the Australian rappel, where men went down the rope face-front with a weapon in one hand. She'd never seen it done, except on television and in adventure movies. She'd never seen anyone doing it with a hostage over one shoulder. This man was very skillful. She wondered if he really was a rival drug lord, or if perhaps he was one of Eb Scott's mercenaries. Was it possible that Micah would have cared enough to ask Eb to mount her rescue? Her heart leaped at the possibility.

As they reached the ground, she realized that her rescuer wasn't alone. As soon as they were on the ground, he made some sort of signal with one hand, and men dressed in black, barely visible in the security lights dotted along the dark estate, scattered to the winds. Men in suits, still firing after them, began to run toward the jungle.

A four-wheel-drive vehicle was sitting in the driveway with its engine running and the back seat door open, waiting.

Her rescuer threw her inside, climbed in beside her and slammed the door. She pulled the gag off.

"Hit it!" he bit off.

The vehicle spun dirt and gravel as it took off toward the gate. The windows were open. Gunfire hit the side of the door, and was returned by the man sitting beside Callie and the man in the front passenger seat. The other armed man had a slight, neatly trimmed beard and mustache and he looked as formidable as his comrade. The man who was driving handled the vehicle expertly, dodging bullets even as his companions returned fire at the pursuing vehicle.

Callie had seen other armed men in black running
for the jungle. She revised her opinion that these
were rival drug dealers. From the look of these men,
they were commandos. She assumed that these three
men were part of some sort of covert group sent in
to rescue her. Only one person would have the
money to mount such an expedition, and she'd have
bet money that Eb Scott was behind it somehow.
Micah must have paid him to hire these men to come
after her.

If he had, she was grateful for his intervention,
although she wondered what had prompted it. Perhaps his father had persuaded him. God knew, he'd
never have spent that sort of money on her rescue
for his own sake. Her sudden disappearance out of
his life would have delighted him.

She was chilled and embarrassed, sitting in her
underwear with three strange men, but her clothing
had been ripped beyond repair. In fact, her rescuer
hadn't even stopped to grab it up on his way out of
the room where she was being held. She made herself
as inconspicuous as possible, grateful that there was
no light inside the vehicle, and closed her eyes while
the sound of gunfire ricocheted around her. She
didn't say a word. Her companions seemed quite capable of handling this new emergency. She wasn't
going to distract them. If she caught a stray bullet,
that was all right, too. Anything, even death, would
be preferable to what she would endure if Lopez regained custody of her.

Half a mile down the road, there was a deep curve.
The big man who'd rescued Callie told the man in
front to stop the vehicle. He grabbed a backpack on
the floorboard, jumped out, pulled Callie out, and

motioned the driver and the man with the beard and mustache to keep going. The big man carried Callie out of sight of the road and dashed her down in the dark jungle undergrowth, his powerful body lying alongside hers in dead leaves and debris while they waited for the Jeep that had been chasing them to appear. Thorns dug into her bare arms and legs, but she was so afraid that she hardly noticed.

Suddenly, the pursuing Jeep came into sight. It braked for the curve, but it barely slowed down as it shot along after the other vehicle. Its taillights vanished around the bend. So far, so good, Callie thought, feeling oddly safe with the warmth and strength of the man lying so close beside her. But she hoped the man who was driving their vehicle and his bearded companion made a clean getaway. She wouldn't want them shot, even to save herself.

"That went well," her companion murmured curtly, rising. He pulled out some sort of electronic gadget and pushed buttons. He turned, sighting along it. "Can you walk?" he asked Callie.

His voice was familiar. Her mind must be playing tricks. She stood up, still in her underwear and barefoot.

"Yes. But I...don't have any shoes," she said hoarsely, still half in shock.

He looked down at her, aiming a tiny flashlight at her body, and a curse escaped his mouth as he saw her mangled bra.

"What the hell did they do to you?" he asked through his teeth.

Amazing, how familiar that deep voice was. "Not as much as they planned to, thanks to you," she said, trying to remain calm. "It's not a bad cut, just a graze. I'll have to have some sort of shoes if we're going to walk. And I...I don't suppose you have an extra shirt?'' she added with painful dignity.

He was holding a backpack. He pulled out a big black T-shirt and stuffed her into it. He had a pair of camouflage pants, too. They had to be rolled up, but they fit uncannily well. His face was solemn as he dug into the bag a second time and pulled out a pair of leather loafers and two pairs of socks.

''They'll be too big, but the socks will help them fit. They'll help protect your feet. Hurry. Lopez's men are everywhere and we have a rendezvous to make.''

She felt more secure in the T-shirt and camouflage pants. Not wanting to hold him up, she slipped quickly into the two pairs of thick socks and rammed her feet into the shoes. It was dark, but her companion had his small light trained ahead. She noticed that huge knife in his left hand as he started ahead of her. She remembered that Micah was left-handed...

The jungle growth was thick, but passable. Her companion shifted his backpack, so dark that it blended in with his dark gear and the jungle.

''Stay close behind me. Don't speak unless I tell you to. Don't move unless I move.''

''Okay,'' she said in a husky whisper, without argument.

''When we get where we're going, I'll take care of that cut.''

She didn't answer him. She was exhausted. She was also dying of thirst and hunger, but she knew there wasn't time for the luxury of food. She concentrated on where she was putting her feet, and prayed that she wouldn't trip over a huge snake. She knew there were snakes and lizards and huge spiders in the jungle. She was afraid, but Lopez was much more terrorizing a threat than a lonesome snake.

She followed her taciturn companion through the jungle growth, her eyes restless, her ears listening for any mechanical sound. The darkness was oddly comforting, because sound traveled so well in it. Once, she heard a quick, sharp rustle of the underbrush and stilled, but her companion quickly trained his light on it. It was only an iguana.

She laughed with delight at the unexpected encounter, bringing a curt jerk of the head from her companion, who seemed to find her amusement odd. He didn't say anything, though. He glanced at his instrument again, stopped to listen and look, and started off again.

Thorns in some of the undergrowth tore at her bare arms and legs, and her face. She didn't complain. Remembering where she'd been just before she was rescued made her grateful for any sort of escape, no matter how physically painful it might be.

She began to make a mental list of things she had to do when they reached safety. First on the list was to phone and see if Jack Steele was all right. He must be worried about her sudden disappearance. She didn't want him to suffer a setback.

Her lack of conversation seemed to puzzle the big man leading her through the jungle. He glanced back at her frequently, presumably to make sure she was behind him, but he didn't speak. He made odd movements, sometimes doubling back on the trail he made, sometimes deliberately snapping twigs and stepping on grass in directions they didn't go. Callie just followed along mindlessly.

At least two hours passed before he stopped, near a small stream. "We should be safe enough here for the time being," he remarked as he put down the backpack and opened it, producing a small bottle of water. He tossed it to Callie. "I imagine you're thirsty."

She opened it with trembling hands and swallowed half of it down at once, tears stinging her eyes at the pleasure of the wetness on her tongue, in her dry mouth.

He set up a small, self-contained light source, revealing his companion. He moved closer, frowning at her enthusiastic swallowing as he drew a first aid kit from his backpack. "When did you last have anything to drink?" he asked softly.

"Day...before yesterday," she choked.

He cursed. In the same instant, he pulled off the mask he'd been wearing, and Callie dropped the water bottle as her eyes encountered the dark ones of her stepbrother, Micah, in the dim light.

He picked up the water bottle and handed it back to her. "I thought it might come as a shock," he said grimly, noting her expression.

"You came after me yourself?" she asked, aghast. "But, how? Why?"

"Lopez has an agent in one of the federal agencies," he told her flatly. "I don't know who it is. I couldn't risk letting them come down here looking for you and having someone sell you out before I got here. Not that it would have been anytime soon. They're probably still arguing over jurisdictions as we speak." He pulled out a foil-sealed package and tossed it to her. "It's the equivalent of an MRE—a meal ready to eat. Nothing fancy, but if you're hungry, you won't mind the taste.''

"Thanks," she said huskily, tearing into it with urgent fingers that trembled with hunger.

He watched her eat ravenously, and he scowled. "No food, either?"

She shook her head. "You don't feed people you're going to kill," she mumbled through bites of chicken and rice that tasted freshly cooked, if cold.

He was very still. "Excuse me?"

She glanced at him while she chewed a cube of chicken. "He gave me to three of his men and told them to kill me." She swallowed and averted her eyes. "He said they could do whatever they liked to me first. So they did. At least, they started to, when you showed up. I was briefly alone with a smaller man, Arabic I think, and I tried to make him mad enough to release me so I had one last chance at escape. It made him mad, all right, but instead of untying me, he…put his knife into me." She chewed another cube of chicken, trying not to break down. "He said it was a…a taste of what to expect if I resisted him again. When you came in through the window, he was just about to violate me."

"I'm going to take care of that cut right now. Infection sets in fast in tropical areas like this." He opened the first-aid box and checked through his supplies. He muttered something under his breath.

He took the half-finished meal away from her and stripped her out of the T-shirt. She grimaced and lowered her eyes as her mutilated bra and her bare breast were revealed, but she didn't protest.

"I know this is going to be hard for you, considering what you've just been through. But try to remember that I'm a doctor,'' he said curtly. ''As near as not, anyway.''

She swallowed, her eyes still closed tight. ''At least you won't make fun of my body while you're working on it,'' she said miserably.

He was opening a small bottle. ''What's that?''

''Nothing,'' she said wearily. ''Oh God, I'm so tired!''

''I can imagine.''

She felt his big, warm hands reach behind her to unfasten the bra and she caught it involuntarily.

He glanced at her face in the small circle of light from the lantern. ''If there was another way, I'd take it.''

She drew in a slow breath and closed her eyes, letting go of the fabric. She bit her lip and didn't look as he peeled the fabric away from her small, firm breasts.

The sight of the small cut made him furious. She had pretty little breasts, tip-tilted, with dusky nipples. He could feel himself responding to the sight of her, and he had to bite down hard on a wave of desire.

He forced himself to focus on the cut, and nothing else. The bra, he stuffed in his backpack. He didn't dare leave signs behind them. There wasn't much chance that they were closely followed, but he had to be careful.

He had to touch her breast to clean the small cut, and she jerked involuntarily.

''I won't hurt you any more than I have to,'' he promised quietly, mistaking her reaction for pain. ''Grit your teeth.''

She did, but it didn't help. She bit almost through her lip as he cleaned the wound. The sight of his big, lean hands on her body was breathtaking, arousing even under the circumstances. The pain was secondary to the hunger she felt for him, a hunger that had lasted for years. He didn't know, and she couldn't let him know. He hated her.

She closed her eyes while he put a soft bandage over the cleaned wound, taping it in place.

"God in heaven, I thought I'd seen every kind of lowlife on earth, but the guy who did this to you was a class all by himself," he growled.

She remembered the man and shuddered. Micah was pulling the shirt down over her bandaged breast. "It probably doesn't seem like it, but I got off lucky," she replied.

He looked into her eyes. "It's just a superficial wound so you won't need stitches. It probably won't even leave a scar there."

"It wouldn't matter," she said quietly.

"It would." He got up, drawing her up with him. "You're still nervous of me, after all this time."

She didn't meet his eyes. "You don't like me."

"Oh, for God's sake," he burst out, letting go of her shoulders. He turned away to deal with the medical kit. "Haven't you got eyes?"

She wondered what that meant. She was too tired to work it out. She sat down again and picked up her half-eaten meal, finishing it with relish. It was hard to look at him, after he'd seen her like that.

She fingered the rolled-up pair of camouflage pants she was wearing. "These aren't big enough to be yours," she remarked.

"They're Maddie's. She gave me those for you, and the shoes and socks, on the way out of Texas," he commented when he noticed her curious exploration of the pants.

He worked with some sort of electronic device.

"What's that thing?" she asked.

"GPS," he explained. "Global positioning. I can give my men a fix on our position, so they can get a chopper in here to pick us up and pinpoint our exact location. There's a clearing just through there where we'll rendezvous," he added, nodding toward the jungle.

Suddenly she frowned. "Who's Maddie?" she asked.

"Maddie's my scrounger. Anything we need on site that we didn't bring, Maddie can get. She's quite a girl. In fact," he added, "she looks a lot like you. She was mistaken for you at a wedding I went to recently in Washington, D.C."

That was disturbing. It sounded as though he and this Maddie were in partnership or something. She hated the jealousy she felt, when she had no right to be jealous. Old habits died hard.

"Is she here?" she asked, still puzzled by events and Micah's strange skills.

"No. We left her back in the States. She's working on some information I need, about the mole working for the feds, and getting some of your things together to send on to Miami."

She blinked. "You keep saying 'we,'" she pointed out.

His chin lifted. He studied her, unsmiling. "Exactly what do you think I do for a living, Callie?" In the dim light, his blond hair shone like muted moonlight. His handsome face was all angles and shadows. Her vision was still a little blurred from whatever the kidnapper had given her. So was her mind.

"Your mother left you a trust," she pointed out.

"My mother left me ten thousand dollars," he replied. "That wouldn't pay to replace the engine on the Ferrari I drive in Nassau."

Her hands stilled on the fork and tray. Some odd ideas were popping into her head. "You finished your residency?" she fished.

He shook his head. "Medicine wasn't for me."

"Then, what…?"

"Use your mind, Callie," he said finally, irritated. "How many men do you know who could rappel into a drug lord's lair and spirit out a hostage?"

Her breath caught. "You work for some federal agency?"

"Good God!" He got up, moved to his backpack and started repacking it. "You really don't have a clue, do you?"

"I don't know much about you, Micah," she confided quietly as she finished her meal and handed him the empty tray and fork. "That was the way you always wanted it."

"In some cases, it doesn't pay to advertise," he said carelessly. "I used to work with Eb Scott and Cy Parks, but now I have my own group. We hire out to various world governments for covert ops." He glanced at her stunned face. "I worked for the justice department for a couple of years, but now I'm a mercenary, Callie."

She was struck dumb for several long seconds. She swallowed. It explained a lot. "Does your father know?" she asked.

"He does not," he told her. "And I don't want

him to know. If he still gives a damn about me, it would only upset him.''

"He loves you very much,'' she said quietly, avoiding his angry black eyes. "He'd like to mend fences, but he doesn't know how. He feels guilty, for making you leave and blaming you for what...what my mother did.''

He pulled out a foil sealed meal for himself and opened it before he spoke. "You blamed me as well.''

She wrapped her arms around herself. It was cold in the jungle at night, just like they said in the movies. "Not really. My mother is very beautiful,'' she said, recalling the older woman's wavy jet-black hair and vivid blue eyes and pale skin. "She was a model just briefly, before she married my...her first husband.''

He frowned. "You were going to say, your father.''

She shivered. "He said I wasn't his child. He caught her in bed with some rich man when I was six. I didn't understand at the time, but he pushed me away pretty brutally and said not to come near him again. He said he didn't know whose child I was. That was when she put me in foster care.''

Micah stared at her, unspeaking, for several long seconds. "Put you in what?''

She swallowed. "She gave me up for adoption on the grounds that she couldn't support me. I went into a juvenile home, and from there to half a dozen foster homes. I only saw her once in all those years, when she took me home for Christmas. It didn't last long.'' She stared down at the jungle floor. "When she married your father, he wanted me, so she told him I'd been staying with my grandmother. I was in a foster home, but she got me out so she could convince your father that she was a good mother.'' She laughed hollowly. ''I hadn't seen her or heard from her in two years by then. She told me I'd better make a good job of pretending affection, or she'd tell the authorities I'd stolen something valuable—and instead of going back into foster care for two more years, I'd go to jail.''

Chapter Three

Micah didn't say a word. He repacked the first-aid kit into his backpack with quick, angry movements. He didn't look at Callie.

"I guess you know how to use that gun," she said quietly. "If we're found, or if it looks like Lopez is going to catch us, I want you to shoot me. I'd rather die than face what you saved me from."

She said it in such a calm, quiet tone that it made all the more impact.

He looked up, scanning her drawn, white face in the soft light from the lantern. "He won't get you. I promise."

She drew a slow breath. "Thanks." She traced a fingernail over the camouflage pants. "And thanks for coming to get me. Lopez said he didn't have any plans to ransom me. He was going to let his men kill me because he thought it would make you suffer."

"What did you tell him?"

"That you were my worst enemy and you wouldn't care if he killed me," she said carelessly. "But he said you did care about your father, and he was the next victim. I hope you've got someone watching Dad," she added fervently. "If anything happens to him…!"

"You really love him, don't you?" he asked in an odd tone.

"He's the only person in my whole life who ever loved me," she said in a strained whisper.

A harsh sound broke from his lips. He got up and started getting things together. He pulled out what looked like a modified cell phone and spoke into it. A minute later, he put it back into the backpack.

"They're on the way in." He stood over her, his face grim as he picked up the small lantern and extinguished the light. "I know you must be cold. I'm sorry. I planned a quick airlift, so I didn't pack for a prolonged trek."

"It's all right," she said at once. "Cold is better than tortured."

He cursed under his breath as he hefted the backpack. "We have to get to that small clearing on the other side of the stream. It isn't deep, but I can carry you…"

"I'll walk," she said with quiet dignity, standing up. It was still painful to move, because she'd been tied up for so long, but she didn't let on. "You've done enough already."

"I've done nothing," he spat. He turned on his heel and led the way to the bank of the small stream, offering a hand.

She didn't take it. She knew he found her repulsive. He'd even told her mother that. She'd enjoyed taunting Callie with it. Callie had never understood why her mother hated her so much. Perhaps it was because she wasn't pretty.

"Walk where I do," he bit off as he dropped his hand. "The rocks will be slippery. Go around them, not over them."

"Okay."

He glanced over his shoulder as they started over the shallow stream. "You're damned calm for someone who's been through what you have in the past two days."

She only smiled. "You have no idea what I've been through in my life."

He averted his eyes. It was as if he couldn't bear to look at her anymore. He picked his way across to the other bank. Callie followed obediently, her feet cold and wet, her body shivering. Only a little longer, she told herself, and she would be home with Jack. She would be completely safe. Except...Lopez was still out there. She shivered again.

"Cold?" he asked when they were across.

"I'll be fine," she assured him.

He led her through one final tangle of brush, which he cut out of the way with the knife. She could see the silver ripple of the long blade in the dim light of the small flashlight he carried. She put one foot in front of the other and tried to blank out what would happen if Lopez's men caught up with them. It was terrifying.

They made it to the clearing just as a dark, noisy silhouette dropped from the sky and a door opened.

"They spotted us on radar!" came a loud voice

from the chopper. "They'll be here in two minutes. Run!"

"Run as if your life depended on it!" Micah told Callie, giving her a push.

She did run, her mind so affected by what she'd already endured that she almost kept up with her long-legged stepbrother. He leaped right up into the chopper and gave her a hand up. She landed in a heap on the dirty floor, and laughed with relief.

The door closed and the chopper lifted. Outside, there were sounds like firecrackers in the wake of the noise the propellers made. Gunfire, Callie knew.

"It always sounds like firecrackers in real life," she murmured. "It doesn't sound that way in the movies."

"They augment the sound in movies, mademoiselle." A gentle hand eased her into a seat on the edge of the firing line Micah and two other men made at the door.

She looked up. There was barely any light in the helicopter, but she could make out a beard and a mustache on a long, lean face. "You made it, too!" she exclaimed with visible relief. "Oh, I'm glad. I felt bad that you and the other man had to be decoys, just to get me out."

"It was no trouble, mademoiselle," the man said gently, smiling at her. "Rest now. They won't catch us. This is an Apache helicopter, one of the finest pieces of equipment your country makes. It has some age, but we find it quite reliable in tight situations."

"Is it yours?" she asked.

He laughed. "You might say that we have access to it, and various other aircraft, when we need them."

"Don't bore her to death, Bojo," a younger voice chuckled.

"Listen to him!" Bojo exclaimed. "And do you not drone on eternally about that small computer you carry, Peter, and its divine functions?"

A dark-haired, dark-eyed young man with white teeth came into view, a rifle slung over his shoulder. "Computers are my specialty," he said with a grin. "You're Callie? I'm Peter Stone. I'm from Brooklyn. That's Bojo, he's from Morocco. I guess you know Micah. And Smith over there—" he indicated a huge dark-eyed man "—runs a seafood restaurant in Charleston, along with our Maddie and a couple of guys we seem to have misplaced…"

"We haven't misplaced them," Micah said curtly. "They've gone ahead to get the DC-3 gassed up."

Bojo grinned. "Lopez will have men waiting at the airport for us."

"While we're taking off where we landed—at Laremos's private airstrip," Micah replied calmly. "And Laremos will have a small army at his airstrip, just in case Lopez does try anything."

"But what about customs?" Callie voiced.

Everybody laughed.

She flushed, realizing now that her captors hadn't gone through customs, and neither had these men. "Okay, I get it, but what about getting back into the States from here? I don't have a passport…"

"You have a birth certificate," Micah reminded her. "It'll be waiting in Miami, along with a small bag containing some of your own clothes and shoes. That's why Maddie didn't come with us," he added smugly.

"Miami?" she exclaimed, recalling belatedly that he'd mentioned that before. "Why not Texas?"

"You're coming back to the Bahamas with me, Callie," Micah replied. "You'll be Lopez's priority now. He'll be out for revenge, and it will take all of us to keep you safe."

She gaped at him. "But, Dad..." she groaned.

"Dad is in good hands. So are you. Now try not to worry. I know what I'm doing."

She bit her lower lip. None of this was making sense, and she was still scared, every time she thought about Lopez. But all these men surrounding her looked tough and battle-hardened, and she knew they wouldn't let her be recaptured.

"Who's Laremos?" Callie asked curiously, a minute later.

"He's retired now," Micah said, coming away from the door. "But he and 'Dutch' van Meer and J. D. Brettman were the guys who taught us the trade. They were the best. Laremos lives outside Cancún on a plantation with his wife and kids, and he's got the equivalent of a small army around him. Even the drug lords avoid his place. We'll get out all right, even if Lopez has his men tracking us."

She averted her eyes and folded her arms tightly around her body.

"You are shivering," Bojo said gently. "Here." He found a blanket and wrapped it around her.

That one simple act of compassion brought all her repressed fear and anguish to the surface. She bawled. Not a sound touched her lips. But tears poured from her eyes, draping themselves hot and wet across her pale cheeks and down to the corner of her pretty bow mouth.

Micah saw them and his face hardened like rock.

She turned her face toward the other side of the helicopter. She was used to hiding her tears. They mostly angered people, made them more hostile. Or they showed a weakness that was readily exploited. It was always better not to let people know they had the power to hurt you.

She wrapped the blanket closer and didn't speak the rest of the way. She closed her eyes, wiping at them with the blanket. Micah spoke in low tones to the other men, and although she couldn't understand what he was saying, she understood that rough, angry tone. She'd heard it enough at home.

For now, all she wanted to do was get to safety, to a place where Lopez and the animals who worked for him couldn't find her, couldn't hurt her. She was more afraid now than she had been on the way out of Texas, because now she knew what recapture would mean. The darkness was a friend in which she could hide her fear, conceal her terror. The sound of the propellers became suddenly like a mechanical lullaby in her ears, lulling her, like the whispers of the deep voices around her, into a brief, fitful sleep.

She felt an odd lightness in her stomach and opened her eyes to find the helicopter landing at what looked like a small airstrip on private land.

A big airplane, with scars and faded lettering, was waiting with its twin prop engines already running. Half a dozen armed men in camouflage uniforms stood with their guns ready to fire. A tall, imposing man with a mustache came forward. He had a Latin look about him, dark eyes and graceful movement.

He shook hands with Micah and spoke to him quietly, so that his voice didn't carry. Micah listened, and then nodded. They shook hands again. The man glanced at Callie curiously, and smiled in her direction.

She smiled back, her whole young face drawn and fatigued.

Micah motioned to her. "We have to get airborne before Lopez's men get here. Climb aboard. Thanks, Diego!" he called to the man.

"No es nada," came the grinning reply.

"Was that the man you know, with the plantation?" Callie asked when they were inside and the door was closed.

"That was Laremos," he agreed.

"He and his family won't be hurt on our account, will they?" she persisted.

He glanced down at her. "No," he said slowly. His eyes searched hers until she looked away, made uneasy and shivery by the way he was looking at her.

He turned and made his way down the aisle to the cockpit. Two men poked their heads out of it, grinning, and after he spoke to them, they revved up the engines.

The passengers strapped themselves into their seats. Callie started to sit by herself, but Micah took her arm and guided her into the seat beside his. It surprised her, but she didn't protest. He reached across her to fasten her seat belt, bringing his hard, muscular chest pressing gently against her breasts.

She gasped as the pressure made the cut painful.

"God, I'm sorry! I forgot," he said, his hand going naturally, protectively, to her breast, to cup it gently. "Is it bad?"

She went scarlet. Of course, nobody was near

enough to see what was going on, but it embarrassed her to have him touch her with such familiarity. And then she remembered that he'd had her nude from the waist up on one side while he cleaned and bandaged that cut.

Her eyes searched his while she tried to speak. Her tongue felt swollen. Her breath came jerkily into her throat and her lips parted under its force. She felt winded, as if she'd fallen from a height.

His thumb soothed the soft flesh around the cut. "When we get to Miami, I'll take you to a friend of mine who's in private practice. We'll get you checked out before we fly out to the Bahamas."

His other arm, muscular and warm, was under her head. She could feel his breath, mint-scented and warm, on her lips as he searched her eyes.

His free hand left her breast and gently cupped her softly rounded chin. "Soft skin," he whispered deeply. "Soft heart. Sweet, soft mouth…"

His lips pressed the words against hers, probing tenderly. He caught her upper lip in both of his and tasted it with his tongue. Then he lifted away to look down into her shocked, curious eyes.

"You should hate me," he whispered. "I hurt you, and you did nothing, nothing at all to deserve it."

She winced, remembering how it had been when he'd lived with his father. "I understood. You resented me. My mother and I were interlopers."

"Your mother, maybe. Never you." He looked formidable, angry and bitter. But his black eyes were unreadable. "I've hesitated to ask. Maybe I don't really want to know. When Lopez had you," he began with uncharacteristic hesitation, "were you raped?"

"No," she said quietly. "But I was about to be. I remember thinking that if it hadn't all gone wrong that Christmas…" Her voice stopped. She was horrified at what she was about to say.

"I know," he interrupted, and he didn't smile. "I thought about it, too. What Lopez's damned henchmen did to you at least wouldn't have been your first experience of intimacy, if I hadn't acted like a prize heel with you!"

He seemed maddened by the knowledge. His hand on her face was hard and the pressure stung.

"Please," she whispered, tugging at his fingers.

He relaxed them at once. "I'm sorry," he bit off. "I'm still on edge. This whole thing has been a nightmare."

"Yes." She searched his black eyes, wishing she knew what he was thinking.

His thumb brushed softly over her swollen mouth. "Lopez will never get the chance to hurt you again," he said quietly. "I give you my word."

She bit her lower lip when his hand lifted away, shy of him. "Do you really think he'll come after me again?"

"I think he'll try," he said honestly.

She shivered, averting her eyes to the aisle beside them. "I hate remembering how helpless I was."

"I've been in similar situations," he said surprisingly. "Once I was captured on a mission and held for execution. I was tied up and tortured. I know how it feels."

She gaped at him, horrified. "How did you escape?"

"Bojo and the others came in after me," he said simply. "Under impossible odds, too." He smiled, and it was the first genuine smile he'd ever given her. "I guess they missed being yelled at."

She smiled back, hesitantly. It was new to relax with Micah, not to be on her guard against antagonistic and sarcastic comments.

He touched her face with a curious intensity in his eyes. "You must have been terrified when you were kidnapped. You've never known violence."

She didn't tell him, but she had, even if not as traumatically as she had at Lopez's. She lowered her gaze to his hard, disciplined mouth. "I never expected to be rescued at all, least of all by you. I wasn't even sure you'd agree to pay a ransom if they'd asked for one."

He scowled. "Why not?"

"You don't like me," she returned simply. "You never did."

He seemed disturbed. "It's a little more complicated than that, Callie."

"All the same, thank you for saving me," she continued. "You risked your own life to get me out."

"I've been risking it for years," he said absently while he studied her upturned face. She was too pale, and the fatigue she felt was visible. "Why don't you try to sleep? It's going to be a long flight."

Obviously he didn't want to talk. But she didn't mind. She was worn-out. "Okay," she agreed with a smile.

He moved back and she leaned her head back, closed her eyes, and the tension of the past two days caught up with her all at once. She fell asleep almost at once and didn't wake up until they were landing.

She opened her eyes to find a hard, warm pillow

under her head. To her amazement, she was lying across Micah's lap, with her cheek on his chest.

"Wakey, wakey," he teased gently. "We're on the ground."

"Where?" she asked, rubbing her eyes like a sleepy child.

"Miami."

"Oh. At the airport."

He chuckled. "*An* airport," he corrected. "But this one isn't on any map."

He lifted her gently back into her own seat and got to his feet, stretching hugely. He grinned down at her. "Come on, pilgrim. We've got a lot to do, and not much time."

She let him lead her off the plane. The other men had all preceded them, leaving behind automatic weapons, pistols and other paraphernalia.

"Aren't you forgetting your equipment?" she asked Micah.

He smiled and put a long finger against her mouth. His eyes were full of mischief. He'd never joked with her, not in all the years they'd known each other.

"It isn't ours," he said in a stage whisper. "And see that building, and those guys coming out of it?"

"Yes."

"No," he corrected. "There's no building, and those guys don't exist. All of this is a figment of your imagination, especially the airplane."

"My gosh!" she exclaimed with wide eyes. "We're working for the CIA?"

He burst out laughing. "Don't even ask me who they are. I swore I'd never tell. And I never will. Now let's go, before they get here."

He and the others moved rapidly toward a big

sport utility vehicle sitting just off the apron where they'd left the plane.

"Are you sure you cleared this with, uh—" Peter gave a quick glance at Callie "—the man who runs this place?"

"Eb did," Micah told him. "But just in case, let's get the hell out of Dodge, boys!"

He ran for the SUV, pushing Callie along. The others broke into a run as well, laughing as they went.

There was a shout behind them, but it was still hanging on the air when the driver, one of the guys in the cockpit, burned rubber taking off.

"He'll see the license plate!" Callie squeaked as she saw a suited man with a notepad looking after them.

"That's the idea," the young man named Peter told her with a grin. "It's a really neat plate, too. So is this vehicle. It belongs to the local director of the—" he hesitated "—of an agency we know. We, uh, had a friend borrow it from his house last night."

"We'll go to prison for years!" Callie exclaimed, horrified.

"Not really," the driver said, pulling quickly into a parking spot at a local supermarket. "Everybody out."

Callie's head was spinning. They got out of the SUV and into a beige sedan sitting next to it, with keys in the ignition. She was crowded into the back with Micah and young Peter, while the two pilots, one a Hispanic and the other almost as blond as Micah, crowded Bojo on either side in the front. The driver took off at a sedate pace and pulled out into Miami traffic.

That was when she noticed that all the men were wearing gloves. She wasn't. "Oh, that's lovely," she muttered. "That's just lovely! Everybody's wearing gloves but me. My fingerprints will be the only ones they find, and *I'll* go to prison for years. I guess you'll all come and visit me Sundays, right?" she added accusingly.

Micah chuckled with pure delight. "The guy who owns the SUV is a friend of Eb's, and even though he doesn't show it, he has a sense of humor. He'll double up laughing when he runs your prints and realizes who had his four-wheel drive. I'll explain it to you later. Take us straight to Dr. Candler's office, Don," he told the blond guy at the wheel. "You know where it is."

"You bet, boss," came the reply.

"I'm not going to prison?" Callie asked again, just to be sure.

Micah pursed his lips. "Well, that depends on whether or not the guy at customs recognizes us. I was kidding!" he added immediately when she looked ready to cry.

She moved her shoulder and grimaced. "I'll laugh enthusiastically when I get checked out," she promised.

"He'll take good care of you," Micah assured her. "He and I were at medical school together."

"Is he, I mean, does he do what you do?"

"Not Jerry," he told her. "He specializes in trauma medicine. He's chief of staff at a small hospital here."

"I see," she said, nodding. "He's a normal person."

Micah gave her a speaking glance while the others chuckled.

* * *

The hospital where Micah's friend worked was only a few minutes from the airport. Micah took Callie inside while the others waited in the car. Micah had a private word with the receptionist, who nodded and left her desk for a minute. She came back with a tall, dark-headed man about Micah's age. He motioned to Micah.

Callie was led back into an examination room. Micah sank into a chair by the desk.

"Are you going to sit there the whole time?" Callie asked Micah, aghast, when the doctor asked her to remove the shirt she was wearing so he could examine her.

"You haven't got anything that I haven't seen, and I need to explain to Jerry what I did to treat your wound." He proceeded to do that while Callie, uncomfortable and shy, turned her shoulder to him and removed the shirt.

After checking her vital signs, Dr. Candler took the bandage off and examined the small red cut with a scowling face. "How did this happen?" he asked curtly.

"One of Lopez's goons had a knife and liked to play games with helpless women," Micah said coldly.

"I hope he won't be doing it again," the physician murmured as he cleaned and redressed the superficial wound.

"That's classified," Micah said simply.

Callie glanced at him, surprised. His black eyes met hers, but he didn't say anything else.

"I'm going to give you a tetanus shot as a precaution," Dr. Candler said with a professional smile. "But I can almost guarantee that the cut won't leave a scar when it heals. I imagine it stings."

"A little," Callie agreed.

"I need to give her a full examination," Dr. Candler told him after giving Callie the shot. "Why don't you go outside and smoke one of those contraband Cuban cigars I'm not supposed to know you have?"

"They aren't contraband," Micah told him. "It isn't illegal if you get given one that someone has purchased in Cuba. Cobb was down there last month and he brought me back several."

"Leave it to you to find a legal way to do something illegal," Candler chuckled.

"Speaking of which, I'd better give a mutual acquaintance a quick call and thank him for the loan of his equipment." He glanced at Callie and smiled softly. "Then maybe Callie can relax while you finish here."

She didn't reply. He went out and closed the door behind him. She let out an audible sigh of relief.

"Now," Dr. Candler said as he continued to examine her. "Tell me what happened."

She did, still shaken and frightened by what she'd experienced in the last two days. He listened while he worked, his face giving nothing away.

"What happened to the man who did it?" he persisted.

She gave him an innocent smile. "I really don't know," she lied.

He sighed. "You and Micah." He shook his head. "Have you known him long?"

"Since I was fifteen," she told him. "His father and my mother were briefly married."

"You're Callie!" the doctor said at once.

Chapter Four

The look on Callie's face was priceless. "How did you know?" she asked.

He smiled. "Micah talks about you a lot."

That was a shocker. "I didn't think he wanted anybody to know I even existed," she pointed out.

He pursed his lips. "Well, let's just say that he has ambiguous feelings about you."

Ambiguous. Right. Plainly stated, he couldn't stand her. But if that was true, why had he come himself to rescue her, instead of just sending his men?

She drew in a breath as he tended to her. "Am I going to be okay?"

"You're going to be good as new in a few days." He smiled at her. "Trust me."

"Micah seems to."

"He should. I taught him everything he knows

about surgery," he chuckled. "I was a year ahead of him when we were in graduate school, and I took classes for one of the professors occasionally."

She smiled. "You're very good."

"So was he," he replied grimly.

She hesitated, but curiosity prodded her on. "If it wouldn't be breaking any solemn oath, could you tell me why he didn't finish his residency?"

He did, without going into details. "He realized medicine wasn't his true calling."

She nodded in understanding.

"But you didn't hear that from me," he added firmly.

"Oh, I never tell people things I know," she replied easily, smiling. "I work for a lawyer."

He chuckled. "Do tell?"

"He's something of a fire-eater, but he's nice to me. He practices criminal law back in Jacobsville, Texas."

He put the medical equipment to one side and told her she could get dressed.

"I'm going to put you on some antibiotics to fight off infection." He studied her with narrowed eyes. "What you've been through is traumatic," he added as he handed her the prescription bottle. "I'd advise counseling."

"Right now," she said on a long breath, "I'm occupied with just trying to stay alive. The drug dealer is still after me, you see."

His jaw tautened. "Micah will take care of you."

"I know that." She stood up and smiled, extending her hand. "Thanks."

He shook her hand and shrugged. "Think nothing

of it. We brilliant medical types feel obliged to minister to the masses…''

''Oh, for God's sake!'' Micah groaned as he entered the room, overhearing his friend.

Dr. Candler gave him a look full of frowning mock-hauteur. ''And aren't you lucky that I don't have to examine *you* today?'' he drawled.

''We're leaving. Right now.'' He took Callie by the hand and gave the other man a grin. ''Thanks.''

''Anytime. You take care.''

''You do the same.''

Callie was herded out the door.

''But, the bill,'' she protested as he put her out a side door and drew her into the vehicle that was waiting for them with the engine running.

''Already taken care of. Let's get to the airport.''

Callie settled into the seat, still worrying. ''I don't have anything with me,'' she said miserably. ''No papers, no clothes, no shoes…''

''I told you, Maddie got all that together. It will be waiting for us at the airport, along with tickets and boarding passes.''

''What if Lopez has people there waiting for us?'' she worried aloud.

''We also have people waiting there for us,'' Bojo said from the front seat. ''Miami is our safest domestic port.''

''Okay,'' she said, and smiled at him.

He smiled back.

Micah and Bojo exchanged a complicated glance. Bojo turned his attention back to the road and didn't say another word all the way to the airport. Callie understood. Micah didn't want her getting too friendly with his people. She didn't take offense. She was used to rejection, after so many years in foster care. She only shrugged and looked out the window, watching palm trees and colorful buildings slide past as they wove through side streets and back onto the expressway.

The airport was crowded. Micah caught her by the arm and guided her past the ticket counter on the way to the concourses.

"But…" she protested.

"Don't argue. Just walk through the metal detector."

He followed close behind her. Neither of them was carrying anything metallic, but Micah was stopped when a security woman passed a wand over the two of them and her detector picked up the residual gunpowder on his hands and clothing. The woman looked at her instrument and then at him, with a wary, suspicious stare.

He smiled lazily at the uniformed woman holding the wand. "I'm on my way to a regional skeet shooting tournament," he lied glibly. "I sent my guns on ahead by express, unassembled. Can't be too careful these days, where firearms are concerned," he added, catching Callie's hand in his. "Right, honey?" he murmured softly, drawing her close.

To Callie's credit, she didn't faint at the unexpected feel of Micah's arm around her, but she tingled from head to toe and her heart went wild.

The airport security woman seemed to relax, and she smiled back. She assumed, as Micah had intended, that he and Callie were involved. "Indeed you can't. Have a good trip."

Micah kept that long, muscular arm around Callie

as they walked slowly down the concourse. He
looked down, noting the erratic rhythm of her heartbeat at her neck, and he smiled to himself.

"You have lightning-quick reflexes," he remarked
after a minute. "I noticed that in Cancún. You didn't
argue, you didn't question anything I told you to do,
and you moved almost as fast as I did. You're good
company in tight corners."

She shrugged. "When you came in through the
window, I didn't know who you were, because of
that face mask. Actually," she confessed with a
sheepish smile, "at first, I figured you were a rival
drug dealer, but I had high hopes that you might be
kind enough to just kill me and not torture me first
if I didn't resist."

He drew in a sharp breath and the arm holding her
contracted with a jerk. "Strange attitude, Callie," he
remarked.

"Not at the time. Not to me, anyway." She shivered at the memory and felt his arm tighten almost
protectively. They were well out of earshot and sight
of the security guard. "Micah, what was that wand
she was checking us with?"

"It detects nitrates," he replied. "With it, they can
tell if a passenger has had any recent contact with
weapons or explosives."

She was keenly aware of his arm still holding her
close against his warm, powerful body. "You can,
uh, let go now. She's out of sight."

He didn't relent. "Don't look, but there's a security guard with a two-way radio about fifteen feet to
your right." He smiled down at her. "And I'll give
you three guesses who's on the other end of it."

She smiled back, but it didn't reach her eyes. "The

lady with the nitrate wand? We're psyching them out, right?''

He searched her eyes and for a few seconds he stopped walking. ''Psyching them out,'' he murmured. His gaze fell to her soft, full mouth. ''Exactly.''

She couldn't quite get her breath. His expression was unreadable, but his black eyes were glittering. He watched her blouse shake with the frantic rate of her heartbeats. He was remembering mistletoe and harsh words, and that same look in Callie's soft eyes, that aching need to be kissed that made her look so very vulnerable.

''What the hell,'' he murmured roughly as his head bent to hers. ''It's an airport. People are saying hello and goodbye everywhere…''

His warm, hard mouth covered hers very gently while the sounds of people in transit all around them faded to a dull roar. His heavy brows drew together in something close to anguish as he began to kiss her. Fascinated by his expression, by the warm, ardent pressure of his mouth on hers, she closed her eyes tight, and fantasized that he meant it, that he wasn't pretending for the benefit of security guards, that he was enjoying the soft, tremulous response of her lips to the teasing, expert pressure of his own.

''Boss?''

They didn't hear the gruff whisper.

It was followed by the loud clearing of a throat and a cough.

They didn't hear that, either. Callie was on tiptoe now, her short nails digging into the hard muscles of his upper arms, hanging on Micah's slow, tender kiss with little more than willpower, so afraid that he was going to pull away…!

"Micah!" the voice said shortly.

Micah's head jerked up, and for a few seconds he seemed as disoriented as Callie. He stared blankly at the dark-headed man in front of him.

The man was extending a small case toward him. "Her papers and clothes and shoes and stuff," the man said, nodding toward Callie and clearing his throat again. "Maddie had me fly them over here."

"Thanks, Pogo."

The big, dark man nodded. He stared with open curiosity at Callie, and then he smiled gently. "It was my pleasure," he said, glancing again at Micah and making an odd little gesture with his head in Callie's direction.

"This is Callie Kirby," Micah said shortly, adding, "my…stepsister."

The big man's eyebrows levered up. "Oh! I mean, I was hoping she wasn't a real sister. I mean, the way you were kissing her and all." He flushed, and laughed self-consciously when Micah glared at him. Callie was scarlet, looking everywhere except at the newcomer.

"You'll miss your flight out of here," Micah said pointedly.

"What? Oh. Yeah." He grinned at Callie. "I'm Pogo. I'm from Saint Augustine. I used to wrestle alligators until Micah here gave me a job. I'm sort of a bodyguard, you know…"

"You're going to be an unemployed bodyguard in twenty seconds if you don't merge with the crowd," Micah said curtly.

"Oh. Well…sure. Bye, now," he told Callie with an ear-to-ear smile.

She smiled back. He was like a big teddy bear. She was sorry they wouldn't get to know each other.

Pogo almost fell over his own feet as he turned, jerking both busy eyebrows at his boss, before he melted into the crowd and vanished.

"Stop doing that," Micah said coldly.

She looked up at him blankly. "Doing what?"

"Smiling at my men like that. These men aren't used to it. Don't encourage them."

Her lips parted on a shaken breath. She looked at him as if she feared for his sanity. "Them?" she echoed, dazed.

"Bojo and Peter and Pogo," he said, moving restlessly. He was jealous, God knew why. It irritated him. "Come on."

He moved away from her, catching her hand tightly and pulling her along with him.

"And don't read anything into what just happened," he added coldly, without looking at her.

"Why would I?" she asked honestly. "You said it was just for appearances. I haven't forgotten how you feel about me, Micah."

He stopped and stared intently down into her eyes. His own were narrow, angry, impatient. She wore her heart where anyone could see it. Her vulnerability made him protective. Odd, that, when she was tough enough to survive captivity by Lopez and still keep her nerve during a bloody breakout.

"You don't have a clue how I feel about you," he said involuntarily. His fingers locked closer into hers. "I'm thirty-six. You're barely twenty-two. The sort of woman I prefer is sophisticated and street-smart and has no qualms about sex. You're still at the kissing-in-parked-cars stage.''

She flushed and searched his eyes. "I don't kiss people in parked cars because I don't date anybody,'' she told him with blunt honesty. "I can't leave Dad alone in the evenings. Besides, too many men around Jacobsville remember my mother, and think I'm like her.'' Her face stiffened and she looked away. "Including you.''

He didn't speak. There was little softness left in him after all the violent years, but she was able to touch some last, sensitive place with her sweet voice. Waves of guilt ran over him. Yes, he'd compared her to her mother that Christmas. He'd said harsh, cruel things. He regretted them, but there was no going back. His feelings about Callie unnerved him. She was the only weak spot in his armor that he'd ever known. And what a good thing that she didn't know that, he told himself.

"You don't know what was really going on that night, Callie,'' he said after a minute.

She looked up at him. "Don't you think it's time I did?'' she asked softly.

He toyed with her fingers, causing ripples of pleasure to run along her spine. "Why not? You're old enough to hear it now.'' He glanced around them cautiously before he looked at her again. "You were wearing an emerald velvet dress that night, the same one you'd worn to your eighteenth birthday party. They were watching a movie while you finished decorating the Christmas tree,'' he continued absently. "You'd just bent over to pick up an ornament when I came into the room. The dress had a deep neckline. You weren't wearing a bra under it, and your breasts were visible in that position, right to the nipples. You looked up at me and your nipples were suddenly hard.''

She gaped at him. The comment about her nipples was disturbing, but she had no idea what he meant by emphasizing them. ''I had no idea I was showing like that!''

''I didn't realize that. Not at first.'' He held her fingers tighter. ''You saw me and came right up against me, drowning me in that floral perfume you wore. You stood on tiptoe, like you did a minute ago, trying to tempt me into kissing you.''

She averted her embarrassed eyes. ''You said terrible things…''

''The sight of you like that had aroused me passionately,'' he said frankly, nodding when her shocked eyes jumped to his face. ''That's right. And I couldn't let you know it. I had to make you keep your distance, not an easy accomplishment after the alcohol you'd had. For which,'' he added coldly, ''your mother should have been shot! It was illegal for her to let you drink, even at home. Anyway, I read you the riot act, pushed you away and walked down the hall, right into your mother. She recognized immediately what you hadn't even noticed about my body, and she thought it was the sight of her in that slinky silver dress that had caused it. So she buried herself against me and started kissing me.'' He let out an angry breath. ''Your father saw us like that before I could push her away. And I couldn't tell him the truth, because you were just barely eighteen. I was already thirty-two.''

The bitterness in his deep voice was blatant. She didn't feel herself breathing. She'd only been eighteen, but he'd wanted her. She'd never realized it. Everything that didn't make sense was suddenly crystal clear—except that comment about his body. She wondered what her mother had seen and recognized about him that she hadn't.

"You never told me."

"You were a child, Callie," he said tautly. "In some ways, you still are. I was never low enough to take advantage of your innocence."

She was almost vibrating with the turmoil of her emotions. She didn't know what to do or say.

He drew in a long, slow breath as he studied her. "Come on," he said, tugging her along. "We have to move or we'll miss our flight." He handed her the case and indicated the ladies' room. "Get changed. I'll wait right here."

She nodded. Her mind was in such turmoil that she changed into jeans and a long-sleeved knit shirt, socks and sneakers, without paying much attention to what was in the small travel case. She didn't take time to look in any of the compartments, because he'd said to hurry. She glanced at herself in the mirror and was glad she had short hair that could do without a brush. Despite all she'd been through, it didn't look too bad. She'd have to buy a brush when they got where they were going, along with makeup and other toiletries. But that could wait.

Micah was propping up the wall when she came out. He nodded, approving what Maddie had packed for her, and took the case. "Here," he said, passing her a small plastic bag.

Inside were makeup, a brush, a toothbrush, toothpaste and deodorant. She almost cried at the thoughtful gift.

"Thanks," she said huskily.

Micah pulled the tickets and boarding passes out of his shirt pocket. "Get out your driver's license and birth certificate," he said. "We have to have a photo ID to board."

She felt momentary panic. "My birth certificate is in my file at home, and my driver's license is still in my purse, in my car...!"

He laid a lean forefinger across her pretty mouth, slightly swollen from the hard contact with his. "Your car is at your house, and your purse is inside it, and it's locked up tight. I told Maddie to put your birth certificate and your driver's license in the case. Have you looked for them?"

"No. I didn't think..."

She paused, putting the case down on the carpeted concourse floor to open it. Sure enough, her driver's license was in the zipped compartment that she hadn't looked in when she was in the bathroom. Besides that, the unknown Maddie had actually put her makeup and toiletries inside as well, in a plastic bag. She could have wept at the woman's thoughtfulness, but she wasn't going to tell Micah and make him feel uncomfortable that he'd already bought her those items. She closed it quickly and stuck her license in her jeans pocket.

"Does Maddie really look like me?" she asked on the way to the ticket counter, trying not to sound as if she minded. He'd said they resembled one another earlier.

"At a distance," he affirmed. "Her hair is shorter than yours, and she's more muscular. She was a karate instructor when she signed on with me. She's twenty-six."

"Karate."

"Black belt," he added.

"She seems to be very efficient," she murmured a little stiffly.

He gave her a knowing glance that she didn't see and chuckled softly. "She's in love with Colby Lane, a guy I used to work with at the justice department," he told her. "She signed on with us because she thought he was going to."

"He didn't?"

He shook his head. "He's working for Pierce Hutton's outfit, as a security chief, along with Tate Winthrop, an acquaintance of mine."

"Oh."

They were at the ticket counter now. He held out his hand for her driver's license and birth certificate, and presented them along with his driver's license and passport and the tickets to the agent on duty.

She put the tickets in a neat folder with the boarding passes in a slot on the outside, checked the ID, and handed them back.

"Have a nice trip," she told them. "We'll be boarding in just a minute."

Callie hadn't looked at her boarding pass. She was too busy trying to spot Bojo and Peter and the others.

"They're already en route," Micah told her nonchalantly, having guessed why she was looking around her.

"They aren't going with us?"

He gave her a wry glance. "Somebody had to bring my boat back. I left it here in the marina when I flew out to Jacobsville to help Eb Scott and Cy Parks shut down Lopez's drug operation. It's still there."

"Why couldn't we have gone on the boat, too?"

"You get seasick," he said before he thought.

Her lips fell open. She'd only been on a boat once, with him and her mother and stepfather, when she was sixteen. They'd gone to San Antonio and sailed down the river on a tour boat. She'd gotten very sick and thrown up. It had been Micah who'd looked after her, to his father's amusement.

She hadn't even remembered the episode until he'd said that. She didn't get seasick now, but she kept quiet.

"Besides," he added, avoiding her persistent stare, "if Lopez does try anything, it won't be on an international flight out of the U.S. He's in enough trouble with the higher-ups in his organization without making an assault on a commercial plane just to get even for losing a prisoner."

She relaxed a little, because that had been on her mind.

He took her arm and drew her toward a small door, where a uniformed man was holding a microphone. He announced that they were boarding first-class passengers first, and Micah ushered her right down the ramp and into the plane.

"First class," she said, dazed, as he eased her into a wide, comfortable seat with plenty of leg room. Even for a man of his height, there was enough of it.

"Always," he murmured, amused at her fascination. "I don't like cramped places."

She fastened her seat belt with a wry smile. "Considering the size of you, I can understand that. Micah, what about Dad?" she added, ashamed that she was still belaboring the point.

"Maddie's got him under surveillance. When Pogo goes back, he'll work a split shift with her at your apartment to safeguard him. Eb and Cy are keeping their eyes out, as well. I promise you, Dad's going to be safe." He hesitated, searching her wide, pale blue eyes. "But you're the one in danger."

"Because I got away," she agreed, nodding.

He seemed worried. His dark eyes narrowed on her face. "Lopez doesn't lose prisoners, ever. You're the first. Someone is going to pay for that. He'll make an example of the people who didn't watch you closely enough. Then he'll make an example of you and me, if he can, to make sure his reputation doesn't suffer."

She shivered involuntarily. It was a nightmare that would haunt her forever. She remembered what she'd suffered already and her eyes closed on a helpless wave of real terror.

"You're going to be safe, Callie. Listen," he said, reading her expression, "I live on a small island in the Bahamas chain, not too far from New Providence. I have state-of-the-art surveillance equipment and a small force of mercenaries that even Lopez would hesitate to confront. Lopez isn't the only one who has a reputation in terrorist circles. Before I put together my team and hired out as a professional soldier, I worked for the CIA."

Her eyes widened. She hadn't known that. She hadn't known anything about him.

"They approached me while I was in college, before I changed my course of study to medicine. I was already fluent in French and Dutch, and I picked up German in my sophomore year. I couldn't blend in very well in an Arabic country, but I could pass for

German or Dutch, and I did. During holidays and vacations, I did a lot of traveling for the company.'' He smiled, reminiscing. ''It was dangerous work, and exciting. By the time I was in my last year of residency, I knew for a fact that I wouldn't be able to settle down into a medical practice. I couldn't live without the danger. That's when I left school for good.''

She was hanging on every word. It was amazing to have him speak to her as an equal, as an adult. They'd never really talked before.

''I wondered,'' she said, ''why you gave it up.''

He stretched his long legs out in front of him and crossed his arms over his broad chest. ''I had the skills, but as I grew older, the less I wanted roots or anything that hinted at permanence. I don't want marriage or children, so a steady, secure profession seemed superfluous. On the other hand, being a mercenary is right up my alley. I live for those surges of adrenaline.''

''None of us ever knew about that,'' she said absently, trying not to let him see how much it hurt to know that he couldn't see a future as a husband and father. Now that she knew what he really did for a living, she could understand why. He was never going to be a family man. ''We thought it was the trust your mother left you that kept you in Armani suits,'' she added in a subdued tone.

''No, it wasn't. I like my lifestyle,'' he added with a pointed glance in her direction. He stretched lazily, pulling the silk shirt he was wearing taut across the muscles of his chest. A flight attendant actually hesitated as she started down the aisle, helplessly drinking in the sight of him. He was a dish, all right. Callie didn't blame the other woman for staring, but the flight attendant had blond hair and blue eyes and she was lovely. Her beauty was like a knife in the ribs to Callie, pointing out all the physical attributes she herself lacked. If only she'd been pretty, she told herself miserably, maybe Micah would have wanted more than an occasional kiss from her.

"Would you care for anything to drink, sir?" the flight attendant asked, smiling joyfully as she paused by Micah's side.

"Scotch and soda," he told her. He smiled ruefully. "It's been a long day."

"Coming right up," the woman said, and went at once to get the order.

Callie noticed that she hadn't been asked if she wanted anything. She wondered what Micah would say if she asked for a neat whiskey. Probably nothing, she told herself miserably. He might have kissed her in the airport, but he only seemed irritated by her now.

The flight attendant was back with his drink. She glanced belatedly at Callie and grimaced. "Sorry," she told the other woman. "I didn't think to ask if you'd like something, too?"

Callie shook her head and smiled. "No, I don't want anything, thanks."

"Are you stopping in Nassau or just passing through?" the woman asked Micah boldly.

He gave her a lingering appraisal, from her long, elegant legs to her full breasts and lovely face. He smiled. "I live there."

"Really!" Her eyes lit as if they'd concealed fires. "So do I!"

"Then you must know Lisette Dubonnet," he said.

"Dubonnet," the uniformed woman repeated, frowning. "Isn't her father Jacques Dubonnet, the French ambassador?"

"Yes," he said. "Lisette and I have known each other for several years. We're...very good friends."

The flight attendant looked suddenly uncomfortable, and a little flushed. Micah was telling her, in a nice way, that she'd overstepped her introduction. He smiled to soften the rejection, but it was a rejection, just the same.

"Miss Dubonnet is very lovely," the flight attendant said with a pleasant, if more formal, smile. "If you need anything else, just ring."

"I will."

She went on down the aisle. Beside him, Callie was staring out the window at the ocean below without any real enthusiasm. She hated her own reaction to the news that Micah was involved with some beautiful woman in Nassau. And not only a beautiful woman, but a poised sophisticate as well.

"You'll like Lisse," he said carelessly. "I'll ask her to go shopping with you. You'll have to have a few clothes. She has excellent taste."

Implying that Callie had none at all. Her heart felt like iron in her chest, heavy and cold. "That would be nice," she said, lying through her teeth. "I won't need much, though," she added, thinking about her small savings account.

"You may be there longer than a day or two," he said in a carefully neutral voice. "You can't wear the same clothes day in and day out. Besides,'' he added curtly, ''it's about time you learned how to dress like a young woman instead of an elderly recluse!''

Chapter Five

Callie felt the anger boil out of her in waves. "Oh, that's nice, coming from you," she said icily. "When you're the one who started me wearing that sort of thing in the first place!"

"Me?" he replied, his eyebrows arching.

"You said I dressed like a tramp," she began, and her eyes were anguished as she remembered the harsh, hateful words. "Like my mother," she added huskily. "You said that I flaunted my body..." She stopped suddenly and wrapped her arms around herself. She stared out the porthole while she recovered her self-control. "Sorry," she said stiffly. "I've been through a lot. It's catching up with me. I didn't mean to say that."

He felt as if he'd been slapped. Maybe he deserved it, too. Callie had been beautiful in that green velvet dress. The sight of her in it had made him ache. She

had the grace and poise of a model, even if she
lacked the necessary height. But he'd never realized
that his own anger had made her ashamed of her
body, and at such an impressionable age. Good God,
no wonder she dressed like a dowager! Then he remembered what she'd hinted in the jungle about the
foster homes she'd stayed in, and he wondered with
real anguish what she'd endured before she came to
live in his father's house. There had to be more to
her repression than just a few regretted words from
him.

"Callie," he said huskily, catching her soft chin
and turning her flushed face toward him. "Something
happened to you at one of those foster homes, didn't
it?"

She bit her lower lip and for a few seconds, there
was torment in her eyes.

He drew in a sharp breath.

She turned her face away again, embarrassed.

"Can you talk about it?" he asked.

She shook her head jerkily.

His dark eyes narrowed. And her mother—her
own mother—had deserted her, had placed her in
danger with pure indifference. "Damn your
mother," he said in a gruff whisper.

She didn't look at him again. At least, she thought
mistakenly, he was remembering the breakup of his
father's marriage, and not her childhood anymore.
She didn't like remembering the past.

He leaned back in his seat and stretched, folding
his arms over his broad chest. One day, he promised
himself, there was going to be a reckoning for Callie's mother. He hoped the woman got just a fraction
of what she deserved, for all the grief and pain she'd

caused. Although, he had to admit, she had changed in the past year or so.

He wondered if her mother's first husband, Kane Kirby, had contacted Callie recently. Poor kid, he thought. She really had gone through a lot, even before Lopez had her kidnapped. He thought about what she'd suffered at Lopez's hands, and he ached to avenge her. The drug lord was almost certain to make a grab for her again. But this time, he promised himself, Lopez was going to pay up his account in full. He owed Callie that much for the damage he'd done.

It was dark when the plane landed in Nassau at the international airport, and Micah let Callie go ahead of him down the ramp to the pavement. The moist heat was almost smothering, after the air-conditioned plane. Micah took her arm and escorted her to passport control. He glanced with amusement at the passengers waiting around baggage claim for their bags to be unloaded. Even when he traveled routinely, he never took more than a duffel bag that he could carry into the airplane with him. It saved time waiting for luggage to be off-loaded.

After they checked through, he moved her outside again and hailed a cab to take them to the marina, where the boat was waiting.

Another small round of formalities and they boarded the sleek, powerful boat that already contained Micah's men. Callie went below and sat quietly on a comfortable built-in sofa, watching out the porthole as the boat flew out of Prince George Wharf and around the bay. From there, it went out to sea.

"Comfortable?" Micah asked, joining her below.

She nodded. "It's so beautiful out there. I love the way the ships light up at night. I knew cruise ships did, but I didn't realize that smaller ones did, too." She glanced at him in the subdued light of the cabin. "You don't light yours, do you?"

He chuckled. "In my line of work, it wouldn't be too smart, would it?"

"Sorry," she said with a sheepish smile. "I wasn't thinking."

He poured himself a scotch and water and added ice cubes. "Want something to drink? If you don't want anything alcoholic, I've got soft drinks or fruit juice."

She shook her head. "I'm fine." She laughed. Her eyes caught and held on a vessel near the lighted dock. "Look! There's a white ship with black sails flying a skull and crossbones Jolly Roger flag!"

He chuckled. "That would be Fred Spence. He's something of a local eccentric. Nice boat, though."

She glanced at him. "This one is nice, too."

"It's comfortable on long hauls," he said noncommittally. He dropped down onto the sofa beside her and crossed his long legs. "We need to talk."

"About what?"

"Lopez. I'm putting you under twenty-four-hour surveillance," he said somberly. "If I'm not within yelling distance, one of my men will be. Even when you go shopping with Lisse, Bojo or Peter will go along. You aren't to walk on the beach alone, ever."

"But surely that would be safe...?"

He sat forward abruptly, and his black eyes glittered. "Callie, he has weapons that could pinpoint your body heat and send a missile after it from a distance of half a mile," he said curtly.

She actually gasped. That brought to mind another worry. She frowned. "I'm putting you in jeopardy by being with you," she said suddenly.

"You've got that backward, honey," he said, the endearment coming so naturally that he wasn't even aware he'd used it until he watched Callie's soft complexion flush. "You were in jeopardy in the first place because of me. Why does it make you blush when I call you honey?" he added immediately, the question quick enough to rattle her.

"I'm not used to it."

"From me," he drawled softly. "Or from any man?"

She shifted. "From Dad, maybe."

"Dad doesn't count. I mean single, datable bachelors."

She shook her head. "I don't date."

He'd never connected her solitary existence with himself. Now, he was forced to. He drew his breath in sharply, and got up from the sofa. He took a long sip from his drink, walking slowly over to stare out the porthole at the distant lights of the marina as they left it behind. "I honestly didn't realize how much damage I did to your ego, Callie. I'm really sorry about it."

"I was just as much at fault as you were," she replied evenly. "I shouldn't have thrown myself at you like some drunk prostitute…"

"Callie!" he exclaimed, horrified at her wording.

She averted her eyes and her hands clenched in her lap. "Well, I did."

He put his drink on the bar and knelt just in front of her. He was so tall that his black eyes were even with soft blue ones in the position. His lean hands went to her waist and he shook her very gently.

"I pushed you away because I wanted you, not because I thought you were throwing yourself at me," he said bluntly. "I was afraid that I wouldn't be able to resist you if I didn't do something very fast. I would have explained it to you eventually, if your mother hadn't stepped in and split the family apart, damn her cold heart!"

Her hands rested hesitantly on his broad shoulders, lifted and then rested again while she waited to see if she was allowed to touch him.

He seemed to realize that, because he smiled very slowly and his thumbs edged out against her flat belly in a sensuous stroking motion. "I like being touched," he murmured. "It's all right."

She smiled nervously. "I'm not used to doing it."

"I noticed." He stood up and drew her up with him. The top of her head only came to his nose. He framed her face in his warm, strong hands and lifted it gently. "Want to kiss me?" he asked in a husky whisper, and his eyes fell to her own soft mouth.

She wasn't sure about that. Her hands were on his chest now, touching lightly over the silky fabric. Under it, she could feel thick hair. She was hopelessly curious about what he looked like bare-chested. She'd never seen Micah without a shirt in all the time she'd lived in his house with his father.

"No pressure," he promised, bending. "And I won't make fun of you."

"Make fun of me?" she asked curiously.

"Never mind." He bent and his lips closed tenderly on her upper lip while he tasted the moist inside of it with his tongue. His lips moved to her lower lip and repeated the arousing little caress. His hands were at her waist, but they began to move up and down with a lazy, sensual pressure that made her body go rigid in his arms.

He lifted his mouth from her face and looked down at her with affectionate amusement. "Relax! Why are you afraid of me?" he asked gently. "I wouldn't hurt you, Callie. Not for any reason."

"I know. It's just that…"

"What?" he asked.

Her eyes met his plaintively. "Don't…tease me," she asked with dignity. "I'm not experienced enough to play that sort of game."

The amusement left his face. "Is that what it seems like to you?" he asked. He searched her worried eyes. "Even if I were into game-playing, you'd never be a target. I do have some idea now of what you've been through, in the past and just recently."

She let out the breath she'd been holding. "This Lisette you mentioned. Is she…important to you?"

"We're good friends," he said, and there was a new remoteness in his expression. "You'll like her. She's outgoing and she loves people. She'll help you get outfitted."

Now she was really worried. "I have my credit card, but I can't afford expensive shops," she emphasized. "Could you tell her that, so I won't have to?"

"I can tell her." He smiled quizzically. "But why won't you let me buy you some clothes?"

"I'm not your responsibility, even if you have been landed with me, Micah," she replied. "I pay my own way."

He wondered if she had any idea how few of his

female acquaintances would ever have made such a statement to him? It occurred to him that he'd never had a woman refuse a wardrobe.

He scowled. "You could pay me back, if you have to."

She smiled. "Thanks. But I'll buy my own clothes."

His black eyes narrowed on her face. "You were always independent," he recalled.

"I've had to be. I've been basically on my own for a long time," she said matter-of-factly. "Since I was a kid, really, and my father—I mean, Mother's first husband—threw us out. Mother didn't want the responsibility for me by herself and Kane Kirby didn't want me at all."

"If your father didn't think you were his, why didn't he have a DNA profile run?" he asked with a watchful look.

She drew away from him. "There was no such thing fifteen years ago."

"You could insist that he have it done now, couldn't you?" He gave her an odd look. "Have you spoken to him?"

"He phoned me recently. But I didn't call him back," she said unwillingly. She'd seen her mother's first husband once or twice, during his rare visits to his Jacobsville home. He'd actually phoned her apartment a few weeks ago and left a strange, tentative message asking her to call him back. She never had. His rejection of her still hurt. She didn't see him often. He lived mostly in Miami these days.

"Why not talk to him and suggest the DNA test?" he persisted.

She looked up at him with tired, sad eyes. "Because it would probably prove what my mother said, that I'm not related to him at all.'' She smiled faintly. ''I don't know whose child I am. And it really doesn't matter anymore. Please, just…leave it alone.''

He sighed with irritation, as if he knew more than he was telling her. She wondered why he was so interested in her relationship with the man who was supposed to be her own father.

He saw that curiosity in her eyes, and he closed up. He could see years of torment in that sad little face. It infuriated him. ''Your mother should be horsewhipped for what she did to you,'' he said flatly.

She folded her arms across her chest, remembering the loneliness of her young life reluctantly. New homes, new faces, new terrors. She turned back to the porthole. ''I used to wish I had someplace to belong,'' she confessed. ''I was always the outsider, in any home where I lived. Until my mother married your father,'' she added, smiling. ''I thought he'd be like all the others, that he'd either ignore me or be too familiar, but he just sort of belonged to me, from the very beginning. He really cared about me. He hugged me, coming and going.'' She drew in a soft breath. ''You can't imagine what it feels like, to have someone hug you, when you've hardly been touched in your whole life except in bad ways. He was forever teasing me, bringing me presents. He became my family. He even made up for my mother. I couldn't help loving him.'' She turned, surprised to see an odd look of self-contempt on Micah's strong face. ''I guess you resented us…''

''I resented your mother, Callie,'' he interrupted,

feeling icy-cold inside. "What I felt for you was a lot more complicated than that."

She gave him a surprised little smile. "But, I'm still my mother's daughter, right? Don't they say, look at the mother and you'll see the daughter in twenty years or so?"

His face hardened. "You'll never be like her. Not in your worst nightmares."

She sighed. "I wish I could be sure of that."

He felt like hitting something. "Do you know where she is?"

"Somewhere in Europe with her new husband, I suppose," she said indifferently. "Dad's lawyer heard from her year before last. She wanted a copy of the final divorce decree, because she was getting married again, to some British nobleman, the lawyer said."

He remembered his own mother, a gentle little brown-eyed woman with a ready smile and open arms. She'd died when he was ten, and from that day on, he and his father had been best friends. Until Anna showed up, with her introverted, nervous teenage daughter. The difference between Anna and his own mother was incredible. Anna was selfish, vain, greedy…he could have laid all seven deadly sins at her feet with ease. But Callie was nothing like her, except, perhaps, her exact opposite.

"You're the sort of woman who would love a big family," he murmured thoughtfully.

She laughed. "What do I know about families?" she responded. "I'd be terrified of bringing an innocent child into this sort of world, knowing what I know about the uncertainties of life."

He shoved his hands into his pockets. Children.

He'd never thought about them. But he could picture Callie with a baby in her arms, and it seemed perfectly natural. She'd had some bad breaks, but she'd love her own child. It was sad that she didn't want kids.

"Anyway, marriage is dead last on my list of things to do," she added, uncomfortable because he wasn't saying anything.

"That makes two of us," he murmured. It was the sort of thing he always said, but it didn't feel as comfortable suddenly as it used to. He wondered why.

She turned away from the porthole. "How long will it take us to get to your place?" she asked.

He shrugged. "About twenty more minutes, at this speed," he said, smiling. "I think you'll like it. It's old, and rambling, and it has a history. According to the legend, a local pirate owned it back in the eighteenth century. He kidnapped a highborn Spanish lady and married her out of hand. They had six children together and lived a long and happy life, or so the legend goes." He studied her curiously. "Isn't there Spanish in your ancestry somewhere?"

Her face closed up. "Don't ask me. My mother always said she descended from what they call 'black Irish,' from when the Spanish armada was shipwrecked off the coast of Ireland. I know her hair was jet-black when she was younger, and she has an olive complexion. But I don't really know her well enough to say whether or not it was the truth."

He bit off a comment on her mother's penchant for lying. "Your complexion isn't olive," he remarked quietly. "It's creamy. Soft."

He embarrassed her. She averted her eyes. "I'm just ordinary."

He shook his head. His eyes narrowed on her pretty bow of a mouth. "You always were unique, Callie." He hesitated. "Callie. What's it short for?" he asked, suddenly curious.

She drew in a slow breath. "Colleen," she replied reluctantly. "But nobody ever calls me that. It's been Callie since I was old enough to talk."

"Colleen what?"

"Colleen Mary," she replied.

He smiled. "Yes. That suits you."

He was acting very strangely. In fact, he had been ever since he rescued her. She wondered if he was still trying to take her mind off Lopez. If he was, it wasn't working. The nightmarish memories were too fresh to forget.

She looked at him worriedly. "Lopez will be looking for me," she said suddenly.

He tautened. "Let him look," he said shortly. "If he comes close enough to make a target, I'll solve all his problems. He isn't getting his hands on you again, Callie."

She relaxed a little. He sounded very confident. It made her feel better. She moved back into the center of the room, wrapping her arms around herself. "How can people like that exist in a civilized world?" she wanted to know.

"Because governments still can't fight that kind of wealth," he said bluntly. "Money and power make criminals too formidable. But we've got the Rico statutes which help us take away some of that illegal money," he added, "and we've got dedicated people enforcing the law. We win more than we lose these days.''

''You sound like a government agent,'' she teased.

He chuckled. ''I do, don't I? I spent several years being one. It sticks.'' He moved forward, taking his hands out of his pockets to wrap them gently around her upper arms. ''I give you my word that I won't let Lopez get you. In case you were worrying about that.''

She grimaced. ''Does it show?''

''I don't know. Maybe I can read your mind these days,'' he added, trying to make light of it.

''You're sure? About Dad being safe, I mean?''

''I'm sure about Dad,'' he returned at once. ''Gator may look dumb, but he's got a mind like a steel trap, and he's quick on the draw. Nobody's going to get past him—certainly nobody's going to get past him and Maddie at the same time.''

''You like her a lot, I guess?''

He chuckled. ''Yes, I do. She's hell on two legs, and one of the best scroungers I've ever had.''

''What does Bojo do?''

He gave her a wary appraisal, and it seemed as if he didn't like the question. ''Bojo is a small arms expert,'' he replied. ''He also has relatives in most of the Muslim nations, so he's a great source of information as well. Peter, you met him on the plane, is new with the group. He's a linguist and he's able to pass for an Arab or an Israeli. He's usually undercover in any foreign operation we're hired to undertake. You haven't met Rodrigo yet—he was the pilot of the DC-3 we flew back to Miami. He does undercover work as well. Don, the blond copilot, is a small arms expert. We have another operative,

Cord Romero, who does demolition work for us, but he had an accident and he's out of commission for a while.''

"What you and your men do—it's dangerous work."

"Living is dangerous work," he said flatly. "I like the job. I don't have any plans to give it up."

Her eyebrows arched and her pale blue eyes twinkled. "My goodness, did I propose marriage just now and get instant amnesia afterward? Excuse *me!*"

He gaped at her. "Propose marriage…?"

She held up both hands. "Now, don't get ruffled. I understand how men feel about these things. I haven't asked you out, or sent you flowers, or even bought you a nice pair of earrings. Naturally you're miffed because I put the cart before the horse and asked you to give up an exciting job you love for marriage to a boring paralegal."

He blinked. "Callie?" he murmured, obviously fearing for her sanity.

"We'll just forget the proposal," she offered generously.

"You didn't propose!" he gritted.

"See? You've already forgotten. Isn't that just like a man?" she muttered, as she went back to the sofa and sat down. "Now you'll pout for an hour because I rejected you."

He burst out laughing when he realized what she was doing. It took the tension away from their earlier discussion and brought them back to normal. He dropped down into an armchair across from her and folded his arms over his chest.

"Just when I think I've got you figured out, you throw me another curve," he said appreciatively.

"Believe me, if I didn't have a sense of humor, I'd already have smeared Mr. Kemp with honey and locked him in a closet with a grizzly bear."

"Ouch!"

"I thought you lived in Nassau?" She changed the subject.

He shrugged. "I did. This place came on the market three years ago and I bought it. I like the idea of having a defendable property. You'll see what I mean when we get there. It's like a walled city."

"I'll bet there are lots of flowers," she murmured hopefully.

"Millions," he confirmed. "Hibiscus and orchids and bougainvillea. You'll love it." He smiled gently. "You were always planting things when I lived at home."

"I didn't think you noticed anything I did," she replied before she thought.

He watched her quietly. "Your mother spent most of that time ordering you around," he recalled. "If she wanted a soft drink, or a scarf, or a sandwich, she always sent you after it. I don't recall that she ever touched a vacuum cleaner or a frying pan the whole time she was around."

"I learned to cook in the last foster home I stayed in," she said with a smile. "It was the best of the lot. Mrs. Toms liked me. She had five little kids and she had arthritis real bad. She was so sweet that it was a joy to help her. She was always surprised that anyone would want to do things for her."

"Most giving people are," he replied. "Ironically they're usually the last ones people give to."

"That's true."

"What else did she teach you?" he asked.

"How to crochet," she recalled. She sighed. "I can't make sweaters and stuff, but I taught myself how to make hats. I give them to children and old people in our neighborhood. I work on them when I'm waiting for appointments with Dad. I get through a lot."

It was another reminder that she was taking care of his father, something he should have been doing himself—something he would be doing, if Callie's mother hadn't made it impossible for him to be near his parent.

"You're still bitter about Dad," she said, surprising him. "I can tell. You get this terrible haunted look in your eyes when I talk about him."

It surprised him that at her age she could read him so well, when his own men couldn't. He wasn't sure he liked it.

"I miss him," he confessed gruffly. "I'm sorry he won't let me make peace."

She gaped at him. "Whoever told you that?"

He hesitated. "I haven't tried to talk to him in years. So I phoned him a few days ago, before you were kidnapped. He listened for a minute and hung up without saying a word."

"What day was it?"

"It was Saturday. What difference does that make?"

"What time was it?" she repeated.

"Noon."

She smiled gently. "I go to get groceries at noon on Saturdays, because Mrs. Ruiz, who lives next door, comes home for lunch and makes it for herself and Dad and stays with him while I'm away."

"So?"

"So, Mrs. Ruiz doesn't speak English yet, she's still learning. The telephone inhibits her. She'll answer it, but if it's not me, she'll put it right down again." She smiled. "That's why I asked when you called."

"Then, Dad might talk to me, if I tried again," he said after a minute.

"Micah, he loves you," she said softly. "You're the only child he has. Of course he'll talk to you. He doesn't know what really happened with my mother, no more than I did, until you told me the truth. But he realizes now that if it hadn't been you, it would have been some other younger man. He said that, after the divorce was final, she even told him so."

"He didn't try to get in touch with me."

"He was upset for a long time after it happened. So was I. We blamed you both. But that's in the past. He'd love to hear from you now," she assured him. "He didn't think you'd want to talk to him, after so much time had passed and after what he'd said to you. He feels bad about that."

He leaned forward. "If that's so, when he had the heart attack, why wasn't I told?"

"I called the only number I had for you," she said. "I never got an answer. The hospital said they'd try to track you down, but I guess they didn't."

Could it really be that simple? he wondered. "That was at the old house, in Nassau. It was disconnected three years ago. The number I have now is unlisted."

"Oh."

"Why didn't you ask Eb Scott or Cy Parks?"

"I don't know them," she said hesitantly. "And until very recently, when this Lopez thing made the

headlines, I didn't know they were mercenaries.''
She averted her eyes. "I knew you were acquainted
with them, but I certainly didn't know that you were
one of them.''

He took a slow breath. No, he remembered, she
didn't know. He'd never shared that bit of information with either her or Jack Steele.

"I wrote to you, too, about the heart attack, at the
last address you left us.''

"That would have been forwarded. I never got it.''

"I sent it,'' she said.

"I'm not doubting that you did. I'm telling you
that it never got to me.''

"I'm really sorry,'' she told him. "I did try, even
if it doesn't look like it. I always hoped that you'd
eventually phone someone and I'd be able to contact
you. When you didn't, well, I guess Dad and I both
figured that you weren't interested in what happened
back here. And he did say that he'd been very cruel
in what he said to you when you left.''

"He was. But I understood,'' he added.

She smiled sadly. "He loves you. When this is
over, you should make peace with him. I think you'll
find that he'll more than meet you halfway. He's
missed you terribly.''

"I've missed him, too.'' He could have added that
he'd missed her as well, but she wasn't likely to believe him.

He started to speak, but he felt the boat slowing.
He smiled. "We must be coming up to the pier.
Come on. It will be nice to have a comfortable bed
to sleep in tonight.''

She nodded, and followed him up to the deck.

Her eyes caught sight of the house, on a small rise
in the distance, long and low and lighted. She could

see arches and flowers, even in the darkness, because of the solar-powered lights that lined the walkway from the pier up to the walled estate. She caught her breath. It was like a house she'd once seen in a magazine and daydreamed about as a child. She had the oddest feeling that she was coming home…

Chapter Six

"What do you think?" Micah asked as he helped her onto the ramp that led down to the pier.

"It's beautiful," she said honestly. "I expect it's even more impressive in the daylight."

"It is." He hesitated, turning back toward the men who were still on the boat. "Bojo! Make sure we've got at least two guards on the boat before you come up to the house," he called to his associate, who grinned and replied that he would. "Peter can help you," he added involuntarily.

Callie didn't seem to notice that he'd jettisoned both men who'd been friendly with her. Micah did. He didn't like the idea of his men getting close to her. It wasn't jealousy. Of course it wasn't. He was...protecting her from complications.

She looked around as they went up the wide graveled path to the house, frowning as she became aware of odd noises. "What's that sound?" she asked Micah.

He smiled lazily. "My early warning radar."

"Huh?"

He chuckled. "I keep a flock of geese," he explained, nodding toward a fenced area where a group of big white birds walked around and swam in a huge pool of water. "Believe it or not, they're better than guard dogs."

"Wouldn't a guard dog or two be a better idea?"

"Nope. I've got a Mac inside."

Before she could ask any more questions, the solid wood front door opened and a tall, imposing man in khakis with gray-sprinkled black wavy hair stood in their path. He was holding an automatic weapon in one big hand.

"Welcome home, boss," he said in deep, crisply accented British. He grinned briefly and raised two bushy eyebrows at the sight of Callie. "Got her, did you?"

"Got her, and with no casualties," Micah replied, returning the grin. "How's it going, Mac?"

"No worries. But it'll rain soon." He shifted his weight, grimacing a little.

"At least you're wearing the prosthesis, now," Micah muttered as he herded Callie into the house.

Mac rubbed his hip after he closed the door and followed them. "Damned thing feels funny," he said. "And I can't run." He glowered at Micah as if the whole thing was his fault.

"Hey," Micah told him, "didn't I say 'duck'? In fact, didn't I say it twice?"

"You said it, but I had my earphones in!"

"Excuses, excuses. We even took up a collection

for your funeral, then you had to go mess everything up by living!'' Micah grumbled.

''Oh, sure, after you lot had divided up all my possessions! Bojo's still got my favorite shirt and he won't give it back! And he doesn't even wear shirts!''

''He's using it to polish his gun,'' Micah explained. ''Says it's the best shine he's ever put on it.''

Callie was openly gaping at them.

Micah's black eyes twinkled. ''We're joking,'' he told her gently. ''It's the way we let off steam, so that we don't get bogged down in worry. What we do is hard work, and dangerous. We have to have safety valves.''

''I'll blow Bojo's safety valve for him if he doesn't give back my shirt!'' Mac assured his boss. ''And you haven't even introduced us.''

Callie smiled and held out her hand. ''Hi! I'm Callie Kirby.''

''I'm MacPherson,'' he replied, shaking it. ''I took a mortar hit on our last mission, so I've got KP until I get used to this damned prosthesis,'' he added, lifting his right leg and grimacing.

''You'd better get used to it pretty soon, or you're going to be permanent in that kitchen,'' Micah assured him. ''Now I'd like to get Callie settled. She's been through a lot.''

The other man became somber all at once. ''She's not what I expected,'' Mac said reluctantly as he studied her.

''I can imagine,'' she said with a sad little smile. ''You were expecting a woman who was blond and as good-looking as Micah. I know I don't look like him…''

Before she could add that they weren't related, the older man interrupted her. "That isn't what I meant," Mac replied at once.

She shrugged and smiled carelessly. "Of course not. I really am tired," she added.

"Come on," Micah said. "Have you got something for sandwiches?" Micah asked Mac. "We didn't stop for food."

"Sure," Mac replied, visibly uncomfortable. "I'll get right to it."

Micah led Callie down the long hall and turned her into a large, airy room with a picture window overlooking the ocean. Except for the iron bars, it looked very touristy.

"Mac does most of the cooking. We used to take turns, but after he was wounded, and we found out that his father once owned a French restaurant, we gave him permanent KP." He glanced at her with a wry smile. "We thought it might encourage him to put on the prosthesis and try to be rehabilitated. Apparently it's working."

"He's very nice."

He closed the door and turned to her, his face somber. "He meant that the sort of woman I usually bring here is blond and long-legged and buxom, and that they usually ignore the hired help."

She flushed. "You didn't have to explain."

"Didn't I?" His eyes narrowed on her face as a potential complication presented itself when he thought about having Lisette take Callie on that shopping trip. The woman was extremely jealous, and Callie had been through enough turmoil already.

"I haven't told Mac or Lisette that we aren't related. It might be as well to let them continue thinking we are, for the time being."

She wondered why, but she wasn't going to lower her pride by asking. "Sure," she said with careful indifference. "No problem." Presumably this Lisette would be jealous of a stepsister, but not of a real one. Micah obviously didn't want to cause waves. She smiled drowsily. "I think I could sleep the clock around."

"If Maddie's her usual efficient self, she should have packed a nightgown for you."

"I don't have a gown," she murmured absently, glancing at the case he'd put down beside the bed.

"Pajamas, then."

"Uh, I don't wear those, either."

He stood up and looked at her pointedly. "What *do* you sleep in?"

She cleared her throat. "Never mind."

His eyebrows arched. "Well, well. No wonder you locked your bedroom door when you lived with us."

"That wasn't the only reason," she said before she thought.

His black eyes narrowed. "You've had a hell of a life, haven't you? And now this, on top of the past."

She bit her lower lip. "This door does have a lock?" she persisted. "I'm sorry. I've spent my life behind locked doors. It's a hard habit to break, and not because of the way I sleep."

"The door has a lock, and you can use it. But I hope you know that you're safe with me," he replied quietly. "Seducing innocents isn't a habit with me, and my men are trustworthy."

"It's not that."

"If you're nervous about being the only woman here, I could get Lisette to come over and spend the night in this room with you," he added.

"No," she said, reluctant to meet his paramour. "I'll be fine."

"You haven't been alone since it happened," he reminded her. "It may be more traumatic than you think, especially in the dark."

"I'll be all right, Micah," she said firmly.

He drew in an irritated breath. "All right. But if you're frightened, I'm next door, through the bathroom."

She gave him a curious look.

"I'll wear pajama bottoms while you're in residence," he said dryly, reading her mind accurately.

She cleared her throat. "Thanks."

"Don't you want to eat something before you go to bed?"

She shook her head. "I'm too tired. Micah, thanks for saving me. I didn't expect it, but I'm very grateful."

He shrugged. "You're family," he said flatly, and she grimaced when he wasn't looking. He turned and went out, hesitating before he closed the door. "Someone will be within shouting distance, night or day."

Her heart ached. He still didn't see her as a woman. Probably, he never would. "Okay," she replied. "Thanks."

He closed the door.

She was so tired that she was sure she'd be asleep almost as soon as her head connected with the pillow. But that wasn't the case. Dressed only in her cotton briefs, she lay awake for a long time, staring at the ceiling, absorbing the shock of the past two days. It seemed unreal now, here where she was safe. As her strung muscles began to relax, she tugged the cool, expensive designer sheet in a yellow rose pattern over her and felt her mind begin to drift slowly into peaceful oblivion.

"Callie? Callie!"

The deep forceful voice combined with steely fingers on her upper arms to shake her out of the nightmare she'd been having. She was hoarse from the scream that had dragged Micah from sleep and sent him running to the connecting door with a skeleton key.

She was sitting up, both her wrists in one of his lean, warm hands, her eyes wide with terror. She was shaking all over, and not from the air-conditioning.

He leaned over and turned on the bedside lamp. His eyes went helplessly to the full, high thrust of her tip-tilted little breasts, their nipples relaxed from sleep. She was so shaken that she didn't even feel embarrassment. Her pale blue eyes were wild with horror.

"You're safe, baby," he said gently. "It's all right."

"Micah!" came a shout from outside the bedroom door. It was Bojo, alert as usual to any odd noise.

"Callie just had a nightmare, Bojo. It's okay. Go back to bed!"

"Sure thing, boss."

Footsteps faded down the corridor.

"I was back in the chair, at Lopez's house. That man had the knife again, and he was cutting me," she choked. Her wild, frightened eyes met Micah's.

"You'll shoot me, if they try to take me and you can't stop them, right?" she asked in a hoarse whisper.

"Nobody is going to take you away from here by force," he said gently. "I promise. I can protect you on this island. It's why I brought you here in the first place."

She sighed and relaxed a little. "I'm being silly. It was the dream. It was so real, and I was scared to death, Micah! It all came back the minute I fell asleep!" She shivered. "Can't you hold me?" she asked huskily, her eyes on his muscular, hair-roughened chest. Looking at it made her whole body tingle. "Just for a minute?"

"Are you out of your mind?" he ground out.

She searched his eyes. He looked odd. "Why not?"

"Because..." His gaze fell to her breasts. They were hard-tipped now, visibly taut with desire. His jaw clenched. His hands on her wrists tightened roughly.

"Oh, for heaven's sake. I forgot! Sorry." She tried to cover herself, but his hands were relentless. She cleared her throat and grimaced. "That hurts," she complained on a nervous laugh, tugging at his hands. They loosened, but only a fraction.

"Did you take those pills I gave you to make you sleep?" he asked suddenly.

"Yes. But they didn't keep me asleep." She blinked. She smiled drowsily. She felt very uninhibited. He was looking at her breasts and she liked it. Her head fell back, because he hadn't turned her loose. His hands weren't bruising anymore, but they were holding her wrists firmly. She arched her back sensuously and watched the way his eyes narrowed and glittered on her breasts. She saw his body tense, and she gave a husky, wicked little laugh.

"You like looking at me there, don't you?" she asked, vaguely aware that she was being reckless.

He made a rough sound and met her eyes again. "Yes," he said flatly. "I like it."

"I wanted to take my clothes off for you when I was just sixteen," she confided absently as her tongue ran away with her. "I wanted you to see me. I ached all over when you looked at me that last Christmas. I wanted you to kiss me so hard that it would bruise my mouth. I wanted to unbutton your shirt and pull my dress down and let you hold me like that." She shivered helplessly at the images that rushed into her reeling mind. "You're so sexy, Micah," she whispered huskily. "So handsome. And I was just plain and my breasts were small, nothing like those beautiful, buxom women you always dated. I knew you'd never want me the way I wanted you."

He shook her gently. "Callie, for God's sake, hush!" he grated, his whole body tensing with desire at the imagery she was creating.

She was too relaxed from the sleeping pills to listen to warnings. She smiled lazily. "I never wanted anybody to touch me until then," she said softly. "Men always seemed repulsive to me. Did I ever tell you that my mother's last lover tried to seduce me? I ran from him and he knocked me down the stairs. I broke my arm. My mother said it was my fault. She took me back to the foster home. She said I was a troublemaker, and told lies about what happened."

"Dear God!" he exclaimed.

"So after that, I wore floppy old clothes and no makeup and pulled my hair back so I looked like the plainest old maid on earth, and I acted real tough. They left me alone. Then my mother married your dad," she added. "And I didn't have to be afraid anymore. Except it was worse," she murmured drowsily, "because I wanted you to touch me. But you didn't like me that way. You said I was a tramp, like my mother..."

"I didn't mean it," he ground out. "I was only trying to spare you more heartache. You were just a baby, and I was old enough to know better. It was the only way I knew to keep you at arm's length."

"You wanted my mother," she accused miserably.

"Never!" he said, and sounded utterly disgusted. "She was hard as nails, and her idea of femininity was complete control. She was the most mercenary human being I ever met."

Her pale blue eyes blinked as she searched his black ones curiously. "You said I was, too."

"You're not mercenary, honey," he replied quietly. "You never were."

She sighed, and her breasts rose and fell, drawing his attention again. "I feel so funny, Micah," she murmured.

"Funny, how?" he asked without thinking.

She laughed softly. "I don't know how to describe it. I feel...like I'm throbbing. I feel swollen."

She was describing sexual arousal, and he was fighting it like mad. He drew in a long, slow breath and forced himself to let go of her wrists. Her arms fell to her sides and he stared helplessly at the thrust of her small, firm breasts.

"It's so sad," she sighed. "The only time you've

ever looked at me or touched me was because I was hurt and needed medical attention.'' She laughed involuntarily.

"You have to stop this. Right now,'' he said firmly.

"Stop what?'' she asked with genuine curiosity.

He lifted the sheet and placed it over her breasts, pulling one of her hands up to hold it there.

She glowered at him as he got to his feet. "That's great,'' she muttered. "That's just great. Are you the guy at a striptease who yells 'put it back on'?''

He chuckled helplessly. "Not usually, no. I'll leave the door between our rooms and the bathroom open. You can sing out if you get scared again.''

"Gosh, you're brave,'' she said. "Aren't you afraid to leave your door unlocked? I might sneak in and ravish you in your sleep.''

"I wear a chastity belt,'' he said with a perfectly straight face.

Her eyes widened and suddenly she burst out laughing.

He grinned. "That's more like it. Now lie back down and stop trying to seduce me. When you wake up and remember the things you've said and done tonight, you'll blush every time you look at me.''

She shrugged. "I guess I will.'' She frowned. "What was in those pills?''

"A sedative. Obviously it has an unpredictable reaction on you,'' he commented with a long, amused look. "Either that or I've discovered a brand-new aphrodisiac. It makes retiring virgins wanton, apparently.''

She glared up at him. "I am not wanton, and it wasn't my fault, anyway. I was very scared and you came running in here to flaunt your bare chest at me," she pointed out.

"You were the one doing the flaunting," he countered. "I'm going to have Lisette buy you some gowns, and while you're here, you'll wear them. I don't keep condoms handy anymore," he added bluntly.

She flushed and gasped audibly. "Micah Steele!" she burst out, horrified at the crude remark.

"Don't pretend you don't know what one is. You're not that naive. But that's the only way I'd ever have sex with you, even if I lost my head long enough to stifle my conscience," he added bluntly. "Because I don't want kids, or a wife, ever."

"I've already told you that I'm not proposing marriage!"

"You tried to seduce me," he accused.

"You tempted me! In fact, you drugged me!"

He was trying valiantly not to laugh. "I never!" he defended himself. "I gave you a mild sedative. A very mild sedative!"

"It was probably Spanish Fly," she taunted. "I've read about what it's supposed to do to women. You gave it to me deliberately so that I'd flash my breasts at you and make suggestive remarks, no doubt!"

He pursed his lips and lifted his chin, muffling laughter. "For the record, you've got gorgeous breasts," he told her. "But I've never seen myself as a tutor for a sensuous virgin. In case you were thinking along those lines."

She felt that compliment down to her toes and tried not to disgrace herself by showing it. Apparently he didn't think her breasts were too small at all. Imagine that! "There are lots of men who'd just love to have sex with me," she told him haughtily.

"What a shame that I'm the only one you'd submit to."

She glared at him. "Weren't you going back to bed?" she asked pointedly.

He sighed. "I might as well, if you're through undressing for me."

"I didn't undress for you! I sleep like this."

"I'll bet you didn't before you moved in with my father and me," he drawled softly.

Her flush was a dead giveaway.

"*And* you never locked your bedroom door at home," he added.

"For all the good it did me," she said grimly.

"I never got my kicks as a voyeur, especially with precocious teenagers," he told her. "You're much more desirable now, with a little age on you. Not," he added, holding up one lean hand, "that I have any plans to succumb. You're a picket-fence sort of woman."

"And you like yours in combat gear, with muscles," she retorted.

His eyes sketched her body under the sheet. "If I ever had the urge to marry," he said slowly, "you'd be at the top of my list of prospects, Callie. You're kindhearted and honest and brave. I was proud of you in the jungle."

She smiled. "Were you, really? I was terribly scared."

"All of us are, when we're being hunted. The trick is to keep going anyway." He pushed her down gently with the sheet up to her neck and her head on the pillow, and he tucked her in very gently. "Go back to sleep," he said, tracing a path down her cheek with a lean forefinger. He smiled. "You can dream about having wild sex with me."

"I don't have a clue about how to have wild sex," she pointed out. She lifted both eyebrows and her eyes twinkled as she gave him a wicked smile. "I'll bet you're great in bed."

"I am," he said without false modesty. "But," he added somberly, "you're a virgin. First times are painful and embarrassing, nothing like the torrid scenes in those romance novels you like to read."

She drew in a drowsy breath. "I figured that."

He had to get out of here. He was aroused already. It wouldn't take much to tempt him, and she'd been through enough already. He tapped her on the tip of her nose. "Sleep well."

"Micah, can I ask you something?" she murmured, blinking as she tried to stay awake.

"Go ahead."

"What did my mother see that made her think she'd enticed you that night we had the blowup?"

"Are you sure you want to know?" he asked. "Because if you do, I'll show you."

Her breath caught in her throat and her heart pounded. She looked at him with uninhibited curiosity and hunger. "I'm sure."

"Okay. Your choice." He unsnapped his pajama bottoms, and let them fall. "She saw this," he said quietly.

Her eyes went to that part of him that the pajamas had hidden. She wasn't so naive that she hadn't seen statues, and photographs in magazines, of naked men. But he sure didn't look like any of the pictures. There were no white lines on him anywhere. He was solid muscle, tanned and exquisitely male. Her eyes went helplessly to that part of him that was most male, and she almost gasped. He was impressive, even to an innocent.

"Do you understand what you're seeing, Callie?" he asked quietly.

"Yes," she managed in a husky whisper. "You're…you're aroused, aren't you?"

He nodded. "When I got away from you that Christmas night, I was like this, just from being close to you," he explained quietly, his voice strained. "The slacks I was wearing were tailored to fit properly, so it was noticeable. Your mother was experienced, and when she saw it, she thought it was because of her. She was wearing a strappy little silver dress, and she had an inflated view of her own charms. I found her repulsive."

"I didn't know men looked like that." Her lips parted as she continued to stare at him. "Are you…I mean, is that…normal?"

"I do occasionally inspire envy in other men," he murmured with a helpless laugh. He pulled his pajama trousers back up and snapped them in place, almost shivering with the hunger to throw himself down on top of her and ravish her. She had no idea of the effect that wide-eyed curiosity had on him. "Now I'm getting out of here before it gets any worse!" he said in a tight voice. "Good night."

She stretched, feeling oddly swollen and achy. She stretched, feeling unfamiliar little waves of pleasure washing over her at the intimacy they'd just shared. She noticed that his face went even tauter as he watched her stretch. It felt good. But she was really sleepy and her eyelids felt heavy. Her eyes began to close. "Gosh, I'm tired. I think I can sleep…now." Her voice trailed off as she sighed heavily and her whole body relaxed in the first stages of sleep.

He looked at her with pure temptation. She'd been sedated, of course, or she'd never have been so un-inhibited with him. He knew that, but it didn't stop the frustrated desire he felt from racking his powerful body.

"I'm so glad that one of us can sleep," he murmured with icy sarcasm, but she was already asleep. He gave her one last, wistful stare, and went out of the room quickly.

The next morning, Callie awoke after a long and relaxing sleep feeling refreshed. Then she remembered what had happened in the middle of the night and she was horrified.

She searched through the bag Micah's friend had packed for her, looking for something concealing and unnoticeable, but there wasn't a change of clothing. She only had the jeans and shirt she'd been wearing the day before. Grimacing, she put them back on and ran a brush through her short dark hair. She didn't bother with makeup at all.

When she went into the kitchen, expecting to find it empty, Micah was going over several sheets of paper with a cup of black coffee in one big hand. He gave her a quick glance and watched the blush cover her high cheekbones. His lean, handsome face broke into a wicked grin.

"Good morning," he drawled. "All rested, are we? Ready for another round of show and tell?"

She ground her teeth together and avoided looking directly at him as she poured herself a cup of coffee from the coffeemaker on the counter and added creamer to it.

"I was drugged!" she said defensively, sitting down at the table. She couldn't make herself look him in the eye.

"Really?"

"You should know," she returned curtly. "You drugged me!"

"I gave you a mild sedative," he reminded her. He gave her a mischievous glance. "But I'll be sure to remember the effects."

She cleared her throat and sipped her coffee. "Can you find me something to do around here?" she asked. "I'm not used to sitting around doing nothing."

"I phoned Lisse about thirty minutes ago," he said. "She'll be over at ten to take you shopping."

"So soon?" she asked curiously.

"You don't have a change of clothes, do you?" he asked.

She shook her head. "No."

"Maddie travels light and expects everyone else to, as well," he explained. "Especially in tight corners. I'll give you my credit card..."

"I have my own with my passport," she said at once, embarrassed. "Thanks, but I pay my own way."

"So you said." He eyed her over his coffee cup. "I won't expect anything in return," he added. "In case that thought crossed your mind."

"I know that. But I don't want to be obligated to you any more than I already am."

"You sound like me, at your age," he mused. "I

never liked to accept help, either. But we all come to it, Callie, sooner or later.''

She let out a slow breath and sipped more coffee. ''I couldn't repay you in a hundred years for what you did for me,'' she said gently. ''You risked your life to get me out of there.''

''All in a day's work, honey,'' he said, and smiled. ''Besides,'' he added, ''I had a score to settle with Lopez.'' His face hardened. ''I've got an even bigger one to settle, now. I have to put him out of action, before he organizes his men and goes after Dad!''

Chapter Seven

Callie felt her heart go cold at the words. She'd been through so much herself that she'd forgotten briefly that Jack Steele was in danger, too. Micah had said that Pogo and Maddie would watch over him, but obviously he still had fears.

"You don't think he'll be safe with your people?" she asked worriedly.

"Not if Lopez gets his act together," he said coolly. "Which is why I've had Bojo send him a message in the clear, rubbing it in that I took you away from him."

She felt uneasy. "Isn't that dangerous, with a man like Lopez?"

"Very," he agreed. "But if he's concentrating on me, he's less likely to expend his energy on Dad. Right?"

"Right," she agreed. "What do you want me to do?"

He lowered his eyes to his coffee cup and lifted it to his chiseled mouth. "You do whatever you like. You're here as my guest."

She frowned. "I don't need a holiday, Micah."

"You're getting one, regardless. Today you can go shopping with Lisse. Tomorrow, I'll take you sight-seeing, if you like."

"Is it safe?"

He chuckled. "We won't be alone," he pointed out. "I intend taking Bojo and Peter and Rodrigo along with us."

"Oh."

"Disappointed?" he asked with faint arrogance. "Would you rather be alone with me, on a deserted beach?"

She glared at him. "You stop that."

"Spoilsport. You do rise to the bait so beautifully." He leaned back in his chair and the humor left his eyes. "Bojo's going with you to Nassau. Buy what you like, but make sure you don't bring home low-cut blouses and short-shorts or short skirts. There aren't any other women on this island, except a couple of married middle-aged island women who live with their husbands and families. I don't want anything to divert the men's attention with Lopez on the loose."

"I don't wear suggestive clothing," she pointed out.

"You do around me," he said flatly. "Considering last night's showing, I thought the warning might be appropriate."

"I was drugged!" she repeated, flushing.

"I don't mind if you show your body to me," he continued, as if she hadn't spoken. "I enjoy looking at it. But I'm not sharing the sight. Besides, for the next week or two, you're my sister. I don't want anyone speculating about our exact relationship."

"Why? Because of your friend Lisette?" she asked bitterly.

"Exactly," he said with a poker face. "Lisette and I are lovers," he added bluntly. "The last thing I need is a jealous tug-of-war in a crisis."

She caught her breath audibly. It was cruel of him to say such a thing. Or maybe he was being cruel to be kind, making sure that she didn't get her hopes up.

She lifted her head with postured arrogance. "That's wishful thinking," she said firmly. "I know you're terribly disappointed that I haven't proposed, but you'd better just deal with it."

For an instant he looked shocked, then he laughed. It occurred to him that he'd never laughed as much in his life as he had with her, especially the past couple of days. Considering the life or death situation they'd been in, it was even more incredible. Callie was a real mate under fire. He'd heard stories about wives of retired mercs walking right into fire with their husbands. He'd taken them with a grain of salt until he'd seen Callie in a more desperate situation than any of those wives had ever been in.

"You made me proud, in Cancún," he said after a minute. "Really proud. If we had campfires, you're the sort of woman we'd build into legend around them."

She flushed. "Like Maddie?"

"Maddie's never been in the situation you were

in," he said somberly. "I don't even know another woman who has. Despite the nightmares, you held up as well as any man I've ever served with."

She smiled slowly. "A real compliment, wow," she murmured. "If you'll write all that down, I'll have it notarized and hang it behind my desk. Mr. Kemp will be very impressed."

He glowered at her. "Kemp's more likely to hang you on the wall beside it. You're wasted in a law office."

"I love what I do," she protested. "I dig out little details that save lives and careers. Law isn't dry and boring, it's alive. It's history."

"It's a job in a little hick Texas town while you'll eventually dry up and blow away like a sun-scorched creosote bush."

She searched his dark eyes. "That's how it felt to you, I know. You never liked living in Jacobsville. But I'm not like you," she added softly. "I want a neat little house with a flower garden and neighbors to talk to over the fence, and a couple of children." Her face softened as she thought about it. "Not right away, of course. But someday."

"Just the thought of marriage gives me chest pain," he said with veiled contempt. "More often than not, a woman marries for money and a man marries for sex. What difference does a sheet of paper with signatures make?"

"If you have to ask, you wouldn't understand the answer," she said simply. "I guess you don't want kids."

He frowned. He'd never thought about having kids. It was one of those "someday" things he didn't give much time to. He studied Callie and pictured her again with a baby in her arms. It was surprisingly nice.

"It would be hard to carry a baby through jungle undergrowth with a rifle under one arm," she answered her own question. "And in your line of work, I don't suppose leaving a legacy to children is much of a priority."

He averted his head. "I expect to spend what I make while I'm still alive," he said.

She looked out over the bay, her eyes narrowing in the glare of the sunlight. The casuarinas lining the beach were towering and their feathery fronds waved gracefully in the breeze that always blew near the water. Flowers bloomed everywhere. The sand was like sugar, white and picturesque.

"It's like a living travel poster," she remarked absently. "I've never seen water that color except in postcards, and I thought it was just a bad color job."

"There are places in the Pacific and the Caribbean like it," he told her. He glanced toward the pier as he heard the sound of a motor. "There's Lisse," he said. "Come and be introduced."

She got up and followed along behind him, feeling like a puppy that couldn't be left alone. As she watched, a gorgeous blonde in a skimpy yellow sundress with long legs and long hair let Micah help her onto the pier. Unexpectedly he jerked her against him and kissed her so passionately that Callie flushed and looked away in embarrassment. He was obviously terrified that she might read something into last night, so he was making his relationship with Lisse very plain.

A few minutes later, Micah put something into Lisse's hand and spoke softly to her. Lisse laughed breathily and said something that Callie couldn't hear. Micah took the blonde by the hand and led her down the pier to where Callie was waiting at a respectful distance.

Up close, the blonde had a blemishless complexion and perfect teeth. She displayed them in a smile that would do credit to a supermodel, which was what the woman really looked like.

"I'm Lisette Dubonnet, but everyone calls me Lisse," she introduced herself and held out a hand to firmly shake Callie's.

"I'm Callie…" she began.

"My sister," Micah interrupted, obviously not trusting her to play along. "She's taking a holiday from her job in Texas. I want you to help her buy some leisure wear. Her suitcase didn't arrive with her."

"Oh," Lisse said, and laughed. "I've had that happen. I know *just* how you feel. Well, shall we go? Micah, are you coming with us?"

Micah shook his head. "I've got things to do here, but Bojo wants to come along, if you don't mind. He has to check on a package his brother is sending over from Georgia."

"He's perfectly welcome," Lisse said carelessly. "Come along, Callie. Callie…what a pretty name. A little rare, I should say."

"It's short for Colleen," Callie told her, having to almost run to keep up with the woman's long strides.

"We'll go downtown in Nassau. There are lots of chic little boutiques there. I'm sure we can find something that will do for you."

"You're very kind…"

Lisse held up an imperative hand as they reached

the boat she'd just disembarked from. "It's no bother. Micah never speaks of you. Did he have you hidden in a closet or something?"

"We don't get along very well," Callie formulated. It was the truth, too, mostly.

"And that's very odd. Micah gets along wonderfully with most women."

"But then you're not related to him," Callie pointed out, just managing to clamber aboard the boat before the line was untied by Bojo, who was already there and waiting to leave.

"No, thank God I'm not." Lisse laughed. Even her laugh was charming. "I'd kill myself. Hurry up, Bojo, Dad and I have to go to an embassy ball tonight, so I'm pressed for time!"

"I am coming, mademoiselle!" he said with a grin and leaped down into the boat.

"Let's go, Marchand!" she called to the captain, who replied respectfully and turned the expensive speedboat back into the bay and headed it toward Nassau.

"We could postpone this trip, if you don't have time," Callie offered.

"Not necessary," Lisse said. "I'll have less time later on. I try to do anything Micah asks me to. He's always *so* grateful," she added in a purring tone.

And I can just imagine what form that takes, Callie thought, but she didn't say it. Even so, Bojo heard their conversation, caught Callie's eye, and grinned so wickedly that she cleared her throat and asked Lisse about the history of Nassau to divert her.

Nassau was bustling with tourists. The colorful straw market at the docks was doing a booming business, and fishing boats rocked gently on the waves made by passing boats. Seagulls made passes at the water and flew gracefully past the huge glass windows of the restaurant that sat right on the bay. It was beautiful. Just beautiful. Callie, who'd never been anywhere—well, except for the road trip to Cancún with the drug lord's minions while she was unconscious—thought it was pure delight.

"Don't gawk like a tourist, darling," Lisse scoffed as they made their way past the fishing boats and into an arcade framed in an antique stone arch covered in bougainvillea. "It's only Nassau."

But Callie couldn't help it. She loved the musical accents she caught snatches of as they strolled past shops featuring jewelry with shell motifs and handcrafts from all over Europe, not to mention dress shops and T-shirt shops galore. She loved the stone pathways and the flowers that bloomed everywhere. They went past a food stand and her nose wrinkled.

"I thought I smelled liquor," she said under her breath.

"You did," Lisse said nonchalantly, waving her painted fingernails in the general direction of the counter. "You can buy any sort of alcoholic drink you want at any of these food stands."

"It's legal?"

"Of course it's legal. Haven't you been anywhere?"

Callie smiled sheepishly. "Not really. Now this is the sort of shop I need," she said suddenly, stopping at a store window displaying sundresses, jeans and T-shirts and sneakers. It also displayed the cards it accepted, and Callie had one of them. "I'll only be a minute…"

"Darling, not there!" Lisse lamented. "It's one of those cheap touristy shops! Micah wants you to use his charge card. I've got it in my pocket. He wants you to wear things that won't embarrass him." She put her fingers over her mouth. "Oh, dear, I forgot, I wasn't to tell you that he said that." She grimaced. "Well, anyway…"

"Well, anyway," Callie interrupted, following Lisse's lead, "this is where I'm shopping, with *my* card. You can wait or come in. Suit yourself."

She turned and left Lisse standing there with her mouth gaping, and she didn't care. The woman was horrible!

After she'd tried on two pairs of jeans, two sundresses, a pair of sandals, one of sneakers and four T-shirts, she felt guilty for the way she'd talked to Micah's woman. But Lisse was hard-going, especially after that kiss she'd witnessed. It had hurt right to the bone, and Lisse's condescending, snappy attitude didn't endear her to Callie, either.

She came back out of the shop with two bags. "Thank you very much. I'd like to go back to the house, now," she told Lisse, and she didn't smile.

Lisse made a moue with her perfect mouth. "I've hurt your feelings. I'm sorry. But Micah told me what to do. He'll be furious with me now."

What a pity. She didn't say it. "He can be furious with me," Callie said, walking ahead of Lisse back the way they'd come. "I buy my own clothes and pay my own way. I'm not a helpless parasite. I don't need a man to buy things for me."

There was a stony silence from behind her. She stopped and turned and said, "Oh, my, did I hurt your feelings? I'm sorry." And with a wicked gleam in her eyes at the other woman's furious flush, she walked back toward the boat.

Bojo knew something was going on, but he was too polite to question Lisse's utter silence all the way back to the pier. He got out first to tie up the boat and reached down to help Callie out, relieving her of her packages on the way. Micah had heard the boat and was strolling down the pier to meet them. There was a scramble as Lisse climbed out of the boat, cursing her captain for not being quick enough to spare her a stumble. She sounded like she was absolutely seething!

"We'd better run for it," Callie confided to Bojo.

"What did you do?" he asked under his breath.

"I called her a parasite. I think she's upset."

He muffled a laugh, nodded respectfully at his boss and herded Callie down the pier at very nearly a run while Micah stood staring after them with a scowl. Seconds later Lisse reached him and her voice carried like a bullhorn.

"She's got the breeding of a howler monkey, and the dress sense of an octopus!" she raged. "I wouldn't take her to the nearest tar pit without a bribe!"

Callie couldn't help it. She broke down and ran even faster, with Bojo right beside her.

Later, of course, she had to face the music. She'd changed into a strappy little blue-and-white-striped sundress. It was ankle-length with a square bodice and wide shoulder straps. Modest even enough for her surroundings. She was barefoot, having disliked the fit of the sandals she'd bought that rubbed against her big toe. Micah came striding toward her where she was lounging under a sea grape tree watching the fishing boats come into the harbor.

Micah was in cutoff denims that left his long, powerful legs bare, and he was wearing an open shirt. His chest was broad and hair-roughened and now Callie couldn't look at it without feeling it under her hands.

"Can't you get along with anyone?" he demanded, his fists on his narrow hips as he glared down at her.

"My boss Mr. Kemp thinks I'm wonderful," she countered.

His eyes narrowed. "You gave Lisse fits, and she only came over to do you a favor, when she was already pressed for time."

Her eyebrows arched over shimmering blue eyes. "You don't think I'm capable of walking into a shop and buying clothes all by myself? Whatever sort of women are you used to?"

"And you called her a parasite," he added angrily.

"Does she work?"

He hesitated. "She's her father's hostess."

"I didn't ask you about her social life, I asked if she worked for her living. She doesn't. And she said that when she did you favors, you repaid her handsomely." She cocked her head up at him. "I suppose, in a pinch, you could call that working for her living. But it isn't a profession I'd want to confess to in public."

He just stood there, scowling.

"I make my own living," she continued, "and pay my own way. I don't rely on men to support me, buy me clothes, or chauffeur me around."

"Lisse is used to a luxurious lifestyle," he began slowly, but without much conviction.

"I'm sure that I've misjudged her," she said placatingly. "Why, if you lost everything tomorrow, I know she'd be the first person to rush to your side and offer to help you make it all back with hard work."

He pursed his lips and thought about that.

"That's what I thought," she said sweetly.

He was glaring again. "I told you to put everything on my card, and get nice things."

"You told Lisse to take me to expensive dress shops so that I wouldn't buy cheap stuff and embarrass you," she countered, getting to her feet. She brushed off her skirt, oblivious to the shocked look on his face, before she lifted her eyes back to his. "I don't care if I embarrass you," she pointed out bluntly. "You can always hide me in a closet when you have guests if you're ashamed of me."

He made a rough sound. "You'd walk right into the living room and tell them why you were hidden."

She shrugged. "Blame it on a rough childhood. I don't like people pushing me around. Especially model-type parasites."

"Lisse is not—" he started.

"I don't care what she is or isn't," she cut him off, "she's not bossing me around and insulting me!"

"What did you tell her about our relationship?" he demanded, and he was angry.

"I told her nothing," she countered hotly. "It's none of her business. But, for the record, if you really were my brother, I'd have you stuffed and mounted and I'd use you for an ashtray!"

She walked right past him and back into the house. She heard muffled curses, but she didn't slow down. Let him fume. She didn't care.

She didn't come out for supper. She sat in a peacock chair out on the patio overlooking the bay and enjoyed the delicious floral smell of the musty night air in the delicious breeze, while sipping a piña colada. She'd never had one and she was curious about the taste, so she'd had Mac fix her one, along with a sandwich. She wasn't really afraid of Micah, but she was hoping to avoid him until they both cooled down.

He came into her room without knocking and walked right out onto the patio. He was wearing a tuxedo with a faintly ruffled fine white cotton shirt, and he looked so handsome that her heart stopped and fluttered at just the sight of him.

"Are you going to a funeral, or did you get a job as a waiter?" she asked politely.

He managed not to laugh. It wasn't funny. She wasn't funny. She'd insulted Lisse and the woman was going to give him fits all night. "I'm taking Lisse to an embassy ball," he said stiffly. "I would have invited you, but you don't have anything to wear," he added with a vicious smile.

"Just as well," she murmured, lifting her glass to him in a mock toast. "It would have blood all over it by the end of the night, if I'm any judge of miffed women."

"Lisse is a lady," he said shortly. "Something you have no concept of, with your ignorance of proper manners."

That hurt, but she smiled. "Blame it on a succession of foster homes," she told him sweetly. "Manners aren't a priority."

He hated being reminded of the life she'd led. It made him feel guilty, and he didn't like it. "Pity," he said scathingly. "You might consider taking lessons."

"I always think that if you're going to fight, you should get down in the mud and roll around, not use words."

"Just what I'd expect from a little savage like you," he said sarcastically.

The word triggered horrible memories. She reacted to it out of all proportion, driven by her past. She leaped to her feet, eyes blazing, the glass trembling in her hand. "One more word, and you'll need a shower and a dry cleaner to get out the door!"

"Don't you like being called a savage?" He lifted his chin as her hand drew back. "You wouldn't daaa....re!"

He got it right in the face. It didn't stay there. It dribbled down onto his spotless white shirt and made little white trickles down over his immaculate black tuxedo.

She frowned. "Damn. I forgot the toast." She lifted the empty glass at him. *"Salud y pesetas!"* she said in Spanish, with a big furious smile. Health and wealth.

His fists clenched at his sides. He didn't say a word. He didn't move a muscle. He just looked at her with those black eyes glittering like a coiling cobra.

She wiggled her eyebrows. "It will be an adventure. Lisse can lick it off! Think of the new experiences you can share…now, Micah,'' she shifted gears and started backing up.

He was moving. He was moving very slowly, very deliberately, with the steps of a man who didn't care if he had to go to jail for homicide. She noticed that at once.

She backed away from him. He really did look homicidal. Perhaps she'd gone a little too far. Her mouth tended to run away from her on good days, even when she wasn't insulted and hadn't had half a glass of potent piña colada to boot. She wasn't used to alcohol at all.

"Let's be reasonable," she tried. She was still backing up. "I do realize that I might have overreacted. I'll apologize."

He kept coming.

"I'm really sorry," she tried again, holding up both hands, palms toward him, as if to ward him off.

He still kept coming.

"And I promise, faithfully, that I will never do it…*aaaaahh!*"

There was a horrific splash and she swallowed half the swimming pool. She came up soaked, sputtering, freezing, because the water was cold. She clamored over the softly lit water to the concrete edge and grabbed hold of the ladder to pull herself up. It was really hard, because her full skirt was soaked and heavy.

"Like hell you do," he said fiercely, and started to push her back in.

She was only trying to save herself. But she grabbed his arms and overbalanced him, and he went right into the pool with her, headfirst.

This time when she got to the surface, he was right beside her. His black eyes were raging now.

She pushed her hair out of her eyes and mouth. "I'm *really* sorry," she panted.

He was breathing deliberately. "Would you like to explain why you went ballistic for no reason?" he demanded.

She grimaced, treading water and trying not to sink. She couldn't swim *very well.* She was ashamed of her behavior, but the alcohol had loosened all her inhibitions. She supposed she owed him the truth. She glanced at him and quickly away again. "When that man hit on me and made me break my arm, he told my mother I was a lying little savage and that I needed to be put away. That's when my mother took me back to my foster family and disowned me," she bit off the words, averting her eyes.

There was a long silence. He swam to the ladder, waiting for her to join him. But she was tired and cold and emotionally drained. And when she tried to dog-paddle, her arms were just too tired. She sank.

Powerful arms caught her, easing her to the surface effortlessly so that she could breathe. He sat her on the edge and climbed out, reaching down to lift her out beside him. He took her arm and led her back up the cobblestoned walkway to the patio.

"I can pack and go home tomorrow," she offered tautly.

"You can't leave," he said flatly. "Lopez knows where you are."

She lifted her weary eyes to his hard, cold face. "Poor you," she said. "Stuck with me."

His eyes narrowed. "You haven't dealt with any

of it, have you?'' he asked quietly. ''You're still carrying your childhood around on your back.''

''We all do, to some extent,'' she said with a long sigh. ''I'm sorry I ruined your suit. I'm sorry I was rude to Lisse. I'll apologize, if you like,'' she added humbly.

''You don't like her.''

She shrugged. ''I don't know her. I just don't have a high opinion of women who think money is what life is all about.''

He scowled. ''What *is* it all about?'' he challenged.

She searched his eyes slowly. ''Pain,'' she said in a husky tone, and she winced involuntarily before she could stop herself. ''I'm going to bed. Good night.''

She was halfway in the door when he called her back.

She didn't turn. ''Yes?''

He hesitated. He wanted to apologize, he really did. But he didn't know how. He couldn't remember many regrets.

She laughed softly to herself. ''I know. You wish you'd never been landed with me. You might not believe it, but so do I.''

''If you'll give me the name of the shop where you bought that stuff, I'll have them transfer it to my account.''

''Fat chance, Steele,'' she retorted as she walked away.

Chapter Eight

After a restless night, but thankfully with no night-mares, Callie put on a colorful sundress and went out onto the beach barefoot to pick up shells. She met Bojo on the way. He was wearing the long oyster silk hooded djellaba she'd never seen him out of.

He gave her a rueful glance. "The boss had to send to town for a new tuxedo last night," he said with twinkling dark eyes. "I understand you took him swimming."

She couldn't help chuckling. "I didn't mean to. We had a name-calling contest and he lost."

He chuckled, too. "You know, his women rarely accost him. They fawn over him, play up to him, stroke his ego and live for expensive presents."

"I'm his sister," she said neutrally.

"You are not," he replied gently. He smiled at her surprised glance. "He does occasionally share

things with me,'' he added. "I believe the fiction is
to protect you from Lisse. She is obsessively jealous
of him and not a woman to make an enemy of. She
has powerful connections and little conscience.''

"Oh, I got to her before I got to him, if you recall,'' Callie said with a wry glance. She scuffed her
toes in the sand, unearthing part of a perfect shell.
She bent to pick it up. "I guess I'll be fish food if
she has mob connections.''

He chuckled. "I wouldn't rule that out, but you
are safe enough here," he admitted. "What are you
doing?''

"Collecting shells to take back home," she said,
her eyes still on the beach. "I've lived inland all my
life. I don't think I've ever even seen the ocean. Gal-
veston is on the bay, and it isn't too far from Jacobsville, but I've never been there, either. It just
fascinates me!'' She glanced at him. "Micah said
you were from Morocco. That's where the Sahara
Desert is, isn't it?''

"Yes, but I am from Tangier. It is far north of the
desert.''

"But it's desert, too, isn't it?'' she wondered.

He laughed pleasantly. "Tangier is a seaport, mademoiselle. In fact, it looks a lot like Nassau. That's
why I don't mind working here with Micah.''

"Really?'' She just stared at him. "Isn't it funny,
how we get mental pictures of faraway places, and
they're nothing like what you see when you get
there? I've seen postcards of the Bahamas, but I
thought that water was painted, because it didn't
even look real. But it is. It's the most astonishing
group of colors…''

"Bojo!''

He turned to see his boss coming toward them, taciturn and threatening. It was enough for Callie to hear the tone of his voice to know that he was angry. She didn't turn around, assuming he had chores for Bojo.

"See you," she said with a smile.

He lifted both eyebrows. "I wonder," he replied enigmatically, and went down the beach to speak to Micah.

Minutes later, Micah strolled down the beach where Callie was kneeling and sorting shells damp with seawater and coated with sand. He was wearing sand-colored slacks with casual shoes and an expensive silk shirt under a sports coat. He looked elegant and so handsome that Callie couldn't continue looking at him without letting her admiration show.

"Are you here for an apology?" she asked, concentrating on the shells instead of him. Her heart was pounding like mad, but at least her voice sounded calm.

There was a pause. "I'm here to take you sightseeing."

Her heart jumped. She'd thought that would be the last thing on his mind after their argument the night before. She glanced at his knees and away again. "Thanks for the offer, but I'd rather hunt shells, if it's all the same to you."

He stuck his hands into his pockets and glared at her dark, bent head, his mouth making a thin line in a hard face. He felt guilty about the things he'd said to her the night before, and she'd made him question his whole lifestyle with that remark about Lisse. When he looked back, he had to admit that most of the women in his life had been out for material re-

wards. Far from looking for love, they'd been looking for expensive jewelry, nights out in the fanciest
nightclubs and restaurants, sailing trips on his yacht.
Callie wouldn't even let him buy her a decent dress.

He glared at the dress she was wearing with bri-
dled fury. Lisse had spent the evening condemning
Callie for everything from her Texas accent to her
lack of style. It had been one of the most unpleasant
dates of his life, and when he'd refused her offer to
stay the night at her apartment, she'd made furious
comments about his "unnatural" attraction to his sister. Rather than be accused of perversion, he'd been
forced to tell the truth. That had only made matters
worse. Lisse had stormed into her apartment house
without a word and he knew that she was vindictive.
He'd have to watch Callie even more carefully now.

"I guess she gave you hell all night, huh?" Callie
asked his shoes. "I'm really sorry."

He let out a harsh breath. His dark eyes went to
the waves caressing the white sand near the shore.
Bits of seaweed washed up over the occasional shell,
along with bits of palm leaves.

"Why don't you want to see Nassau?"

She stood up and lifted one of her bare feet. There
was a noticeable blister between her big toe and the
next one, on both feet. "Because I'd have to go barefoot. I got the wrong sort of sandals. They've got a
thong that goes between your toes, and I'm not used
to them. Sneakers don't really go with this dress."

"Not much would," he said with a scathing scrutiny of it. "Half the women on New Providence are
probably wearing one just like it."

She glared at him. "Assembly line dresses are part
of my lifestyle. I have to live within my means," she

said with outraged pride. "I'm sorry if I don't dress up to your exacting standards, but I can't afford haute couture on take-home pay of a little over a hundred and fifty dollars a week!" Her chin tilted with even more hostility. "So spare your blushes and leave me to my shells. I'd hate to embarrass you by wearing my 'rags' out in public."

"Oh, hell!" he burst out, eyes flashing.

He was outraged, but she knew she'd hit the nail on the head. He didn't even try to pretend that he wasn't ashamed to take her out in public. "Isn't it better if I stay here, anyway? Surely I'm safer in a camp of armed men that I would be running around Nassau."

"You seem to be surgically attached to Bojo lately," he said angrily.

She lifted both eyebrows. "I like Bojo," she said. "He doesn't look down on the way I dress, or make fun of my accent, or ignore me when I'm around."

He was almost vibrating with anger. He couldn't remember any woman in his life making him as explosively angry as Callie could.

"Why don't you take Lisse sight-seeing?" she suggested, moving away from him. "You could start with the most expensive jeweler in Nassau and work your way to the most expensive boutique…Micah!"

He had her up in his arms and he was heading for the ocean.

She pushed at his broad chest. "Don't you dare, don't…you…dare, Micah!"

It didn't work. He swung her around and suddenly was about to toss her out right into the waves when the explosion came. There was a ricochet that was unmistakable to Micah, and bark flew off a palm tree nearby. "Bojo!" Micah yelled.

The other man, who was still within shouting distance, came running with a small weapon in his hands. Out beyond the breakers, there was a ship, a yacht, moving slowly. A glint of sunlight reflecting off metal was visible on the deck and the ricocheting sound came again.

"What the…!" she exclaimed, as Micah ran down the beach with her in his arms.

"This way!" Bojo yelled to him, and a sharp, metallic ripple of gunfire sounded somewhere nearby.

The firing brought other men to the beach, one of whom had a funny-looking long tube. It was Peter. Bojo called something to him. He protested, but Bojo insisted. He knelt, resting the tube on his shoulder, sighted and pulled the trigger. A shell flew out of it with a muffled roar. Seconds later, there was a huge splash in the water just off the yacht's bow.

"That'll buy us about a minute. Let's go!" Micah grabbed Callie up in his arms and rushed up the beach to the house at a dead run. His men stopped firing and followed. Micah called something to Bojo in a language Callie had never heard before.

"What was that?" she asked, shocked when he put her down inside the house. "What happened?"

"Lopez happened, unless I miss my guess. I was careless. It won't happen twice," Micah said flatly. He walked away while she was still trying to form questions.

Moments later, Micah went to find Bojo.

"The yacht is gone now, of course," Bojo said

angrily. "Peter is upset that I refused to let him blow her up."

"Some things require more authority than I have, even here," Micah said flatly. "But don't think I wasn't tempted to do just that. Lopez knows I have Callie, and he knows where she is now. He'll make a try for her." He looked at Bojo. "She can't be out of our sight again, not for a second."

"I am aware of that," the other man replied. His dark eyes narrowed. "Micah, does she have any idea at all that you're using her as bait?"

"If you so much as mention that to her…!" Micah threatened softly.

"I would not," he assured the older man. "But you must admit, it hardly seems the action of someone who cares for her."

Micah stared him down. "She's part of my family and I'll take care of her. But she's only part of my family because my father married her tramp of a mother. She's managed to endear herself to my father and it would kill him if anything happened to her," he said in a cold tone. "I can't let Lopez get to my father. Using Callie to bait him here, where I can deal with him safely, is the only way I have to get him at all, and I'm not backing down now!"

"As you wish," Bojo said heavily. "At least she has no idea of this."

Micah agreed. Neither of them saw the shadow at the door behind them retreat to a distance.

Callie went back to her room and closed the door very quietly before she let the tears roll down her white face. She'd have given two years of her life not to have heard those cold words from Micah's lips. She knew he was angry with her, but she didn't

realize the contempt with which he was willing to
risk her life, just to get Lopez. All he'd said about
protecting her, keeping her safe, not letting Lopez
get to her—it was all lies. He wanted her for bait.
That was all she meant to him. He was doing it to
save his father from Lopez, not to save her. Apparently she was expendable. Nothing in her life had
ever hurt quite so much.

She seemed to go numb from the pain. She didn't
feel anything, except emptiness. She sat down in the
chair beside the window and looked out over the
ocean. The ship that had been there was gone now,
but Lopez knew where the house was, and how well
it was guarded. Considering his record, she didn't
imagine that he'd give up his quest just because Micah had armed men. Lopez had armed men, too, and
all sorts of connections. He also had a reputation for
never getting bested by anyone. He would do everything in his power to get Callie back, thinking Micah
really cared for her. After all, he'd rescued her hadn't
he?

She wrapped her arms around herself, remembering how it had been at Lopez's house, how that
henchman had tortured her. She felt sick all over.
This was even worse than being in the foster care
system. She was all alone. There was no one to offer
her protection, to comfort her, to value her. Her
whole life had been like that. For just a little while,
she'd had some wild idea that she mattered to Micah.
What a joke.

At least she knew the truth now, even if she'd had
to eavesdrop to learn it. She could only depend on
herself. She was going to ask Bojo for a gun and get
him to teach her to shoot it. If she had to fend for

herself, and apparently she did, she wanted a chance for survival. Micah would probably turn her over to Lopez if he got a guarantee that Lopez would leave his father alone, she reasoned irrationally. The terror she felt was so consuming that she felt her whole body shaking with it.

When Micah opened the door to her room, she had to fight not to rage at him. It wasn't his fault that he didn't care for her, she told herself firmly. And she loved his father as much as he did. She managed to look at him without flinching, but the light in her eyes had gone out. They were quiet, haunted eyes with no life in them at all.

Micah saw that and frowned. She was different. "What's wrong? You're safe," he assured her. "Lopez was only letting us know he's nearby. Believe me, if he'd wanted you dead, you'd be dead."

She swallowed. "I figured that out," she said in a subdued tone. "What now?"

The frown deepened. "We wait, of course. He'll make another move. We'll draw back and let him think we didn't take the threat seriously. That will pull him in."

She lifted her eyes to his face. "Why don't you let me go sight-seeing alone?" she offered. "That would probably do the trick."

"And risk letting him take you again?" he asked solemnly.

She laughed without humor and turned her eyes back to the ocean. "Isn't that what you have in mind already?"

The silence behind her was arctic. "Would you like to explain that question?"

"In ancient times, when they wanted to catch a

lion, they tethered a live kid goat to a post and baited him with it. If the goat lived, they turned him loose, but if the lion got him, it didn't really matter. I mean, what's a goat more or less?''

Micah had never felt so many conflicting emotions at the same time. Foremost of them was shame. "You heard me talking to Bojo?''

She nodded.

His indrawn breath was the only sound in the room. "Callie," he began, without knowing what he could say to repair the damage.

"It's okay," she said to the picture window. "I never had any illusions about where I fit in your family. I still don't.''

His teeth ground together. Why should it be so painful to hear her say that? She was the interloper. She and her horrible mother had destroyed his relationship with his own father. He was alone because of her, so why should he feel guilty? But he did. He felt guilty and ashamed. He hadn't really meant everything he'd said to Bojo. Somewhere there was a vague jealousy of the easy friendship she had with his right-hand man, with the tenderness she gave Bojo, when she fought Micah tooth and nail.

"I'll do whatever you want me to," she said after a minute. "But I want a gun, and I want to learn how to use it." She stood up and turned to face him, defiant in the shark-themed white T-shirt and blue jeans she'd changed into. "Because if Lopez gets me this time, he's getting a dead woman. I'll never go through that again.''

Micah actually winced. "He's not getting you," he said curtly.

"Better me than Dad," she said with a cold smile. "Right?"

He slammed the door and walked toward her. She didn't even try to back up. She glared at him from a face that was tight with grief and misery, the tracks of tears still visible down her cheeks.

"Do you actually think I'd let him take you, even to save Dad?" he demanded furiously. "What sort of man do you think I am?"

"I have no idea," she said honestly. "You're a stranger. You always have been."

He searched her blue eyes with irritation and impatience. "You're a prime example of the reason I prefer mercenary women," he said without thinking. "You're nothing but a pain in the neck."

"Thank you. I love compliments."

"You probably thrive on insults," he bit off. Then he remembered how she'd had to live all those years, and could have slapped himself for taunting her.

"If they're all you ever hear, you get used to them," she agreed without rancor. "I'm tough. I've had to be. So do your worst, Micah," she added. "Tie me to a palm tree and wait in ambush for Lopez to shoot at me, I don't care."

But she did care. There was real pain in those blue eyes, which she was trying so valiantly to disguise with sarcasm. It hurt her that Micah would use her to draw Lopez in. That led him to the question of why it hurt her. And when he saw that answer in her eyes, he could have gone through the floor with shame.

She…loved him. He felt his heart stop and then start again as the thought went through him like electricity. She almost certainly loved him, and she was doing everything in her power to keep him from seeing it. He remembered her arms around him, her mouth surrendering to his, her body fluid and soft under his hands as she yielded instantly to his ardor. A woman with her past would have a hard time with lovemaking, yet she'd been willing to let him do anything he liked to her. Why hadn't he questioned that soft yielding? Why hadn't he known? And she'd heard what he said to Bojo, feeling that way...

"I swear to you, I won't let Lopez get you," he said in a firm, sincere tone.

"You mean, you'll try," she replied dully. "I want a gun, Micah."

"Over my dead body," he said harshly. "You're not committing suicide."

Her lower lip trembled. She felt trapped. She looked trapped.

That expression ignited him like fireworks. He jerked her into his tall, powerful body, and bent to her mouth before she realized his intent. His warm, hard mouth bit into her lips with ardent insistence as his arms enveloped her completely against him. He felt his body swell instantly, as it always did when he touched her. He groaned against her mouth and deepened the kiss, lost in the wonder of being loved...

Dizzily he registered that she was making a half-hearted effort to push him away. He felt her cold, nervous hands on his chest. He lifted his head and looked at her wary, uncertain little face.

"I won't hurt you," he said softly.

"You're angry," she choked. "It's a punishment..."

"I'm not and it isn't." He bent again, and kissed

her eyelids. His hands worked their way up into the thickness of her hair and then down her back, slowly pressing her to him.

She shivered at the feel of him against her hips.

He chuckled at that telltale sign. "Most men would kill to have such an immediate response to a woman. But I don't suppose you know that."

"You shouldn't..."

He lifted his head again and gave her a look full of amused worldly wisdom. "You think I can will it not to happen, I guess?"

She flushed.

"Sorry, honey, but it doesn't work that way." He moved away just enough to spare her blushes, but his hands slid to her waist and held her in front of him. "I want you to stay in the house," he said, as if he hadn't done anything outrageous at all. "Stay away from windows and porches, too."

She searched his eyes. "If Lopez doesn't see me," she began.

"He knows you're here," he said with faint distaste. "I don't want him to know exactly where you are. I'll have men on every corner of the property and the house for the duration. I won't let you be captured."

She leaned her forehead against him, shivering. "You can't imagine...how it was," she said huskily.

His arms tightened, holding her close. He cursed himself for ever having thought of putting her deliberately in the line of fire. He couldn't imagine he'd been that callous, even briefly. It had been the logical thing to do, and he'd never let emotion get in the way of work. But Callie wasn't like him. She had feelings that were easily bruised, and he'd done a lot of damage already. Those nightmares she had should have convinced him how traumatic her captivity had been, but he hadn't even taken that into consideration when he was setting up Lopez by bringing Callie here.

"I'm sorry," he bit off the words. He wondered if she knew how hard it was to say that.

She blinked away sudden tears. "It's not your fault, you're just trying to save Dad. I love Dad, too, Micah," she said at his chest. "I don't blame you for doing everything you can to keep him safe."

His eyes closed and he groaned silently. "I'm going to do everything I can to keep you safe, too," he told her.

She shrugged. "I know." She pulled away from him with a faint smile to soften the rejection. "Thanks."

He studied her face and realized that he'd never really looked at her so closely before. She had a tiny line of freckles just over her straight little nose. Her light blue eyes had flecks of dark blue in them and she had the faintest little dimple in her cheek when she smiled. He touched her pretty mouth with his fingertips. It was slightly swollen from the hungry, insistent pressure of his lips. She looked rumpled from his ardor, and he liked that, too.

"Take a picture," she said uncomfortably.

"You're pretty," he murmured with an odd smile.

"I'm not, and stop trying to flatter me," she replied, shifting away from him.

"It isn't flattery." He bent and brushed his mouth lightly over her parted lips. She gasped and hung there, her eyes wide and vulnerable on his face when he drew back. Her reaction made him feel taller. He smiled softly. "You don't give an inch, do you? I suppose it's hard for you to trust anyone, after the life you've led."

"I trust Dad," she snapped.

"Yes, but you don't trust me, do you?"

"Not an inch," she agreed, pulling away. "And you don't have to kiss me to make me feel better, either."

"It was to make me feel better," he pointed out, smiling at her surprise. "It did, too."

She shifted her posture a little, confused.

His dark eyes slid over her body, noting the little points that punctuated her breasts and the unsteady breathing she couldn't control. Yes, she wanted him.

She folded her arms over her breasts, curious about why he was staring at them. They felt uncomfortable, but she didn't know why.

"I didn't tell Lisse that you were an embarrassment to me," he said suddenly, and watched her face color.

"It's okay," she replied tersely. "I know I don't have good dress sense. I don't care about clothes most of the time."

"I'm used to women who do, and who enjoy letting men pay for them. The more expensive they are, the better." He sounded jaded and bitter.

She studied his hard face, recognizing disillusionment and reticence. She moved a step closer involuntarily. "You sound…I don't know…cheated, maybe."

"I feel cheated," he said shortly. His eyes were full of harsh memories. "No man likes to think that he's paying for sex."

"Then why do you choose women who want expensive gifts from you?" she asked him bluntly.

His teeth met. "I don't know."

"Don't you, really?" she asked, her eyes soft and curious. "You've always said you don't want to get married, so you pick women who don't want to, either. But that sort of woman only lasts as long as the money does. Or am I wrong?"

He looked down at her from his great height with narrowed eyes and wounded pride. "I suppose you're one of those women who would rush right over to a penniless man and offer to get a second job to help him out of debt!"

She smiled sheepishly, ignoring the sarcasm. "I guess I am." She shrugged. "I scare men off. They don't want me because I'm not interested in what sort of car they drive or the expensive places they can afford to take me to. I like to go walking in the country and pick wildflowers." She peered up at him with a mischievous smile. "The last man I said that to left town two days before he was supposed to. He was doing some accounts for Mr. Kemp and he left skid marks. Mr. Kemp thought it was hilarious. He was a notorious ladies' man, it seems, and he'd actually seduced Mr. Kemp's last secretary."

Micah didn't smile, as she'd expected him to. He looked angry.

She held up a hand. "I don't have designs on you, honest. I know you don't like wildflowers and Lisse is your sort of woman. I'm not interested in you that way, anyhow."

"Considering the way you just kissed me, you might have trouble proving that," he commented dryly.

She cleared her throat. "You kiss very nicely, and I have to get experience where I can."

"Is that it?" he asked dubiously.

She nodded enthusiastically. She swallowed again as the terror of the last hour came back and the eyes she lifted to his were suddenly haunted. "Micah, he's never going to stop, is he?"

"Probably not, unless he has help." He lifted an eyebrow. "I have every intention of helping him, once I've spoken with the authorities."

"What authorities?"

"Never mind. You know nothing. Got it?"

She saluted him. "Yes, sir."

He made a face. "Come on out. We'll have Mac make some sandwiches and coffee. I don't know about you, but I'm hungry."

"I could eat something."

He hesitated before he opened her door. "I really meant what I told you," he said. "Lopez won't get within fifty yards of you as long as there's a breath in my body."

"Thanks," she said unsteadily.

He felt cold inside. He couldn't imagine what had made him tell such lies to Bojo, where she might overhear him. He hadn't meant it, that was honest, but he knew she thought he had. She didn't trust him anymore.

He opened the door to let her go through first. A whiff of the soft rose fragrance she wore drifted up into his nostrils and made his heart jump. She always smelled sweet, and she had a loving nature that was miraculous considering her past. She gave with both hands. He thought of her with Bojo and something snapped inside him.

"Bojo's off limits," he said as she slid past him. "So don't get too attached to him!"

She looked up at him. "What a bunch of sour grapes," she accused, "just because I withdrew my proposal of marriage to you!" She stalked off down the hall.

He opened his mouth to speak, and just laughed instead.

Chapter Nine

They ate lunch, but conversation among the mercenaries was subdued and Callie got curious glances from all of them. One man, the Mexican called Rodrigo, gave her more scrutiny than the rest. He was a handsome man, tall, slender, dark-haired and dark-eyed, with a grace of movement that reminded her of Micah. But he had a brooding look about him, and he seemed to be always watching her. Once, he smiled, but Micah's appearance sent him away before he could speak to her.

After lunch, Callie asked Bojo about him.

"Rodrigo lost his sister to Lopez's vicious temper," he told her. "She was a nightclub singer who Lopez took a fancy to. He forced himself on her after she rejected Lopez's advances and… She died trying to get away from him. Rodrigo knows what was done to you, and he's angry. You remind him of his sister. She, too, had blue eyes.''

"But he's Latin," she began.

"His father was from Denmark," he said with a grin. "And blond."

"Imagine that!"

He gave her a wry glance. "He likes you," he said. "But he isn't willing to risk Micah's temper to approach you."

"You do," she said without thinking.

"Ah, but I am indispensable," he told her. "Rodrigo is not. He has enemies in many countries overseas and also, Lopez has a contract out on him. This is the only place he has left to go where he has any hope of survival. He wouldn't dare risk alienating Micah."

She frowned. "I can't think why approaching me would do that. Micah tolerates me, but he still doesn't really like me," she pointed out. "I overheard what he said to you, about using me as bait."

He smiled. "Yes. Curious, is it not, that when one of the other men suggested the same thing, he paid a trip to the dentist?"

"Why?"

"Micah knocked out one of his teeth," he confided. "The men agreed that no one would make the suggestion twice."

She caught her breath. "But I heard him tell you that very thing…!"

"You heard what he wanted me to think," he continued. "Micah is jealous of me," he added outrageously, and grinned. "You and I are friendly and we have no hostility between us. You don't want anything from me, you see, or from him. He has no idea how to deal with such a woman. He has become used to buying expensive things at a woman's whim, yet you refuse even the gift of a few items of necessary clothing." He shrugged. "It is new for him that neither his good looks nor his wealth make an impression on you. I think he finds that a challenge and it irritates him. He is also very private about his affairs. He doesn't want the men to see how vulnerable he is where you are concerned," he mused. "He had to assign me, along with Peter and Rodrigo, to keep a constant eye on you. He didn't like that. Peter and Rodrigo are no threat, of course, but he is afraid that you are attracted to me." He grinned at her surprise. "I can understand why he thinks this. I hardly need elaborate on my attributes. I am urbane, handsome, sophisticated, generous..." He paused to glance at her wide-eyed, bemused face. "Shall I continue? I should hate to miss acquainting you with any of my virtues."

She realized he was teasing then, and she chuckled. "Okay, go ahead, but I'm not making you any marriage proposals."

His eyebrows arched. "Why not?"

"Micah's put me off men," she said, tongue-in-cheek. "He's already upset because I won't propose to him." She gave him a wicked grin. "Gosh, first Micah, then you! Having this much sex appeal is a curse. Even Lopez is mad to have me!"

He grinned back. She was a unique woman, he thought, and bristling with courage and character. He wondered why Micah didn't see her as he did. The other man was alternately scathing about and protective of Callie, as if his feelings were too ambiguous to unravel. He didn't like Bojo spending time with her, but he kept her carefully at arm's length, even dragging Lisse over for the shopping trip and using her as camouflage. Callie didn't know, but Lisse had been a footnote in Micah's life even in the days when he was attracted to her. She hadn't been around much for almost a year now.

"After we deal with Lopez, you must play down your attractions," he teased. "Providing twenty-four-hour protection is wearing on the nerves."

"You're not kidding," she agreed, wandering farther down the beach. "I'm getting paranoid about dark corners. I always expect someone to be lurking in them." She glanced up at him. "Not rejected suitors," she added wryly.

He clasped his hands behind him and followed along with her, his keen eyes on the horizon, down the beach, up the beach—everywhere. Bojo was certain, as Micah was, that Lopez wasn't likely to give them time to attack him. He was going to storm the island, and soon. They had to be constantly vigilant, if they wanted to live.

"Do you know any self-defense?" Bojo asked her curiously.

"I know a little," she replied. "I took a course in it, but I was overpowered too fast."

"Show me what you know," he said abruptly. "And I will teach you a little more. It never hurts to be prepared.

She did, and he did. She learned enough to protect herself if she had time to use it. She didn't tell him, but she was really scared that Lopez might snatch her out of sight and sound of the mercs. She prayed that she'd have a fighting chance if she was in danger again.

* * *

Callie had convinced herself that an attack would come like a wave, with a lot of men and guns. The last thing she expected was that, when she was lying in her own bed, a man would suddenly appear by the bed and slap a chloroformed handkerchief over her mouth and nose. That was what happened. Outside her patio a waiting small boat on the beach was visible only where she was situated. The dark shadow against the wall managed to bypass every single safeguard of Micah's security system. He slipped into Callie's bedroom with a cloth and a bottle of chloroform and approached the bed where she was asleep.

The first Callie knew of the attack was when she felt a man's hand holding her head steady while a foul-smelling cloth was shoved up under her nose. She came awake at once, but she kept her head, even when she felt herself being carried roughly out of her bedroom onto the stone patio. She knew what to expect this time if she were taken, and she remembered vividly what Bojo had taught her that afternoon. She twisted her head abruptly so that the chloroform missed her face and landed in her hair. Then she got her hands up and slammed them against her captor's ears with all her might.

He cried out in pain and dropped her. She hit the stone-floored patio so hard that she groaned as her hip and leg crashed down onto the flagstones, but she dragged herself to her feet and grabbed at a shovel that the yardman had left leaning against a stone bench close beside her. As her assailant ignored the pain in his fury to pay her back, she swung the shovel and hit him right in the head with it. He made a strange sound and crumpled to the patio. Callie stared out toward the boat, where a dark figure was waiting.

Infuriated by the close call, and feeling very proud of the fact that she'd saved herself this time, she raised the shovel over her head. "Better luck next time, you son of a bitch!" she yelled harshly. "If I had a gun, I'd shoot you!"

Her voice brought Micah and two other men running out onto the patio. They were all armed. The two mercs ran toward the beach, firing as they made a beeline toward the little boat, which had powered up and was sprinting away with incredible speed and very little noise.

Micah stood in front of Callie wearing nothing but a pair of black silk boxer shorts. He had an automatic pistol in one hand. His hair was tousled, as if he'd been asleep. But he was wide-awake now. His face was hard, his dark eyes frightening.

He moved close to her, aware of her body in the thin nylon gown that left her breasts on open display in the light from inside the house. She didn't seem to notice, but he did. He looked at them hungrily before he dragged his gaze back up to her face, fighting a burst of desire as he tried to come to grips with the terror he'd felt when he heard Callie yelling. Thank God she'd had the presence of mind to grab that shovel and knock the man out.

"Are you okay?" he asked curtly.

"I'm better off than he is," she said huskily, swallowing hard. Reaction was beginning to set in now, and her courage was leaking away as the terror of what had almost happened began to tear at her nerves. "He had chloroform. I...I fought free, but...oh, Micah, I was scared to...death!"

She threw herself against him, shuddering in the aftermath of terror. Now that the danger was past, reaction set in with a vengeance. Her arms went under his and around him. Her soft, firm breasts were flattened against his bare stomach because she was so much shorter than he was. Her hands ran over the long, hard muscles of his back, feeling scars there as she pressed closer. He felt the corner of her mouth in the thick hair that covered the hard muscles of his chest. His body reacted predictably to the feel of a near-naked woman and he gasped audibly and stiffened.

Her hips weren't in contact with his, but she felt a tremor run through his powerful body and she pulled back a little, curious, to look up at his strained face. "What's wrong?"

He drew in a steadying breath and moved back. "Nothing! We'll get this guy inside and question him. You don't need to see it," he added firmly. "You should go back into your room..."

"And do what?" she asked, wide-eyed and hurt by his sudden withdrawal. "You think I can go to sleep now?"

"Stupid assumption," he murmured, moving restively as his body tormented him. "I can call Lisse and let her stay with you."

"No!" She lifted her chin with as much pride as she had left. "I'll get dressed. Bojo will sit up with me if I ask him..."

"The hell he will!" he exploded, his eyes glittering.

She took a step backward. He was frightening

when he looked like that. He seemed more like the stranger he'd once been than the man who'd been so kind to her in past days.

"I'll get dressed and you can stay with me tonight," he snapped. "Obviously it's asking too much to expect you to stay by yourself!" That was unfair, he realized at once, and he ground his teeth. He couldn't help it. He was afraid to be in the same room with her in the dark, but not for the reason she thought.

She took another step backward, pride reasserting itself. Her chin came up. "No, thanks!" she said. "If you'll just get me a gun and load it and show me how to shoot it, I won't have any problem with being alone."

She sounded subdued, edgy, still frightened despite that haughty look she was giving him. He was overreacting. It infuriated him that she'd had to rescue herself. It infuriated him that he wanted her. He was jealous of his men, angry that she was vulnerable, and fighting with all his might to keep from giving in to his desire for her. She was a marrying woman. She was a virgin. It was hopeless.

Worst of all, she'd almost been kidnapped again and on his watch. He'd fallen asleep, worn-out by days of wear and tear and frustrated desire. Lopez had almost had her tonight. He blamed himself for not taking more precautions, for putting her in harm's way. He should have protected her. He should have realized that Lopez was desperate enough to try anything, including an assault on the house itself. So much for his security net. Upgrades were very definitely needed. But right now, she needed comfort, and he wasn't giving it to her.

He glanced toward the beach. Out beyond it, the little boat had stilled in the water and seemed to be sinking. A dark figure struck out toward the shore.

"Peter, get him!" Micah yelled.

The young man gave him a thumbs-up signal. The tall young man tossed down his weapon, jerked off his boots and overclothes and dived into the water. The assailant tried to get away, but Peter got him. There was a struggle and seconds later, Peter dragged the man out of the water and stood over him where he lay prone on the beach.

Rodrigo came running back up from the beach just about the time the man who'd tried to carry Callie off woke up and rubbed his aching head.

"I told Peter to take the other man around the side of the house to the boat shed."

"Good work," Micah said.

"Oh, look, he's all right," Callie murmured, her eyes narrowed on the downed man who was beginning to move and groan. "What a shame!"

Micah glanced at her. "Bloodthirsty girl," he chided, and grinned despite his churning emotions.

"Well, he tried to kidnap me," she bit off, finally getting her nerve and her temper back. She remembered the chloroform and her eyes blazed. "All I had to hand was a lousy shovel, that's why he's all right."

He turned to the other man. "Rodrigo, get this guy around to the boat shed to keep Peter's captive company. Strip them both, tie them up and gag them. I've got to make a few preparations and I'll be along to question them. Do *not* tell Bojo anything, except that the police have been notified. You can phone them to pick up Lopez's henchmen an hour from now, no sooner.''

"I know what you're thinking. It won't work," Rodrigo said, trying to reason with him. "Lopez will be expecting his men back, if he hasn't already seen what happened."

"Have you got the infrareds on you?"

Rodrigo nodded and pulled out what looked like a fancy pair of binoculars.

"Check the area off the beach for Lopez's yacht."

"It's clear for miles right now. No heat signatures."

"Heat signatures?" Callie murmured.

"We have heat-seeking technology," Micah explained. "We can look right into a house or a room in the dark and see everything alive in it, right through the walls."

"You're kidding!" she exclaimed.

"He's not," Rodrigo said, his dark eyes narrowing as he noted the gown and the pretty form underneath.

Micah knew what the other man was seeing, and it angered him. He stepped in front of Callie, and the action was blatant enough to get Rodrigo moving.

"Where do you think Lopez's yacht is?" Callie asked.

"It'll be somewhere close around. Let's just hope the man Peter caught was too rattled to call Lopez while he was being shot at. I'm sure he had a cell phone. Get out my diving gear and some C-4. And don't say a word to Bojo. Got that? It will work."

"What will work?" Callie asked.

"Never mind," Micah said. "Thanks, Rodrigo. I'm going to get Callie back inside."

"I'll deal with our guest," Rodrigo said, and turned at once to his chore.

Micah drew Callie along with him, from the patio to the sliding glass doors her assailant had forced, and down the hall to her bedroom. On the way, he noticed that two other doors had been opened, as if her captor had looked in them in search of her. His bedroom was closer to the front of the house.

He drew her inside her room and closed the door behind them, pausing to lay the automatic on a table nearby. "Did he hurt you?" he asked at once.

"He dropped me on the patio. I bruised my hip…Micah, no!" she exclaimed, pushing at the big, lean hand that was pulling up her nylon gown.

"I've seen more of you than this," he reminded her.

"But…"

He swept her up in his arms and carried her to the bed, easing her down gently onto the sheet where the covers had been thrown back by her captor. He sat down beside her and pulled up the gown, smiling gently at the pale pink cotton briefs she was wearing.

"Just what I'd expect," he murmured. "Functional, not sexy."

"Nobody sees my underthings except me," she bit off. "Will you stop?"

He pushed the gown up to her waist, ignoring her protests, and winced when he saw her upper thigh and hip. "You're going to have a whopper of a bruise on your leg," he murmured, drawing down the elastic of the briefs. "Your hip didn't fare much better."

His thumb was against the soft, warm skin of her lower stomach and the other one was poised beside her head on the pillow while he looked at her bruises. She didn't think he was doing it on purpose, but that thumb seemed to be moving back and forth in a very arousing way. Her body liked it. She moved restlessly on the sheet, shivering a little with unexpected pleasure.

"A few bruises are…are better than being kidnapped," she whispered shakily. Her wide eyes met his. "I was so scared, Micah!"

His hand spread on her hip. His narrow black eyes met hers. "So was I, when I heard you shouting," he said huskily. "He almost had you!"

"Almost," she agreed, her breath jerking out. "I'm still shaking."

His fingers contracted. "I'm going to give you a sedative," he said, rising abruptly. "You need to sleep. You never will, in this condition."

He left her there and went to get his medical kit. He was back almost at once. He opened the bag and drew out a small vial of liquid and a prepackaged hypodermic syringe. This would alleviate her fear of being alone tonight and give him time to get his rampaging hormones under control.

She watched him fill the syringe effortlessly. It was a reminder that he'd studied medicine.

"Have you ever thought of going back to finish your residency?" she asked him.

He shook his head. "Too tame." He smiled in her general direction as he finished filling the syringe. "I don't think I could live without adrenaline rushes."

"Doctors have those, too," she pointed out, watching him extend her arm and tap a vein in the curve of her elbow. "You're going to put it in there?" she asked worriedly.

"It's quicker. You won't get addicted to this," he added, because she looked apprehensive. "Close your eyes. I'll try not to hurt you."

She did close her eyes, but she felt the tiny prick of the needle and winced. But it was over quickly and he was dabbing her arm with alcohol on a cotton ball.

"It won't knock you out completely," he said when he'd replaced everything in the kit. "But it will relax you."

She blinked. She felt *very* relaxed. She peered up at him with wide, soft eyes. "I wish you liked me," she said.

His eyebrows levered up. "I do."

"Not really. You don't want me around. I'm not pretty like her."

"Her?"

"Lisse." She sighed and stretched lazily, one leg rising so that the gown fell away from her pretty leg, leaving it bare. "She's really beautiful, and she has nice, big breasts. Mine are just tiny, and I'm so ordinary. Gosh, I'd love to have long blond hair and big breasts."

He glanced at the bag and back at her. "This stuff works on you like truth serum, doesn't it?" he murmured huskily.

She sat up with a misty smile and shrugged the gown off, so that it fell to her waist. Her breasts had hard little tips that aroused him the instant he saw them. "See?" she asked. "They look like acorns. Hers look like cantaloupes."

He couldn't help himself. He stared at her breasts helplessly, while his body began to swell with an urgency that made him shiver. He was vulnerable tonight.

"Yours are beautiful," he said softly, his eyes helplessly tracing them.

"No, they're not. You don't even like feeling them against you. You went all stiff and pushed me away, out on the patio. It's been like that since...Micah, what are you...doing?" she gasped as his hungry mouth abruptly settled right on top of a hard nipple and began to suckle it. "Oh...glory!" she cried out, arching toward him with a lack of restraint that was even more arousing. Her nails bit into his scalp through his thick hair, coaxing him even closer. "I like that. I...really like that!" she whispered frantically. "I like it, I like it, I...!"

"I should be shot for this," he uttered as he suckled her. "But I want you. Oh God, I want you so!" His teeth opened and nipped her helplessly.

She drew back suddenly, apprehensively as she felt his teeth, her eyes questioning.

He could barely breathe, and he knew there was no way on earth he was going to be able to stop. It was already too late. Danger was an aphrodisiac. "You don't like my teeth on you," he whispered. "All right. It's all right. We'll try this."

His fingers traced around her pert breast gently and he bent to take her mouth tenderly under his lips. She had no willpower. She opened her lips for him and clung as he eased her down onto the cool sheets.

"Don't let me do this, Callie," he ground out in a last grab at sanity, even as he shed his boxer shorts. "Tell me to stop!"

"I couldn't, not if it meant my life," she murmured, her body on fire for him. Her mind wasn't even working. She held on for dear life and pulled his mouth down harder on hers. She was shivering with pleasure. "I want you to do it," she whispered brazenly. "I want to feel you naked in my arms. I want to make love...!"

"Callie. Sweet baby!" he whispered hoarsely as he felt her hands searching down his flat belly to the source of his anguish. She touched him and he was lost, totally lost. He pressed her hard into the mattress while his mouth devoured hers. It was too late to pull back, too late to reason with her. She was drugged and uninhibited, and her hands were touching him in a way that pushed him right over the edge.

Callie lifted against him, aware of his nudity and the delight of touching him where she'd never have dreamed of touching him if she hadn't been drugged. But she'd always wanted to touch him like that, and it felt wonderful. Her body moved restlessly with little darts of pleasure as he began to discover her, too.

She enjoyed the feel of his body, the touch of his hands. Her skin felt very hot, and when she realized that the gown and her underwear were gone, it didn't matter, because she felt much more comfortable. Then he started touching her in a way she'd never been touched. She gasped. Her body tensed, but she moved toward his hand, burying her face in his neck as the delicious sensations made her pulse with delight. His skin was damp and very hot. She could hear the rasp of his breathing, she could feel it in her hair as he began to caress her very intimately.

Of course, it was wrong to let him do something so outrageous, but it felt too good to stop. She kept coaxing him with sharp little movements of her hips until he was touching her where her body wanted him to. Now the pleasure was stark and urgent. She opened her legs. Her nails bit into his nape and she clung fiercely.

"It's all right," he whispered huskily. "I won't stop. I'll be good to you."

She clung closer. Her body shivered. She was suddenly open to his insistent exploration and with embarrassment she felt herself becoming very damp where his fingers were. She stiffened.

"It's natural," he breathed into her ear. "Your body is supposed to do this."

"It is?" She couldn't look at him. "It isn't repulsive to you?"

"It's the most exciting thing I've ever felt," he whispered. His powerful body shifted so that he was lying directly over her, his hair-roughened legs lazily brushing against hers while he teased her mouth with his lips and her body with his fingers.

Her arms were curled around his neck and the sensations were so sweet that she began to gasp rhythmically. Her hips were lifting and falling with that same rhythm as she fed on the delicious little jabs of pleasure that accompanied every sensual movement.

He began to shudder, too. It was almost as if he weren't in control of himself. But that was ridiculous. Micah was always in control.

His teeth tugged at her upper lip and then at her lower one, his tongue sliding sinuously inside her mouth in slow, teasing thrusts. She felt her breasts going very tight. He was lying against her in an unexpectedly intimate way. She felt body hair against her breasts and her belly. Then she felt him there, *there,* in a contact that she'd never dreamed of sharing with him.

Despite her languor, her eyes opened and looked straight into his. She could actually see the desire that was riding him, there in his taut face and glittering eyes and flattened lips. He was shivering. She liked seeing him that way. She smiled lazily and deliberately brushed her body up against him. He groaned.

Slowly he lifted himself just a little. "Look down," he whispered huskily. "Look at me. I want you to see how aroused I am for you."

Her eyes traced the path of thick, curling blond-tipped hair from the wedge on his muscular chest, down his flat belly, and to another wedge…heavens! He had nothing on. And more than that, he was…he was…

Her misty gaze shot back up to meet his. She should be protesting. He was so aroused that a maiden lady with silver hair couldn't have mistaken it. She felt suddenly very small and vulnerable, almost fragile. But he wanted her, and she wanted him so badly that she couldn't find a single word of protest. Even if he never touched her again, she'd have this one time to live on for the rest of her miserable, lonely life. She'd be his lover, if only this once. Nothing else mattered. Nothing!

Her body lifted to brush helplessly against his while she looked at him. She was afraid. She was excited. She was on fire. She was wanton…

His hand went between their hips and began to invade her body, where it was most sensitive. Despite the pleasure that ensued, she felt a tiny stab of discomfort.

"I can feel it," he whispered, his eyes darkening as his body went taut. "It's wispy, like a spiderweb.'' He shifted sensuously. His body began to invade hers in a slow, teasing motion, and he watched her the whole time. "Are you going to let me break it, Callie?" he whispered softly.

"Break…it?"

"Your maidenhead. I want it." He moved his hips down and his whole face clenched as he felt the veil of her innocence begin to separate. His hands clenched beside her head on the pillow and the eyes that looked down into hers were tortured. His whole body shuddered with each slow movement of his hips. "I want…you! Callie!" he groaned hoarsely, his eyes closing. "Callie …baby…let me have you," he whispered jerkily. "Let me have…all of you! Let me teach you pleasure…"

He seemed to be in pain. She couldn't bear that. She slid her calves slowly over his and gasped when she felt his body tenderly penetrating hers with the action, bringing a tiny wave of pleasure. She gasped again.

He arched above her, groaning. His eyes held hers as he moved slowly, carefully. He watched her wince and he hesitated. He moved again, and she bit her lip. He moved one more time, and she tensed and then suddenly relaxed, so unexpectedly that his possession of her was complete in one involuntary movement.

It was incredible, he thought, his body as taut as steel as he looked down into her wide, curious eyes with awe as he became her lover. He could feel her, like a warm silk glove. She was a virgin. He was having her. She was giving herself. He moved experimentally, and her lips parted on a helpless breath.

His lean hands slid under her dark hair and cradled

her head while he began to move on her. One of his thighs pushed at hers, nudging it further away from the throbbing center of her body. The motion lifted her against him in a blind grasp at pleasure.

"I never thought…it would be you," she whispered feverishly.

"I never thought it would be anyone else," he replied, his eyes hot and narrow and unblinking. "I watched you when I went completely into you," he whispered and smiled when she gasped. "Now, you can watch me," he murmured roughly. "Watch me. I'll let you see…everything I feel!"

She shivered as his hips began to move sinuously, more insistently, increasing the pleasure.

He caught one of her hands and drew it between them, coaxing it back to his body. He groaned at the contact and guided her fingers to the heart of him.

She let him teach her. It was so sweet, to lie naked in his arms, and watch him make love to her. He was incredibly tender. He gave her all the time in the world before he became insistent, before his kisses devoured, before his hand pinned her hips and his whole body became an instrument of the most delicious torture. He looked down at her with blazing dark eyes, his face clenched in passion, his body shivering with urgency as he poised over her.

"Don't close your eyes," he groaned when stars were exploding in his head. "I want to see them…the very second…that you go over the edge under me!"

The words were as arousing as the sharp, violent motion of his hips as he began to drive into her. She thought he became even more potent as the tempo and the urgency increased. He held her eyes until she became blind with the first stirrings of ecstasy and her sharp, helpless cry of surprised pleasure was covered relentlessly by his mouth.

She writhed under him, sobbing with the sensation of fulfillment, her body riveted to his as convulsions made her ripple like a stormy wave. She clutched his upper arms, her nails biting in, as the ripples became almost painful in their delight. Seconds later, she felt him climax above her. His harsh, shuddering groan was as alien a sound as her own had been seconds before. She wrapped her arms around him and held on for dear life, cuddling him, cradling him, as he endured the mindless riptide and finally, finally, went limp and heavy in her arms with a whispery sigh.

"You looked at me...when it happened," she whispered with wonder. "And I saw you, I watched you." She shivered, holding him tight. Her body rippled with the tiny movement, and she laughed secretly and moaned as she felt the pleasure shoot through her. "Do it again," she pleaded. "Make me scream this time...!"

He was still shivering. "Oh, God, ...no!" he bit off. "Be still!" He held her down, hard, drawing in a sharp breath as he fought the temptation to do what she asked. He closed his eyes and his teeth clenched as he jerked back from her abruptly.

She gasped as his weight receded. There was a slight discomfort, and then he was on his feet beside the bed, grabbing up his boxer shorts with a furious hand.

She stared at him with diminishing awareness. She was deliciously relaxed. She felt great. Why was he cursing like that. She blinked vacantly. "You're very angry. What's wrong?"

DIANA PALMER 173

"What's wrong!" He turned to look down at her. She was sprawled nude in glorious abandon, looking so erotic that he almost went to his knees with the arousal that returned with a vengeance.

She smiled lazily and yawned. "Gosh, that was good. So good!" Her eyelids felt very heavy. She sprawled even more comfortably. "Even better than the last time."

"What last time?" he demanded, outraged.

She yawned again. "That other dream," she mumbled, rolling onto her side. "So many dreams. So embarrassing. So erotic! But this was the best dream, though. The very...best..."

Her voice trailed away and he realized all at once that she'd fallen asleep. She didn't understand what had happened. She'd been full of sedative and she'd let him seduce her, thinking she was just dreaming. She thought the whole thing was nothing more than another dream. No wonder she hadn't protested!

"God in heaven, what have I done!" he asked her oblivious form. There was a smear of blood on the white sheet.

Micah ground his teeth together and damned his lack of control. He hadn't had a woman in a very long time, and he'd wanted Callie since the day he'd met her. But that was no excuse for taking advantage of her while she was under the influence of a sedative. Even if she had come on to him with the most incredibly erotic suggestions. He'd seduced her and that was that.

He went to the bathroom, wet a washcloth and bathed her body as gently as he could. She was sleeping so soundly that she never noticed a thing. He put her briefs and gown back on her and put her under the sheet. He'd have to hope she didn't notice the stain, or, if she did, assumed it was an old one.

He dressed, hating himself, and went out of the room after checking the security net. He still had to go after Lopez, and now his mind was going to be full of Callie sobbing with pleasure under the crush of his body. And what if there were consequences?

Chapter Ten

With a face as grim as death, Micah pulled on his black wet suit and fins and checked the air in his tanks and the mouthpiece and face mask. He sheathed the big knife he always carried on covert missions. To the belt around his waist, he attached a waterproof carry pack. He'd interrogated one of the men, who'd been far too intimidated not to tell him what he wanted to know about Lopez's setup on the yacht, the number and placement of his men and his firepower.

"I should go with you," Rodrigo told him firmly.

"You can't dive," Micah said. "Besides, this is a one-man job. If I don't make it, it will be up to you and Bojo to finish it. But whatever happens," he added curtly, and with a threatening stare, "don't let them get Callie."

"I won't. I swear it," Rodrigo said heavily.

"Tell Bojo where I've gone after I've gone, but only after I'm gone," he added. "Don't let him follow me." He picked up a small device packed with plastique and shoved it into the waterproof bag on his belt and sealed it.

"Once you set the trigger, you'll only have a few minutes to get free of the ship. If the engines fire up while you're placing the bomb, you'll be chum," Rodrigo said worriedly. "You already look exhausted. Even if everything goes right, how will you make that swim and turn around and come back in time?"

"If I can't get free in that amount of time, I'm in the wrong business," he told Rodrigo. "I'd disgrace my expensive government training. How many men on the yacht right now?"

Rodrigo nodded toward the yacht, which had just come into view in the past ten minutes. It was out very far, almost undetectable without exotic surveillance devices. But they had a device that used a heat sensor with a telescopic lens, and they could see inside the ship. "The crew, Lopez, and six henchmen. It's suicide to do this alone."

"I'm not letting him try again," he said shortly, and his eyes were blazing. "I've put Callie's life at risk already, because I was arrogant enough to think she was safe here. She could have been killed tonight while I was asleep in my bed. I won't get over that in a hurry. I'm not going to give her to Lopez, no matter what it costs me." He put a hand on Rodrigo's shoulder. "Listen to me. If anything goes wrong, you tell Bojo that I want him to take care of her from now on. There's enough money in my Swiss account to support her and my father for life, in any style they like. You tell Bojo I said to see that she gets it, less the sum we agreed on for all of you. Promise me!''

"Of course I promise." Rodrigo's eyes narrowed. "You look...different."

I've just seduced a virgin who thinks she was having an erotic dream, he thought with black humor. *No wonder I look different.* "It's been a long night," he said. "Call the police an hour from now." He looked at his expensive commando watch, the one with a tiny sharp knife blade that could be released from the edge of the face with a light touch. "Coming up on fourteen hundred and ten hours...almost... almost...hack!''

Rodrigo had set his watch to the same time. He gave Micah a long, worried look as the taller man put on his face mask and adjusted the mouthpiece.

"Dios te protégé," Rodrigo said gently. God protect you.

Micah smiled and put the mouthpiece in. Seconds later, he was in the water, under the water, headed out toward the yacht. It was a distance of almost half a mile, and Rodrigo was uneasy. But Micah had been a champion swimmer in his school days, and he held some sort of record for being able to hold his breath underwater. He looked very tired, though, and that was going to go against him. Odd, Rodrigo thought, that a man who'd just gotten out of bed should look exhausted. And after the culprits had been dealt with so quickly and effectively, which couldn't have tired him. He hoped Micah would succeed. He checked his watch, glanced at the bound and gagged captives in their underwear, and shrugged.

"How sad for you, *compadres,* that your futures will be seen through vertical bars. But, then, your choice of employer leaves so much to be desired!''

He turned away, recalling that Micah had told him to phone the police an hour after he'd gone. But he hesitated to do that, orders or not. Timing was going to be everything here. If there was a holdup planting the charge, and if Lopez had someone on the payroll in Nassau, the show was over. Lopez would get word of the failed kidnapping attempt in time to blow Micah out of the water. Micah couldn't have been thinking straight. Rodrigo would do that for him. He would watch Micah's back. Now he prayed that his boss could complete this mission without discovery. If ever a man deserved his fate, it was Manuel Lopez. He gave Mexicans a bad name, and for that alone Rodrigo was anxious to see him go down.

It took Micah a long time to reach the boat. He was exhausted from the mindless pleasure Callie had given him. Making love with her just before the most dangerous mission of recent years had to be evidence of insanity. But it had been so beautiful, so tender. He could still hear her soft, surprised cries of pleasure. The memory was the sort a man wouldn't mind going down into the darkness for. Of course, it wasn't helping him focus on the task at hand. He forcibly put the interlude to the back of his mind and swam on.

He paused as he reached the huge yacht, carefully working his way toward the huge propellers at the stern, which were off right now but would start again eventually. If they started while he was near them, he'd be caught in their turbulent wake and dragged right into those cruel blades to be dismembered before he set the charge. *Not* the end he hoped for.

He kept himself in place with slow movements of his fins while he shone an underwater light hooked to his belt on the bomb package enclosed in the waterproof bag. He drew it out, very carefully, and secured it to a metallic connection behind the propellers. It stuck like glue. He positioned the light so that he could work with his hands while he wired the charge into the propeller system. It was meticulous work, and he was really tired. But he finally secured the connection and double-checked the explosive package. Yes. The minute the turbine engines fired, the ship would blow up.

The problem was, he was almost too tired to swim back. He was going to have to give himself thirty minutes to get back to the shore, and pray that Lopez didn't have his men fire up those propellers until he was out of harm's way.

He gave the ship's hull a gentle pat, with a momentary twinge of regret at having to destroy such a beautiful yacht. Then he turned and moved slowly, cautiously, around toward the bow of the ship. There was a ladder hanging down from the side. He passed it with idle curiosity and held onto it while he floated, letting his body relax and rest. He just happened to look up while he was hanging from it.

Just above the surface, a man was aiming an automatic weapon down at him through the water.

He couldn't get away. He was too tired. Besides, the man wasn't likely to miss at this range. Salute the flag and move on, he mused philosophically. Nobody lived forever, and his death would serve a noble cause. All he had to do was make them think he'd come aboard to use the knife on Lopez, so they wouldn't start looking for bombs. They had enough time to find and disarm it if he didn't divert them. The waterproof bag on his hip was going to be hard to explain. So was his flashlight. Fortunately the light fit into the bag and weighed it down. He unhooked the bag and closed it out of sight while the man above motioned angrily for him to come up the ladder. He let the bag drop and it sank even as he started the climb to his own death. He might get a chance at Lopez before they killed him, because Lopez would want to gloat.

He padded onto the deck in his breathing equipment and fins, which the man ordered him in Spanish to take off.

Micah tossed his gear aside, carefully, because the man with the gun was nervous. If he had any chance at all to escape, he could make the distance without his equipment if he swam—assuming he wasn't shot to death in the process. He had to hope for a break, but it wasn't likely. This was the situation that every working mercenary had to consider when he chose the lifestyle. Death could come at any moment, unexpectedly.

He stood glaring down at the smaller man. Even with his automatic weapon, the drug lord's man didn't seem too confident. He backed up two more steps. Micah noted the hasty retreat and tensed to make his move. But only seconds later, Lopez and two more men—armed men—came up on deck.

Lopez stared at Micah for a minute and then recognition flashed in his dark eyes. "Micah Steele, I presume," he drawled in accented English. He put his hands behind him and walked around Micah like an emperor inspecting a new slave. "You lack proficiency, don't you? Were you planning to use this on me while I slept?" he added, jerking the big bowie knife out of its sheath. "A nasty weapon. Very nasty." He put the point against Micah's wet suit just below the nipple. "A hard thrust, and you cease to exist. You were careless. Now you will pay the price for it.'' His face hardened. ''Where are my two men that I sent to reclaim your stepsister?''

Micah smiled calmly. ''The police have them by now. I expect they'll spill their guts trying to save themselves.''

''They would not dare,'' Lopez said easily. ''They fear me.''

''They won't fear you if you're in prison,'' he replied easily. ''Or dead.''

Lopez laughed. It amused him that this mercenary wasn't begging for his life. He was used to men who did.

''Your attempt at diversion serves no purpose. We both know that my men are on the way back with their captive even now. In fact,'' he added with a deliberate smile, ''I had a phone call just before you were discovered, telling me that she was safely bound and gagged. Your men are too numerous for them to fight, so they are hiding her some distance from your house until the coast is clear and they can get here with the boat.'' He chuckled maliciously.

Micah surmised that a cell phone had been discovered on one of the men, and Rodrigo had used it to reassure Lopez. A stroke of genius, and it might have worked, if Micah hadn't been careless and let himself get captured like a raw recruit.

''I am fond of knives,'' Lopez murmured, and ran his fingers over the carved bone handle almost like a caress. He looked at Micah as he traced the pattern in it. ''This time, I will not give your stepsister to my men. I will use the knife on her myself.'' His eyes were cold, hard, unfeeling. ''I will skin her alive,'' he said softly. ''And with every strip that comes off, I will remind her that you were careless

enough to let her be apprehended a second time.''
His eyes blazed. ''You invaded my home to take her
from me. No one humiliates me in such a manner
and lives to gloat about it. You will die and your
sister will die, and in such a way that it will frighten
anyone who sees it.''

Micah studied the little man with contempt, seeing
the years of death and torture that had benefited Lopez. The drug lord could buy people, yachts, countries. He had enormous power. But it was power built
on a foundation of greed, floored with blood and
tears. If ever a man deserved to go down, it was
Lopez.

''You are very quiet, Micah Steele,'' Lopez said
suddenly, and his eyes narrowed suspiciously.

''I was thinking that I've never encountered anyone as evil as you, Lopez,'' he said quietly. ''You
have no conscience at all.''

Lopez shrugged. ''I am what I am,'' he said simply. ''In order to accumulate great wealth, one has
to be willing to take great risks. I have been poor. I
never want to be poor again.''

''Plenty of people prefer it to murder.''

Lopez only laughed. ''You are, how is it said,
stalling for time,'' he said abruptly. ''Are you hoping
to be rescued? Or are you hoping that perhaps one
of your men has checked on your stepsister and
found her missing from her room? That is not likely.
My men are quite expert. Playing for time will avail
you nothing.''

Micah could have told him that he was using the
time to rest from his exhaustive swim, marshaling
his strength for an all-out assault. If they took him
down, he vowed, he was at least going to take Lopez

with him, even if he died with the drug lord's neck in his hands.

"Or you might think it possible to overpower all of us and escape." He laughed again. "I think that I will wait to begin your interrogation until your stepsister is on board with us. Carlos!" he called to a henchman. "Tell the captain to start the engines and move us a little closer to the island."

Micah's heart stopped dead, but not a trace of fear or apprehension showed on his face. Lopez was watching him very closely, as if he suspected something. Micah simply smiled, considering that it was the fortunes of war that sometimes you didn't win. At least Callie was safe. He hadn't lost completely as long as she survived. He took a relaxing breath and waited for the explosion.

Lopez's henchman was almost up the steps to the pilothouse when Lopez wheeled suddenly.

"Wait!" Lopez called his man back suddenly and Micah fought to keep from showing his relief. "I do not trust you, Steele," Lopez added. "I think perhaps you want me to go closer to your island, to give your men a shot at us, here on the deck. If so, you are going to be disappointed." He turned to the man, Carlos. "Take him below and tie him up. Then I want you and Juan to take one of the boats and follow in the steps of Ramon and Jorge. They must be somewhere near the house waiting for the mercenaries to give up the search or locate it elsewhere. You can help them bring the girl back."

"Si, señor," Carlos said at once, and stuck the automatic weapon in Micah's back. "You will go ahead of me, *señor,*" he told Micah. "And remember, there will be an armed man at the foot of the steps. Escape is not possible. *¡Vaya!*"

Micah gave Lopez one last contemptuous look before he went down the steps into the bowels of the ship. So far, so good. They were convinced that their men on shore were safe and had Callie. They weren't going to start the ship just yet, thank God. He had one last chance to absolve himself. He was going to take it, regardless of the price.

The henchman tied him up in a chair with nylon cord at his wrists and ankles. The cord was tight enough to cut off the circulation. Micah felt his hands and feet going numb, but he wasn't going to protest.

"What a nice fish we caught," Lopez's man chuckled. "And soon, big fish, we will fillet you and your stepsister together." His eyes narrowed and he smiled coldly. "You have embarrassed my boss. No one is allowed to do that. You must be made an example of. I would not wish to be in your shoes." He looked pointedly at Micah's bare feet. "Hypothetically speaking," he added. "Enjoy your last minutes of life, *señor.*"

The small man left Micah in the stateroom, which was obviously some sort of guest room. There was a bed and a dresser and this chair in it, and it was very small. One of the officers of the ship might sleep here, he reasoned.

Now that he was alone—and he wouldn't be for long—he might have just enough time to free himself. Micah touched the button on his watch that extended the small but very sharp little knife blade concealed in the watch face. He cut himself free with very little effort. But the most dangerous part was yet to come. There were men everywhere, all armed. The one thing he had going for him was that it was dark and Lopez had very few lights on deck at the moment, hoping not to be noticed by Micah's men.

He eased out into the corridor and listened. He heard a man's voice humming a Mexican drinking song off-key nearby. Watching up and down the hall with every step, he eased into the galley. A man just a little smaller than he was stirring something in a very big stainless-steel pot. He was wearing black slacks and a black sweater with an apron over them. Micah smiled.

He caught the man from behind and stunned him. Carefully he eased the cook back behind the stove and began to strip him. He pulled off his scuba gear and donned the cook's outerwear, taking time to dress the cook in his own diving suit. The cook had dark hair, but it wouldn't matter. All he had to do was look like Micah at a distance.

He got the cook over his shoulder and made his way carefully to the ladder that led up onto the deck. Lopez was talking to two other men, and not looking in Micah's direction. What supreme self-confidence, Micah thought. Pity to spoil it.

He slapped the cook and brought him around. In the next instant, he threw the man overboard on the side that faced away from Micah's island.

"¡Steele ha escapado!" Micah yelled in Spanish. *"¡Se fue alla, a la izquierda, en el Mar!"* Steele has escaped, he went there, to the left, in the sea!

There was a cry of fury from Lopez, followed by harsh orders, and the sound of running feet. Micah followed the other men, managing to blend in, veering suddenly to the other side of the ship.

Just as he got there, he was faced with a henchman who hadn't followed the others. The man had an automatic weapon in his hands and he was hesitating, his eyes trying to see Micah, who was half in shadow so that his blond hair didn't give the game away. If the man pulled that trigger…

"*Es que usted esta esperando una cerveza?*" he shot at the man angrily. "*¡Vaya! ¡Steele esta alla!*" What are you waiting for, a beer? Get going, Steele's over there!

He hesitated with his heart in his throat, waiting, waiting…

All at once, there was a shout from the other side of the ship. The man who was holding Micah at bay still hesitated, but the noise got louder.

"*¡Vaya!*" he repeated. He waved the man on urgently with a mumbled Spanish imprecation about Steele and his useless escape attempt. In that space of seconds before they discovered the man in the water was not Micah, their escaping captive got over the rail and into the ocean and struck out back toward the shore. He kept his strokes even and quick, and he zigzagged. Even if Lopez's men spotted him, they were going to have to work at hitting him from that distance. Every few yards, he submerged and swam underwater. Any minute now, he told himself, and thanked God he'd had just enough rest to allow him a chance of making it to shore before he was discovered and killed.

He heard loud voices and a searchlight began sweeping the water. Micah dived under again and held his breath. With a little bit of luck, they might pass right over him, in his black clothing. He blended in very well with the ocean.

There was gunfire. He ground his teeth together and prayed they'd miss him. Probably they were shooting blind, hoping to hit him with a lucky shot.

Odd, though, the gunfire sounded closer than that…

He came up for air, to snatch a breath, and almost collided with his own swift motorboat, with Bojo driving it and firing an automatic rifle toward Lopez and his men at the same time.

"Climb in, boss!" Bojo called, and kept shooting.

"Remind me to give you a raise," Micah panted as he dragged himself over the side and into the rocking boat. "Good work. Good work! Now get the hell out of here before they blow us out of the water!"

Bojo swung the boat around masterfully and imitated the same zigzag pattern that Micah had used when he swam.

"Lopez is mad now," Micah said with a glittery smile. "If there's any justice left in the world, he'll try to move in closer to get a better shot at us."

"We hope," Bojo said solemnly, still dodging bullets.

Micah looked back toward the ship, now clearly visible against the horizon. He thought of all Lopez's helpless victims, of whole families in tiny little Mexican towns who had been mowed down with automatic weapons for daring to help the authorities catch the local pushers. He thought of the hard fight to shut down Lopez's distribution network slated for operation in Jacobsville, Texas. He thought of Callie in that murderous assassin's hands, of the knife cut on her pretty little breast where the point had gone in. He thought of Callie dead, tortured, an anguished expression locked forever into those gentle features. He thought of his father, who would have been Lopez's next target. He thought of Lisa Monroe Parks's young husband in the DEA who'd been killed on Lopez's orders. He thought of all the law enforcement people who'd risked their lives and the lives of their families to stop Lopez.

"It's retribution time, Lopez," Micah said absently, watching the big ship with somber eyes. "Life calls in the bets for us all, sooner or later. But you're overdue, you drug-dealing son of a…!"

Before the last word left his lips, there was a huge fireburst where the ship had been sitting in the water. Flames rolled up and up and up, billowing black smoke into the atmosphere. The sound rocked the boat, and pieces of the yacht began falling from the sky in a wide circumference. Micah and Bojo ducked down in the boat and covered their heads as Bojo increased their speed and changed direction, hoping to miss the heavier metal parts that were raining down with wood and fabric.

They made it to the boat dock and jumped out as the last pieces of what had been Lopez's yacht fell into the water.

Mercenaries came rushing down from the house, all armed, to see what had happened.

"Say goodbye to Lopez," Micah told them, eyes narrowed with cold scrutiny.

They all watched the hull of the ship, still partially intact, start to sink. To their credit, none of them cheered or laughed or made a joke. Human lives had been lost. It was no cause for celebration, not even when the ringleader was as bad as Lopez. It had been necessary to eliminate him. He was crazed with vengeance and dangerous to the world at large.

Rodrigo came up beside them. "Glad to see you still alive, boss," he said.

Micah nodded. "It was close. I was too tired to swim back. He caught me at the ladder like a raw recruit."

There was a faint sound from Peter, the newest of

the group. "I thought slips were my signature," he told Micah.

"Even veterans can step the wrong way and die for it," Micah told him gently. "That's why you always do it by the book and make sure you've got backup. I broke all the rules, but I didn't want to put anyone else at risk. I got lucky. Sometimes you don't." He watched the last of Lopez's yacht sink. "What about our two guests?"

"They're still in the shed."

"Load them up and take them in to Nassau and say we'll file charges for trespassing," Micah told Rodrigo.

"I'm on my way."

"We'll have federal agents combing the island by dawn, I guess," one of the other mercenaries groaned.

Micah shook his head. "I was sanctioned. And that's all I intend to say about this, ever," he added when the man seemed set to protest. "Let's see if we can get a little more sleep before dawn."

Mumbled agreement met the suggestion. He walked back into the house and down the hall to his bedroom. Callie's door was still closed. He felt a horrible pang of guilt when he remembered what had happened before he went after Lopez. He was never going to get over what he'd done.

He took a shower and changed into a pair of white striped shorts and a white-and-red patterned silk shirt. He padded down the hall to the kitchen and started to get a beer out of the refrigerator. But it hadn't been a beer sort of night. He turned on his heel and went to the liquor cabinet in his study. He poured himself two fingers of Kentucky bourbon with a little ice and took it back down the hall with him.

At the door of Callie's room, he paused. He opened the door gently and moved in to stand by the bed and look down at her. She was sound asleep, her cheek pillowed on a pretty hand devoid of jewelry. She'd kicked off the sheet and bedspread and her long legs were visible where the gown had fallen away from them. She looked innocent, untouched. He remembered the feel of that soft mouth under his lips, the exquisite loving that had driven every sane thought out of his mind. His body went rigid just from the memory.

She stirred, as if she sensed his presence, but she didn't wake up. The sedative had really kicked in now. She wouldn't wake until dawn, if then.

He reached down a gentle hand and brushed the hair away from the corner of her mouth and her cheek. She wasn't conventionally pretty, but she had an inner beauty that made him feel as if he'd just found spring after a hard winter. He liked to hear her laugh. He liked the way she dressed, so casually and indifferently. She didn't take hours to put on makeup, hours to dress. She didn't complain about the heat or the cold or the food. She was as honest as any woman he'd ever known. She had wonderful qualities. But he was afraid of her.

He'd been a loner most of his life. His mother's death when he was ten had hit him hard. He'd adored his mother. After that, it had been Jack and himself, and they'd grown very close. But when Callie and her mother moved in, everything had changed. Suddenly he was an outsider in his own family. He despised Callie's mother and made no secret of his resentment for both women. That had caused a huge rift between his father and himself, one that had inevitably grown wide enough to divide them altogether.

He'd blamed Callie for the final blow, because he'd convinced himself that she'd found Jack and sent him to the hall to find Micah and Anna kissing. Callie had always denied it, and finally he believed her. It hadn't been pique because he'd rejected her.

He took a sip of the whiskey and stared down at her broodingly. She was part of his life, part of him. He hated knowing that. He hated the memory of her body moving sensuously under his while he seduced her.

And she thought she was dreaming. What if she woke up still believing that? They'd not only had sex, but thanks to him they'd had unprotected sex. His dark eyes slid down her body to her flat belly. Life might already be growing in her womb.

His breath caught. Callie might have his baby. His lips parted as he thought about a baby. He'd never wanted one before. He could see Callie with an infant in her arms, in her heart, in her life. Callie would want his baby.

He felt an alien passion gripping him for the first time. And just as quickly, he considered the difficulty it would engender. Callie might be pregnant. She wouldn't remember how she got that way, either.

He pursed his lips, feeling oddly whimsical for a man who was facing the loss of freedom and perhaps even the loss of his lifestyle and his job. Wouldn't it be something if Callie was pregnant and he was the only one who knew?

Chapter Eleven

Callie felt the sun on her face. She'd been dreaming. She'd been in Micah's warm, powerful arms, held tight against every inch of him, and he'd been making ardent love to her. He'd looked down into her wide eyes at the very instant he'd possessed her. He'd watched her become a woman. It seemed so real…

Her eyes opened. Sure it was real. And any minute now, the tooth fairy was going to fly in through the open patio windows and leave her a shiny quarter!

She sat up. Odd, that uncomfortable feeling low in her belly. She shifted and she felt sore. Talk about dreams that seemed real!

She swung her legs off the bed and stood up, stilling for a moment so that the sudden dizziness passed. She turned to make up the bed and frowned. There was a stain on the bottom sheet. It looked like dried blood. Well, so much for the certainty that her period wasn't due for another two weeks, she thought. Probably all the excitement had brought it on sooner. She went into the bathroom, wondering what she was going to do for the necessary equipment in a house full of men.

But she wasn't having her period. That would mean some spotting had occurred and that frightened her because it wasn't natural. She'd always been regular. She'd have to see a doctor when she got home, she supposed.

She bathed and frowned when she was standing in front of the mirror. There were some very bad bruises on her hip and thigh, and that was when she remembered the terror of the night before. Half asleep, she hadn't really been thinking until she saw the bruises and it began to come back. A man, Lopez's man, had tried to kidnap her. She'd actually knocked him out with a shovel. She smiled as she remembered it. Sadly she'd been less brave when Micah came running out to see about her. He'd carried her in here and given her a sedative. She hoped she hadn't said anything revealing to him. Sedatives made her very uninhibited. But she had no memory past the shot. That might, she concluded, be a good thing.

Dressed in a pink Bermuda shorts set that she'd bought on her shopping trip in Nassau, she put her feet into a new pair of sneakers. Unlike the sandals she couldn't wear, the sneakers were a perfect fit.

She walked back into the bedroom worriedly, wondering what Micah had done with Lopez's men. It seemed very quiet this morning. She was certain Micah had all sorts of surveillance systems set up to make sure Lopez couldn't sneak anybody else in here to make another attempt at kidnapping her. But she felt uneasy, just the same. Lopez would never stop. She knew that she was still in the same danger she'd been in when she first arrived here with Micah.

She felt as if she had a hangover, probably because of that sedative Micah gave her. That explained the erotic dream as well. She blushed, remembering what an erotic dream it was, too. She brushed her hair, not bothering with makeup, and went down the hall to the kitchen to see if coffee was available.

Bojo was helping himself to a cup. He grinned as she came into the room. "You slept very late."

"I was very tired. Besides, Micah drugged me. That's the second time he's given me a sedative since I've been here. I'm not used to them." She laughed as she took the fresh cup of coffee Bojo handed her. "It's a good thing I fell asleep right away, too, because sedatives generally have a very odd effect on me. I get totally swept away. Where is everybody?" she added, noting that Bojo was the only person in the house.

"Micah has gone to Nassau on business," he told her with a grin. "Lopez seems to have vanished in the night. Not only Lopez, but his very expensive yacht and several of his men. The authorities are justifiably curious."

"Lopez has gone?" she asked, excited. "You mean, he's gone away?"

"Very far away," he said with a grin.

"But he'll just come back." He gave her a wry look and she frowned. "Don't you still have his two henchmen? Micah was going to give those two men to the police," she reminded him. "Maybe they know where he is."

"They were handed over to the police," he agreed. "But they don't know where Lopez is, either."

"You look smug," she accused.

He smiled. "I am. I do know where Lopez is. And I can promise you that he won't be making any more raids on this island."

"Great!" she exclaimed, relieved. "Can you hand him over to the police, too?"

"Lopez can't be handed over." He paused to think. "Well, not in one piece, at least," he added.

"You're sounding very strange," she pointed out.

He poured his own cup of coffee and sat back down at the table. "Lopez's yacht went up in flames last night," he said matter-of-factly. "I am amazed that you didn't hear the explosion. It must have been a fault in the engine, or a gas leak," he added, without meeting her eyes. He shook his head. "A very nasty explosion. What was left of the yacht sank within sight of here."

"His boat sank? He was on it? You're sure? Did you see it go down?" she asked, relieved and horrified at the same time.

"Yes, yes, and yes." He studied her. "Lopez will never threaten you or Micah's father again. You will be able to return home now, to your job and your stepfather. I shall miss you."

"I'll miss you, too, Bojo," she said, but her mind was racing ahead. Lopez was dead. She was out of danger. She could go home. She had to go home, she amended. She would never see Micah again…

Bojo was watching the expressions chase themselves across her face. She was vulnerable, and besides that, she was in love with Micah. It didn't take much guesswork to figure that out, or to make sense of Micah's strange attitude about her. Obviously the boss knew she was in love with him, and he was trying to be kind while making his position to her clear.

He grimaced. The musical tones of his cell phone interrupted his gloomy thoughts. He answered it quickly.

"Yes," he said, glancing warily at Callie. "She's here, having coffee. I'll ask her." He lifted both eyebrows. "Micah is having lunch with Lisse on the bay in Nassau. If you want to join them, I can take you over in the small boat."

Lisse. Why should she think anything had changed? she wondered. Lisse was beautiful and Micah had told her at the beginning that he and Lisse were lovers. They'd been together for a long time, and she was important in the Bahamas as well as being beautiful. A few teasing kisses for Callie meant nothing to him. She'd been a complete fool. Micah had been kind to her to get her to stay and bait Lopez. That was all it had been. It was an effort to smile, but she did.

"Tell him thanks, but I've got to start packing. If Lopez is really out of the way, I have to go home. Mr. Kemp won't keep my job open forever."

Bojo looked really worried. "Boss, she says she'd rather not." He hesitated, nodded, glanced again at Callie. "Okay. I'll make sure he knows. We'll expect you soon. Yes. Goodbye."

"You look like a bad party," she commented.

"He's bringing Lisse here for lunch," he said reluctantly.

Her heart jumped but she only smiled. "Why not?

It's obvious to anybody that he's crazy about her. She's a dish,'' she added, and then wondered why she should suddenly think about Lisse's bust size when compared to her own.

''She's a cat,'' Bojo replied tersely. ''Don't let her walk on you.''

''I never have,'' she commented. ''If we're having lunch, I guess I need to get started fixing it, huh?''

''We have a cook...''

''I'm good,'' she told him without conceit. ''I cook for Dad and me every night. I'm not *cordon-bleu,* but I get compliments.''

''Very well.'' Bojo gave in, hoping the boss wasn't going to fire him for letting her into the kitchen. ''Mac went to Nassau with the boss and the other guys, so it would have been cold cuts anyway.''

''I make homemade rolls,'' she told him with a grin. ''And I can bake a pound cake.''

She got up, looked through the cupboards and refrigerator, found an apron and got busy. It would give her something to do while her heart was breaking.

Two hours later, Micah and Lisse came into the living room together, laughing. Callie peered out from the kitchen. ''Food's on the table if you want to sit down,'' she called gaily.

Micah gaped at her. He'd told Bojo to get Mac to fix lunch. What was Callie doing in the kitchen?

Bojo came out of it, and Micah's face hardened. ''I thought I told you to monitor communications for traffic about Lopez,'' he said coldly.

Bojo knew what was eating him, so he only

smiled. "I am. I was just asking Callie for another pot of coffee. We drank the other, between us," he added deliberately.

Micah's eyes flashed like black lightning, but he didn't say another word as Bojo nodded politely at Lisse and walked back toward the communications room.

"Sit down, Lisse," Micah said quietly, pulling out a chair for her at the dining-room table, already laid with silverware and plates and fresh flowers. "I'll be back in a minute."

"I do hope it's going to be something light," Lisse said airily. "I can't bear a heavy meal in the middle of the day."

Micah didn't answer her. He'd run into Lisse in town and she'd finagled him into lunch. He'd compromised by bringing her here, so that he could see how Callie was feeling after the night before. He was hoping against hope that she remembered what had happened. But the instant she looked at him, he knew she hadn't.

"Hi," she said brightly and with a forced smile. "I slept like two logs. I hope you've got an appetite. I made homemade bread and cake, and steak and salad."

"Lisse will probably only want the salad," he murmured. "But I love cake."

"I remember. Go sit down. I'll bring it."

"You only set two places," he said quietly.

She shrugged. "I'm just cooking it. I wouldn't want to get in the way...Micah!"

While she was talking, he picked her up and carried her out of the kitchen the back way and into the first sprawling bathroom he came to, closing the door behind them.

"You're not the hired help here," he said flatly, staring into her eyes without putting her down. "You don't wait at table. You don't cook. I have a man for that."

"I'm a good cook," she pointed out. "And it's going to get cold if you don't put me down and let me finish."

His eyes dropped to her mouth and lingered there hungrily. "I don't want food." He brought her close and his mouth suddenly went down against hers and twisted ardently, until he forced her lips apart and made her respond to him. He groaned under his breath as her arms reached up to hold him. She made a husky little sound and gave in all at once. It felt so familiar to be held like this, kissed like this. She opened her mouth and felt his tongue go into it. Her body was on fire. She'd never felt such desire. Odd, that her body seemed to have a whole different knowledge of him than her mind did.

He couldn't get enough of her mouth. He devoured it. His powerful arms had a faint tremor when he was finally able to draw back. He looked straight into her eyes, remembering her headlong response the night before, feeling her body yield to him on crisp, white sheets in the darkness. He'd thought of nothing else all day. It was anguish to know that she was totally oblivious to what they'd done together, when the memories were torturing him.

"How long have you been talking to Bojo?" he demanded gruffly.

"Just…just a little while." Her mouth was swollen, but her body was shivering with secret needs.

She looked at the tight line of his lips and impulsively reached up to kiss him. Amazingly he kissed her back with ardent insistence.

"Micah!" Lisse's strident voice came floating down the hall, followed by the staccato sound of high heels on wood.

Micah heard her and lifted his head. His mouth, like Callie's, was swollen. He searched her misty eyes intently.

"It's Lisse," she whispered dazedly.

"Yes." He bent and brushed his lips lazily over her own, smiling as she followed them involuntarily.

"She wants her lunch," she persisted.

"I want you," he murmured against her mouth.

The words shocked. Her fingers, linked behind his nape, loosened and she looked worried. "I can't!" she whispered huskily.

"Why can't you?"

"Because I've never..." she began.

Until last night. He almost said it. He thought it. His face hardened as he forced his tongue to be silent. He couldn't tell her. He wanted to. But it was too soon. He had to show her that it wasn't a one-night thing with him. Even more important, he had to convince himself that he could change enough, settle down enough, to give her some security and stability. He knew that he could have made her pregnant. Oddly it didn't worry him. The thought of a child was magical, somehow. He didn't know much about children, except that he was certain he'd love his own. Callie would make a wonderful mother.

He smiled as he bent and kissed her eyelids shut. "Wouldn't you?" he whispered. "If I insisted?"

"I'd hate you," she bit off, knowing that she wouldn't. She loved him endlessly.

"Yes, you might," he said after a minute. "And that's the last thing I want."

"Micah!" Lisse's voice came again, from even farther down the hall.

"Sit. Stay," Callie whispered impishly.

He bit her lower lip and growled deep in his throat. "She insisted on lunch. I compromised. Kiss me again." His mouth drifted lazily over hers.

She did kiss him, because she had no willpower when it came to this. She loved being in his arms, being held by him. She loved him!

After a minute he lifted his head and put her down, with obvious reluctance. "We'd better go before she starts opening doors," he said in a husky tone.

"Would she?" she asked, curious.

"She has before," he confessed with a wry grin. He brushed back her hair with exquisite tenderness. His eyes held an expression she'd never seen in them. "You look like I've been making love to you," he whispered with a faint smile. "Better fix your face before you come out."

She reached up and touched his swollen mouth with wonder. She was still trying to make herself believe that he'd dragged her in here and kissed her so hungrily. There was something in the back of her mind, something disturbing. She couldn't grasp it. But the most amazing thing was the tenderness he was showing her. It made her breathless.

His lean hand spread against her cheek. His thumb parted her lips as he bent again, as if he couldn't help himself. He kissed her softly, savoring the trembling response of her lips.

"Micah!" Lisse was outside, almost screeching now.

He lifted his head again with a long sigh. "I need to take you out in the boat and drop anchor five miles out," he said heavily. He tapped her nose. "Okay, let's go see if everything's cold before Lisse loses her voice."

He opened the door, checking to see if the coast was clear. "Fix your face," he whispered with a wicked grin and closed the door behind him.

She heard his footsteps moving toward the dining room. Two minutes later, staccato heels made an angry sound passing the bathroom door.

"Micah…!"

"I'm in the dining room, Lisse! Where were you? I've been looking everywhere!"

He was good at improvising, Callie thought as she repaired the damage to her face. She combed her hair with a comb from a tray on the vanity table and wondered at the change in her relationship with Micah. He was very different. He acted as if she'd become suddenly important to him, and not in a conventional way. She couldn't help smiling. It was as if her whole life had changed.

She went back into the kitchen and put everything on the table, after checking that the steak had kept warm on the back of the stove. It had.

Micah got up and set a third place at the table, giving Callie a deliberate look. "You eat in here with us," he said firmly, ignoring Lisse's glare.

"Okay." She put out the last of the food, and butter for the rolls, and sat down. "Micah, will you say grace?" she added.

"Grace?" Lisse's beautiful face widened into shock.

Micah flashed her a disapproving glance and said a brief prayer. He was digging into the food while Lisse, in her gold-trimmed white pantsuit, was still gaping.

"We're very conventional at home," Callie pointed out.

"And traditional," Micah added. "Tradition is important for families."

"But you don't have a family, really, darling," Lisse protested. She helped herself to a couple of forkfuls of salad and a hint of dressing. "Rolls? Thousands of calories, darling, especially with butter!" she told Micah.

"Callie made them for me, from scratch," he said imperturbably. He bit into one and smiled. "These are good," he said.

Callie shrugged. "It's the only thing I do really well. My mother couldn't boil water." That had slipped out and she looked horrified as she met Micah's eyes.

"I think Micah could do very well without hearing about your tramp of a mother, dear," Lisse said haughtily. "He's suffered enough at her hands already. Who was it she threw you over for, darling, that British earl?"

"She didn't throw me over," Micah said through his teeth.

"But she was staying here with you last year…?"

Callie's eyes exploded. She got up, throwing down her napkin. "Is that true?" she demanded.

"It is, but not the way you're assuming it is," he

said flatly. "Callie, there's something you need to know."

She turned and walked out of the room.

"What the hell was that in aid of?" Micah demanded of Lisse, with real anger.

"You keep secrets, don't you?" she asked with cold delight. "It's dangerous. And she isn't really your sister, either. I got that out of Bojo. You've even slept with her, haven't you, darling?" she added venomously.

Micah threw down his own napkin and got to his feet. *"Bojo!"* he yelled.

The tall Berber came rushing into the room. His boss never raised his voice!

Micah was almost vibrating with rage. "See Lisse back to Nassau. She won't be coming here again," he added with ice dropping from every syllable.

Lisse put down her fork and wiped her mouth before she got leisurely to her feet. She gave him a cool look. "You use people," she accused quietly. "It's always what *you* want, what *you* need. You manipulate, you control, you…use. I loved you," she added in a husky undertone. "But you didn't care. I was handy and good in bed, and that was what mattered to you. When you didn't want me so much anymore, you threw me out. I was only invited over here this time so that you could show your houseguest that she wasn't the only egg in your basket." She gave him a cold smile. "So how does it feel to be on the receiving end for once, Micah? It's your turn. I wish, I really wish, I could stick around to see the result. She doesn't look like the forgiving sort to me. And I'd know, wouldn't I?"

She turned, leaving Bojo to follow her after a complicated glance in Micah's direction. The boss didn't say a word. Not a single word.

Callie was packing with shaking hands. Micah came to the doorway and leaned against it with his hands in his pockets, watching her glumly.

"Nothing to say?" she asked curtly.

"Nothing you'd listen to," he replied. He shrugged. "Lisse just put me in my place. I didn't realize it, but she's right. I do use people. Only I never meant to use you, in any way."

"You said you weren't having an affair with my mother," she accused as she folded a pair of slacks and put them in her case.

"I'm not. I never have." His chest rose and fell heavily. "But you're not in any mood to listen, are you, baby?"

Baby. She frowned. Baby. Why did that word make her uneasy? She looked at him with honest curiosity.

"I called you that," he said quietly. "You don't remember when, do you?"

She sighed, shaking her head.

"It may be just as well," he said, almost to himself. "For now, it's safe for you to go home. Lopez is dead. His top lieutenants died with him. There's no longer any threat to you or to Dad."

"Yes. What a lucky explosion it was," she added, busy with her case.

"It wasn't luck, Callie," he said shortly. "I swam out to the yacht and planted a block of C-4 next to his propeller shaft."

She turned, gasping. Her hands shook as she fumbled the case closed and sat down heavily on the bed.

So that was what they'd been talking about the night
before, when Micah had said that "it might work."
He could have been killed!

"It was a close call," he added, watching her. "I
let myself get caught like a rank beginner. I was too
tired to make it back in a loop, so I stopped to rest.
One of Lopez's men caught me. Lopez made a lot
of threats about what he planned to do to you and
Dad, and then he got stupid and had me tied up down
below." He extended his arm, showed her his watch,
pressed a button, and watched her expression as a
knife blade popped out. "Pity his men weren't astute
enough to check the watch. They knew what I do for
a living, too."

Her eyes were full of horror. Micah had gone after
Lopez alone. He'd been captured. If it hadn't been
for that watch, he'd be dead. She stared at him as if
she couldn't get enough of just looking at him. What
difference did it make if he'd had a full-blown affair
with her mother? He could be out there with Lopez,
in pieces...

She put her face in her hands to hide the tears that
overflowed.

He went to the bed and knelt beside her, pulling
her wet face into his throat. He smoothed her hair
while she clung to him and let the tears fall. It had
been such a traumatic week for her. It seemed that
her whole life had been uprooted and stranded. Micah could have been dead. Or, last night, she could
have been dead. Pride seemed such a petty thing all
of a sudden.

"You could have died," she whispered brokenly.

"So could you." He moved, lifting her into his
arms. He dropped into a wide cushioned rattan chair

and held her close while the anguish of the night before lanced through her slender body like a tangible thing. She clung to him, shivering.

"I wish I'd known what you were planning," she said. "I'd have stopped you, somehow! Even if it was only to save you so you could go to my...my mother."

He wrapped her up even closer and laid his cheek against her hair with a long sigh. "You still don't trust me, do you, honey?" he murmured absently. "I suppose it was asking too much, considering the way I've treated you over the years." He kissed her dark hair. "You go back home and settle into your old routine. Soon enough, this will all seem like just a bad dream."

She rubbed her eyes with her fists, like a small child. Curled against him, she felt safe, cherished, treasured. Odd, to feel like that with a man who was a known playboy, a man who'd already told her that freedom was like a religion to him.

"You'll be glad to have your house to yourself again," she said huskily. "I guess it really cramped your style having me here. With Lisse, I mean."

He chuckled. "I lied."

"Wh...what?"

"I lied about Lisse being my lover now. What was between us was over years ago." He shrugged. "I brought her over here when you arrived as a buffer."

She sat up, staring at him like a curious cat. "A buffer?"

He smiled lazily. His fingers brushed away the tears that were wetting her cheeks. "Bachelors are terrified of virgins," he commented.

"You don't even like me," she protested.

His dark eyes slid down to her mouth, and even farther, over her breasts, down to her long legs. "You have a heart like marshmallow," he said quietly. "You never avoid trouble or turn down people in need. You take in all sorts of strays. Children love you." He smiled. "You scared me to death."

"Past tense?" she asked softly.

"I'm getting used to you." He didn't smile. His dark eyes narrowed. "It hurt me that Lopez got two men onto my property while I was lying in bed asleep. You could have been kidnapped or killed, no thanks to me."

"You were tired," she replied. "You aren't superhuman, Micah."

He drew in a slow breath and toyed with the armhole of her tank top. His fingers brushed against soft, warm flesh and she had to fight not to lean toward them. "I didn't feel comfortable resting while we were in so much danger. It all caught up with me last night."

She was remembering something he'd said. "You were almost too tired to swim back from Lopez's yacht, you said," she recalled slowly. She frowned. "But you'd just been asleep," she added. "How could you have been tired?"

"Oh, that's not a question you should ask yet," he said heavily. "You're not going to like the answer."

"I'm not?"

He searched her eyes for a long moment. All at once, he stood up, taking her with him. "You'd better finish getting your stuff together. I'll put you on a commercial flight home."

She didn't want to go, but she didn't have an excuse to stay. She looked at him as if she were lost and alone, and his face clenched.

"Don't do that," he said huskily. "The idea is to get you out of here as smoothly as possible. Don't invite trouble."

She didn't understand that taut command. But then, she didn't understand him, either. She was avoiding the one question she should be asking. She gave in and asked it. "Why was my mother here?"

"Her husband has cancer," he said simply. "She phoned here and begged for help. It seems the earl is penniless and she does actually seem to love him. I arranged for him to have an unorthodox course of treatment from a native doctor here. They both stayed with me until he got through it." He put his hands in his slacks pockets. "As much as I hate to admit it, she's not the woman she was, Callie," he added. "And she did one other thing that I admired. She phoned your father and told him the truth about you."

Her heart skipped. "What father? What truth?" she asked huskily.

"Your father was going to phone you and ask you to meet him. Did he?"

She moved restlessly back to her packing. "He phoned and left a message. I didn't have anything to say to him, so I didn't call him back."

"He knows that you're his child," he told her. "Your mother sent him your birth certificate. That's why he's trying to contact you. I imagine he wants to apologize. Your mother does, too, to you and Dad, but she told me she wasn't that brave."

Her eyes met his, haunted. "I went through hell because of her and my father," she said in a tight tone. "You don't know…you can't imagine…what it was like!"

"Yes, I can," he said, and he sounded angry. "He's apparently counting his regrets. He never remarried. He doesn't have any children, except you."

"Then he still doesn't have a child," she said through her teeth.

He didn't reply for several long seconds. "I can understand why you feel that way, about him and your mother. I don't blame you. I just thought I'd tell you what I know. It's up to you, what you do or don't do about it."

She folded one last shirt and put it into the case. "Thanks for telling me." She glanced at him. "Lisse wanted to make trouble."

"Yes, she did, and she was entitled. She's right. I did use her, in a way. Your mother left me very embittered about women," he confessed. "I loved my own mother, but I lost her when I was still in grammar school. In later years, your mother was the very worst example of what a wife should be. She made a very bad impression on me."

"On me, too." She closed the case and turned back to him, her eyes trying to memorize his lean face. "I wish you'd liked me, when I lived in your house," she said abruptly. "It would have meant more than you know."

His eyes narrowed. "I couldn't afford to like you, Callie," he said quietly. "Every time I looked at you, I burned like fire inside. You were just a teenager, a virgin. I couldn't take advantage of you that way."

"We could have been friends," she persisted.

He shook his head. "You know we couldn't. You know why."

She grimaced, averting her face. "It's always sex with you, isn't it?"

"Not anymore." His voice was quiet, solemn. "Those days are past. I'm looking ahead now. I have a future to build."

A bigger army of mercenaries, she decided, and more money. She smiled to herself. Once a mercenary, always a mercenary. He'd be the last mercenary who would ever be able to give up the lifestyle.

"I wish you well," she said. She picked up her case and looked around to make sure she hadn't left anything. "Thanks for saving my life. Twice," she added with a forced grin.

"You're welcome." He moved forward to take the case from her. He studied her face for a long time with narrowed eyes. It was as if he was seeing her for the first time. "It's amazing," he murmured involuntarily, "that it took me so long."

"What took you so long?"

"Never mind," he murmured, and he smiled. "You'll find out soon enough. Come on. I'll drive you into Nassau to the airport."

"Bojo could…"

He put his fingers against her soft mouth, and he didn't smile. "I'll drive you."

She swallowed. The tip of his finger was tracing her upper lip, and it was making her knees weak. "Okay," she said.

He took her hand and led her out to the car.

Chapter Twelve

Two weeks later, Callie was back at work and it was as if she'd never been kidnapped by Lopez's men or gone to Nassau with Micah. Despite the excitement and adventure, she hadn't told anyone except Mr. Kemp the truth about what had happened. And she let him think that Lopez had died in a freak accident, to protect Micah.

Micah had walked her to the concourse and kissed her goodbye in such a strange, breathlessly tender way that it had kept her from sleeping much since she'd been back. The look in his eyes had been fascinating, but she was still trying to decide what she'd seen there. He'd said he'd see her soon. She had no idea what he meant. It was like leaving part of herself behind when she got on the plane. She cried all the way to Miami, where she got on a plane to San Antonio and then a charter flight to Jacobsville from there.

Micah's father was much better, and so glad to see her that he cried, too. She dismissed the nurse who'd been staying with him with gratitude and a check, but the nurse refused the check. She'd already been paid her fee, in advance, she told a mystified Callie. She left, and Callie and Jack Steele settled back into their comfortable routine.

"I feel better than I have in years," Jack Steele told her with a grin at supper one evening. "It makes me proud that my son wanted to protect me as well as you."

"Micah loves you terribly," she assured him. "He just has a hard time showing it, that's all."

"You really think so?"

"I do. I'm sure he'll come and see you, if you'll let him."

He gave her a peculiar look and pursed his lips. "I'll let Micah come here if you'll do something for me."

"What?"

He leaned back in his chair, and his features reminded her of Micah in a stubborn mood. "If you'll make peace with your father," he said.

She let out a surprised gasp.

"I knew you'd take it like that," he said. "But he's phoned here every single day since you left. He told me some cock-and-bull story about a drug dealer named Lopez. He said he'd heard from a friend in law enforcement that Lopez had kidnapped you and taken you to Mexico. I thought he was full of bull and I told him so. But he kept phoning. I guess it was a good excuse to mend fences. A man that persistent should at least have a hearing.''

She gaped at him. ''You...didn't believe him, about Lopez?''

Her tone surprised him. ''No, of course not.'' Her expression was very disturbing. He scowled. ''Callie...it wasn't true? You really did go to take care of that aunt Micah told me about?''

''Jack, I don't have a aunt,'' she said heavily. ''Lopez did kidnap me. Micah came and got me out himself. He went right into Lopez's house and rescued me.''

''My son, storming drug dealers' lairs?'' he exclaimed. ''Are you kidding?''

''Oh, I didn't want you to have to find out like this,'' she groaned. ''I should have bitten my tongue through!''

He was shocked. ''Micah got you out,'' he repeated.

She leaned across the table and took his arthritic hands in hers and held them tight. ''There's no easy way to say this, but you'll have to know. I'm not sure Micah wants you to know, but I don't have a choice anymore. Dad, Micah is a professional mercenary,'' she told him evenly. ''And he's very good at it. He rappelled from Lopez's roof right into a bedroom and rescued me from a man who was going to kill me. We're both fine. He got me away and out of the country, and took me home with him to Nassau. He lured Lopez in, and...Lopez's boat was blown up in a freak accident.''

Jack let out the breath he'd been holding. ''The things you learn about people you thought you knew. My own son, and he never told me.''

She grimaced. "I'm not sure he ever would. He's very brave, Jack. He isn't really money-hungry, although it sounds as if he is. I'd never have survived without him. His men are just the same, dedicated professionals who really care about what they do. They're not a gang of thugs."

Jack sat back in his chair again, scowling. "You know, it does make some sort of sense. He came home bandaged, you remember that time? And he said he'd had a bad fall. But I saw him accidentally without the bandage and it looked like a bullet wound to me."

"It probably was," she said. "He has scars on his back, too."

She frowned, trying to understand how she knew that. She'd seen Micah with his shirt unbuttoned in Nassau, but never with it off completely. How would she know he had scars down his back?

She put that thought out of her mind. "There's something else I found out," she added. "My mother was there last year, staying with him."

Jack's face hardened at once.

"No, it's not what you're thinking," she said quickly. "That was my thought, too, but she asked Micah for help. She's married to a British earl who has cancer. There was a clinic near Micah and he let them stay with him while the earl was treated. He's impoverished, and I suspect that Micah paid for the treatments, too, although he didn't admit it." She smiled. "He says Mother is really in love this time. She wanted to make peace with both of us as well, but she didn't think it would be possible."

"Not for me," Jack said quietly. "She cost me a lot."

"She cost me more," she agreed. "But you can't hate people forever. It only hurts you in the end. You have to forgive unless you want to live in torment forever."

"How did you get so wise, at your age?" he asked, smiling as he tried to lighten the mood.

"I had a lot of hard knocks. I learned early how terrible a thing hatred is." She touched his hand gently. "Micah loves you so much. You can't imagine how it hurt him when we thought he'd betrayed you with Mother. He's been bitter, too."

"I wouldn't let him talk about it," he said. "I should have listened. He's never lied to me, except maybe by omission." He sighed with a wry smile. "I never would have guessed he'd have been in such a profession."

She laughed. "Neither would I." She sighed. "He can't give it up, of course. He told me he had no ambition whatsoever to settle down and have a family. I never really saw him as a family man."

He studied her curiously. "But you wish he was," he said perceptibly.

Her gaze fell to the table. "I love him," she said heavily. "I always have. But he's got all the women in his life that he needs already. Beautiful women. One of them took me shopping when we first got to Nassau."

"You have ties with him that no other woman will ever have. If he didn't care about you, he certainly wouldn't have risked his own life to rescue you," he remarked.

"He did it for you, because he knows you love me," she said. "That's why."

He pursed his lips and his eyes narrowed as he studied her. "Think so? I wonder."

She got up. "I'll fix dinner. Then I guess I'll try to phone my father."

"Remember what you said, about forgiving people, Callie," he reminded her. "Your mother told him a lot of lies. He believed her, but maybe it was easier to believe her, when he knew she was taking you away. He was going to lose you anyway."

"She didn't take me away," she said coldly. "He threw me out, and she put me in foster care immediately."

He grimaced. "Yes, I know. Your father told me. He'd only just found out."

"Found out, how?" she exclaimed.

"Apparently he hired a private detective," he said gently. "He was appalled at how you'd been treated, Callie. He blames himself."

She moved restlessly, her eyes glancing at him. "You're the only father I've ever known."

He grinned. "You'll always have me. But give the man a chance. He's not as bad as you remember him being." The smile faded. "Maybe, like your mother, he's found time to face himself and his mistakes."

She turned away. "Okay. I guess it wouldn't hurt to talk to him."

She phoned, but her father was out of the country. She left a message for him on his answering machine, a stumbling sort of greeting and her phone number. If he hadn't given up on her, he might try again.

The next week dragged. She missed Micah. She felt tired. She wondered if all the excitement of the past few weeks wasn't catching up with her. She also seemed to have stopped having a period. She'd always been regular and never skipped, and then she remembered that odd spotting in Nassau. She grimaced. It must be some sort of female problem. She'd have to make an appointment to see Dr. Lou Coltrain.

She made the appointment from work, just after she got back from lunch. When she hung up, her boss, Blake Kemp, was speaking to someone in his office, the door just having opened so that he could show his client out.

"...yes, he phoned me a couple of days ago," the client was saying. "He used to hate Jacobsville, which makes it even stranger. We were all shocked."

"Yes," Kemp replied. "He had a whole island, didn't he? He's already sold up there, and he's got big plans for the Colbert Ranch property. He owns several thoroughbreds, which he's having shipped here from New Providence. He plans to have one of the best racing stables in Texas, from what he says."

"He says he's giving up the business as well and coming back here to live."

"That's another odd thing, he mentioned going back to medical school and finishing his residency," Kemp chuckled.

"He's good at what he used to do. He's patched me up enough over the years." The tall man with the green eyes, favoring a burned forearm and hand glanced at Callie and noted her shocked face. "Yes, Callie, I'm talking about your stepbrother. I don't guess you and Jack Steele knew a thing about this, did you?"

She shook her head, too stunned to speak.

"That's like Micah." The client chuckled. "He always was secretive. Well, Callie, you look none the worse for wear after your ordeal."

She finally realized who the client was. That was Cy Parks! She knew that he and Micah were friends, but until recently she hadn't known that they shared the same profession.

"Micah's moving here?" she asked involuntarily.

"He is," Cy told her. "But don't tell him you heard me say so," he added with a twinkle in his green eyes. "I don't need to lose any more teeth."

"Sure thing, Mr. Parks," she said with a smile.

"He couldn't stop talking about how brave you were, you know," he added unexpectedly. "He was so proud of you."

She flushed. "He never said so."

"He doesn't, usually." He smiled. "Your father will enjoy having him home, too."

She nodded. "He's proud of Micah. I had to tell him the truth. He'll be over the moon to think that Micah's coming home. He's missed him."

"That cuts both ways. I'm glad to see him making an attempt to settle down," he added with a chuckle. "I can recommend it highly. I never expected so much happiness in my own life. Lisa's pregnant, you know," he added. "It's going to be a boy. We're both over the moon."

"Babies are nice," Callie said wistfully. "Thanks for telling me about Micah, Mr. Parks."

"Make it Cy," he told her. "I expect we'll be seeing each other again. Kemp, walk me out, I want to ask you something."

"Sure thing."

The men walked out onto the sidewalk and Callie

stared at her computer screen with trembling fingers on the keyboard. Micah had sold his island. He was coming to live in Jacobsville. Was Lisse coming with him? Had they made up in spite of what he'd said about her? Was he going to marry the beautiful blonde and set up housekeeping here? If he was, she couldn't bear to stay in Jacobsville!

She felt like bawling. Her emotions had been all over the place lately. Along with the sudden bouts of fatigue and an odd nausea at night, and a missing period, she was likely to cry at the drop of a hat. She remembered a girlfriend having all those same symptoms, but of course, the girlfriend had been pregnant. That wasn't possible in her case. An erotic dream did not produce conception, after all. She was going to see the doctor the next day, anyway. She'd know what was wrong then, if anything was. She hoped it was nothing too terrible.

When she got home that evening, the doctor, the office, everything went right out of her head. There was a black Porsche convertible sitting in the driveway. With her heart pounding like mad, she got out and rushed up the front steps and into the apartment house.

She opened her own door, which was unlocked, and there was Micah, sitting at the dining-room table with Jack Steele while they shared a pot of coffee.

"Micah!" she exclaimed, everything she felt showing helplessly on her face.

He got to his feet, his face somber and oddly watchful. "Hello, Callie," he said quietly.

"I thought...I mean, I didn't think..." The room

was swirling around her. She felt an odd numbness in her face and everything went white.

Micah rushed forward and caught her up in his arms before she hit the floor.

"Her bedroom's through there," Jack told him. "She's been acting very odd, lately. Tired and goes to bed early. I'll make another pot of coffee."

"Thanks, Dad."

Micah carried her to her room and laid her down gently on the white coverlet of her bed. Her fingers were like ice. He brushed back her disheveled hair and his heart clenched at just the sight of her. He'd missed her until it was anguish not to hear her voice, see her face.

She moaned and her eyes opened slowly, looking up into his. She was faintly nauseous and her throat felt tight.

"I feel awful, Micah," she whispered. "But I'm so happy to see you!"

"I'm happy to see you, too," he replied, but he didn't look it. He looked worried. His big hand flattened on her belly, resting there very gently. He leaned close and his lips touched her eyelids, closing them. They moved down her face, over her cheeks, to her soft lips and he kissed her with breathless tenderness. "Callie," he whispered, and his lips became hard and insistent, as if he couldn't help himself.

She opened her mouth to him unconsciously, and her arms went around his neck, pulling him down. She forgot about Lisse, about everything. She kissed him back hungrily. All the weeks apart might never have been. She loved him so!

After a long minute, he forced himself to lift his head. He drew in a long, hard breath. He looked down where his hand was resting on her belly. It wasn't swollen yet, but he was certain, somehow, that she was carrying his child.

"Why...are you doing that?" she asked, watching his hand smooth over her stomach.

"I don't know how to tell you," he replied gently. "Callie...do you remember the night Lopez's men tried to kidnap you again? Do you remember that I gave you a sedative?"

"Yes," she said, smiling nervously.

"And you had an...erotic dream," he continued.

"Yes." She shifted on the cover. "I'd rather not talk about it."

"But we have to. Callie, I..."

"How about some coffee?" Jack Steele asked, poking his head through the doorway. "I just made a fresh pot."

"I'd like some," Callie said with a forced smile. "I'd like something to eat, too. I'm so empty!"

"That's what you think," Micah said under his breath. He stared down at her with twinkling eyes and a smile unlike any smile she'd ever seen on his lips before.

"You look very strange," she commented.

He shrugged. "Don't I always?"

She laughed gently. "Cy Parks was in Mr. Kemp's office today," she said as he helped her to her feet. "He said you were moving here...oops! I promised not to say anything, too. Please don't get mad at him, Micah."

"It's no big secret," he said gently. "In small towns, everybody knows what's going on. It's all right."

"You really are coming back here?"

Her wide eyes and fascinated expression made him tingle all over. "I am. I'm going to breed thoroughbreds. It's something I've always had an interest in. I might finish my residency as well. Jacobsville can always use another doctor."

"I guess so. I have to go see Dr. Lou Coltrain tomorrow. I think I may have a female problem," she said absently as they started out of the bedroom.

"Tomorrow?"

"After lunch," she said. "Don't tell Dad," she said, holding him back by the sleeve before they left the room. "I don't want him to worry. It probably scared him when I fainted. It scared me, too," she confessed.

He touched her hair gently. He wanted to tell her, but he didn't know how. He needed to talk to Lou Coltrain first. This had to be done very carefully, so that Callie didn't feel he was being forced into a decision he didn't want to make.

She searched his eyes. "You look so tired, Micah," she said softly.

"I don't sleep well since you left the island," he replied. "I've worried about you."

"I'm doing okay," she said at once, wanting to reassure him. "I don't even have nightmares." She looked down at her hand on his sleeve. "Micah, is Lisse…I mean, will she come, too?"

"Lisse is history. I told you that when you left. I meant it."

"She's so beautiful," she said huskily.

He frowned, tipping her face up to his with a hand under her chin. "You're beautiful yourself. Didn't you know?" he asked tenderly. "You have this big, open heart that always thinks of other people first.

You have a generosity of spirit that makes me feel selfish by comparison. You glow, Callie.'' He smiled softly. ''That's real beauty, the kind you don't buy in the cosmetic section of the department store. Lisse can't hold a candle to you.'' The smile faded. ''No woman on earth could, right now. You're pure magic to me, Callie. You're the whole world.''

That sounded serious. She just stared at him, transfixed, while she tried to decipher what he was saying.

''Coffee?'' Jack Steele repeated, a little more loudly.

They both jumped when they saw him there. Then they laughed and moved out of the bedroom. Jack poured coffee into mugs and Micah carried Callie hers.

''Feeling better?'' Jack asked.

''Oh, yes,'' she said, the excitement she was feeling so plain on her face that Micah grinned. ''Much better!''

Micah stayed near Callie for the rest of the evening, until he had to go. She'd fixed them a meal and had barely been able to eat a bite of it. She had little appetite, but mostly she was too excited. Micah was watching her as if everything she did fascinated him. All her dreams of love seemed to be coming true. She couldn't believe the way he was looking at her. It made her tingle.

She walked out with him after he'd said his goodnights to his father. ''You could stay,'' she said.

''I can't sleep on that dinky little sofa, and Dad's in a twin bed. So unless you're offering to share your nice big double bed...?'' he teased as they paused by the driver's side of his car.

She flushed. "Stop that."

He touched her cheek with his fingertips. "There's something I wanted to ask you. I can't seem to find a way to do it."

"What? You can ask me anything," she said softly.

He bent and brushed his mouth over hers. "Not yet. Come here and kiss me."

"We have neighbors…" she protested weakly.

But he'd already lifted her clear of the ground and he was kissing her as if there was no tomorrow. She held on and kissed him back with all her might. Two young boys on skateboards went whizzing by with long, insinuating wolf whistles.

Micah lifted his head and gave them a hard glare. "Everyone's a critic," he murmured.

"I'm not complaining," she whispered. "Come back here…"

He kissed her again and then, reluctantly, put her back on her feet. "Unless you want to make love on the hood of the car, we'd better put on the brakes." He looked around. More people had appeared. Incredible that there would be hordes of passersby at this hour in a small Texas town. He glared at two couples sauntering by. They grinned.

"That's Mr. and Mrs. Harris, and behind them is Mr. Harris's son and Jill Williams's daughter. They're going steady," she explained. "They know me, but I'm not in the habit of being kissed by handsome men in Porsches. They're curious."

He nodded over her shoulder. "And her?"

She followed where he was looking. "That's old Mrs. Smith. She grows roses."

"Yes. She seems to be pruning them." He

checked his watch. "Ten o'clock at night is an odd hour to do that, isn't it?"

"Oh, she just doesn't want to look as if she's staring," she explained. "She thinks it would embarrass us." She added in a whisper, "I expect she thinks we're courting."

He twirled a strand of dark hair around his fingers. "Aren't we?" he asked with a gentle smile.

"Courting?" She sounded breathless. She couldn't help it.

He nodded. "You're very old-fashioned, Callie. In some ways, so am I. But you'd better know up-front that I'm not playing."

"You already said you didn't want to settle down," she said, nodding agreement.

"That isn't what I mean."

"Then what do you mean?"

"Hello, Callie!" came an exuberant call from the window upstairs. It was Maria Ruiz, who was visiting her aunt who lived upstairs. She was sixteen and vivacious. "Isn't it a lovely night?"

"Lovely."

"Who's the dish?" the younger woman asked with an outrageous grin. "He's a real hunk. Does he belong to you, or is he up for grabs?"

"Sorry, I'm taken," Micah told her.

"Just my luck," she sighed. "Well, good night!"

She closed the window and the curtain and went back inside.

Callie laughed softly. "She's such a doll. She looks in on Dad when her aunt's working. I told you about her aunt, she doesn't speak any English."

He bent again and kissed her lazily. "You taste like roses," he whispered against her mouth. He enfolded her against him, shivering a little as his body responded instantly to the feel of hers against it and began to swell. He groaned softly as he kissed her again.

"Micah, you're..." She felt the hard crush of his mouth and she moaned, too. It was as if she'd felt him like this before, but in much greater intimacy. It was as if they'd been lovers. She held on tight and kissed him until she was shivering, too.

His mouth slid across her cheek to her ear, and he was breathing as roughly as she was. "I want you," he bit off, holding her bruisingly close. "I want you so much, Callie!"

"I'm sorry," she choked. "I can't...!"

He took deep breaths, trying to keep himself in check. He had to stop this. It was too soon. It was much too soon.

"It may not seem like it, but I'm not asking you to," he said. "It's just that there are things you don't know, Callie, and I don't know how to tell them to you."

"Bad things?"

He let out a slow breath. "Magical things," he whispered, cradling her in his arms as he thought about the baby he was certain she was carrying. His eyes closed as he held her. "The most magical sort of things. I've never felt like this in my life."

She wanted, so much, to ask him what he was feeling. But she was too shy. Perhaps if she didn't push him, he might like her. He sounded as if he did. She smiled, snuggling close to him, completely un-intimidated with the hard desire of his body. She loved making him feel this way.

He smoothed over her hair with a hand that wasn't

quite steady. His body ached, and even that was sweet. The weeks without her had been pure hell.

"Soon," he said enigmatically. "Very soon."

"What?"

He kissed her hair. "Nothing. I'd better go. Mrs. Smith is cutting the tops off the roses. Any minute now, there won't even be a bud left."

She glanced past his shoulder. She giggled helplessly. The romantic old woman was so busy watching them that she was massacring her prize roses!

"She wins ribbons for them, you know," she murmured.

"She won't have any left."

"She's having the time of her life," she whispered. "Her boyfriend married her sister. They haven't spoken in thirty years and she's never even looked at another man. She reads romance novels and watches movies and dreams. This is as close as she's likely to get to a hot romance. Even if it isn't."

"It certainly is," he whispered wickedly. "And if I don't get out of here *very* soon, she's going to see more than she bargained for. And so are you."

"Really?" she teased.

His hand slid to the base of her spine and pushed her close to him. His eyes held a very worldly amusement at her gasp. "Really," he whispered. He bent and kissed her one last time. "Go inside."

She forced herself to step back from him. "What about Bojo and Peter and Rodrigo and Pogo and Maddie?" she asked suddenly.

"Bojo was being groomed to take over the group. He's good at giving orders, and he knows how we operate. I'll be a consultant."

"But why?" she asked, entranced. "And why come back to Jacobsville to raise horses?"

"When you're ready for those answers I'll give them to you," he said with a gentle smile. "But not tonight. I'll be in touch. Good night."

He was in the car and gone before she could get another word out. Several doors down, Mrs. Smith was muttering as she looked at the rosebuds lying heaped around her feet. The skateboarders went past again with another round of wolf whistles. The couples walking gave her long, wicked grins. Callie went back inside, wondering if she should give them all a bow before she went inside.

Chapter Thirteen

Micah was ushered back into Dr. Lou Coltrain's office through the back door, before she started seeing her patients. He shook hands with her and took the seat she indicated in her office. She sat down behind her desk, blond and attractive and amused.

"Thanks for taking time to see me this morning," he said. He noted her wry look and chuckled. "Is my head on backward?" he asked.

"You may wish it was," she replied with twinkling dark eyes. "I think I know why you're here. At least two people have hinted to me that Callie Kirby's having what sounds like morning sickness."

He sighed and smiled. "Yes."

"And you're the culprit, unless I miss my guess. Are you here to discuss alternatives?" she asked, suddenly serious.

"I am not!" he said at once. "I want a baby as much as Callie will, when she knows about it."

"When she knows? She doesn't suspect?" she asked, wide-eyed.

He grimaced. "Well, it's like this. Lopez and his thugs—you know about them?" When she nodded, he sighed. "I was careless and they almost got her a second time in Nassau. She knocked her assailant out with a shovel, but she was really shaken up afterward. I gave her a sedative." His high cheekbones colored and he averted his eyes. "She got amorous and I was already upset and on the edge, and I'd abstained for so damned long. And…well…"

"Then what?" she asked, reading between the lines with avid curiosity.

He shifted in the chair, still avoiding eye contact. "She doesn't remember anything. She thinks it was an erotic dream."

Her intake of breath was audible. "In all my years of medicine…" she began.

"I haven't had that many, but it's news to me, too. The thing is, I'm sure she's pregnant, but she'll have a heart attack if you tell her she is. I have to break it to her. But first I have to find a way to convince her to marry me," he added. "So that she won't spend the rest of our lives together believing that the baby forced me into marriage. It's not like that," he said. He rubbed at a spot on his slacks so that he wouldn't have to meet Lou's intent stare. "She's everything. Everything in the world."

Lou smiled. He wasn't saying the words, but she was hearing them. He loved Callie. So it was like that. The mercenary was caught in his own trap. And, amazingly, he didn't want to get out of it. He wanted the baby!

"What do you want me to do?" she asked.

"I want you to do a blood test and see if she really is pregnant. But if she is, I want you to make some excuse about the results being inconclusive, and you can give her a prescription for some vitamins and ask her to come back in two weeks."

"She'll worry that it's something fatal," Lou advised. "People do."

"Tell her you think it's stress, from her recent ordeal," he persisted. "Please," he added, finding the word hard to say even now. "I just need a little time."

"Just call me Dr. Cupid Coltrain," she murmured. "I guess I'll get drummed out of the AMA, but how can I say no?"

"You're in the business of saving lives," he reminded her. "This will save three of them."

"I hear you're moving back here," she said.

"I am. I'm going to raise thoroughbreds," he added, smiling. "And act as a consultant for Eb Scott when he needs some expertise. That way, I'll not only settle down, I'll have enough of a taste of the old life to satisfy me if things get dull. I might even finish my residency and hit you and Coltrain up for a job."

"Anytime," she said, grinning. "I haven't had a day off in two years. I'd like to take my son to the zoo and not have to leave in the middle of the lions on an emergency call."

He chuckled. "Okay. That's a dare."

She stood up when he did and shook hands again. "You're not what I expected, Mr. Steele," she said after a minute. "I had some half-baked idea that you'd never give up your line of work, that you'd want Callie to do something about the baby."

"I do. I want her to have it," he said with a smile. "And a few more besides, if we're lucky. Callie and I were only children. I'd like several, assorted."

"So would we, but one's all we can handle at the moment. Of course, if you finish your residency and stand for your medical license, that could change," she added, tongue-in-cheek.

He grinned. "I guess it's contagious."

She nodded. "Very. Now get out of here. I won't tell Callie I've ever seen you in my life."

"Thanks. I really mean it."

"Anything for a future colleague," she returned with a grin of her own.

Callie worried all morning about the doctor's appointment, but she relaxed when she was in Lou's office and they'd drawn blood and Lou had checked her over.

"It sounds to me like the aftereffects of a very traumatic experience," Lou said with a straight face. "I'm prescribing a multiple vitamin and I want you to come back and see me in two weeks."

"Will the tests take that long?" Callie asked.

"They might." Lou sighed. "You're mostly tired, Callie. You should go to bed early and eat healthy. Get some sun, too. And try not to worry. It's nothing serious, I'm positive of that."

Callie smiled her relief. "Thanks, Dr. Coltrain!" she said. "Thanks, so much!"

"I hear your stepbrother's moving back to town,'

Lou said as she walked Callie to the door of the cubicle. "I guess you'll be seeing a lot of him now."

Callie flushed. "It looks that way." Her eyes lit up. "He's so different. I never could have imagined Micah settling for small-town life."

"Men are surprising people," Lou said. "You never know what they're capable of."

"I suppose so. Well, I'll see you in two weeks."

"Count on it," Lou said, patting her on the shoulder. "Lots of rest. And take those vitamins," she added, handing over the prescription.

Callie felt as if she were walking on air. No health problems, just the aftereffects of the kidnapping. That was good news indeed. And when Micah phoned and asked her to come out to the ranch with him and see the house, she was over the moon.

He picked her up after work at her apartment house. "I took Dad out there this morning," he told her with a grin. "He's going to move in with me at the weekend."

Callie's heart jumped. "This weekend?"

He nodded, glancing at her. "You could move in, too."

Her heart jumped, but she knew he didn't mean that the way it sounded. "I like living in town," she lied.

He smiled to himself. He knew what she was refusing. She wasn't about to live in sin with him in Jacobsville, Texas.

He reached for her hand and linked her fingers with his. "Did you go see the doctor?"

"Yes. She said it was stress. I guess it could be. At least, it's nothing extreme."

"Thank God," he said.

"Yes."

He turned down onto a long winding graveled road. Minutes later, they pulled up in front of a big white Victorian house with a turret room and a new tin roof. "It's really old-fashioned and some of the furniture will have to be replaced," he said, helping her out of the car. "But it's got potential. There's a nice rose garden that only needs a little work, and a great place out to the side for a playground. You know, a swing set and all those nice plastic toys kids love so much."

She stared at him. "You have kids?" she asked with an impish smile.

"Well, not yet," he agreed. "But they're definitely in the picture. Don't you like kids?" he asked with apparent carelessness.

"I love them," she said, watching him warily. "I didn't think you did."

He smiled. "I'll love my own, Callie," he said, his fingers contracting in hers. "Just as you'll love them."

"I'll love your kids?" she blurted out.

He couldn't quite meet her eyes. He stared down toward the big barn a few hundred yards behind the house and he linked his fingers tighter with hers. "Have you ever thought," he said huskily, "about making a baby with me?"

Her heart went right up into her throat. She flushed scarlet. But it wasn't embarrassment. It was pure, wild, joy.

He looked down at her then. Everything she thought, felt, was laid out there for him to see. He caught his breath at the depth of those emotions she didn't know he could see. It was more than he'd ever dared hope for.

"I want a baby, Callie," he whispered huskily. He framed her red face in his hands and bent to kiss her eyelids closed. His fingers were unsteady as he held her where he wanted her, while his mouth pressed tender, breathless little kisses all over her soft skin. "I want one so much. You'd make…the most wonderful little mother," he bit off, choked with emotion. "I could get up with you in the night, when the baby cried, and take turns walking the floor. We could join the PTA later. We could make memories that would last us forever, Callie—you and me and a little boy or a little girl."

She slid her arms tight under his and around him and held on for dear life, shaking with delighted surprise. He wasn't joking. He really meant it. Her eyes closed. She felt tears pouring down her cheeks.

He felt them against his thin silk shirt and he smiled as he reached in his pocket for a handkerchief. He drew her away from him and dabbed at the tears, bending to kiss away the traces. "We can build a big playground here," he continued, as if he hadn't said anything earthshaking. "Both of us were only kids. I think two or three would be nice. And Dad would love being a grandfather. He can stay with us and the kids will make him young again."

"I'd love that. I never dreamed you'd want to have a family or settle down. You said…"

He kissed the words back against her lips. "Freedom is only a word," he told her solemnly. "It stopped meaning anything to me when I knew that Lopez had you." The memory of that horror was suddenly on his face, undisguised. "I couldn't rest until I knew where you were. I planned an assault in a day that should have taken a week of preparation. And then I went in after you myself, because I couldn't trust anyone to do it but me.'' His hands clenched on her shoulders. ''When I saw you like that, saw what that animal had done to you...'' He stopped and swallowed hard. ''My God, if he'd killed you, I'd have cut him to pieces! And then,'' he whispered, folding her close, shivering with the depth of his feelings, ''I'd have picked you up in my arms and I'd have jumped off the balcony into the rocks with you. Because I wouldn't want to live in a world...that didn't hold us both. I couldn't live without you. Not anymore.''

There was a faint mist in his black eyes. She could barely see it for the mist in her own. She choked on a sob as she looked up at him. ''I love you,'' she whispered brokenly. ''You're my whole life. I never dared to hope that you might care for me, too!''

He folded her against him and held her close, rocking her, his cheek on her dark hair as he counted his blessings. They overwhelmed him. She loved him. His eyes closed. It seemed that love could forgive anything, even his years of unkindness. ''I wish I could take back every single hurtful thing I've ever done or said to you.''

She smiled tearfully against his broad chest. ''It's all right, Micah. Honest it is. Do you really want babies?'' she asked dreamily, barely aware of anything he'd said.

''More than anything in the world!''

''I won't sleep with you unless you marry me,'' she said firmly.

He chuckled. ''I'll marry you as soon as we can

get a license. But,'' he added on a long sigh, drawing back, ''I'm afraid it's too late for the sleeping together part.''

Her thin eyebrows arched up. ''What?''

He traced around her soft lips. ''Callie, that erotic dream you had…'' He actually flushed. ''Well, it wasn't a dream,'' he added with a sheepish grin.

Her eyes widened endlessly. All those explicit things he'd done and said, that she'd done and said, that had seemed like something out of a fantasy. The fatigue, the spotting, the lack of a period, the…

''Oh my God, I'm pregnant!'' she exclaimed in a high-pitched tone.

''Oh my God, yes, you are, you incredible woman!'' he said with breathless delight. ''I'm sorry, but I went to Lou Coltrain behind your back and begged her not to tell you until we came to an understanding. I was scared to death that you'd be off like a shot if you knew it too soon.'' He shook his head at her surprise. ''I've never wanted anything as much as I want this child—except you,'' he added huskily. ''I can't make it without you, Callie. I don't want to try.'' He glanced around them at the house and the stable. ''This is where we start. You and me, a new business, a new life—in more ways than one,'' he added with a tender hand on her soft abdomen. ''I know I'm something of a risk. But I'd never have made the offer to come here unless I'd been sure, very sure, that I could make it work. I want you more than I want the adventure and the freedom. I love you with all my heart. Is that enough?''

She smiled with her heart in her eyes. ''It's enough,'' she said huskily.

He seemed to relax then, as if he'd been holding

his breath the whole while. His eyes closed and he shivered. "Thank God," he said reverently.

"You didn't think I was going to say no?" she asked, shocked. "Good Lord, the sexiest man in town offers me a wedding ring and you think I'm going to say no?"

He pursed his lips. "Sexy, huh?"

"You seduced me," she pointed out. "Only a very sexy man could have managed that." She frowned. "Of course, you did drug me first," she added gleefully.

"You were hysterical," he began.

"I was in love," she countered, smiling. "And I wasn't all that sedated." She blushed. "But I did think it was a dream. You see, I'd had sort of the same dream since I was...well, since I was about sixteen."

His lips parted on a shocked breath. "That long?"

She nodded. "I couldn't even get interested in anybody else. But you didn't want me..."

"I did want you," he countered. "That's why I was horrible to you. But never again," he promised huskily. "Never again. I'm going to work very hard at being a good husband and father. You won't regret it, Callie. I swear you won't."

"I know that. You won't regret it, either," she promised. She placed her hand over his big one, that still lay gently against her stomach. "And I never guessed," she whispered, smiling secretly. Her eyes brimmed over with excitement. "I'm so happy," she told him brokenly. "And so scared. Babies don't come with instruction manuals."

"We have Lou Coltrain, who's much better than an instruction manual," he pointed out with a grin.

"And speaking of Lou, did you get those vitamins she prescribed?"

"Well, not yet," she began.

"They're prenatal vitamins," he added, chuckling. "You're going to be amazed at how good you feel. Not to mention how lucky you are," he added blithely, "to have a husband who knows exactly what to expect all through your pregnancy." He kissed her softly. "After the baby comes, I might finish my residency and go into practice with the Coltrains," he added.

That meant real commitment, she realized. He was giving up every vestige of the old life for her. Well, almost. She knew he'd keep his hand in with Eb Scott's operation. But the last of Jacobsville's mercenaries was ready to leave the past behind and start again.

So many beautiful memories are about to be created here, she thought as she looked around her from the shelter of Micah's hard arms. She pressed close with a sigh. "After the pain, the pleasure," she whispered.

"What was that?"

"Nothing. Just something I heard when I was younger." She didn't add that it was something her father had said. That was the one bridge she hadn't yet crossed. It would have to be faced. But, she thought, clinging to Micah in the warmth of the sun, not right now...

Micah drove her by the pharmacy on the way back to her apartment. He stood with her while Nancy, the dark-haired, dark-eyed pharmacist filled the prescription, trying not to grin too widely at the picture they made together.

"I suppose you know what these are for?" Nancy asked Callie.

Callie smiled and looked up at Micah, who smiled back with the same tenderness. "Oh, yes," she said softly.

He pulled her close for an instant, before he offered his credit card to pay for them. "We're getting married Sunday at the Methodist church," Micah told her and the others at the counter. "You're all invited…2:00 p.m. sharp."

Nancy's eyes twinkled. "We, uh, heard that from the minister already," she said, clearing her throat as Callie gaped at her.

Micah chuckled at Callie's expression. "You live in a small town, and you didn't think everybody would know already?"

"But you hadn't told me yet!" she accused.

He shrugged. "It didn't seem too smart to announce that I'd arranged a wedding that you hadn't even agreed to yet."

"And they say women keep secrets!" she said on a rough breath.

"Not half as good as men do, sweetheart," Micah told her gently. He glanced around at a sudden commotion behind them. The two remaining bachelor Hart brothers, Rey and Leo, were almost trampling people in their rush to get to the prescription counter.

"Have to have this as soon as possible, sorry!" Rey exclaimed, pressing a prescription into Nancy's hands with what looked like desperation.

"It's an emergency!" Leo seconded.

Nancy's eyes widened. She looked at the brothers with astonishment. "An emergency? This is a prescription for anti-inflammatories…"

"For our cook," Leo said. "Her hands hurt, she said. She can't make biscuits. We rushed her right over to Lou Coltrain and she said it was arthritis." He grimaced. "*Pleaaase* hurry? We didn't get any breakfast at all!"

Callie had her hand over her mouth trying not to have hysterics. Micah just looked puzzled. Apparently he didn't know about the famous biscuit mania.

Leo sounded as if he was starving. Amazing, a big, tall man with a frame like that attempting to look emaciated. Rey was tall and thin, and he did look as if he needed a feeding. There had been some talk about a new woman out at the ranch recently who was rather mysterious. But if they had a cook with arthritis, she surely wasn't a young cook.

Nancy went to fill the prescriptions.

"Sorry," Rey muttered as he glanced behind him and Leo at the people they'd rushed past to get their prescription filled. He tried to smile. He wasn't really good at it. He cleared his throat self-consciously. "Chocolates," he reminded Leo.

"Right over there," Leo agreed somberly. "We'd better get two boxes. And some of that cream stuff for arthritis, and there's some sort of joint formula…"

"And the We're Sorry card," Rey added, mumbling something about shortsightedness and loose tongues as they stomped off down the aisle with two pairs of spurs jingling musically from the heels of their boots.

Nancy handed Micah the credit card receipt, which he signed and gave Callie a pert grin as she went back to work.

Callie followed Micah out the door, letting loose

a barrage of laughter when they reached the Porsche. By the time they got to her apartment, he was laughing, too, at the town's most notorious biscuit eaters.

Jack Steele was overjoyed at the news they had for him. For the next week he perked up as never before, taking a new interest in life and looking forward to having a daughter-in-law and a grandchild. The news that he was going to live with them disturbed him, he thought they needed privacy, but they insisted. He gave in. There was no mistaking their genuine love for him, or their delight in his company. He felt like the richest man on earth.

Callie, meanwhile, had an unexpected phone call from her father, who was back in town and anxious to see her. She met him in Barbara's café on her lunch hour from the law office, curious and nervous after so many years away from him.

Her father had black hair with silver at his temples and dark blue eyes. He was somber, quiet, unassuming and guilt was written all over him.

After they'd both ordered salads and drinks, her father gave her a long, hesitant scrutiny.

"You look so much like my mother," he said unexpectedly. "She had the same shaped eyes you do, and the same color."

Callie looked down at her salad. "Do I?"

He laid down his fork and leaned forward on his elbows. "I've been an idiot. How do I apologize for years of neglect, for letting you be put through hell in foster homes?" he asked quietly. "When I knew what had happened to you, I was too ashamed even to phone. Your mother had only just told me the truth and after the private detective I hired gave me the file on you, I couldn't take it. I went to Europe and stayed for a month. I don't even remember what I did there.'' He grimaced at Callie's expression. "I'm so ashamed. Even if you hadn't been my biological child, you'd lived in my house, I'd loved you, protected you.'' He lowered his shamed eyes to his plate. "Pride. It was nothing but pride. I couldn't bear thinking that you were another man's child. You paid for my cruelty, all those years.'' He drew in a long breath and looked up at her sadly. "You're my daughter. But I don't deserve you.'' He made an awkward motion. "So if you don't want to have anything to do with me, that's all right. I'll understand. I've been a dead bust as a father.''

She could see the torment in his eyes. Her mother had done something unspeakably cruel to both of them with her lies. The bond they'd formed had been broken, tragically. She remembered the loneliness of her childhood, the misery of belonging nowhere. But now she had Micah and a child on the way, and Jack Steele as well. She'd landed on her feet, grown strong, learned to cope with life. She'd even fought off drug dealing thugs, all by herself, that night in Nassau when her child had been conceived. She felt so mature now, so capable. She smiled slowly. She'd lectured Micah about forgiveness. Here was her best chance to prove that she believed her own words.

"You're going to be a grandfather," she said simply. "Micah and I are getting married Sunday afternoon at two o'clock in the Methodist church. You and Jack Steele could both give me away if you like.'' She grinned. "It will raise eyebrows everywhere!''

He seemed shocked. His blue eyes misted and he

bit his lip. "A grandfather." He laughed self-consciously and looked away long enough to brush away something that looked suspiciously wet. "I like that." He glanced back at her. "Yes. I'd like to give you away. I'd like to get you back even more, Callie. I'm…sorry."

When he choked up like that, she was beyond touched. She got up from her seat and went around to hug him to her. The café was crowded and she didn't care. She held him close and laid her cheek on his hair, feeling his shoulders shake. It was, in so many ways, one of the most poignant experiences of her young life.

"It's okay, Papa," she whispered, having called him that when she was barely school age. "It's okay now."

He held her tighter and he didn't give a damn that he was crying and half of Jacobsville could see him. He had his daughter back, against all the odds.

Callie felt like that, too. She met Barbara's eyes over the counter and smiled through her tears. Barbara nodded, and smiled, and reached for a napkin. It was so much like a new start. Everything was fresh and sweet and life was blessed. She was never again going to take anything for granted as long as she lived!

The wedding was an event. Callie had an imported gown from Paris, despite the rush to get it in time. Micah wore a morning coat. All the local mercenaries and the gang from the island, including Bojo, Peter, Rodrigo and Mac were there, along with Pogo and Maddie. And, really, Callie thought, Maddie did resemble her, but the older woman was much more athletic and oddly pretty. She smiled broadly at Callie as she stood beside a man Callie didn't recognize, with jet-black hair and eyes and what was obviously a prosthetic arm. There were a lot of men she didn't know. Probably Micah had contacts everywhere, and when word of the marriage had gotten out, they all came running to see if the rumors were true. Some of them looked astonished, but most were grinning widely.

The ceremony was brief, but beautiful. Micah pulled up the veil Callie wore, and kissed her for the first time as his wife.

"When we're finished, you have to read the inscription in your wedding band," he whispered against her soft mouth.

"Don't make me wait," she teased. "What does it say?"

He clasped her hand to his chest, ignoring the glowing faces of the audience. "It says 'forever,' Callie. And it means forever. I'll love you until I close my eyes for the last time. And even afterward, I'll love you."

She cried as he kissed her. It was the most beautiful thing he'd ever said to her. She whispered the words back to him, under her breath, while a soft sound rippled through the church. The couple at the rose-decked altar were so much in love that they fairly glowed with it.

They walked out under a cloud of rose petals and rice and Callie stopped and threw her bouquet as they reached the limousine that would take them to the airport. They were flying to Scotland for their honeymoon, to a little thatched cottage that belonged to Mac and had been loaned to them for the occasion.

A romantic gesture from a practical and very unromantic man, that had touched Callie greatly.

Jack Steele, who was staying at the ranch with Micah's new foreman and his wife, waved them off with tears in his eyes, standing next to Kane Kirby, who was doing the same. The two men had become friends already, both avid poker players and old war movie fanatics.

A flustered blond Janie Brewster had caught the bouquet that Callie threw, and she looked down at it as if she didn't quite know what to do next. Nearby, the whole Hart family was watching, married brothers Corrigan and Simon and Cag, and the bachelor boys, Rey and Leo. It was Leo who was giving Janie an odd look, but she didn't see it. She laughed nervously and quickly handed the bouquet to old Mrs. Smith, Callie's neighbor. Then she ducked into the crowd and vanished, to Callie's amusement.

"The last mercenary," she whispered. "And you didn't get away, after all."

"Not the last," he murmured, glancing toward his old comrades and Peter, their newest member, all of whom were silently easing away toward the parking lot. He smiled down at her. "But the happiest," he added, bending to kiss her. "Wave bye at both our papas and let's go. I can't wait to get you alone, Mrs. Steele!"

She chuckled and blushed prettily. "That makes two of us!"

She waved and climbed into the car with her acres of silk and lace and waited for Micah to pile in beside her. The door closed. The car drove away to the excited cries of good luck that followed it. Inside, two newlyweds were wrapped up close in each others' arms, oblivious to everything else. Micah cradled Callie in his arms and thanked God for second chances. He recalled Callie's soft words: After the pain, the pleasure. He closed his eyes and sighed. The pleasure had just begun.

* * * * *

Look for a new Diana Palmer novel,
Boss Man, *coming in October 2006*
from Silhouette Desire.

A Man Apart
GINNA GRAY

GINNA GRAY

A native Houstonian, Ginna Gray admits that, since childhood, she has been a compulsive reader as well as a head-in-the-clouds dreamer. Long accustomed to expressing her creativity in tangible ways Ginna also enjoys painting and needlework—she finally decided to try putting her fantasies and wild imaginings down on paper. The result? The mother of two now spends eight hours a day as a full-time writer.

Chapter One

More than a dozen policemen stood vigil in the corridor outside the hospital operating room. Every few minutes, more officers arrived to join the silent watch. When one of their own took a hit, the men and women in blue rallied around.

Less than an hour earlier, the frantic call had gone out over the police radio frequency.

"Shots fired! Shots fired! Officer down! We need assistance!"

Within seconds, every available man and woman on the Houston police force had raced to aid the besieged detectives at the scene of a drug bust gone bad.

Now, grim-faced and tense, those same men and women waited for news of their fellow officer's condition.

John Werner and Hank Pierson, the two men who were closest to the wounded officer, paced like caged lions, their faces dark and stony.

Guilt and worry ate at Hank like sharp-toothed animals. Dammit, it was his duty to protect his partner's back, and he had let Matt down. Now he might die. Matt had taken two bullets, and for that he blamed himself. Under a hail of automatic weapons' fire, hunkered down behind their squad car, he had radioed in the frantic call for assistance and fired random shots at the attackers over the hood of the vehicle, but beyond that he had been helpless.

Hank suddenly stopped pacing, and with an oath, he slammed the side of his fist against the wall. Several of the other policemen eyed him askance, but no one said a word.

Lieutenant Werner understood his detective's frustration and ignored the outburst.

As chief of detectives, John Werner felt a personal responsibility for every man and woman on his squad, but he shared a special friendship with the wounded officer. John had gone through the police academy with Matt's father. Patrick Dolan had been John's best friend and one of the finest officers the city had ever had.

That it was Matt Dolan who had been shot had spread like wildfire through the Houston Police Department. The news had stunned everyone and left them shaken. Matt was a smart, straight-arrow, tough cop, a twelve-year veteran on the force. He had seemed invincible.

The double doors of the operating room swung open and every officer in the hallway sprang to attention. A middle-aged man dressed in green scrubs emerged and flashed a look around at the crowd, meeting the anxious expressions with a grim look.

"I'm Dr. Barnes. Who's in charge here?" He raked the paper scrub cap off his head and absently massaged the tense muscles in his neck.

"I am." John Werner stepped forward. Hank edged up beside him. "How is he, Doc?"

"Alive. Just barely. The first bullet nicked his right lung. The second caused severe damage to his right leg. Plus, he lost a lot of blood before he arrived here. He's a tough nut, though, I'll give him that. If he weren't, he'd never have made it this far. But he is in bad shape."

"I see." John's jaw clenched and unclenched for several seconds. At last he asked the question that was foremost on his and every other officer's mind, the question to which they all dreaded the answer. "Is Matt going to make it, Doc?"

"Barring complications, yes."

"Thank God for that."

"Yes, well…I feel it's only fair to warn you, given the condition of that leg…well…"

"What? What're you trying to say, Doc?" Hank demanded.

"Just that…well…I think you should know that it's unlikely he will ever be able to return to police work. At least, not on the streets."

Matt turned his head on the pillow and gazed out the window at nothing in particular. The lady in the mist had come to him again last night.

The fanciful thought brought a hint of a smile to his stern mouth. Nevertheless, that was how he thought of the recurring dream that had plagued him all his life: a visitation by a phantom figure.

It was strange. For the past fifteen or twenty years he'd had the dream very infrequently—once or twice a year at the most—but since awaking in the hospital two weeks ago, it had been nightly. Not even the sleeping tablets the staff administered so faithfully had helped.

Absently, Matt fingered the jagged fragment of silver that hung from a chain around his neck, his thumb rubbing back and forth over the lines etched on either side. The pie-shaped wedge had been roughly cut from a silver medallion approximately two inches in diameter.

The instant Matt had regained consciousness he'd reached for the piece, and he'd panicked when he discovered it was no longer around his neck.

The medallion piece had been returned to him only because he had threatened to tear the place apart if it wasn't. The hospital prohibited patients from wearing jewelry of any kind. Matt, however, had worn the medallion fragment since he was a small boy, never taking it off.

Matt's fingers continued to rub the etched surface and jagged edges. Somehow, merely touching it seemed to soothe him. Particularly after a night of chasing after the lady in the mist.

He smiled again. The lady in the mist. He'd named the dream that years ago. It wasn't scary or in any way threatening—just him and others he couldn't identify, chasing through swirling mist after the shadowy figure of a woman, calling out to her, reaching for her as she backed away and disappeared—yet the experience always disturbed him. Invariably, he awoke with a start, his heart pounding. Last night had been no different. He wondered, as he had countless times, if he'd ever decipher the meaning behind the subconscious message.

Pushing the futile thought aside, Matt sighed and focused his attention elsewhere.

The impersonal atmosphere of the hospital made him feel adrift, removed from the world outside, a spectator with no part to play. Which, he supposed, was appropriate, since the life he had built for himself was most likely finished.

"Dammit, Matt, are you listening to me?"

John Werner stepped between the bed and the window, blocking Matt's view of the street and giving him no option but to acknowledge him. The older man glared, his jaw thrust forward. "I've put up with your silent treatment long enough. If you think you can just clam up and pretend I'm not here, like you've been doing to me and everyone else for the past two weeks, think again. I won't stand for it, you hear?"

John was a big bull of a man, standing six foot seven and weighing more than three hundred pounds. He had a broad, menacing face that looked as though it had been hewn from oak with a blunt ax and a voice that rumbled out like the wrath of God when he was angry. Most of the detectives on his squad cringed when he got on their cases.

Matt didn't turn a hair.

"I don't know what you're talking about."

"The hell you don't. You've had a steady stream of visitors—family and friends, the guys on the force, the department psychologist, even your doctors—but you barely talk to any of them. You just turn away and tune them out. The few times you have bothered to speak was just to bite someone's head off. Well, it won't work with me. Like it or not, we're going to talk about this."

"There's nothing to talk about."

"Oh, no? How about the fact that you've refused all the offers of help you've received? Huh? How about that? Hank here has practically begged you to come stay with him and his wife while you recuperate. So have several others, but you've turned them all down flat." He nodded toward Hank Pierson, who stood on the other side of the room watching his partner with a worried expression. "Isn't that right, Hank?"

"Sure is. Look, old buddy, it's no problem. Patty and I really want you to stay with us."

"Patty's got enough on her hands with three kids to look after."

"Hey, one more won't bother Patty. Really. In fact, she insists. You know she thinks of you as family. We all do."

"Thanks all the same, but no." Matt shook his head and looked away.

"If you don't want to stay with Hank and Patty, then how about someone else?" John persisted. "Several of the other guys and their wives have offered to look after you."

"The answer is still no. I don't need anyone to look after me. Besides, I don't want to impose on my friends."

"All right. I think you're wrong and full of stiff-necked pride, but I understand. Trust me, though, like it or not, you will need someone to look after you when you leave here. At least for a while. So why don't you let the department pay for a nurse to stay with you?"

"Forget it. I don't want some stranger in my house. Anyway, I prefer to be alone. As soon as I get those discharge papers tomorrow, I'm going home."

"You're in no condition to stay in that town house alone," John roared. "Dammit, man, you've got a long recuperation ahead of you, and once your body is healed you're going to be in for some grueling rehab work before you'll be ready to return to duty."

Matt snorted. "What makes you think I'll ever be?"

"Because I know you, you bullheaded Irishman. You're not a quitter, any more than your old man was. And you love police work too much to throw in the towel without a fight."

Matt shrugged. "The doctor doesn't share your confidence."

"So what does he know? You're going to have to work your tail off for weeks, maybe even months, to pass the reentry physical, but if anyone can do it, you can."

Matt gave another scornful snort. "You have more faith in me than I do.'"

"Probably, but that will change. Now, the way I see it, you've got two choices. You can either hire a live-in nurse or you can spend the summer up at my fishing lodge on Lake Livingston."

"Your *fishing lodge?*"

"Why not? It's the perfect place to recuperate. The fresh air and peace and quiet of the country will be good for you. You can go for walks in the woods and fish off the pier at first. Later, when you're stronger, you can go sailing or take the fishing boat out onto the lake."

"Don't you have tenants at the lodge?"

"Just one right now, but that's no problem. It's a big place. You'll probably never run into each other. Anyway, you can use my quarters. There's a private entrance off the side veranda."

"I still don't—"

"This isn't a suggestion, Dolan, it's an order."

Matt bristled. "You can't order me to do anything when I'm not on duty."

Smiling benignly, the lieutenant crossed his arms over his chest and rocked back on his heels. "Oh, yeah? Don't forget, you need my permission to even take the reentry physical. You spend the summer getting well at the lodge or you can forget about working the streets again. Got that, Dolan?"

"You'd do it, too, wouldn't you?" Matt snarled. "You'd

refuse to let me take the physical for street duty and stick me behind a desk.''

John shrugged and spread his hands wide. ''Hey. It's up to you, Dolan. All you have to do is recuperate and get back in shape up at Lake Livingston.''

''That's blackmail.''

''Maybe,'' John agreed with a shrug. ''But I don't see it that way. I'm just trying to help one of my men get back on his feet.''

''Listen to him, Matt,'' Hank urged. ''You gotta recuperate somewhere, and shoot, any way you look at it, that's not bad duty. A carefree summer at a lake in a comfortable fishing lodge. If I thought Patty would allow it, I'd almost be tempted to go out and get myself shot if it meant a summer at the lake.'' He paused and gave his partner a lopsided grin. ''So whaddaya say?''

A muscle worked in Matt's jaw as his gaze slid back and forth between his two friends. Hank's expression was coaxing. John's, though pleasant, was adamant, and unyielding as granite.

''Excuse me. Am I interrupting something?''

The heads of the other two men snapped around, but Matt merely gritted his teeth. He know that drawling voice with its underlay of laughter only too well. Turning his head slowly on the pillow, he stabbed the new arrival with a hard stare.

The man stood in the doorway, one shoulder propped against the frame, an amused smile on his roguishly handsome face. Everything about him—his loose stance, the careless panache of his attire, the smooth nonchalance—made him appear friendly and harmless, but Matt knew that beneath that laid-back charm was a sharp mind and a pitbull determination when he smelled a story.

Their gazes locked, one pair of vivid blue eyes narrowed and hard, with no trace of welcome, the other pair twinkling with curiosity and mischief and humor. Neither wavered.

"Who let you in here?" John snarled, putting an end to the silent battle. "I specifically told the staff that Matt's room was off-limits to reporters."

"C'mon, Lieutenant. Can't a guy drop by to see an old friend?"

"Just because we've known each other for a few years doesn't make us friends, Conway," Matt growled.

"All right, then, a close acquaintance. And it's been more than a few years. More like ten or eleven."

"Whatever. I still don't want you here. I have nothing to say to the press."

"You heard the man."

J. T. Conway straightened away from the doorjamb and stepped into the room, ignoring Hank's warning. "Look, I just want to do a small piece on your recovery. The public want to know how their local hero is doing."

"Yeah, right. We both know that if that was all you wanted, your paper would've sent a cub reporter, not their ace."

A rueful grin hiked up one corner of J.T.'s mouth. "Okay, maybe I was hoping to get a quote or two about the raid. Word is, the dealer was tipped off. That someone in the department is on the take. How does it feel to know that you nearly bought the farm because one of your own is dirty?"

Matt's eyes narrowed. "Get out."

"Look, Matt, I know—"

"All right, that's it. You're outta here," Hank growled. Both he and John took a menacing step toward the reporter.

"Whoa now. Look, guys, I'm just doing my job. The readers have a right to know—"

"How about I show you how it feels to eat teeth? How about that for a story? Your readers ought to love that."

J.T. looked from one determined face to the other, weighing his chances. He was a big man, matching Matt's six foot one and broad-shouldered build, but he knew when to back off. Raising both hands, palms out, he retreated. "Okay, okay. I'm going." His blue eyes darted to Matt and he winked. "You get well, buddy."

"Boy, the nerve of that guy," Hank muttered after J.T. left.

The lieutenant, with his usual tenacity, turned his attention back to Matt. "If you go home to that town house of yours, you can expect more of that sort of thing. And there won't be anyone there to run interference. If you go to the lake, you'll have privacy. No one but Hank and me and a few others will even know you're there."

"Jeez! Don't you ever give up?" Matt groaned. "Oh, all right! I'll go to your damned fishing lodge."

John beamed. "Good, good." He rubbed his palms together. "I'll make the arrangements. Hank will go by your place and pack your clothes, then be here tomorrow at checkout time to drive you up to the lake."

"I'm thrilled," Matt drawled.

"We'll get out of here now and let you rest," John returned, ignoring the sarcastic comment. "C'mon, Hank."

Out in the hallway Hank fell into step with the lieutenant. When they were out of earshot of the room, he cleared his throat and asked, "Uh, does Matt know who your tenant at the lodge is?"

"Nope. We made our deal after he was shot."

"That's what I thought. Are you sure you know what you're doing boss?"

They reached the bank of elevators and John punched the down button. The doors of the waiting elevator opened and the two men stepped inside.

"Absolutely. I've given this a lot of thought," John replied, punching the button for the lobby. "Matt's like an injured animal right now, snapping and snarling at everyone and trying his best to curl up in the dark alone and lick his wounds. Well, I'll be damned if I let him."

The lieutenant leaned back against the elevator wall and shot his detective a self-satisfied look. "Tender loving care and nurturing—that's the best medicine for what ails him. In other words, what Matt needs most right now is a good dose of Maude Ann."

Chapter Two

Matt felt every pothole and bump as the car bounced along the dirt road through the woods. Clutching the armrest, he gritted his teeth against the pain and tried to maintain a stoic expression, but a hard jar made him groan. "Ahhh…damn, doesn't the lieutenant ever grade this excuse for a road?"

"Sorry." Hank slanted him a sheepish look. "I'm going as slow as I can. Hang on. The lodge is just around the next bend."

"Yeah, I know." Matt had been to the lodge with John several times to fish.

He looked around at the thick woods on either side of the road. Through the trees on the right he caught an occasional glimpse of the lake, but there were no houses or people in sight. That was the main reason he had agreed to come here. The lodge was about two miles down the gravel

road from the highway and the only structure on this finger
of land, so he would have plenty of privacy.

John had inherited the lodge and all the land between it
and the highway from an uncle. At present he was merely
renting out a few boats, and occasionally a tenant occupied
the building. When John retired, his plan was to reopen the
place as a fishing lodge and run it himself.

"You know, I really do envy you, getting to spend the
summer here," Hank said as he brought the car to a stop
in the circular drive in front of the lodge. "This is a real
nice place, in a rustic sort of way."

The large, two-story building sat in a clearing about a
hundred yards from the lakeshore. Made of rough cedar, it
had a covered veranda that ran all the way around, with
porch swings and groupings of wicker furniture at intervals
so that the fishermen who came here could sit and enjoy
the view. John's uncle had built the lodge to cater to people
who preferred a quiet place where they could go fishing
and boating, and just relax and enjoy good family-style
meals and the peace and quiet of the country.

In addition to John's quarters, the place had a huge living
room, kitchen and dining room on the first floor and eight
bedrooms and six bathrooms on the second floor.

"It's easy to see why the lieutenant is so proud of it,"
Hank continued. "You're gonna be real comfortable here."

Matt doubted that. These days he wasn't comfortable
anywhere. His wounds still throbbed and ached, and every
step he made was pure agony, causing the mutilated muscles and tendons in his thigh to scream in protest.

With assistance from Hank and leaning heavily on a
cane, Matt climbed the veranda steps. However, when he
reached the top he was so wobbly he had to sit down in
the first swing he reached, while Hank unloaded his bags

from the car and carried them to his room. In no time his
partner reappeared. ''There's something that smells delicious cooking in two big pots in the kitchen, but other than
that there's no sign of John's tenant.''

''Good. I hope it stays that way.''

Hank looked away and shifted uneasily from one foot to
the other. ''Yeah, well, I guess I'd better be heading back
so you can unpack and get settled. Is there anything else
you need before I go?''

''Don't think so.'' Matt knew his partner was worried
about leaving him alone, but the truth was, that was exactly
what he wanted. He was in no mood for socializing, not
even with his best friend. ''Look, don't worry about me,
okay. I'll be fine.''

''Well…if you're sure. And remember, if you need anything—anything at all—you just give me a call.''

As his partner drove away, Matt looked around. In addition to being a fisherman and guide, John's uncle had
been an avid gardener. Though isolated on wooded lakeshore, the lodge was surrounded by a neat lawn and a bed
of roses, and other flowers Matt couldn't name bordered
the porch all around. From previous visits, Matt knew that
there was also a vegetable garden out back, plus a large
garage and storage shed.

Along one side and across the back, the forest came right
up to the yard but a small, open meadow separated the lawn
from the woods on the west side. At the front of the lodge
the lawn went all the way down to the lake. The boat dock
and fishing pier was a quarter mile or so farther along the
shore, out of sight of the lodge and reached by a path
through the woods.

It was a great place, and under other circumstances, Matt
would have enjoyed being here to soak up the sunshine and

nature, but now he resented being forced to stay when all he wanted was to go home and shut out the world.

The lieutenant had been right about one thing, Matt thought, looking around at the peaceful scene. He certainly shouldn't have any trouble with nosy reporters out here in the boonies.

The sound of voices drew Matt's attention to the woods along the east side of the yard just as a woman and a gang of children emerged. Annoyance firmed his mouth as they headed across the lawn toward the lodge. Great. Just what he needed.

They were either lost or trespassing, since all the land between there and the highway belonged to John Werner. Either way, Matt intended to send them packing.

The children were of different ages and, from what he could tell from that distance, different ethnic backgrounds. Dressed in shorts, T-shirts and dirty tennis shoes, they were sweaty, grubby and bedraggled. Oddly, each child carried a pan or bucket.

It was the woman, however, who drew his attention. She also wore shorts and a T-shirt, but on her, the common garments were unbelievably sexy, showing off full breasts, long legs and a curvy figure that made a man's mouth go dry. Her auburn hair, a wild mane of curls that billowed around her face and shoulders, glinted red in the sunlight. It was that slow, hip-rolling walk, though, that distracted him most. Just watching her approach, he felt a surge of heat in his loins. It was the first time he'd experienced that particular reaction since he'd been shot, and it both pleased and annoyed him.

Putting as much weight as he could on his cane, Matt struggled to his feet. As the group drew nearer and he was about to launch into a blistering lecture about intruding on private property, the woman waved to him and called out, "Hi, there! I'm sorry we weren't here when you arrived."

Matt stiffened, his eyes narrowing as an uneasy feeling crept up his spine. There was something vaguely familiar about the woman, but she wasn't the kind of female any red-blooded male was likely to forget.

"Hey, mister! Lookit what we gots," a little blond cherub with a dirty face exclaimed.

Before he could stop them, the pack of children clambered noisily up the porch steps and the woman followed. The little blond cherub held up her bucket for him to admire, but the rest of the kids just eyed him with suspicion, as though he was the one who shouldn't be there.

"All right, kids, take your blackberries inside and rinse them in the colander with cold water. Debbie, sweetheart, don't bother the man." She shot him a grin. "Sorry about that. She's just proud of picking so many berries."

Before he could reply, the woman turned back to the kids and clapped her hands. "Okay, introductions will come later. Everybody inside. Marshall, you and Yolanda see to the younger ones. And Tyrone, you and Dennis knock off that shoving."

Matt stared at her, his uneasiness growing.

She turned back to Matt and cocked one auburn eyebrow. "Detective Dolan? You haven't said a word. Is something wrong?"

"I know you from somewhere, don't I?"

The woman tossed back her head and laughed, and instantly he knew who she was. No man could ever forget that low, husky sound.

"Goodness. I know it's been a couple of years, but surely I haven't changed that much."

Matt's eyes narrowed. "You're Maude Ann Henley,

Tom Henley's widow. You're that shrink who used to work for the department.''

And she had changed all right. The woman he remembered had been reserved and perfectly groomed at all times, her makeup flawless. She'd dressed in tailored suits, wore her hair pulled severely back in a chignon and exuded an air of cool professionalism. Now she stood before him in ragged cutoffs, a form-fitting T-shirt, her hair a cloud of unruly curls, and apparently not wearing a speck of makeup. There was even a splattering of freckles across her nose, for Pete's sake.

"Yes. Although, my name is actually Edwards. Dr. Maude Ann Edwards to be exact. I kept my maiden name for professional reasons. And just so you know, Detective, I prefer the term *psychiatrist* to *shrink.*"

"Just what the hell are you doing here, *Dr.* Edwards?"

She looked taken aback, whether by the question or his curt tone he neither knew nor cared. He just wanted an answer. Then he wanted her gone. He had avoided her when she worked at the precinct. He sure as hell didn't want her around now.

"Why, I live here. Didn't Lieutenant Werner tell you?"

"You live here? No, he didn't tell me," Matt ground out through clenched teeth. "Somehow he neglected to mention that particular piece of information. He just told me he had one tenant. I assumed it was a summer fisherman. That son of a—"

"Detective Dolan, please. I must ask that you refrain from cursing in front of the children." Noticing that the kids hadn't moved, she shooed them toward the door. "Go on in and wash those berries like I told you. Jane will be back from the store soon. If the berries aren't ready, she won't be able to make that cobbler you want for dessert. So get. All of you.''

The departure of the younger children sounded like a herd of wild mustangs clattering across the wooden porch. Amid shouts and squeals and a round of pushing and shoving to see who could be first, and the repeated squeak and bang of the front door, they disappeared into the lodge. A few of the older children, however, were reluctant to leave, They dragged their feet, looking balefully at Matt as they shuffled inside.

When the last straggler disappeared through the door, Maude Ann turned her attention back to Matt.

''Actually, to be fair, Lieutenant Werner didn't lie to you, Detective. I am the only tenant at the lodge.''

''Why are you here?'' She opened her mouth to reply, but he held up his hand and stopped her. ''No, don't bother. It's obvious. Well, you can tell the lieutenant that I don't need anyone to play nursemaid, and I sure as hell don't need a shrink. So this little scheme of his was a waste of time.''

Laughter twinkled in Maude Ann's whiskey-colored eyes. ''My, my, what an ego you have, Dolan. Funny, I worked with you for two years and I never realized that. It so happens that my being here has nothing whatever to do with you. I leased the lodge from the lieutenant to house the foster home I established for abused and neglected children who have been taken away from their parents or guardians. I call it Henley Haven, in honor of my late husband.''

''A foster home? You mean, that mob of kids *lives* here?''

''Yes. And they're hardly a mob. There are only seven children here at the moment. Henley Haven can accom-

modate ten easily. A dozen in an emergency. But whatever
the number, the children keep me much too busy to have
time to spend on you. Actually, it should relieve your mind
to know that I no longer see patients. I prefer to use my
training and experience helping these children adjust and
heal, so you needn't worry that I'll be analyzing you.''

"You're not going to get the chance, lady.''

"Good. I'm glad that's settled. When the lieutenant
called he merely asked if I would mind if you stayed in his
quarters while you recuperated and drive you into Houston
for your checkups. I go into Houston regularly anyway, and
since he's giving me a good deal on this place, I couldn't
very well refuse. Besides, his room isn't part of my lease
agreement. That's always kept ready for him when he visits, so you're not putting anyone out.

"I did agree that you could eat with us. Jane and I must
cook for the children, anyway, so even that isn't an im-
position. I assure you, meals, housekeeping and an occasional ride into town are all the help you'll receive from
me.''

"I won't be needing those, either,'' he snapped. "Dammit, I only agreed to come out here to soak up some sunshine and peace and quiet. Instead, what do I find? A lady
shrink and a bunch of rug rats.''

"Hey, pig, who you calling a rat?''

"Tyrone!'' Maude Ann admonished as a small black boy
charged out onto the porch.

The door banged shut as he stepped between Matt and
Maude Ann. Assuming a challenging stance that was com-
ical in a youngster, he glared at Matt and thrust out his
chin.

Surprise shot through Matt. He recognized the kid instantly. Tyrone Washington was the child of a female

junkie from the section of Houston known as Denver Harbor.

Only seven, the kid was already headed for trouble. Most of the time his mother was stoned out of her mind, and Tyrone ran virtually wild through the slum neighborhood. The kid had a mouth on him like a longshoreman's and an eye for larceny. Tyrone might be only seven, but in the ways of the world he was about forty-five.

Matt looked the kid up and down and returned his glare with a cynical half smile. "Well, well, well, if it isn't Tyrone Washington. The Denver Harbor tough guy."

"That's right, pig, an' there ain't nothin' you kin do 'bout it, so kiss my a—"

"Tyrone!" Maude Ann admonished again. "You're to watch your language, young man. Furthermore, you are not to call Detective Dolan by that derogatory name. Do you understand?"

The boy looked back at her over his shoulder. "Daroga what? Whazzat mean?"

"Derogatory. It means insulting and degrading. You're new, but you've been here long enough to know that we don't treat people that way."

A perplexed frown wrinkled Tyrone's forehead. "Not even stinkin' cops?"

"No. Especially not cops. Remember I told you my husband was a policeman and a wonderful man. Now apologize."

Tyrone's face turned mulish. "I ain't gonna 'pologize to no—"

"Tyrone, either apologize or you stay here with Jane tomorrow while the rest of us go to the movies. The choice is yours."

"Ah, Miz Maudie—"

"You heard me, Tyrone."

"Look, can we drop this?" Matt snapped. "I don't care if the little punk apologizes or not."

"Mr. Dolan! I said no name calling. The rules I've given the children apply to everyone who stays here."

"Then we don't have a problem, because I'm not staying."

"That is entirely up to you, Detective," she replied with a pleasant smile. "I have no feelings on the matter one way or another, I assure you."

"Fine, then you won't mind if I call the lieutenant and tell him to send someone to pick me up, will you," he snapped back.

"Not at all. There's a telephone in your room."

Matt gave her a curt nod. Leaning on his cane, he gritted his teeth and turned to leave.

"Humph. Good riddance," Tyrone muttered, but this time Maude Ann was too distracted to correct him.

She bit her lower lip and watched Matt Dolan limp away. She recalled how he used to look, striding around the station house, often without his suit jacket and his shirtsleeves rolled up. A big man with broad shoulders, a lean muscular build and a self-confident demeanor, he had emitted an aura of masculine invincibility and strength.

His back was still ramrod straight and his head high, but he had lost weight during his stay in the hospital, and his progress was so slow and so obviously painful it wrung her heart. It was all she could do not to rush forward and help him.

The only thing that stopped her was the certain knowledge that he would rebuff the offer, probably none too politely. That, and the promise she had made to herself.

When John Werner had contacted her and asked if Matt

Dolan could stay at the lodge for a few months, she had vowed she would give the man his space and not let herself become involved in his recovery in any way. She had enough on her hands with the children. Nor did she need or want to be drawn back into the world of law enforcement and the dark psychological and physical trauma that came with it.

She had left all that behind two years ago when her husband Tom had been killed during a bank holdup. Her life now was devoted to the children.

Self-deception had never been one of Maude Ann's shortcomings, and she had to admit there was another reason for steering clear of Matt. She didn't ever want to take a chance of falling for another law-enforcement officer.

Not that the risk of that happening was great. During the three years that she had worked for the HPD, Matt had been polite but distant. Maude Ann couldn't recall ever having had a personal conversation with the man, nor had he ever consulted her about any of his cases unless a superior had ordered him to.

He wasn't anything like Tom, not at all her type, and given their history, there was little danger of an attraction developing between them.

Still, Maude Ann wasn't stupid. Matt Dolan was a handsome devil, in a tough-as-nails kind of way. With his black-as-coal hair and vivid blue eyes, those chiseled features and his general ''go to hell'' attitude, he stirred something deep in the female psyche that even the most intelligent of women would have a difficult time resisting.

Yes, it was definitely best, all around, if she gave Detective Dolan a wide berth.

Chapter Three

Matt sat on the edge of the bed with the receiver to his ear, impatiently counting the rings on the other end of the line.

"Lieutenant Werner."

"You sorry, sneaky, scheming, back-stabbing bastard. You set me up."

"Ah, good afternoon to you, too, Matt. I take it you've met Maudie and her charges."

Matt ground his teeth and tightened his grip on the receiver. John didn't even try to hide the amusement in his voice. Matt could almost see him leaning back in his chair, grinning like a jackass eating briars. "At least you have the good sense not to pretend you don't know what I'm talking about," he snarled.

"Not much point in that, is there. So how is Maudie?"

"Maudie is fine. I'm mad as hell. I swear, Werner, if I was there right now, I'd knock your teeth out."

"C'mon, Dolan, in your condition you couldn't whip a flea, and you know it. Of course, you're welcome to try, but if I were you I'd wait until I recovered."

"Funny. Real funny. Did you really think I'd go along with this? I refused to see a shrink at the hospital, so you figured you'd maroon me in the boonies with one. Maude Ann Edwards, for Pete's sake! I steered clear of the woman when she worked for the department. Why the devil would I want to spend time with her now? Radio Hank right away and tell him to turn around and come get me. I'm outta here."

"No way, Dolan. We have a deal and you're sticking to it. Look, don't go jumping to conclusions. Maudie doesn't take patients anymore. But she is a doctor. I figured if you needed medical attention, she would be handy to have around. That's all. She's too busy with her kids to bother with the likes of you, boyo, so just relax, will ya?"

"Forget it. I'm not staying here with that woman and all those kids. You got that? Send Hank back for me. Now."

"No can do, buddy. Tell Maudie hi for me and call me at the end of the summer. We'll talk then about you coming back for that physical."

"Wait a minute! Don't you—"

A click sounded and the dial tone droned. Matt jerked the receiver away from his ear and glared at it, then slammed the instrument down so hard it jumped off the base and he had to hang it up again.

With a frustrated growl he flung himself back on the bed and turned the air blue with curses. He didn't give a rat's nose if Dr. Maude Ann Edwards heard him. In fact, he hoped she did. Maybe she'd give him the boot.

"The children will be down in a minute," Maude Ann announced as she returned to the kitchen. "I left Yolanda supervising their hand-washing."

"Humph, somebody has to," Jane said. That scamp Dennis acts like soap and water are poison. So does Tyrone."

Maude Ann's throaty laugh rolled out. "I know. Dennis just tried to convince me his hands weren't dirty because he'd kept them in his pockets all day."

Jane rolled her eyes. "What those two don't think of the devil hasn't invented yet." Standing in front of the big, six-burner commercial stove, she stirred a pot of gravy. "If that policeman fella is going to join us for dinner he'd better shake a leg, 'cause it's almost ready."

Maude Ann removed an enormous pan of biscuits from the oven. Steam rose from them filling the kitchen with a delicious aroma. She glanced at the door that connected Matt's room to the kitchen. "He hasn't so much as stuck his head out of there, has he?"

"Nope. I got back three hours ago and I haven't seen hide nor hair of the man. Haven't heard a sound outta him, either. You sure he's in there? Maybe he decided to walk up to the highway and hitch a ride back to Houston."

"Not likely. In his condition he wouldn't make it a hundred yards." Maude Ann chewed on her lower lip. "I suppose I should knock on his door and let him know it's dinnertime."

"Humph," Jane poured the gravy into a gravy boat and set it on the table with a decisive thud. "I'd let him stew in his own juice, if it was me. Never could abide a foul-tempered man."

"Detective Dolan isn't foul-tempered, exactly. He's just...well, intense is the word, I guess." Maude Ann pulled two crocks of butter from the refrigerator and placed one at each end of the table. Unable to resist, she picked off a chunk of hot biscuit and popped it into her mouth, and immediately closed her eyes in ecstasy. "Mmm, heaven. Jane, you really are going to have to teach me how to make biscuits like these."

"I'm willing. The problem is you never have a spare minute."

Maude Ann sighed. "True." She glanced at the closed bedroom door again and resigned herself. "Well, I guess I'll have to call him. I can't let him skip dinner. In his condition he needs all the nourishment he can get."

"Suit yourself. While you roust him out, I'm going to go see what's keeping those young'uns. It's too quiet up there by far."

Jane marched out of the kitchen with a militant step and headed for the stairs.

Wiping her hands on the towel slung over her shoulder, Maude Ann went to the door and tapped on it lightly. "Detective? Dinner is ready."

She waited a few seconds, but there was only silence on the other side of the door. "Detective Dolan?" she called again.

She hesitated, then turned the knob, eased the door open and stuck her head inside. "Detective Dolan, are you in here?"

The sun had almost set and the light coming through the windows was rosy and dim. At first Maude Ann thought the room was empty, but as she crept inside she saw him through the gloaming, lying back motionless across the bed, his arms flung over his head.

Her heart leapt with fear and guilt. Dear Lord, was he dead? If so, it was her fault. How could she have let him stay in here by himself for so long without bothering to check on him? The man had just gotten out of the hospital a few hours ago.

Holding her breath, she moved closer to the bed. When she finally stood over him and spotted the steady rise and fall of his chest, she closed her eyes. Thank God. He had only fallen asleep.

She opened her eyes and stepped even closer, intending to nudge him, but she hesitated. Tipping her head to one side, she took shameless advantage of his unguarded state to study him.

As her gaze ran over his face, her own softened and her tender heart contracted. He looked so exhausted, so pale. So defenseless. How sad it was, she thought, for this proud, strong man to be reduced to a state of near helplessness.

He had incredibly long eyelashes for a man, she noticed for the first time. They lay like feathery black fans against his skin. Beneath their sweep, bruiselike shadows formed dark circles under his eyes.

Her eyes trailed down his body and her concern deepened. Though a big man, Matt had always kept himself trim, but now he looked much too thin.

Never in a million years would she have thought to see Matt Dolan brought down to such a state. How very close he'd come to losing his life, Maude Ann thought. As her darling Tom had two years ago.

Through Matt's light blue shirt she could see the faint outline of a bandage on his right side and the bulge of another one beneath the denim covering his right thigh.

They were sure to need changing regularly, yet she knew that any offer to help him would meet with a curt refusal.

Suddenly Maude Ann realized that Matt must have fallen into a deep sleep, no doubt involuntarily, soon after making his telephone call. His sneakered feet were still flat on the floor and around his body the cream-colored chenille bed-spread was undisturbed.

Compassion softened her face. Poor man. The trip from Houston must have exhausted him. Apparently he hadn't moved so much as a muscle in more than three hours.

She hated to disturb him. Still, to regain his strength he needed nourishment. Bending over, she reached out to touch his shoulder, but she drew her hand back when he jerked and mumbled something in his sleep. From the way he was thrashing around on the bed, he appeared to be having a nightmare.

"Detective? Detective Dolan, wake up."

His hand shot up like a striking snake and clamped around her wrist, and Maude Ann let out a shriek as she was jerked down on top of him.

The sound cut off almost before it started as his other hand clamped over her mouth.

Matt's head came up off the mattress, and Maude Ann's eyes widened above his fingers as she found herself looking into his dark, furious face, just inches from the end of her nose.

His wounds may have weakened him, but there was still a surprising amount of strength left in those powerful arms and shoulders.

"Just what the hell do you think you're doing, sneaking around in my room?"

She tried to answer, but her words came out in an indecipherable mumble against his palm. She gave up and glared at him, and he finally got the message and removed his hand.

Maude Ann shook back her hair and tried for a haughty look, which was difficult to achieve when one was sprawled, half-dressed, on top of a man. "I was *not* sneaking around in your room," she informed him. "I came in to tell you that dinner is ready."

"Yeah, right. Have you ever heard of knocking?"

"I did knock. Several times. But you didn't answer. I was worried that something had happened to you, so I came inside to check. You seemed to have been having a bad dream."

Those deep-set blue eyes narrowed as he searched her face for the truth. In the rosy glow of sunset they glittered like sapphires in his dark face. After a time he seemed to come to a decision and gave an almost imperceptible nod.

"I'm fine, as you can see." He paused, his eyes locked with hers. Suddenly the air seemed thick, and an odd tautness surrounded them. "And feel," he added.

Maude Ann's eyes widened. Horrified, she realized several things at once. First, that he still gripped her right forearm in an unbreakable hold, and his other hand was splayed across her bottom. Second, not only was she sprawled on top of him, her bare right thigh was nestled intimately between his legs, and his body had responded to the contact. He might have been weakened by the gunshot wounds, but there was certainly nothing wrong with his sex drive.

Heat raced through Maude Ann like a warm flood, and to her dismay, she felt her own body tighten. Even in the dim light, she could see that Matt was aware of her reaction.

Color flooded her face. She told herself to get up, but she seemed to have lost the power of movement. She could feel his heat all along her body, his breath feathering her face, warm and moist, that masculine hand kneading her buttocks ever so slightly.

Her own breathing was shallow and drew painfully

through her constricted throat. With every labored breath her breasts swelled against the solid wall of his chest.

Had her life depended on it, Maude Ann could not have looked away from his hot stare. Just when she thought she would surely burst into flames, Matt broke eye contact. She experienced a momentary relief, but when his gaze slid downward over her face and zeroed in on her mouth, her heart took off at a gallop.

He stared at her lips for what seemed like forever. His eyes darkened. Maude Ann swallowed hard. Slowly, Matt tipped his head to one side and raised it closer to hers, and her heart began to boom.

Her eyes drifted shut. She felt his breath caressing her mouth and her entire body tingled with anticipation. Before contact could be made the sound of clattering feet and high-pitched chatter announced the arrival of the children in the kitchen.

Aghast, Maude Ann jerked back and tried to scramble off Matt, but at the first move he groaned. She froze.

"Oh, I'm sorry! I'm so sorry! Your wound! Did I hurt you?"

A grimace contorted his face. "I'm…okay," he ground out through gritted teeth. "Just…take it…slow and easy."

"Yes. Of course. I should have realized—"

"Ah, jeez! Watch that knee, will you?"

A fresh wave of color climbed Maude Ann's face, but she bit her lower lip and eased up off him. She was acutely conscious of the open door and the children taking their places at the table in the next room, of Jane issuing orders. She prayed that no one looked this way, or if they did, that they couldn't see anything in the fading light.

With excruciating slowness, she got to her knees beside him on the mattress, then backed off the bed and regained her feet. She smoothed her hair away from her face and brushed at her shorts, more out of nervousness than need.

Then she noticed that Matt still lay flat on his back with his eyes closed and his face contorted.

"Are you all right? Do you need help getting up?" She stepped closer and held out her hand, but he opened his eyes and gave her a baleful look.

"No, I don't need your help," he growled. "I'm not so pathetic that I can't get up off the damned bed by myself." He grabbed hold of the brass railing at the foot of the bed and tried to haul himself up, but his face clenched with pain and he couldn't hold back a groan.

"Oh, for heaven's sake!" Her patience at an end, Maude Ann bent over and slipped her arms around his chest and tugged him upward. "You men and your stubborn pride! It doesn't make you any less of a man to need a little help now and then, you know," she admonished as she gently assisted him to his feet.

"I don't like to be a burden," he gasped when he could catch his breath.

"No one does, but sometimes it can't be helped. Although, I must say, that was foolish of you to jerk me down like that. You could have reopened your wounds."

His gaze met hers. "If those kids hadn't arrived when they did, I probably would have."

Maude Ann felt a blush heat her cheeks again. She hoped it wasn't visible in the dimness, but even if it was, she wasn't one to back away from a challenge. Tossing her head, she gave a throaty chuckle. "In your dreams, Detective. At this point you haven't got the strength for an amorous encounter. But since you brought it up, let me make this much clear. You are welcome to stay here and recuperate for as long as it takes, but I am not part of your physical therapy. Now, if you don't mind, dinner is ready, and Jane and the children are waiting.''

She turned to leave the room, but he grasped her forearm and stopped her. "Just a minute, Dr. Edwards. I woke up and found someone hovering over me. Grabbing you was a perfectly natural reflex reaction.'' He paused a beat, then added, "Just as what happened after that was a natural reaction when a man finds a woman lying on top of him. I don't apologize for that.''

Pursing her lips, Maude Ann considered that. After a moment she nodded. "All right. I can accept that.''

"Good. And just to set the record straight, I wasn't the only one on that bed who was aroused.''

Never one to play games or prevaricate, Maude Ann gave him a rueful half smile and a nod. "Fair enough. So why don't we just chalk up what happened as a freak occurrence? Propinquity, if you will. Despite your wounds, you're still a red-blooded male, and there hasn't been a man in my life since Tom died.''

A startled look flashed in his eyes, but she ignored it. "Add to that combination a dimly lit room, a bed and close contact, and naturally one thing leads to another. We know it didn't mean anything, so let's just forget it happened, shall we?''

Pulling her arm free of his grasp, she smiled cordially and tipped her head toward the kitchen. "Now we really had better get out there before Jane comes looking for us.''

Without waiting for a reply, Maude Ann turned and strolled out, aware of Matt's gaze drilling into her back.

She had already taken her seat at the head of the table when Matt emerged from his room.

Instantly the childish chatter around the table ceased and a tense silence descended. Seven pairs of wary young eyes watched Matt's slow progress as he leaned heavily on his cane and limped to the table.

When he was seated, Maude Ann, acting as though Matt's presence was nothing out of the ordinary, smiled at her charges and said, "Children, this is Detective Matthew Dolan. He works for the Houston Police Department and he's going to be staying with us while he recovers from an injury."

"You mean he gots an ouchie like me?" the tiny blond girl asked. She raised her arm and proudly displayed a wide Band-Aid on her elbow.

"Yes, Debbie. Only Detective Dolan's ouchies are really bad ones, so he's going to be staying with us until they get all better."

The child turned big, pansy-blue eyes on Matt. "You needs to put a Band-Aid on 'em. I can show you where they are. Miz Maudie has all kinds of pretty ones. Some even gots flowers and fairies on 'em."

Despite his foul mood, a smile tugged at Matt's mouth. He resented being stuck here. He especially resented being here with a shrink and a pack of kids. However, he would have had to have a heart of iron to resist those innocent blue eyes and that face like an angel.

"Dumb girl," Tyrone muttered. "He ain't got that kinda ouchie. He's prob'ly been shot."

Gasps and frightened exclamations erupted around the table.

"That's quite enough, Tyrone. You're scaring the other children."

"Yes'um, Miz Maudie," he replied in a meek voice, ducking his head. Under his breath he added just loud enough for Matt to hear, "Fool shoulda got his head blown clean off, messing with them guys. I sure wouldn't'a cried none if he had. Be one less pig on the streets.''

The boy cut his gaze toward Matt and stuck out his chin. Matt met the boy's surly gaze steadily.

''What was that, Tyrone?''

He turned his head and looked at Maude Ann with an expression of wide-eyed innocence. ''Nothin', Ms. Edwards. I was just sayin' how lucky he was.''

''Hmm.'' The glint in Maude Ann's eyes said that she did not believe him, but she let the matter slide.

''My mommy got shot,'' the girl of about six or seven sitting next to Maude Ann said quietly. She sat staring at her clasped hands resting against the edge of the table. Then she turned her solemn gaze on Matt. ''My daddy did it. I saw him. My mommy died.''

Matt didn't know what to say. The blank expression in the child's eyes was chilling. Dammit, it wasn't right that a kid should witness such grotesque violence. ''I'm... sorry.''

Maude Ann reached over and laid her hand over the child's smaller one. ''It was a horrible thing, but Jennifer is going to be okay, aren't you, sweetheart?''

The blank look left the little girl's eyes, replaced by trust and abject adoration as she met Maude Ann's reassuring smile. She nodded. ''Yes, ma'am.''

She wasn't a pretty child. Not like the little blond cherub, Debbie, Matt thought, but she appeared so fragile and vulnerable just looking at her made your heart contract.

Deftly, Maude Ann diverted everyone's attention by making introductions, starting with Jane Beasley, the chunky, middle-aged woman who was her assistant, and working her way around the table.

In addition to Tyrone, Debbie and Jennifer, there was

ten-year-old Marshall, his eight-year-old brother, Dennis, an eleven-year-old Mexican girl named Yolanda and five-year-old Timothy.

Matt sat through the introductions in tight-lipped silence, acknowledging the children and Jane Beasley with no more than a curt nod. He had no desire to know any of them. He may be stuck there, but he intended to keep his distance.

When dinner was over, the children cleared the table, then Maude Ann sent them off to brush their teeth, though not without protests.

"Ah, do I gotta, Miz Maudie?" Tyrone groaned.

"Yes. Now shoo. All of you. And don't think you can pull a fast one on me, either, because I'm going to inspect those teeth when you're done."

Muttering under his breath, Tyrone shuffled out, deliberately dragging his feet on the brick kitchen floor and trailing the other children.

Matt sipped his coffee and watched them go. When their footsteps faded away, he switched his gaze to Maude Ann. "If you're hoping to reform that kid, you're wasting your time. Take it from me—he's bad news."

"Nonsense." Dismissing his comment, Maude Ann left the table and joined Jane at the sink, where she picked up a towel and began drying dishes.

"Do you know anything about his background?" Matt probed.

"If you mean do I know that his mother is a drug addict who never took care of him, yes."

"Do you also know that at seven he's already got a rap sheet? The kid's been picked up for everything from shoplifting to acting as a lookout for a couple of thugs who robbed a liquor store. Being a minor, there's nothing we can do to him, and he and his friends know it. Judges won't even send him to Juvie at his tender age. That's why the older guys like to use him.''

''So? All that proves is he's a little boy who's had a horrible life so far.''

''Lady, Tyrone Washington is a juvenile delinquent in the making. Six months ago I caught him acting as a numbers runner for a gang running a bookmaking operation. I grabbed the kid by the scruff of the neck and hauled him down to the station house myself.''

Maude Ann stopped drying a plate and shot him an accusing glare. ''You arrested a seven-year-old boy?''

''I didn't cuff him and throw him in a cell, if that's what you mean. I just to tried to scare the kid. Anyway, it didn't work. A few days later he was running errands for the same gang.''

''All the more reason for removing him from that environment. Tyrone needs love and guidance and structure in his life. He needs to be shown that someone cares and will be there for him, that life doesn't have to be the squalid existence he's known.''

Matt shot her a sardonic look. ''Watch those rose-colored glasses, Dr. Edwards. They distort your vision.''

''Sounds pretty cynical to me,'' Jane said, speaking up for the first time. ''What's the matter, Mr. Dolan—don't you like kids?''

Matt shrugged. ''I like them okay. Actually I haven't been around children a lot, so I haven't thought much about it one way or another.''

''Ah, I see,'' Jane said as though that explained everything, and turned back to the sinkful of dishes.

''Look, this has nothing to do with me. Those kids are your problem, not mine. I just thought you ought to know Tyrone's background.''

"Thank you, Detective. However, I assure you, I am apprised of every child's case history before he or she ever comes here."

"Fine. Suit yourself. It makes no difference to me." Matt downed the last of his coffee and struggled to his feet. "It appears I'm stuck here whether I like it or not. You're probably not any more thrilled than I am, so I just want you to know that, other than mealtimes, I'll stay out of your way. I'd appreciate the same courtesy in return."

Gritting his teeth against the vicious stabs of pain, he limped to the doorway that connected his room to the kitchen. There he paused and turned back to look at Maude Ann.

"As for the kid, just don't say I didn't warn you."

Chapter Four

Matt didn't come out of his room the rest of the evening, nor did Maude Ann catch so much as a glimpse of him during the next four days, except during meals.

At those times he was distant, speaking only when necessary. He made no effort to join in the mealtime conversations. Inexplicably, little Debbie seemed to find him fascinating, but he barely acknowledged her chatter, and he ignored Tyrone's muttered digs. Matt simply ate his food as quickly as good manners allowed and left.

Maude Ann told herself that was fine with her. If he did not want to be sociable, then she, Jane and the children would keep their distance.

His physical condition troubled her. He was in a great deal of pain, she could tell, and it did not seem to be lessening, nor was he regaining strength as he should. However, she reminded herself repeatedly that Matthew Dolan was not her responsibility. Besides, Matt made it crystal clear with every word, look and action that he did not want her help.

It wasn't easy for Maude Ann to remain aloof. Nurturing came as naturally to her as breathing, and no matter how antisocial his behavior or how hard she tried not to, she still worried about him. Whether or not he wanted to accept it, he did need help.

Still, Matt was a proud man, and she knew any offer of help would not be appreciated. Maude Ann promised herself that she would respect his wishes and leave him alone.

Her resolve held only until his fourth night at the lodge.

That evening, after cleaning the kitchen and supervising baths and teeth brushing, Maude Ann, Jane and the pajama-clad children settled down in the huge living room as they did every night. While the younger ones watched an animated movie on television, Maude Ann and the older boys and girls played a board game. Jane sat in a rocking chair by the massive stone fireplace, contentedly crocheting an afghan.

Maude Ann was feeling smug and proud of herself for the self-restraint she had shown. Not only had she resisted the urge to aid Matt in any way, she had behaved as though she wasn't even aware of his struggles.

However, as had happened every night since he'd been there, while she laughed and talked with the children, she found that she was also keeping one ear cocked for sounds of distress from Matt's room.

Between chores and play and picking berries in the woods, the children had worn themselves out that day. When all her exhausted charges were settled in for the night, Maude Ann went from room to room for one last peek, pausing in each to gaze at the sleeping children snuggled in their beds, their young faces slack and vulnerable and so heartbreakingly innocent. As she studied them, her chest swelled with emotion.

Henley Haven was an enormous responsibility that required long hours of hard work, patience and sacrifice. Many people thought she was crazy for taking on such a burden, and there were times when she questioned her own sanity. Yet, as always at night during this quiet time, she knew a sense of peace and fulfillment that erased all doubt and made it all worthwhile.

Maude Ann closed the door on the last pair of sleeping children and made her way down the hall to her own quarters.

There she filled the tub and treated herself to a long hot soak. Afterward, she showered and shampooed her hair, then crawled into bed, sighing with pleasure. Though only a little after ten, it had been a busy day and she was exhausted.

The clean smell of soap and bath talc clung to her skin and mingled with the fresh, outdoorsy scent of cool cotton sheets that had been dried in the sunshine. Smiling, she closed her eyes and snuggled her face into the down-filled pillow and waited for sleep to claim her.

An hour later she was still waiting. Finally, thoroughly irritated, she threw back the covers donned her robe and stomped, barefoot, out of the room. She loped down the stairs, her clean hair dancing around her shoulders with each impatient step, and her long batiste gown and robe fluttering out behind her.

In the kitchen she started to flip on the overhead light, but thought better of it after a glance at the closed door of Matt's room. She had forgotten about him.

A line of light shone from under the door, and she heard

the faint sound of the shower running. She wasn't going to wake him, at least. However, neither was she anxious to have any contact with him. Forcing herself to move with more caution, she crossed the room and turned on the dim light above the kitchen stove.

A few minutes later she had just removed a mug of warm milk from the microwave when she heard a thud from Matt's room, followed immediately by a groan.

Acting on instinct, without stopping to think of what Matt's reaction might be, she put the mug down, dashed to the door of his room and burst inside.

"Detective Dolan? Are you all right?" she called, darting a quick look around.

The bedspread was turned down, but the bed was empty. The lamp on the nightstand gave off a pale glow that barely illuminated the room, but the door to the en suite bathroom stood ajar, and a narrow rectangle of bright light spilled out. Maude Ann headed in that direction. Halfway there another groan sounded.

"Detective, are you—" She gasped and jerked to a halt in the bathroom doorway.

Matt lay sprawled facedown on the shower floor, struggling to climb to his hands and knees. Overhead the steaming spray beat down on him full force. Every time he tried to gain purchase on the slick tile, he slipped and fell flat again, with painful results.

The shower stall had been built to accommodate John Werner's massive proportions, making it bigger than many small bathrooms. Prone in the middle of the floor, Matt could not reach the sides or anything else on which to brace himself.

Recovering her senses, Maude Ann rushed forward and

snatched open the shower door. "For heaven's sake, wait! Don't try to get up by yourself!"

"Hey! What're you...doing in here?" Matt groaned. "Get the hell out. I'm naked."

"Most people are when they shower."

"Funny. Now, will you leave? I can...manage on my own."

"Oh, yes, I can see that," she replied, giving him a dry look. "Really, Detective, you're being foolish. I am a doctor, after all. I have seen naked men before."

"You're a head doctor. And you haven't seen me."

"Oh, please." She made an exasperated sound and rolled her eyes. She reached in and turned off the shower, wetting the front of her gown and robe in the process, and stepped inside. Immediately she skidded and almost fell. "Whoops! Good grief, this thing is slick as goose grease on glass. Why didn't you tell me? I'm surprised you haven't already broken your neck."

"It wasn't important. Now will you...get out of here?" he gasped.

"No. I'm not going anywhere until we get you on your feet and out of this skating rink, so you're just going to have to deal with it."

Holding on to the built-in towel rack, she leaned down and hooked her other hand under his arm. "C'mon, now, just hang on and let me do the lifting. Will you stop pulling away! You're just making it more difficult."

"Dammit, at least get me a towel before you haul me up."

"Oh, honestly!" Releasing his arm, Maude Ann eased out of the shower and snatched a wine-colored towel off the rack, then quickly climbed back inside and dropped the cloth over his bare backside. "There, that should protect your modesty. Now can I have a little cooperation here?"

Groaning, Matt rolled first to one side, then the other and after several tries finally managed to knot the towel around his lean middle.

"Ready now?" She hooked her hand under his arm again and tugged with all her might, hauling him to his knees, but not without causing him to wince and suck in his breath.

"Are you all right?"

"I'm...okay. Just give me a minute." He closed his eyes and breathed hard for several seconds, then he grasped her arm. "Okay, I'm ready. Let's go."

As Maude Ann pulled, Matt braced his other hand on her hip and strained to lever himself up. The agony in his face was awful to see, and her heart squeezed in sympathy.

"Easy, easy. Don't put any weight on that wounded leg."

Matt shot her a blistering look. "You just hold on to that rack and let me worry about my leg. Jeez, are you always this bossy?"

"Sorry." She gave him an abashed grin. "Comes from dealing with children all day, I guess."

"Well, in case you haven't noticed, I'm not ten years old."

Oh, she'd noticed, all right. It was difficult not to, under the circumstances. Still fresh in her mind's eye was the sight of those tight buns of his.

Despite his recent weight loss, Matt's broad shoulders and arms were corded with muscle. So was his impressive chest and flat abdomen and long, powerful legs. Water-beaded tanned, glistening skin and more droplets clung to the jagged piece of silver he wore on a chain around his neck and the mat of dark curls that covered his chest. She could not help but notice how the silky hair arrowed downward to swirl around his navel, then narrow into a thin line that disappeared beneath the maroon terry cloth slung low around his hips.

She was seeing much more of Matt Dolan than she had ever expected to see, and he was most definitely not a boy but an adult male. A very attractive, well-built, virile adult male.

It wasn't easy, but after a lot of struggle and slipping and sliding, she finally managed to pull him to his feet. "Here, just hang on to me," she instructed. Looping his arm over her shoulder and wrapping her free arm around his waist, she carefully stepped out of the shower with him.

The instant his feet touched the bathmat, he released her and grabbed the edge of the basin for support. Stiff-armed, he braced himself against the sink and hung his head, clenching his jaw. Beneath the tanned skin, his face was pale, and his muscles quivered with fatigue.

Without a word, Maude Ann grabbed another towel and began to pat his torso dry, working so briskly she was almost finished before he could protest.

"Hey! Stop that! Look, I can manage from here okay."

"Nonsense. You're so exhausted you can barely stand. You need to lie down before you fall down. Again." Squatting beside him, she ran the towel down one of his legs and up the other before he could dodge her hands, then she tossed the towel onto the rack and grasped him around the waist again.

"Come along, let's get you to bed."

Out of the corner of her eye, she saw his jaw set, but this time he didn't argue. Beneath her encircling arm, she felt his muscles tremble, and she knew by the way he leaned against her that his strength had reached low ebb. She also knew that a man like Matt Dolan would hate for anyone, especially a woman, to see him in such a weakened state.

His cane was propped against the wall, and she grabbed it and hooked it over her arm as they passed by.

Their progress across the large bedroom was slow and painful, but finally they made it.

"There, you go," she said brightly, lowering him onto the side of the bed.

While Maude Ann lifted his feet onto the mattress, Matt gave a sigh, closed his eyes and collapsed on his back with one arm crooked over his head and the other flung wide.

Straightening, Maude Ann stood beside the bed, debating what to do next. Lines of pain and fatigue etched Matt's face, and his skin had a grayish cast. His black hair was tousled and wet, and a lock hung down over his forehead. Her fingers itched to smooth it back off his face, but she resisted the urge.

Her gaze slid downward over the arm flung over his head, tracing the tender underside to its juncture with his body. For no reason, her attention was caught by the tuft of damp, dark hair under his arm. As she stared at it, she felt her stomach tighten.

Helpless to stop herself, she ran her gaze over his shoulders and throat, the sculpted beauty of his collarbone. A glint caught her eye, and she zeroed in on the jagged piece of silver nestled in the thatch of dark hair on his chest. She wondered what it was. It must be important, because he wore it all the time, even while bathing.

The mystery diverted her only seconds before her gaze was again drawn downward, trailing over his ribs, which moved rhythmically up and down with each heavy breath he drew.

Maude Ann's mouth went dry. Lord, he was a magnificent male specimen. She knew she should look away, but she could not. Mesmerized, she continued her study, following that intriguing line of dark hair down over his belly and lower.

Then her gaze encountered the angry, puckered wound on his right leg. Instantly the sensual spell was broken.

Before she could stop herself she sucked in a sharp breath. Quickly she glanced at Matt's face to make sure he hadn't heard and found he was watching her, his eyes steady and glittering beneath half-closed lids.

Hot color rose in her neck and face, but for an interminable moment neither moved nor spoke. They simply stared at each other, their gazes locked.

The air in the room seemed thick, almost suffocating, magnifying every sound. Maude Ann could hear the wind-up clock on the bedside table ticking, the whir of the cicadas outside the window, the thrumming of her heartbeat in her ears. She wondered if Matt could hear it, too.

"See something you like, Dr. Edwards?"

Maude Ann swallowed around the tightness in her throat. "I was just looking at your wounds. They need tending. I'll, uh…I'll rebandage them for you, if you like."

"What are you going to do? Kiss them and make them all better, like you do Debbie's ouchies?"

"Hardly." She forced a chuckle, fighting to regain control of the situation and her wayward senses. "You're not four years old."

She turned to go in search of his medical supplies, but his hand shot out and clamped around her wrist like a vice, jerking her to a halt. His blue eyes glittered dangerously, and when he spoke his voice dropped, becoming rough and steely.

"That's right. I'm not one of your wounded chicks that you can cluck over and mother. I'm a man, with a man's appetites."

His gaze dropped to her chest, and his eyes darkened. Maude Ann was about to protest, but instead, a downward glance made her gasp and clamp her free arm over her breasts. The front of her gown and robe were still sopping wet, and the thin batiste clung to her body like a second skin. The air-conditioned air had cooled the wet cloth, causing her nipples to pucker and harden. They thrust against the wet gown, clearly visible through the semitransparent material.

"Right now I'm not in any shape to do anything about those appetites, but I will be soon. Remember that the next time you come waltzing in here uninvited. You may get more than you bargained for."

Blushing from her hairline to her toes, Maude Ann stammered, "I got wet helping you. I didn't realize…I certainly didn't mean to flaunt myself. Anyway, I was only trying to help."

"Oh? Is that what you were doing just now? *Helping* me?"

"Well, I—"

"Just keep in mind that the next time you're tempted to look at me with that hungry gleam in your eye, you better be prepared for the consequences."

Denial never even occurred to Maude Ann. Though it hadn't been intentional, she had been admiring his body, and she'd been caught red-handed. She nodded. "Fair enough."

She started to move away, but Matt's grip on her arm tightened. She looked at him and arched one eyebrow.

Matt rubbed his thumb over the delicate skin on the inside of her wrist, and his eyes grew slumbrous. "Unless, of course, you'd like me to satisfy that hunger of yours."

Her sense of humor and down-to-earth common sense, neither of which was ever far from the surface, came bubbling up. That she would find herself in such a situation with Matt Dolan, of all people, struck her as absurdly funny. He was the most intimidating, overwhelmingly masculine man she'd ever encountered. When she had worked for the HPD, even before she had met and married Tom Henley, Matt had paid her no more mind than a piece of office equipment.

That had suited her just fine. From their first meeting she'd had the good sense to know that someone like her, a simple homebody at heart, had no business getting involved with an intense, complicated man like Matt.

Shaking her head, Maude Ann gave a throaty chuckle and pulled her arm from his grasp. Matt's eyes narrowed, his expression going from sensual to surprised, then annoyed. Clearly, he had not expected that reaction.

"Tempting as it is, I think I'll pass on that offer, Detective. I may be a frustrated widow, but I know when I'm in over my head. Now if you'll excuse me, I'll go get some bandages for those wounds."

"Don't bother. I can manage."

"Fine. Then I'll say good-night." Only moments ago she would have argued, but now a hasty withdrawal seemed the wisest course.

The instant Maude Ann pulled the door shut behind her, she leaned back against the kitchen wall and fanned her face with her hand. "Whew! That is one potent man," she whispered.

The encounter with Maude Ann served as a wake-up call for Matt.

What his doctor's repeated lectures and weeks of his friends' pleas and cajoling had failed to do, the humiliating episode in the shower accomplished in mere minutes, firing in him an iron-willed determination to regain his strength—and with it, the life he'd had before he'd been shot.

He had allowed the doctor's pessimism to infect him, to rob him of a sense of purpose. He had wanted a guarantee that he would recover. When he didn't get one, he refused to try. It was easier to accept defeat from the start than to fight and struggle for weeks, maybe months, and fail, anyway.

He had been so mired in bitterness and self-pity he couldn't see what a pathetic loser he'd allowed himself to become—not until he'd found himself sprawled helpless as a newborn baby on the shower floor, completely dependent on a woman to help him out.

It had stung to have Maude Ann see him so weak and helpless. So had that husky laugh of hers and her blunt honesty. The easy way she had twice dismissed the flare of desire between them had been downright insulting. Labeling her feelings nothing more than frustration had made it painfully clear that it wasn't him she wanted; her reaction would have been the same with any man. Abstinence, not attraction, had prompted that smoldering inspection she had given him.

Intellectually Matt knew he shouldn't let the incident bother him. Men, after all, had been guilty of the same impersonal lust for eons. The problem was, coming from a warm and sensual woman like Maude Ann, it had seemed doubly insulting to be relegated to nothing more than a sex object.

What the devil. She wasn't his type, anyway, and he sure as hell wasn't interested in getting involved with the woman.

Still...her attitude had rankled.

The way Matt figured it, the sooner he got back in shape and got out of there, away from the maddening woman and her ragtag bunch of kids, the better.

The morning after the shower incident, Matt rose early and did his exercises, this time with vigor, pushing himself almost beyond endurance.

Before going into the kitchen for breakfast, he braced himself for awkwardness, but it was a wasted effort; Maude Ann wasn't there.

Loath to ask where she was, Matt pretended not to notice her empty chair, but the kids had no such inhibitions.

"Where's Miz Maudie?" Tyrone demanded the instant he took his seat.

"Yeth, where ith she?" Debbie echoed.

"She's gone into Cleveland to do some shopping," Jane replied. "She'll be back in an hour or so. Now you kids eat your breakfasts. Soon as we clean up the kitchen we're going to do some chores."

That brought groans all around the table, especially from Tyrone. Fighting the urge to laugh, Matt ducked his head and ate his waffles in silence.

After breakfast he went for a walk, taking the path through the woods that he'd seen Maude Ann and the kids use. Every step was agony. He limped along, sweating and breathless from the exertion and pain, putting most of his weight on his cane and forcing one foot in front of the other.

Jane was in the kitchen when he staggered in at last to get a drink. She looked up from icing a cake and raised an eyebrow when she saw his flushed, sweaty face.

"Gracious me, you look like forty miles of bad road. What on earth have you been doing, Detective?"

His mouth tightened. He crossed to the sink, the soft thud of his cane almost silent on the brick floor. He had made no attempt to cultivate a friendship with the woman or anyone else in the house, but Jane Beasley didn't let that stop her.

She was a gregarious woman with a sometimes caustic forthrightness about her. She didn't believe in formality and had no time for it. Everyone who came within her sphere she treated exactly the same. You could like it or lump it, it made no difference to her.

"I went for a walk in the woods." He drew a glass of water, chugged it down in three long gulps and filled the glass again.

"Are you sure you're up to taking walks just yet? You look ready to keel over to me."

"I'll be fine. I just need some water is all. I got kind of dehydrated."

"Mmm, I'm not surprised, in this heat. Next time take a bottle of water with you. Oh, by the way, your shower is fixed. Maude Ann put some adhesive non-skid strips on the shower floor as soon as she got back from town."

"She told you what happened?"

"Just that you took a fall last night. 'Course, Maudie being Maudie, she fretted about it all night. Took off at first light to buy those strips to remedy the situation. I swear, that woman's a born mother hen."

"*That's* what she went shopping for so early?"

"Sure. What'd you expect?"

He hadn't expected anything, really. Certainly not that she would make a special trip into town just for him.

Jane swirled the last dollop of icing on top of the cake with a flourish. Wiping her hands on a towel, she gave Matt another long look. "Why don't you go out on the veranda and sit in the shade and rest a bit? You look plum peaked. I'm real glad you're making an effort to recover, but it's not good to push yourself too hard, you know. Particularly at first."

"Funny, I don't recall asking for your opinion," Matt said in the cold voice he used to keep people at arm's length.

"Well, you got it, anyway. No charge." She waved both hands in a shooing motion. "Now go on out there and sit down before you fall down."

He was tempted to refuse, just because she'd ordered him, but the veranda did look inviting. Besides, he was tired of being cooped up in his room.

"All right, all right. I'm going."

The first thing Matt saw when he stepped out onto the back veranda was Maude Ann and the children working in the vegetable garden, about thirty feet behind and to one side of the lodge.

He gingerly lowered himself into a swing and settled back against a pillow to observe Maude Ann and her crew of pint-size gardeners.

As he followed her movements, his first thought was the same one he had over and over for the last four days. What the devil was she doing with this motley bunch of kids and only Jane Beasley to help her?

It didn't make sense. She was an educated woman, a

doctor. She could have a successful and lucrative career in Houston. She wasn't his type, but she was an attractive woman. She was also incredibly sensual and responsive. He had firsthand knowledge of that. So why had she buried herself out here in the middle of nowhere?

Despite the nagging questions, a smile teased Matt's mouth when he noticed that every one of the kids wore a straw hat. More of Maude Ann's mothering, no doubt. Probably slathered them all with sun block, as well.

Most of the kids were working diligently. All except Tyrone. He merely leaned on his hoe, looking bored.

All Matt could see of Maude Ann was the top of her straw hat bobbing among the tall stalks of corn. Suddenly two corn stalks parted, and she stuck her head through the opening

"Tyrone, those weeds aren't going to jump out of the ground, you know. Get busy."

"I don't want to hoe no weeds." He shot her a look, his mouth set in a mulish pout. "I ain't no farm boy."

"No, you're not. But you are a boy who likes to eat. Around here everyone does their part, so either get busy with that hoe or come over here and help me with the corn."

For a moment Matt thought the boy would refuse, and he sat up straighter in the swing, preparing to lend a hand if the little hoodlum gave her any trouble. Then Tyrone threw down his hoe and stomped over to the corn patch, high-stepping over the rows of plants and muttering under his breath. He was a city boy, he groused. He didn't belong here.

For the next fifteen minutes or so the seven-year-old miscreant trudged along behind Maude Ann, looking sullen and ready to revolt, while she broke ears of corn off the stalks and dropped them into the basket he carried. By the time she finished, Tyrone's load had grown so heavy he was gripping the handle of the basket with both hands.

Maude Ann wiped her brow with her forearm and arched her back. "Tyrone, sweetie, take the corn into the house and give it to Jane."

"Yes, ma'am!" Before she got all the words out he headed off as fast as the heavy basket would allow. "And come straight back!" she called after him.

Watching the boy move away, Maude Ann shook her head, but a smile curved her mouth.

Turning her attention to the other children, Maude Ann moved around the garden checking their progress, assisting some and correcting technique where necessary.

"She's something, isn't she?"

Startled, Matt looked up and found Jane standing beside the swing holding a tray containing a pitcher of lemonade and glasses, her gaze fixed on Maude Ann.

Matt turned his attention back to the garden and said nothing, but that didn't deter Jane.

"That gal's a natural with children. She's never met one she didn't adore. And they love her back, too. Even the problem ones like Tyrone come around after a while. You ask me, it's a darned shame she and her husband didn't have any of their own. A woman like that should have a houseful."

Matt had to agree, but he merely shrugged and said, "There's time. She's still a young woman."

"Huh. Fat lot of good that does. She hasn't been out on a date with a man since Tom was killed, and she ain't likely to go anytime soon. Where is she going to meet a man, stuck out here in the country with a passel of young'uns seven days a week, I'd like to know? She never takes a day off, though the good Lord knows, I nag her about it enough.'' Jane glanced his way. ''I was hoping when you showed up that something might happen between you two, but I can see now that you're not suited.''

Matt frowned. He agreed, but somehow, hearing it from Jane annoyed him. ''Really? What makes you say that?''

''Well, it's obvious, isn't it? She's a warm, loving woman who adores children. Pardon me for saying so, Detective, but you're about the coldest, most unfeeling man I've yet to meet. You act as though the children don't exist. Why, that poor little angel, Debbie, chatters away at you all the time, and you ignore her. If there's an ounce of tenderness or love in you, I've yet to see it. No insult intended, but Maudie deserves better.

''Now then, I'd best be getting back to work. Those young'uns are going to be starving when they're done in that garden. Here's your lemonade.'' She plunked down the tray on the wicker table beside the swing and went back inside.

That was certainly plain talk, Matt thought, frowning after her. Oh, well, he did ask.

Matt turned his attention back to Maude Ann. It was funny—when she'd worked for the department, he would never have pegged her as a nurturer. He had assumed that all psychiatrists were cool, analytical people who stood a little apart from the rest of the world, observing, rather than participating. That was part of the reason he'd steered clear of her. That and the fact that he had always preferred chic blondes with a bit of an edge.

Maude Ann, however, was neither cool and distant nor chic and sophisticated. She was totally natural and unaffected. She was a woman who went around barefoot in cutoff jeans and T-shirts without a speck of makeup. A woman who opened her arms to children with problems. A woman who was compassionate and loving and maternal, a natural born earth mother.

Her husky laugh rang out, and Matt saw her grab Debbie up and swing her around.

He'd seen her do that sort of thing constantly since his arrival. Daily, she gave each child an equal amount of attention and time, listening to their earnest chatter as though it was the most important thing she'd ever heard, laughing with them and giving them smiles and praise. He'd noticed, too, that she constantly touched the children, ruffling their hair, patting their cheeks or their shoulders, giving them hugs and kisses or squeezing their hands.

No doubt, that sort of thing was important to a child's emotional well-being. The kids certainly seemed to eat it up.

What baffled Matt was, why the devil did those simple actions suddenly seem so damned sexy?

Chapter Five

He was getting stronger. He could feel it.

Matt hobbled along the path through the woods, determination and a feeling of satisfaction driving him on.

Every day he pushed himself a little harder than the day before, walking farther, forcing himself to depend less and less on the cane, and the effort was beginning to pay off. Mostly he used the walking stick for balance, leaning on it only now and then when he stepped wrong and received a jab of pain in his leg.

He went around a bend and through the trees saw the lodge up ahead. Matt chugged down the last of his water, and when he emerged from the woods, he headed for the back steps. On the veranda he paused to do a few cooldown twists and stretches.

He took these walks in the mornings, and in the afternoons he did the exercises and stretching that the hospital's physical therapist had recommended, only Matt did more than prescribed, and he was gradually stepping up the pace and intensity. The pain was still there. So was the limp, but both were gradually lessening.

It had been two weeks since he'd started applying himself to getting back in shape, and already he could walk half a mile or more without undue suffering. Jane's excellent cooking had put back some of the weight he'd lost, and the color had come back to his skin. If he continued to improve at the same rate, he figured he could switch from walking to running within a couple of months.

When he reached that goal, he would get Hank or one of the other guys on the force to bring his set of weights to the lodge so he could begin some strength training.

It was mid-June. By Matt's calculations, he should be ready to return to Houston and take the reentry physical by the end of September. October at the latest.

The back door opened, then banged shut, and footsteps thudded on the wooden boards of the porch, but Matt didn't look around. Grimacing, he grasped his right ankle and pulled his leg up behind his body. More perspiration popped out on his forehead and the tendons in his neck stood out as he stretched the injured thigh muscle as far as he could bear. He couldn't quite bring his heel into contact with his buttocks yet, but he was determined to get there.

"I brought you some water," Jane announced. "If you don't stop torturing yourself and drink it, I'm gonna pour it into my geranium pot."

Matt released his ankle and grinned at her over his shoulder as she plunked the tray down on a wicker table.

"Nag. Nag."

Chuckling, Matt looped the towel around his neck and took the tumbler of water she offered. He chugalugged the water, and when Jane refilled it he drank half without stopping.

Over the past couple of weeks more had changed than just his physical condition. He had made peace with Jane. You could even say they had become friends, if their sparring could be classified as a show of friendship.

He spent a lot of time in her kitchen talking to her while Maude Ann and the kids were outdoors doing chores or playing games or whatever it was she did with them on their daily outings. Jane was plainspoken and saw to the heart of things with crystal clarity, and she wasn't in the least shy about expressing her opinions. She'd given Matt hell often enough about the way he kept his distance from the kids.

Matt knew Tyrone's background, and he'd learned about Jennifer's the first evening he was there. From Jane, he'd learned that Marshall and his brother, Dennis, had been orphaned when their mother had committed suicide, that Timothy had been repeatedly beaten and nearly starved, that Debbie had been abused by her stepfather and that Yolanda had simply been abandoned on the side of a freeway. As yet, the police had no clue who her parents were.

Though Matt pretended indifference, Jane's comments about his treatment of Debbie and the other children bothered him. He didn't want to hurt the little girl—or any of these kids. They'd had enough hard knocks in their young lives already.

Matt knew it was important for a kid to have a role model, an adult they could idolize and learn from. Hell, he'd thought that Patrick Dolan had hung the moon in the sky.

But he saw no point in allowing the children to form an attachment to him. He would be leaving in a few months, after all. Besides, he had his own problems to deal with.

"Where's your boss and her flock of chicks?" he asked

Jane casually, but he didn't fool her. The look in her eyes said she knew exactly why he'd asked.

"Inside, cleaning house. She's assigned them all a job. The little ones are dusting and Maudie and the others are doing the rest."

"Really? What's Tyrone's job?"

Wry humor twinkled in Jane's eyes. "Cleaning toilets."

Matt laughed so hard he had to lean against one of the veranda posts. "Oh, that's rich," he gasped when he caught his breath. "I can just imagine how much he likes that."

"Well, let's just say he's not too happy right now."

"I can imagine."

"You could stick around and see for yourself, if you wanted to, but we both know you won't."

The look in her eyes challenged him to deny the charge, but he merely smiled. "Actually, I'd planned to go fishing."

Jane sniffed. "Figures." Giving him a disgusted look, she picked up the tray and stomped back inside.

Matt shrugged off her disapproval and went to the storage shed behind the garage, where he gathered what he needed from Werner's large stock of fishing gear. Ten minutes later he settled himself in his favorite spot on the end of the long, T-shaped boat dock.

Lake Livingston covered many square miles, and the boat dock sat in a secluded cove. At this hour the tall pines that lined the shore still shaded the pier. Water lapped against the pilings. Farther out, sunshine danced on the water, flashing like diamonds. A bird flew low and skimmed the water.

The dock was a peaceful spot to relax and think or just enjoy the quiet and solitude. When John Werner had inherited the place and announced his plan to retire here, Matt had thought he was crazy. After the fast pace of Houston and the challenge and stimulation, the occasional adrenaline rush of police work, how could he even consider burying himself in the boonies? However, during the past few weeks, Matt had come to appreciate the lieutenant's desire to live here.

He had been fishing for almost an hour when the hammer of footsteps on the wooden dock interrupted his solitude.

Scowling, Matt looked over his shoulder and saw Tyrone carrying a pole and a bucket. Worms, no doubt.

The boy raced out onto the pier, then spotted Matt and pulled up short.

Matt made no effort to hide his annoyance, and Tyrone glared right back at him. Matt had a hunch that Tyrone had known all along that he was there and was taking spiteful pleasure in interrupting his solitude.

Bold as brass, the boy marched out to the end of the pier and plopped himself down on the opposite side of the T from Matt.

"Where'd you get that rod and reel?" Matt demanded

"Same place as you. Outta the shed."

"Oh, yeah? Well the difference is, I have the owner's permission to use his gear."

Tyrone shrugged.

"I thought you were cleaning toilets."

"I'm done with that," the boy muttered in a surly tone that matched his scowl.

An awkward silence fell. For a long time the only sounds were the lap of the wavelets against the pilings beneath the pier, the caw of a crow in the woods, the soft whir, plop, whir when Matt cast his line out and reeled it back in.

Keeping his gaze straight ahead, Matt ignored the boy. After a while, realizing he had not heard Tyrone casting, he glanced over to see what the little hooligan was up to.

He was surprised to discover the kid was still struggling to thread a worm onto his hook.

The tip of Tyrone's tongue stuck out of the corner of his mouth and he scowled with intense concentration.

Matt frowned. He started tell him that he was doing it all wrong, but he changed his mind and cast.

A splash to his left close to the pier drew his gaze back to the boy. Tyrone had finally impaled the worm on the hook, but his first cast had gone no more than a few feet.

Muttering a string of colorful curses no seven-year-old should know, the boy reeled in his line. When the hook and sinker cleared the water he spat out a vivid obscenity. His overzealous cast had slung the worm off.

It took him another ten minutes to rebait his hook, and when he cast he got the same result as before.

Between casting and catching two good-size trout, Matt watched the boy out of the corner of his eye and shook his head. It was obvious the kid had never fished before in his life. Which, he supposed, wasn't so surprising. Until Tyrone came here, he had probably never been more than a mile from that dump where he and his mother had lived. There weren't many fishing holes in the city slums.

Matt tried to ignore the kid, but Tyrone's vivid cursing and mutters made that impossible. Every now and then he glanced over at the boy, and his frustration grew. Finally, when Tyrone got the granddaddy of all backlashes, Matt could stand it no longer.

"Oh, for Pete's sake! Don't yank at it like that—you're just going to make it worse," he snapped, struggling to his feet. "Here, let me show you."

"I don't need no help from you, pig."

"Well, too bad, punk. You're getting it, anyway. I'm tired of listening to you cuss."

"I'll cuss if I wanna. An' I know how to fish."

"Oh, yeah. Then why is it all you've done for the past twenty minutes is fling worms into the lake?"

Ignoring the boy's glare, Matt eased down next to him on the pier and took the rod from his hands. "Jeez, this looks like a bird's nest."

Tyrone muttered a choice expletive about the quality of the rod and spat into the lake.

Matt picked patiently at the tangled mess. "You'd better watch that mouth of yours. It'll get you into big trouble with Dr. Edwards."

"Huh. I ain't scared of Miz Maudie."

Matt kept his gaze on the tangled line and pulled apart another knot. After a while the boy looked out across the lake and swung his legs back and forth over the edge of the pier.

"You do know that you have it pretty good here, don't you, kid?"

Tyrone swung his legs harder. "Yeah. I know," he admitted grudgingly. He let several seconds tick by, then added, "But I still hate cleaning toilets."

Chuckling, Matt pulled another knot loose. "I got news for you, kid, everybody does, but it's just one of those nasty jobs that's gotta be done. Life's full of 'em. In a big family like this one everybody has to take their turn."

"We ain't no family."

"Really? Sure looks like one to me."

"Naw. We're just a bunch of kids nobody wants."

"Is that right? It appears to me that your Miss Maudie wants you. Otherwise, why would she bother to run this place? She doesn't have to, you know."

"Huh. She's just doin' it for the money the state pays her. That's what all fosters do."

"Are you kidding me? Shoot, kid, that's chump change compared to what Dr. Edwards could make seeing patients in Houston. The lady is a psychiatrist. Most of them charge over a hundred dollars an hour.''

The boy frowned. ''Then why ain't she doin' it, instead of taking care of us?''

Matt gave him a long, level look. ''You're a smart kid. You figure it out.''

He returned his attention to the backlash, but he could feel Tyrone's gaze on him as he untied the last knot and rewound the line. Reaching across the boy, he took a worm from the can. ''Okay now, pay attention. Here's how you bait a hook.''

Tyrone rolled his eyes and tried to look bored, but his sharp, sidelong gaze followed every move Matt made.

''All right, now stand up and I'll show you how to cast.''

Kneeling behind the boy on his good leg, his other knee bent and his foot flat on the pier, Matt put his hand over Tyrone's on the grip and guided his arm. ''When you cast, don't throw the rod like you're cracking a whip. All that does is sling your bait off and create a backlash. Draw back and swing forward in a smooth, continuous motion, like so and thro-o-ow it out there. Nice and easy. And control the reel's spin with your thumb, like this. You got a backlash because the reel was spinning off line faster than the weight on the bait end could carry it out.''

He guided Tyrone through the motion three more times, explaining the finer points as they practiced. ''Okay, you got that?''

''Yeah, yeah, I got it,'' the boy muttered.

''Fine. Let's see how you do.''

Scowling with concentration, Tyrone bit his bottom lip, drew his arm back, swung it forward and sent the baited hook sailing out over the water. When the hook and sinker hit with a gentle plop, he shot Matt a wide-eyed look over his shoulder, his grin growing wide. ''I did it!''

"Yeah. Now reel it in. Hey, not so fast! Jeez! How are you going to land a fish if he can't catch the bait? You want him to think that worm is just swimming along without a care."

"I gotcha. You mean like an easy mark. Like some dude struttin' down Lyons Avenue with his wallet stickin' up outta his back pocket, just askin' for somebody to lift it."

Matt rolled his eyes at the analogy. "Yeah, well, something like that. Okay, now you got the hang of it. Bring it in nice and easy now."

When Tyrone reeled the line all the way in and the hook cleared the water with only the worm attached, he looked crestfallen. "There ain't nothin' on it," he said, shooting Matt an accusing look.

"Of course not. If you'd gotten a bite you would've known it. And you don't catch a fish every time you cast, kid. Fishing is an art and it takes patience. Sometimes you can cast all day, but if the fish aren't biting you're not going to catch anything. You just have to keep trying."

On the third try Tyrone had reeled the line in barely halfway when it tightened and the bobber disappeared under the water, nearly jerking the pole out of his hands.

"Hey!"

"You got one!" Matt shouted. "Release the pressure on the line and let him run."

"But he'll get away!"

"No he won't. Not if you do it right. Keep the end of that rod up or you'll lose him!"

"It...ain't...easy, man," the boy gasped, hauling back on the pole with all his might.

"That's right," Matt agreed, reaching over Tyrone's shoulder to lend a hand. "But then, few things in life worth doing are."

Matt doubted that Tyrone heard the subtle moral in the

comment. The boy was so caught up in the excitement of catching his first fish he wasn't aware of anything else.

The fish jumped out of the water, a silver flash, twisting and arcing, and the reel spun with a rapid whir. "Oh, man! Look at that sucker go!" Tyrone shouted gleefully, pulling back on the rod with both hands as his catch took off and the pole bent in an even sharper arc.

"It's a big one, ain't it, Dolan?"

"Sure seems like it," Matt agreed, his excitement only slightly less than the boy's. "And, man, can that devil fight. Give him his head, son," he coached. "But keep that line taut. Now reel him in a little. Just a little. That's it. That's the way. Now play him out again. Let him know he's in a battle. Atta boy. You're doing fine. Just fine."

Over the next two hours, Matt caught five more fish, but threw four of them back because they were too small. Tyrone landed three more keepers and threw one back, though Matt had quite a job convincing the kid to give it up.

The boy was having the time of his life. When Matt announced it was time to quit, he protested loudly.

"Aw, man, I'm just getting started. You can quit if you want to, but I'm staying."

"I don't think so. You know the rules. You kids aren't supposed to go near the water unless an adult is with you. Besides, it's lunchtime. Anyway, fishing is best in the morning and the late afternoon. Fish don't bite much in the middle of the day. So come on, let's go."

"Aw, ma-a-an," Tyrone groused, but he reeled in his line, and when Matt took the pole from him and handed him the stringer full of fish in exchange, the boy slung it over his shoulder and fell into step beside him.

Maude Ann ran down the path to the boat dock, her heart hammering against her ribs. Fear nearly consumed her.

Matt fished off the pier nearly every morning, so she didn't have much hope that Tyrone would be there. Those two avoided contact whenever they could. But she'd looked everywhere else.

"Oh, God, please let him be there. And please let him be all right," she implored. "Please. Please."

What if, despite her rules to the contrary, Tyrone had gone down to the lake by himself and fallen in and drowned? It would be just like him to disobey. What if he'd climbed a tree and fallen and hurt himself, and she had walked right by him when she'd searched the woods? What if he'd broken a leg or gotten a concussion? Or cut himself and bled to death?

Sweet heaven, what if he'd run away and tried to hitch-hike out on the highway, and some pervert had picked him up?

Panic threatened to choke her. Whimpering, Maude Ann hastened her steps. The instant she tore around the next bend she could have wept with relief. Up ahead, Matt and Tyrone came walking toward her.

One look at her disheveled appearance and panic-stricken face and Matt obviously could tell that something was wrong.

He hurried to meet her as fast as his injured leg would allow. "What is it? What's happened?" he demanded, but she barely heard him. Her entire being was focused on the small, dark-skinned boy tripping along beside Matt as though he hadn't a care in the world.

"Tyrone!" Profound relief washed through Maude Ann, nearly turning her legs to rubber. The instant she reached the child, she dropped to her knees and snatched him into her arms. "Tyrone. Oh, thank God you're all right. Thank God, thank God," she gushed, squeezing the startled boy to her bosom in a bear hug.

The kid was dirty and smelled of sweat and fish, but she didn't care. Between raining kisses over his temple and cheek she babbled an almost incoherent stream of gratitude and endearments. Finally, laying her cheek against his sweaty head, she closed her eyes and began to rock the squirming child back and forth, hugging him fiercely.

"Miz...Maudie. Miz Maudie...leggo 'a me! I can't breathe!"

"Oh, I'm sorry!" She released him from the hug, but could not bear to break physical contact with him just yet. She ran her hands and her gaze over his shoulders, his arms, his chest. Framing his face with her palms, she inspected him, reassuring herself that he was, indeed, all right.

"Oh, sweetie, you nearly scared me to death."

"Me? How come?"

"How *come?* Tyrone, I didn't know where you were. Neither did Jane or any of the children. I was so worried. I thought something terrible had happened to you. I spent the past two hours searching the woods."

Tyrone looked dumbfounded. "I was fishing down at the pier with Dolan. See." A grin brightened his face, and he held up the stringer of fish and thumbed his chest. "*I* caught the biggest one." he announced proudly.

Maude Ann's mouth dropped open. Her stunned gaze went from the boy to the fish, then to Matt. "He was with *you* all this time? I've looked everywhere but the pier. I knew you were there fishing. It never occurred to me that Tyrone would be with you." She closed her eyes. "I've been worried sick."

"Tyrone, why the devil didn't you tell anyone where you were going?" Matt snapped.

Immediately the boy bristled. "Why should I? Back home, I went where I wanted, an' I didn't have to tell nobody, neither. My momma, she didn't care."

The statement, issued with such childish bravado, innocently revealed the grim, loveless existence of Tyrone's life before coming to Henley Haven. Maude Ann felt as though her heart were slowly tearing in two.

"Yeah, well, look at the kind of mom—"

Maude Ann flashed Matt a warning look over Tyrone's head, cutting off whatever disparaging remark he had been about to make. This was dangerous ground and they had to tread very carefully. She knew that no matter how awful or neglectful a parent was or how indifferent a child strove to appear, children still loved their mothers and fathers. They needed to love them, needed to believe their parents loved them back, if only a little. She would not strip any child of that illusion.

Cupping the boy's cheek, she looked at him tenderly. "Tyrone, your mother had problems that prevented her from giving you all the attention you needed. But she loved you, and I'm sure if she could have, she would have looked after you better."

"Shoot, she didn't love nothing but crack." Fixing his sullen stare on the ground, Tyrone drew circles in the dirt with the toe of his sneaker. "Told me if I didn't stay outta her sight, she was gonna give me away."

Anger flared inside Maude Ann that any mother, no matter how stoned she was, could say such a horrible thing to a child. A quick glance at Matt told her that he was as appalled and furious as she was.

She battled down the raw emotions and continued in a soft voice, "Maybe she just didn't want you to see what the crack did to her."

Tyrone looked up, and Maude Ann's chest squeezed painfully at the flash of hope in his chocolate-brown eyes.

"I care about you, too, sweetie. I care very much. That's why it's important to me that you are safe and happy. And when I don't know where you are or what's happened to you, I can't help but worry.'' She gave him a coaxing smile and stroked his hair. ''You don't want to worry me, do you?''

Tyrone looked at his sneakers again and shook his head. ''No, ma'am.''

''Good. So from now on you'll ask permission before you go off somewhere, okay?''

''Yes, ma'am.''

''Thank you, Tyrone,'' she said, and hugged him again. This time, he hugged her back.

Holding him close, Maude Ann closed her eyes and smiled, her heart swelling with love for this neglected, difficult child. For a few seconds, she allowed herself to relish the feel of his small, warm body, the scrawny arm clamped around her neck, his sweaty, little-boy smell, but when tears threatened, she released him and stood up.

''Now why don't you run along and take those fish to Jane before they spoil,'' she said briskly, giving him a little push toward the lodge.

Tyrone needed no more urging. He took off at a run, the stringer of fish flopping and bouncing against his backside.

Brimming with emotion, Maude Ann watched him until he rounded the bend and disappeared from sight.

''You are really something, lady.''

She gave a start and turned to see Matt studying her. Until he spoke she had almost forgotten he was there. ''Pardon?''

Matt walked toward her, slowly, purposefully, his slight limp almost undetectable.

Maude Ann watched him, and her heart began to boom. Something in his eyes, something glittering and intense that turned them several shades darker, sent a frisson of apprehension feathering down her spine. Some sixth sense told her to move, to flee while she had the chance, but her feet wouldn't budge.

Then it was too late.

Coming to an abrupt halt just inches away, Matt dropped the two fishing rods, reached out and clamped his hands on her shoulders and jerked her against his chest.

His smoldering gaze zeroed in on her mouth and stayed there.

Despite her best effort to control them, her lips quivered under that intense stare. Nerves danced along her skin, and suddenly she felt parched as a desert. She swallowed hard and licked her lips with the tip of her tongue.

Something flared in the depths of his blue eyes. For the space of several heartbeats, Matt stared at her. His grip on her shoulders tightened, and she felt herself being drawn closer, saw his head tilt ever so slightly and his eyelids grow heavy. Her heart lurched to a stop, then took off at a gallop. All the while his fiery gaze remained fixed on her mouth.

Then he looked into her eyes and stiffened. His black brows came down in a frown.

"Why the hell don't you get married again?" he snapped, and released her so quickly she stumbled backward.

Dazed and confused, Maude Ann touched her mouth with trembling fingers and watched him stomp away. "Now, what in the world was that all about?" she whispered.

Chapter Six

The memory of the encounter with Matt niggled at Maude Ann all during lunch. He had been about to kiss her, she was certain of that. She was no fluttery, naive girl; she knew when a man had amorous intentions. So why had he stopped and stalked off? Not that she *wanted* him to kiss her, but it was a puzzle.

It bothered her that she had no idea whether his actions had been driven by anger or passion. She was a psychiatrist; she was supposed to know these things. However, with someone as intense and moody as Matt, it was difficult to tell.

He had certainly seemed angry when he left, but the fire in his eyes had definitely been sensual. So which had it been? And what had he meant by those cryptic parting words? Her marital state had never before been of any interest to Matt Dolan.

He, of course, wasn't any help at all. Throughout lunch

Matt didn't so much as glance her way, nor did he take part in the conversation, but there was nothing new about that. To Maude Ann's chagrin, from the way he acted, you would never know that sizzling encounter just half an hour earlier had even occurred. Without coming right out and asking him, which she wasn't about to do, it appeared she was never going to find out what that little scene had been all about.

Mealtime with seven active children was not conducive to introspection. With a sigh, she decided that trying to analyze this remote, complicated man was more trouble than it was worth, and she put the matter aside and turned her attention to her charges.

She had promised them that if they were good and did their chores with no arguing, she would take them into town that afternoon to see a movie. By the end of the meal, they were so excited at the prospect they could barely sit still.

"Can we go now, Miz Maudie? Can we?" Jennifer asked, looking at Maude Ann hopefully.

"First clear the table, like always."

A chorus of cheers and the scrape of seven chairs on the brick floor erupted as the children hurried to comply.

"Hey! Take it easy!" Matt barked when Marshall nearly knocked him off his chair darting around the end of the table.

"Sorry, sir," the ten-year-old responded automatically, but he didn't slow down.

Watching them scramble to the sink with their plates and glasses, Maude Ann smiled, but inside dread squeezed her chest at what she was about to do. Still, she had no choice.

"All right now, all of you go wash your hands and meet me on the front veranda. Everyone except Tyrone, that is," she added quickly when they took off for the hallway door.

Tyrone skidded to a stop, his glee vanishing. "Why can't I go too?" he asked, eyeing her with wary suspicion.

The other children slowed their exit just long enough to dart sympathetic glances his way, then clambered out, pushing and shoving to be first through the door.

"I'm afraid you can't go with us, Tyrone. You sneaked out and went fishing this morning without doing your chores. Now you're going to have to stay here and finish the job while the rest of us go to the movies."

"That ain't fair! I promised that little snitch, Dennis, five bucks to clean 'em for me. 'Stead, he ratted on me. He's the one who didn't do the job, so he's the one you oughtta punish."

"To start with, Dennis did not tell on you. I caught him doing your job and made him stop. You cannot buy or bribe your way out of doing your share of the work around here, Tyrone. And by the way, just where did you plan to get this five dollars you were going to give Dennis?"

Tyrone focused his sulky gaze on the floor and shrugged. "I dunno. I'd get it someplace."

"Translation—he was going to lift it from your or Jane's purse," Matt drawled, entering the discussion for the first time. Leaning back in his chair, he sipped his iced tea and eyed the boy over the rim of the glass. "Isn't that right, Tyrone?"

If looks could kill, the one Tyrone aimed at Matt would have toppled him on the spot, but he didn't deny the charge, which in itself was an answer.

"I see." The disappointment in Maude Ann's voice made the boy wince and lower his head again until his chin touched his scrawny chest. "You didn't pull your weight today, Tyrone. On top of that, you bribed another boy and apparently you plotted to steal. You're lucky your punishment isn't more severe."

"But I hate cleaning toilets!" he wailed.

"I know. I feel the same. Nevertheless, we all have to take turns doing it, and this week is your turn, so you'd better get busy. You'll find the cleaning supplies in the bathroom at the top of the stairs where you left them."

His brown eyes snapped fury. For a moment she thought he was going to stage an all-out rebellion. Then what would she do?

"You said you cared 'bout me. I knew you was lying. I knew it! You're just like everybody else!" he accused. "I hate you! I *hate* you!"

"No, that's not true. I do ca— Tyrone, wait!" Maude Ann called, but he ignored her and ran from the room.

She started to go after him, but Matt got to his feet first. "Stay here. I'll go talk to him."

"You? Oh, but—"

"Just sit tight and let me handle this."

Panic surged inside Maude Ann as she watched Matt limp out of the room. No sooner had he disappeared through the doorway than she jumped to her feet to go after him, but Jane put a hand on her forearm and stopped her.

"Now, Maudie, give the man a chance. Could be what that boy needs most is a man to guide him."

"I know, but Matt's so harsh with the boy."

"He may be a little crusty on the outside, but he's a good man. And a fair one. He'll do the right thing. Trust me."

Maude Ann chewed her bottom lip and stared at the empty doorway, worry and misgivings chasing across her face. At last she sighed and sank back down on her chair. "Maybe you're right."

She tapped her foot and drummed her fingers on the table and glanced at the clock four times in fifteen seconds. It was no use.

"I can't stand this," she announced, and shot to her feet again. "I have to know what's going on."

Hurrying out of the room before Jane could stop her, she raced to the large foyer, swung around the newel post and took the stairs two at a time. At the top she spotted Matt standing a few feet away in the open doorway of the first bathroom.

He looked totally at ease, leaning on the cane with one shoulder propped against the jamb, the fingertips of his free hand stuck in the back pocket of his jeans. The casual stance allayed some of Maude Ann's fears. At least he hadn't stormed up here and lit into the boy. Not yet, anyway.

Eavesdropping was not an admirable activity, nor was it one in which Maude Ann would have engaged under normal circumstances. However, her concern for Tyrone drove her to it as she crept closer.

"I done told you—go away, pig."

Standing a few feet behind Matt, Maude Ann couldn't see Tyrone's face, but she heard the surliness in his voice. The child kept his back to the door and scrubbed the bowl of the commode furiously with a long-handled brush.

"Look, punk, you did wrong and you were busted. It's as simple as that."

"Yeah, well, I'm gonna blow this place first chance I get."

Maude Ann's heart lurched. She clasped her hands in front of her and pressed her lips together.

"Now that'd be kinda dumb, wouldn't it? This place and Dr. Edwards are the best thing that ever happened to you. Are you gonna blow it just because you're mad you got caught breaking the rules?"

The boy shot a searing glance over his shoulder. "Whazzit to you, pig?"

"Nothing, really. I just hate stupidity, that's all. This place is your chance at a decent life, kid. All you have to do is keep your nose clean and follow a few simple rules, and you'll be fine. It's not that difficult."

The boy's scrubbing slacked off to a less-intense rhythm, and this time his backward glance held the first sign of relenting. Maude Ann pressed her clasped hands tight against her breasts and said a silent prayer.

"Look, I'll make a deal with you. You don't give Dr. Edwards any more trouble, and I'll take you fishing whenever you want for as long as I'm here."

Tyrone stopped scrubbing altogether and turned. "You mean it?"

"Yeah."

"What if I wanna go every day?"

Matt shrugged. "Then we'll go every day. I fish most mornings, anyway. Afternoons, too, sometimes."

A calculating gleam entered the boy's eyes. "Will you take me out on one of them boats down in the boathouse?"

"Don't push your luck, punk," Matt drawled, but Maude Ann heard the laughter in his voice. "So how about it? Deal?"

Tyrone pursed his lips and appeared to consider. Then he shrugged and rolled his eyes. "Aw right, deal."

"Good. Let's shake on it."

Matt stepped into the bathroom with his hand outstretched. Tyrone stared at it, apparently surprised by the adult gesture, but he quickly wiped his sweaty palm on the leg of his jeans and stuck his small hand in Matt's large one. As they shook, the boy's chest puffed out and a grin nearly split his face.

Touched, Maude Ann retreated to the top of the stairs to wait for Matt.

He spotted her the instant he stepped from the bathroom,

and his mouth thinned as he limped toward her. "What are you doing here?" he demanded in a furious whisper, but he didn't wait for an answer. Grabbing her arm, he began hustling her down the stairs. "I thought I told you to wait in the kitchen."

"I don't take orders well. It's one of my many failings," Maude Ann replied with a saucy grin. She had hoped the cheerful admission would erase the scowl from his face, but it hadn't the least effect. "Anyway, I'm glad I didn't. I wouldn't have missed what just happened for the world. Oh, Matt, you were so wonderful with Tyrone!"

At the bottom of the stairs he turned her to face him. "You came upstairs because you didn't trust me to deal with the kid fairly, isn't that right? What did you think I was going to do—give him a beating? I'm not an ogre, Maude Ann."

He was angry, but she was too happy to care. She gave him a tender smile, her whiskey-brown eyes brimming with warmth as they ran over his face. "No you're not," she agreed in husky voice.

"I may not be a shrink like you, but for your information, in my own way, I've been trying to save that kid ever since he was about three years old."

"Have you? Oh, Matt, that's so sweet. I think you're making headway."

She gazed into those blue eyes and that stern face and tried to think of a way to explain how she felt, how grateful she was, how moved, but words seemed inadequate. She was brimming over with so much emotion she simply could not contain it any longer. Stepping closer, she placed her palms on his chest and gazed up at him with a melting look.

"Thank you," she whispered, and rising on tiptoe, she put her mouth on his.

Matt stiffened and went utterly still.

It was the softest of kisses, a gossamer caress of infinite tenderness and gratitude that lasted only seconds. There was nothing sexual about it—at least, Maude Ann had not intended there to be—but the instant their lips met in that feathery touch, a zing of electricity shot through her from the point of contact all the way to her bare feet.

If Matt felt anything, he gave no sign. Even as her hands curled into the front of his shirt, he stood rigid as a statue.

Shaken, she drew back and looked up into his face with a self-conscious smile, but it froze on her lips when her gaze met his. He was watching her, his eyes blazing. His face was dark and rigid with the emotions that seethed just below the surface.

Maude Ann felt her heartbeat speed up. This close she could see the tiny lines around his eyes, the pores in his skin, each individual eyelash. She could smell the musky maleness of him, the hint of outdoors and sweat, and feel his breath feathering across her forehead.

"If you're going to thank a man with a kiss, at least do it right," he growled, and before she realized his intent, he bent his head and clamped his mouth to hers. At the same time, his arms came around her, jerking her against his chest.

The kiss was powerful, stunning, and so hot and erotic Maude Ann thought surely she would melt into a puddle on the floor. His tongue stabbed into her mouth, dueled with hers, demanding surrender. His hands roamed over her back, and she felt his cane bumping against her backside. Maude Ann's head swam. All she could do was clutch his shirt and hang on.

She experienced a sudden sensation of spinning. Then her back came up against something hard and flat, and she realized he had swung her around so that her back was to the wall. With his hands braced on either side of her shoulders and his mouth still fused to hers, he leaned his weight into her and pressed against the wall.

The feel of that hard body against hers sent a shiver rippling through her. Her knees were so weak she would have slid down and collapsed on the floor had he not kept her pinned in place. Bracing on one arm, he moved his other hand to her waist and slid it slowly upward to cup her breast. When his thumb swept back and forth across her nipple, her toes curled against the hardwood floor of the hall.

At last he raised his head and released her, but he did not step away. Dazed and shaken, Maude Ann leaned weakly against the wall, her mind fogged with passion. Her breath rushed in and out of her lungs like a marathon runner's at the end of a race.

With his forearm still braced against the wall beside her head, Matt leaned in close and trailed his gaze over her flushed face. It lingered for an uncomfortably long time on her wet, slightly swollen lips, then lifted to meet her eyes. "That's the way it's done."

Straightening abruptly, he turned and limped away, leaving her stunned and disoriented.

Maude Ann had been kissed before. Many times and quite thoroughly, but never like that. Tremors still shook her body, and her heart hammered against her ribs like a wild thing.

She watched Matt move through the doorway at the back of the central hall behind the stairs. When he disappeared into the kitchen, she closed her eyes and let out a long, gusty sigh and slid down the wall until her bottom bumped the floor. Leaning her head back, she closed her eyes. She had always thought Matt was handsome in a tough-as-nails sort of way. Sexy, too. But she hadn't realized he was so...so potent. Sweet, merciful heaven. The man was lethal. If she wasn't careful, she could be in big trouble here.

Matt was having similar thoughts about Maude Ann, though his mood was far less genial.

With a barely civil nod for Jane, he stomped through the kitchen and into his room as fast as his injured leg would allow, slammed the door behind him and didn't slow down until he reached the bed. Hooking the cane on the brass rail at the foot of the bed, he flopped on his back on top of the bedspread, clasped his fingers together on top of his chest and stared, tight-jawed, at the ceiling.

He'd been without a woman too long. Kissing Maude Ann had felt too damned good.

Not that she wasn't attractive. Hell, she was beautiful—beautiful, brainy, empathetic, educated, with an earthy sexuality that made a man itch. And not just for sex, although there was that, but for other things, as well—home and hearth, family, commitment—all the things he avoided like the plague.

One thing he'd learned after twelve years with the department was that those things and police work just didn't go together.

Maude Ann was not the kind of woman suited for a casual, no-strings relationship, and he wasn't in the market for anything else.

He had seen too many of his fellow officers' marriages go sour and end in divorce. The stresses of the job, the long hours, put a strain on a marriage, or even a serious relationship, that few could withstand. Even those marriages that managed to weather the strain were less than perfect.

All his life, Matt had watched his mother worry about his father, seen the fear and dread in her eyes whenever Pat Dolan left for work. Eventually, almost inevitably it had seemed, what she had feared became reality. Matt had witnessed his mother's overwhelming grief when her husband had been killed during a routine traffic stop.

Less than a year later, she was gone, too. Congestive heart failure, the doctors had said, but Matt knew better. Maggie Dolan had died of a broken heart. Matt had no intention of ever putting a woman through that misery.

From outside came the sounds of high-pitched, excited voices. Matt rose from the bed and went to the window in time to see Maude Ann and the children heading for the minivan. She had exchanged her shorts and tank top for a swirling floral skirt that came almost to her ankles, a simple yellow T-shirt and a pair of strappy yellow sandals. Strolling along with a huge straw bag slung over her shoulder and her long auburn hair tied up in a ponytail with a yellow scarf, she looked about eighteen, instead of the thirty-four he knew her to be.

Matt watched her straighten collars and tie sashes and pat little rumps as she helped the kids into the vehicle, and his jaw clenched. There they were again, those simple, loving gestures that she handed out so naturally. He ran his hand through his hair and down the back of his neck to massage the tight muscles there. Dammit, why did he find Maude Ann's nurturing ways so appealing? It didn't make any sense.

Oh, he knew what she and her colleagues in the mental-health profession would probably make of it. No doubt they'd say he was starved for a mother's love, but Matt knew that wasn't true. Maggie Dolan had been a wonderful mother to him.

True, she hadn't given birth to him. He had been a little older than two when Patrick and Maggie Dolan had adopted him, but they couldn't have given him more love and attention had he been their own flesh and blood.

And he had loved them the same way, he thought, watching Maude Ann and her brood of misfits drive away. Which, he knew, was why that persistent dream made him feel so damned guilty.

Unconsciously, Matt touched the piece of medallion nestled against his chest. Though he didn't remember her, had no pictures of her and even in his dreams he'd never seen a face, he knew in his gut that the woman in the mist was his natural mother.

Ever since his parents had explained that he was adopted, he'd had the normal curiosity about the woman who had given birth to him. What was she like? Why had she given him up? Who was his father? Now and then Matt wondered what his biological family was like, and what course his life would have taken had his birth mother kept him.

Even so, he'd never felt any powerful yearning for her or any particular desire to search for her. The way he figured it, she had given him away. End of story.

Still, he had to admit that deep inside him was a hollow feeling, a longing that wouldn't go away. For what, he didn't know, except that it wasn't for his mother. Maggie Dolan had been all the mother he had needed. No, it was something else. It was as though something was missing, something vital.

Lost in thought, Matt continued to absently trace the outline of the medallion piece. It had been left to him by his birth mother. The jagged piece of silver was the only link he had with her.

He knew nothing about the woman. According to his parents, she had insisted on only two things when she had given him up for adoption. Being Irish American, she had wanted him to go to an Irish-American couple. Plus, she had stipulated that he be allowed to keep the medallion fragment.

Hungry for a child to call their own, the Dolans had readily agreed to her conditions. However, Matt knew that legally he couldn't be bound by their promise.

Hell, he didn't even know why he kept the thing. It was nothing but a piece of metal—useless, really. With only part of the medallion, he couldn't even make out the message etched on the back or the symbol on the front. He probably should have thrown the thing away years ago. But something inside wouldn't let him discard this last link to the woman who had given him life.

Accepting that, Matt returned to the bed and lay on his back with his fingers laced behind his head. His thoughts swung back to Maude Ann and the puzzling effect she had on him.

No, mothering was definitely not what he wanted from her. Besides, she didn't fit his image of a mother—a plump matron in an apron and a print dress who fussed and fretted over you and knitted sweaters and smelled of lavender and fresh-baked bread. It was a description, he realized, that fit his adoptive mother to a T, but not Maude Ann.

True, she was caring and affectionate with the kids and had a generous nature, but there was nothing in the least bit matronly about that luscious body and those long legs, or that sultry, hip-swinging walk of hers. Or that husky laugh that conjured up thoughts of warm summer nights, cool sheets and hot, sweaty sex. Even barefoot and wearing cutoffs and a tank top and not a speck of makeup, the woman oozed an earthy sex appeal that damn near drove a man crazy. Somehow, her giving nature only intensified that allure, sort of like the icing on a cake.

She was not, however, a woman you could love and leave, which was the only kind of relationship he wanted. Anything else, with a woman like Maude Ann, would only lead to disaster.

So what was he going to do about this attraction? he wondered as his eyes began to droop sleepily. To neutralize this chemistry between them, maybe he ought to work on building a casual friendship with her. Nobody wanted to ruin a good friendship with sex.

It was worth a shot. Keeping his distance sure as hell hadn't made the attraction go away.

"Here they come," Jane announced.

Maude Ann didn't need to ask who she was talking about. She sat the stack of plates on the table and joined the older woman at the sink. Through the window she saw Matt, with Tyrone at his side, emerge from the woods and head for the back veranda.

Thanks to the scorching weather, for the past week he had been taking his two-mile walk before breakfast, instead of after.

As soon as Tyrone had heard about it, he had begged permission to go with him.

"Why, Tyrone, I didn't think you liked Matt," she had gently teased, knowing full well that the boy's feelings about his former nemesis had shifted dramatically.

"Yeah, well...he's okay, I guess. Anyway, somebody oughtta go with him. You know, just in case he needs help."

Maude Ann had not been fooled by the transparent excuse. Since Matt had started taking Tyrone fishing, he had been a different child, and Matt had become his hero. Every chance he got, the boy followed him around like a shadow, mimicking his every move and everything he did, even to the point of getting up before dawn to walk through the woods.

Matt had changed somewhat, too. Nothing miraculous or drastic, but at least he had loosened up a bit and occasion-

ally joined in their mealtime conversations. Only yesterday
morning, he had come out to the garden when she and the
children were working and shown Marshall and Yolanda
the correct way to stake the tomato plants. Little Debbie
had become jealous and demanded that he show her how
to pick beans, which she had already been doing for weeks.
Matt had ended up spending the entire morning in the garden helping the kids.

The other evening, at Tyrone's urging, he'd even joined
her, Jane and the children in the living room after dinner
to watch a movie on television.

Small things, really, but at least he was making an effort
to be cordial, which made for a more pleasant atmosphere
at mealtime. If it wasn't for those unexpected little sparks
of sexual tension that flared between them, he would be the
perfect house guest.

Maude Ann watched Matt brace one foot on the veranda
rail and stretch his hamstring, then reverse feet and stretch
the other. Muscles in his back and legs flexed and rippled
beneath tanned skin that glistened with sweat, and she felt
her pulse race.

Merciful heavens, but he was one delicious hunk of man.

Maude Ann sighed and silently reminded herself how
inappropriate it was for her to be attracted to him. And
dangerous. There had been no repeat kiss. Matt acted as
though it had not happened at all. Which, she supposed,
was just as well. After all, he was a cop.

"Watch it, girl." Jane gave Maude Ann a poke in the
ribs with her elbow. "If you don't stop ogling the man,
your tongue is going to be hanging out soon. I hate to think
what kind of lascivious thoughts are going on in that head
of yours."

Maude Ann grinned at her, not in the least abashed. "It
doesn't hurt to look."

"True enough. Actually, I'm pleased to know a man exists who can get your motor running again."

Maude Ann shot her a look of mild exasperation, but she really couldn't argue with that, and Jane knew it. Matt was the first man to make her aware of her own sexuality since Tom. She stole another look at him through the window and sighed. "Good thing he's a cop. If he weren't, I might attack the poor man."

"You ask me, that'd be the smartest move you could make. And you could relax those rules of yours. It's possible to have a relationship with a man without marrying him, you know."

"Oh, no. Not on your life. Not me. With my luck I could date a dozen men, and if one of them was a cop, that would be the one I'd fall in love with."

"A dozen, huh? Shoot, I'd be happy if you dated just one. And so what if you did fall for another cop? Just because a man is a police officer doesn't mean he's going to go out and get himself killed. Most of them work thirty years or more and never have to fire their guns once."

"Maybe so, but I'm not taking any chances."

Jane clucked her tongue and gave her a disgusted look. "Stubborn. That's what you are. Just plain ol' mule stubborn. Oh, well. Maybe that fella you're meeting for lunch today will be single and gorgeous. He sure sounded sexy over the phone."

Maude Ann groaned. "Oh, no. That's today? I'd forgotten all about it."

"Don't even think about canceling. This is too important."

"I know, I know. It's just that there's so much to do if I'm going to make a good impression. I'd better start getting ready right now."

Two hours later, the woman who looked back at Maude

Ann from the mirror was a far cry from the casual, shorts-and-tank-top-clad foster mother the kids saw every day.

The mint-green, square-necked, princess-style dress skimmed her body perfectly and fell in a slim, straight tube from her hips almost to her ankles. On one side of the skirt a long slit from the hem to about three inches above her knee provided walking ease and a tantalizing flash of leg with each step.

It had been so long since she had dressed up for a social event—court appearance didn't count because then she always wore one of her business suits—that Maude Ann was a bit surprised herself. And pleased.

She picked up her keys and small white purse and headed for the door like a general going into battle.

She was halfway down the stairs when Matt walked in through the front door. Two steps inside the wide foyer, he spied her and stopped in his tracks.

"Maude Ann?" he said with so much shock that she chuckled, but her steps faltered under his hot stare.

Slowly, thoroughly, he took in every inch of her, from the coral-tipped toes peeking out of the sandals to the shining russet hair that swung around her face, controlled for once in a full pageboy. The inspection was blatantly sensual, the look in those vivid blue eyes sizzling. At last that bold gaze met hers, and when he spoke, the husky pitch of his voice made her skin prickle.

"You look beautiful."

The compliment caught her off guard. She had expected sarcasm. Forcing her feet to move, she continued down the stairs. "Thank you. Tom always said that I cleaned up good," she quipped.

"More than good. Spectacular."

"Are you trying to tell me something? Do I really look so awful normally?"

His gaze continued to roam over her as she descended, and when she reached the bottom of the stairs and stepped into the foyer he moved closer. "Maude Ann, you couldn't look awful if you tried. It's just that today you look really incredible."

"Good heavens. Be careful. You'll turn my head."

"I doubt that's possible. You're just about the most down-to-earth person I know." He gave her another quick head-to-toe inspection. "I take it you're going somewhere?"

"Yes. I have an appointment in Houston."

Without her noticing, Matt had somehow inched nearer while they talked. Now he stood so close she could feel his heat radiate along her bare arms. He smelled of soap and shaving cream, and sunshine and maleness. His nearness made her insides quiver and her nerves jump. She had just spent the past three hours indulging in a confidence-building grooming routine for the meeting in Houston. If she wanted to preserve her poise, she knew she had to get out of there. Now.

Maude Ann glanced at her watch. "Oh, look at the time. If I don't hurry, I'm going to be late, so if you'll excuse me..."

The twitch of Matt's mouth told her he knew he was making her nervous, but after a brief hesitation he stepped aside and let her pass. "Sure."

She hurried to the door, aware every step of the way of his gaze burning into her back.

If his expression was anything to go by, she had much the same effect on the man she was meeting for lunch as she'd had on Matt.

Maude Ann spotted him before he saw her. She had never met the man before. Their dealings so far had consisted of two telephone conversations, but since he was the only man sitting alone in the restaurant, it was easy to pick him out.

He sat at a table in a window alcove, absently fiddling with his silverware and looking bored. As she and the maître d' approached, he glanced up, and a look of surprise flashed over his face, followed by a swift but discreet appraisal and a slow smile of masculine appreciation.

He stood up as Maude Ann reached the table. "Mr. Conway?" she asked. "You are J.T. Conway, the reporter with the *Houston Herald,* I hope."

He flashed a charming smile. "Guilty as charged."

Chapter Seven

Maude Ann extended her hand. "How do you do."

He was a tall man, about the same height as Matt Dolan, and he had the same blue eyes and wide-shouldered, muscular build. He also looked about the same age. There, though, all similarity ended. Where Matt's hair was black as midnight, J.T. Conway's was a rich, dark brown. His eyes twinkled with teasing good humor, and she suspected that his smile could charm the hardest heart.

"I do hope I haven't kept you waiting long, Mr. Conway."

"Not at all. I'm delighted to meet you, Doctor. I've heard good things about you from several sources. It's nice to finally put a face with the name. Particularly such a lovely face."

It had been a long time since a man had flirted with Maude Ann, and J.T. Conway did it with such panache that she felt a little rush of pleasure. "Thank you," she replied with a polite smile, taking the chair he held out for her.

"Before we start, I must ask how you heard about Henley Haven. We're not listed in any telephone book and few people know of our existence. I'd like to keep it that way."

"I sorry, Doctor, I'm afraid I can't reveal my sources. But I will promise that I won't pass the information on to anyone."

She looked at him for a long moment. "Well, I suppose I'll have to settle for that."

They made small talk as they perused their menus and the waiter took their drink order.

When the man left, J.T. Conway's blue eyes twinkled at her. "You don't look at all like my image of a doctor. Or a foster mother, for that matter."

"Really? And what do you think a doctor and foster mother looks like?"

"I don't know, but you're much too young and too lovely to be either."

"Thank you, but I assure you, I am both." Maude Ann took a sip of water to hide her smile. "Which, may I remind you, is why I'm here."

"I appreciate your meeting with me." His rueful smile was charming. "I'll be honest with you. When my editor assigned this story to me, I wasn't too enthused about it. But now that I've met you, I'm glad I was given the job. So, tell me, Dr. Edwards, where exactly is this foster home of yours?"

"If you don't mind, I'd rather not say just yet."

That was why she had insisted on meeting him at a restaurant to discuss the possibility of him doing a story on Henley Haven instead of him coming to the lodge, as he had originally requested. Only John Werner and a small number of his officers, along with a few judges and social workers, knew where Henley Haven was located.

This meeting was a chance for both her and J.T. Conway to size each other up. He would decide if a story on Henley Haven would be of sufficient human interest for his newspaper, and Maude Ann would decide if she trusted him enough to allow him to write it.

"You're being kinda cloak-and-dagger about this, aren't you, Doctor?"

"Perhaps I am, Mr. Conway, but—"

"Please, call me J.T."

"Oh. Very well, then. And I'm Maude Ann. Now, as I was saying, until we reach an understanding, I would prefer not to disclose the whereabouts of Henley Haven. I appreciate your enthusiasm for this project, Mr. Con—uh, J.T., but I must warn you, before I grant an interview, there are some things we need to discuss."

His dark eyebrows rose, and Maude Ann could see that he was surprised. Apparently, not many people hedged when he wanted to do a story about them. After a brief hesitation, he shrugged and leaned back in his chair. "Maude Ann, you do realize that a big spread in the Sunday supplement, like the one I'm planning to do, will give your foster home invaluable publicity, and it's free. That can only be of benefit to the children."

"Not necessarily. It depends."

"On what?"

"On the type of story you do. And on whether or not you agree to my conditions."

"Conditions?" He laughed and shook his head. "I'm sorry, Maude Ann, but I don't allow conditions to be imposed on what I write. It's called freedom of the press."

"I see. If that's your final word, then I feel I must exercise my freedom of choice and right to privacy." Her tone was polite. So was her smile, but there was steel in her eyes. "I'm sorry, Mr. Conway, but I'm afraid there will be no story about Henley Haven. And no point in continuing this meeting. Perhaps if you would call the waiter over, you can cancel my lunch order. Good day." She picked up her purse and started to rise, but he reached across the table and grasped her wrist.

"Whoa. Whoa. Don't be so hasty. C'mon, sit down and let's talk about this, Maude Ann. Surely we can work something out."

"I doubt it. Those are my terms and they're not negotiable." Maude Ann's nature was mellow and easygoing, but when it came to the children, she could be as fiercely protective as a lioness. The look she aimed at him left no doubt of that.

J.T. eyed her shrewdly. "You operate mainly on a combination of grants and donations and the pittance the state allows foster parents, right?"

She nodded, and a look of satisfaction flickered in his eyes. He obviously thought he'd hit on the right tactic.

"Well, then, just think what a financial boon a piece like this would be."

Sitting back down, Maude Ann pulled her wrist from his grasp and met his confident gaze. "I am well aware of that, J.T. However, while I'll admit that it would be nice to have more operating capital, there are more important considerations."

He blinked, taken aback. "Like what?"

"Like the safety of the children."

They stared at each other in silence across the linen-covered table, Maude Ann's gaze level and uncompromising, J.T.'s full of disbelief and frustration. Finally he sighed. "You are one tough negotiator, lady. Okay, why don't you tell me what it is you want?"

"First of all, I want your agreement, in writing, that you will not divulge the names of any of the residents of Henley Haven in your story, or show any of their faces in the photos that will accompany the story."

"Why not? There's nothing like sad little faces to stir up public sympathy."

"For the same reason I don't give out the location of the home to people I don't know—for the children's safety. You have to understand that with the exception of a few who were orphaned under harrowing and traumatizing circumstances, these children were forcibly and permanently removed from their mother's and/or father's care. I don't want any disenfranchised parents with a grudge against our judicial system showing up on my doorstep trying to reclaim their child by force. None of them need any more trauma in their lives."

"Mmm. I guess you do have a point there. Anything else?"

"Only that you cannot divulge the whereabouts of the home to *anyone*—either in print or verbally." She waited a beat, then added, "And you must grant me the right to final approval before the story is printed."

"Whoa! Just hold it right there. That isn't going to happen. I might—just might—be able to get my editor to go along with the other conditions, but no way in hell will he allow an outsider to censor a story."

Maude Ann pursed her lips and gave him a considering look, but it was just for appearance' sake. She had expected him to balk at the last condition, which was why she had included it.

In any negotiation each party had to compromise and give in on something. So she threw in a condition that she could forgo if necessary, to which she knew J.T. and his superior would object. Chances were, if she gave in on that point, they would feel victorious and probably wouldn't object to the conditions she *really* wanted to impose.

"Well...I suppose for the sake of compromise, I have to give in on something," she said finally. "If you promise on your honor that you will write a favorable article about Henley Haven without revealing its whereabouts or the identities of the residents, I won't insist on seeing it prior to publication."

"You have my word on it. I'll run your conditions by my editor and get back to you in a few days. If that's okay?"

"That will be fine." She opened her purse and pulled out a long, white envelope and handed it to him. "This is a document outlining in detail my conditions. You can just cross out the prepublishing approval clause, and we'll all initial. If your boss agrees to the other terms, then you both need to sign the document and return both copies to me. When I've signed them, I'll return your copy."

J.T. looked flummoxed, but the waiter returned with their order before he could reply. When the man left, he raised his eyebrows and leaned forward. "You had a *contract* drawn up?"

"Yes. I told you, my number-one concern is keeping the children safe."

J.T. tipped his head to one side and looked at her with renewed interest. "You'd do it, too, wouldn't you? If I reneged on our deal, you'd use this document to sue me, wouldn't you?"

Still smiling sweetly, Maude Ann leaned closer across the table. "In a New York second, Mr. Conway. When it comes to protecting those children, I'd fight the devil himself."

The next morning, Jane awoke with a toothache, and Maude Ann shooed her off to the dentist. Preparing break-

fast for nine people on her own had her thoroughly frazzled
and dashing around the kitchen like a crazy woman, but at
last she put the meal on the table and sat down with Matt
and the kids.

"Can I haff two muffinth thith morning, Mith Maudie?"

Maude Ann looked at Timothy, and her heart wrenched
at the trace of fear in the five-year-old's eyes.

Though he had been with her for ten months, he still
expected a slap for simply asking for food. Because he had
been starved the first four years of his life, the child never
seemed to get enough to eat. Nor could he quite believe
that he was allowed to eat his fill.

Unable to resist, Maude Ann reached over and tousled
the child's blond curls and gave him a warm smile. "You
can have as many muffins as you want, sweetheart. Just
like always."

She glanced up and discovered Matt watching her, his
eyes dark with some unknown emotion. Inexplicably, her
face heated and she felt a little tingle race over her skin.

"What time are we leaving, Miss Maudie?"

Grateful for the diversion, Maude Ann turned her attention to Yolanda, only belatedly registering the barely controlled excitement in the girl's voice.

"Leaving?"

"To go out on the houseboat."

"Oh, dear!" She had been so busy since Jane left she'd
forgotten all about the excursion she'd promised the kids.
"Children, I'm afraid we're going to have to postpone our
outing until another day when Jane can go with us."

"But you promised to take us out on the houseboat today
if the weather was good!" Jennifer whined as groans went
up from the other children. "You promised!"

"I know. And if I could keep that promise I would, but

it's just not possible. Jane will be gone for hours, and I don't imagine she'll feel like doing much when she returns. I can't operate the houseboat and keep an eye on all of you by myself.''

"But you promithed!" Debbie wailed while the other children muttered their own complaints.

Feeling terrible, Maude Ann sent an imploring look around the table. "Kids, I really am sorry. Honest. I know you're disappointed, but—"

"I'll go with you," Matt inserted quietly.

Maude Ann's head snapped around. "Wh-what?"

"I said, I'll go with you. I can operate the boat and you can keep an eye on the kids."

"Oh, but—"

"'Ray! We're going!" Debbie squealed.

All around the table the other children cheered and hooted and pumped their arms in victory.

"Matt, I don't think you realize what you're letting yourself in for."

Instantly the babble of elation around the table faded to a taut silence as seven pairs of eyes switched back and forth between the two adults.

"I told the children we would stay out on the lake all day. We were going to picnic in a cove several miles south of here and go swimming and maybe fish off the boat and just laze the day away. We won't get back until late."

"No problem. I've got nothing else to do. Anyway, I've been promising Tyrone for weeks that I'd take him out in one of the boats. Isn't that right, Tyrone?"

"Yeah, but I thought we was goin' out in one of them hot powerboats. Just you'n me," the boy mumbled with a pout. "Not on some dumb ol' houseboat with everybody else."

In spite of the situation, the boy's reluctance to share his hero with the other kids brought a smile to Maude Ann's lips.

"Yeah, well, you don't start with the most powerful, you know. You have to crawl before you can walk. Besides, I'm not sure I'm up to handling one of those souped-up jobs just yet." Matt reached over and cuffed the boy on the shoulder. "C'mon, punk, don't look so glum. It'll be fun."

The prospect of spending a whole day with Matt filled Maude Ann with a mixture of excitement and apprehension. No matter how appealing, she knew it wasn't a smart thing to do. The attraction between them was too strong. Whenever they were in the same room, even sitting at the table with Jane and the children around them, sexual tension sparked and crackled in the air between them. She couldn't believe Matt didn't feel it, too.

"Matt, I don't think—"

"What's the problem? You said you needed help with the boat and I'm volunteering. Unless, of course, you have some personal objection to my coming along?"

"No, of course not!" she lied. "I, uh…I'm just concerned that you'll get bored."

As one, seven little heads swiveled, and the children looked at Matt, their young faces taut and hopeful.

Leaning back in his chair, he sipped his coffee. Over the rim of the cup his eyes mocked her. "I don't bore easily, Maude Ann." He cocked one brow. "Any other reasons I shouldn't come along?"

Seven pairs of eyes swung back in Maude Ann's direction.

She tried desperately to think of something, but other than the truth, she couldn't come up with a single plausible reason. With what she hoped was a gracious smile, she bowed to the inevitable. "No, of course not. None at all."

"Good. We wouldn't want to disappoint the kids, would we?"

His gaze swept over the expectant faces. "Well? What're you all just sitting there for? Go get your swimsuits and let's get this show on the road."

The kids scattered like a covey of quail, shouting and squealing as they raced to the sink to dump their dishes and silverware. An instant later seven pairs of little feet pounded up the stairs. The decibel level was ear-shattering.

Maude Ann gave Matt a rueful look. "Just remember, you volunteered."

A half hour later they were on board the *Lazy Day,* chugging out into the cove, picking up speed a bit as they left the placid cove and the boat slipped into the lake's main current.

The kids were so excited they ran from one side of the craft to the other, peering over the sides and chattering. Maude Ann had made them all put on life jackets before they left the dock. Even so, she assigned Marshall and Yolanda the job of keeping an eye on the younger children while she went inside to stow their gear.

She put their towels, sunscreen and bug repellent in the bathroom and went into the small galley. As she searched the cabinets for lemonade mix, she wondered how she could have forgotten, even for a minute, that she had promised the children this outing on Lieutenant Warner's house boat.

The screen door slid open with a bang and Tyrone dashed inside. "Miz Maudie! Matt, he says he could sure use somethin' to drink. An' he needs you to come up to the bridge to show him where you want us to go."

"Tell him I'll be up in a bit but in the meantime to just keep heading south."

"Yes, ma'am."

He turned and raced back outside as quickly as he'd come in.

Smiling, Maude Ann shook her head. The change in the boy since Matt had taken him under his wing was nothing short of miraculous.

She wondered why Matt had volunteered to come out with them today. He had never done anything like that before. True, he had mellowed a bit lately. As his physical condition had improved so had his attitude toward her and the kids. So maybe this act of kindness was just more of the same.

That line of reasoning eased her tension, and she smiled and picked up the tray and headed for the forward deck. Apparently, the prospect of returning to Houston and the department had worked wonders on Detective Dolan's disposition.

She left the children eating their snack and climbed the ladder to the bridge.

"Where the devil have you been?" Matt demanded the instant her head poked over the top of the upper deck.

"Looking after the kids." She joined him at the console and pointed ahead. "The cove we want is right around the next bend. We've picnicked there a few times this summer. It has a sandy beach and the water is shallow for fifty feet or so out. It's a good place for the children to swim."

She glanced down at them and smiled. "I really appreciate you doing this, Matt. They're having a wonderful time."

"Like I told you, it's no problem."

Her gaze cut to him, and a little dart of awareness shot through her.

He stared straight ahead, his attention fixed on the water, both hands on the wheel. A baseball cap, dark sunglasses and a pair of boxer-style swimming trunks were his only attire. His skin was bronze from his daily walks and fishing, and it glistened with a fine sheen of sweat. He had regained almost all the weight he had lost, and his face no longer had that drawn look. Well-defined muscles sculpted his broad shoulders, chest and arms. He was an impressive-looking man.

The children's laughter and excited squeals floated up to them. Matt glanced down at the lower deck and snorted. "The way they're acting, you'd think they'd never been on a boat before."

"They haven't. Well…except for Marshall and Dennis. They claim that before he died, their grandfather used to take them out fishing in his skiff. But none of the others have been boating before."

"Why not? I thought you said you'd been here since February."

"We have, but I can't take them out by myself, and Jane is terrified of the water. She can't swim and she's leery of venturing out onto the lake even wearing a life jacket. It's taken me all summer to persuade her to give it a try so that the children could enjoy the treat."

"Why didn't you say something before now? I would have helped you."

"You? Oh, please." She shot him a wry look. "What? Do I look like a masochist?"

Matt had the grace to look embarrassed.

"Okay, okay. I'll admit I've been a bear to you and the kids since I arrived. I apologize for that. It's just that I've been so…down since the shooting. For a long time I was kind of lost, I guess. I wasn't certain of anything—whether I'd ever be able to return to active duty, whether I could live with it if I couldn't go back. Would I still be a good cop if I did? What I would do the first time I heard gunfire again? I guess I took out all my frustrations and uncertainties on you and your bunch.''

"It's okay." Touched that this strong man trusted her enough to make the admission, Maude Ann put her hand on his arm. The contact startled him, and she felt the involuntary contraction of his muscles.

She also felt the jolt she always experienced when their bodies touched. With an effort, she smiled warmly at him. "Really. You don't have to explain or apologize to me, Matt. I understand post-trauma depression."

He stared into her eyes as though searching for something. Finally he nodded. "Yeah, I guess you do."

Maude Ann told herself to break eye contact, to look away from that vivid blue stare, but she could not.

As their gazes held, a subtle tension built. She felt her chest tighten, her pulse race. She saw Matt's pupils dilate, saw the slight flare of his nostrils. A breeze caught a tendril of her hair and whipped it across her mouth. Several strands stuck to her lips, and as she lifted her hand to pull them away, his gaze dropped to her mouth.

The hungry look in his eyes made her heart skip a beat, then take off at a gallop.

Matt's mouth suddenly tightened, and he jerked his gaze away, focusing on the water ahead. His hands gripped the wheel in a white-knuckled hold. "Look, I'd like to forget these past few weeks and start over. I'd like us to be friends, Maude Ann."

Friends? She blinked several times and tried to adjust to the abrupt change in his demeanor. She had been certain he was about to kiss her again. Instead, he was offering friendship?

Was that even possible, given the chemistry between them? True, it was probably the wisest course to take. Anything else was impossible.

Finally she nodded and smiled at him. "I'd like that."

"Good." Letting go of the wheel with one hand, he stuck it out for her to shake. "Pals?"

His slow smile did devastating things to his stern face and her insides, and Maude Ann had the fleeting thought that it was a shame he didn't smile more often. Although, for her own emotional stability, perhaps it was just as well that he didn't.

Ignoring the tingly sensation that raced up her arm when she clasped his hand, she gave him a wry smile. "Pals."

Pulling her hand from his, she glanced ahead. "That's the cove."

Matt throttled down the engine, and immediately, realizing they were nearing their destination, the children's excitement level rose.

"I'd better get down there before somebody falls overboard. Give me a yell when you want me to drop anchor."

"Will do."

Being friends was for the best, Maude Ann told herself as she scrambled down the ladder. She knew that.

Even so, she couldn't seem to banish the tight knot of disappointment that caused her chest to ache.

Chapter Eight

Matt steered the flat-bottomed boat as far into the shallow cove as he dared before cutting the engine and calling down to Maude Ann to drop anchor. The kids were so excited they scampered from one end of the boat to the other, jumping up and down and squealing with delight and anticipation.

The instant the anchor splashed into the water, a babble of pleas to go swimming erupted from the children. The din was so overwhelming Maude Ann couldn't get a word in.

"Hey! Knock it off, you guys," Matt barked, hopping down the ladder on his good leg. "We're going to do this in an orderly manner. Now, I want all of you to line up over here," he ordered, pointing to a spot on the deck in front of him.

To Maude Ann's amazement, not only did the kids scramble to obey, except for a few giggles and elbow pokes, they were quiet about it. None of them appeared to be frightened by Matt's gruffness, nor did they seem to mind his dictatorial manner.

"All right now, if you can swim, raise your hand. Good. Good. Marshall, you, Yolanda and Dennis can help Maude Ann and me keep an eye on the other kids. You nonswimmers keep your life jackets on."

"Uh, Matt," Maude Ann said, "those are a bit bulky. I brought some floaties and inner tubes for the little ones to wear while swimming."

He frowned. "What the hell is a 'floatie'?"

"You'll see. I'll go get them."

When Maude Ann returned, she and Matt spent the next fifteen minutes blowing up the inflatable cuffs and putting them on the upper arms of the three youngest children.

To save Tyrone the indignity of being lumped in with the little ones, Matt slid a red plastic inner tube over his head and ordered him to stick beside him once they were in the water.

When at last they were ready, Matt jumped over the side first to test the depth of the water. Finding it came just to his waist, he signaled to the older kids to join him. Whooping with joy, Marshall picked up his little brother and tossed him over the side. As Dennis hit the water, his brother reached for Yolanda, but the shrieking girl dodged him and jumped in on her own. Marshall followed right behind.

Matt watched them for a few minutes to assess their competence. None of them were Olympic material but they were good enough swimmers to put his mind at ease.

Tyrone's gaze followed his friends with envy, but he eyed the water with a good amount of trepidation. Seeing his dilemma, Matt stepped closer to the side of the boat and murmured, "Just hold on tight to the inner tube with both hands, close your eyes and jump."

The boy flashed him a wild-eyed look. If anything, he appeared more frightened than before.

"C'mon, punk. It's not that deep here. See?" Matt held up both arms to show the boy where the water reached on him. "If you jump, your feet will probably touch the bottom for a second, then you'll bob right back up. Nothing to it."

Tyrone leaned forward and peered over the edge of the boat at the water. He caught his lower lip between his teeth.

"You can do it," Matt quietly urged. "And you know you can trust me. I won't let anything happen to you. Now c'mon, jump. Show 'em you're not afraid."

Tyrone's round-eyed stare went from Matt to the water, then back to Matt. For a second Maude Ann thought he would refuse. Then, setting his jaw, he clutched the inner tube under both arms, closed his eyes, sucked in a deep breath and took the plunge.

He hit the water with a yell and a tremendous splash, but when he surfaced, he was grinning. "I did it!"

"Sure you did," Matt acknowledged matter-of-factly. "Just don't go getting cocky on me. And stay close. As soon as we get the little ones into more-shallow water, you're going to get some swimming lessons, punk."

Tyrone looked ecstatic, and Maude Ann's heart filled with gratitude. She could have kissed Matt for his gruff kindness toward the boy.

Demanding her attention, the three remaining children hopped around on the deck as though it was on fire, squealing, "Me next! Me next, Miz Maudie! I wanna go swimmin' too!" Surreptitiously, Maude Ann wiped the moisture from her eyes and handed Jennifer and Timothy down into Matt's waiting arms. With Debbie straddling her hip, the child's arms locked around her neck in a death grip, she stepped off the side of the boat.

For the next couple of hours the older children swam and played a water game understandable only to them, while Matt and Maude Ann worked with the younger ones in the shallow water near the shore.

Matt showed remarkable patience and gentleness with the children. Within an hour they could all tread water. After two hours, Jennifer and Tyrone were happily paddling around and diving to the bottom to retrieve the coins and other objects that Matt tossed there. Even little Debbie and Timothy learned to float and do the dog paddle. What they lacked in form they more than made up for in joy and enthusiasm.

After a few hours of play, the children were ravenous and clamoring for lunch. Once they had eaten, Maude Ann issued orders that no one could return to the water for at least an hour. The children complained, but she stood her ground. When Matt backed her up, they accepted defeat and wandered off to seek other diversions.

Sitting on the picnic blanket, Maude Ann watched them play, her face soft with fondness. "They're having such a good time." She turned her head and looked at Matt. "Thank you so much for coming with us today. I wanted the children to have this day of fun, particularly Marshall and Dennis. There's a good chance they'll be leaving, so this may be their last outing with us."

Matt shot her a frown. "What do you mean? Where are they going? Jean told me that their mother committed suicide when their father ran out on them and there was no close family to take them. Ah, jeez! Don't tell me Children's Services has found their deadbeat dad and they're going to turn them over to him!"

"No, no. Judge Simpson would never do that. He's a

real children's advocate who puts the welfare of the children first. A distant cousin has petitioned the court for custody of the boys. He and his wife have two sons the boys' ages. Under the judge's orders, Children's Services has done a thorough check on them, including an extensive psychological study. They appear to be just the sort of family the boys need. The final custody hearing will be soon.''

"I see. Do Marshall and Dennis know?''

"Yes. I explained everything to them privately. Naturally, they're nervous about leaving. They feel secure here. But at the same time, they're anxious to be part of a real family again, and after our talk, I think they're okay with leaving. Last night I told the other children. There was some anxiety. Mostly fear that they, too, would have to leave someday, but that's only to be expected.''

"Do they have reason to fear? I mean, is this how it's going to be for all of them? They're here for a while, and just when they begin to feel safe, they're shipped off to strangers?''

The anger in Matt's voice caused surprise to ripple through Maude Ann. She had thought he was a cold and unfeeling man, uninterested in the children or their problems. Lord knew, with the exception of Tyrone and the occasional small kindness to Debbie, he had gone out of his way to avoid them.

A hint of a smile tugged at her mouth. Poor man. He had worked so hard to remain aloof and uninvolved, but the effort had apparently been for nothing. As she knew only too well, children in their innocence had a way of winding their little fingers around your heartstrings whether you wanted them to or not.

Touched by his righteous anger on their behalf, Maude Ann reached out and laid her hand on Matt's arm. ''I won't lie to you, Matt. It's possible. For some of them, at any rate. Others, ones like Tyrone and Jennifer, may never be adopted, in which case, they may remain here. Or they could eventually be transferred to another foster facility.''

''Oh, great! So they're just going to be shuffled around from one foster home to another until they're eighteen, when they'll be booted out into the world to fend for themselves.''

''The system isn't perfect, Matt, but it's all we have.''

''It stinks! Why can't they all just stay here with you?''

''Matt, you have to understand, Henley Haven is just a temporary shelter for these kids, a place to heal and adjust until a better home can be found for them.''

''Better than this?'' he demanded with an expansive wave of his arm. ''Impossible. Hell, Maudie, your place is every kid's dream—a rambling home in the country, with a lake and woods, a bunch of other kids for company, good food, clean clothes and beds, all run by a beautiful mother figure. Trust me, for a kid, it doesn't get any better than this.''

Maude Ann gaped at him, momentarily stunned, not only by his praise of Henley Haven, but to learn that he thought she was beautiful. When he continued to glare, she blinked and gathered her scattered wits.

''Matt, that's sweet of you. I…I don't know what to say. I always thought you didn't like me. And that you disapproved of me running a foster home.''

Some of the harshness faded from his face, and she thought she saw a flash of chagrin in his eyes before his gaze switched to the ground in front of his bare feet. ''That wasn't personal. I just wanted the place to myself.'' He picked up a handful of sand and let it trickle back to the ground, watching the flow as though it was fascinating.

''I never disliked you,'' he added quietly. ''I'll admit I've never had much faith in your profession, particularly in conjunction with police work, but until recently, I was neutral about you on a personal level.''

"I see. And now?''

He looked up and his gaze locked with hers. Something in his eyes, something intense and hungry, almost desperate, sent a thrill coursing through her. His face was dark and somber. His whole body seemed taut, as though he was on the brink of making a life-altering confession. The depths of his eyes, swirling with emotion, were like a seething cauldron.

Then he blinked and it was gone, as though a curtain had been lowered. He gave her a quirky smile. "Now? Now we're pals. Remember?''

Disappointment washed over her, but she returned his smile with a weak one of her own. "Yes. Of course,'' she agreed, but she had the strangest feeling that was not what he had been about to say at all.

The boys came running back at that moment, Marshall in the lead and little Timothy trailing far behind and whining. Skidding to a halt beside the blanket, they were flushed from their run and smelled of sweat and sunshine.

"Miz Maudie, can me'n Marshall an' Dennis go exploring in the woods?'' Tyrone gasped, his chest heaving.

Maude Ann glanced at the thick woods that lined the shore. The kids played in the woods around the lodge all the time, but there they had trails and most of the underbrush had been cleared out. These woods were wild and thick and probably dangerous. "Oh, guys, I don't know…''

"C'mon. Let 'em go, Maude Ann. All boys like to explore,'' Matt said with a hint of admonition in his voice.

"What if they get lost?''

"They won't. But if they do we'll find them.'' Taking her agreement for granted, he turned a stern face on the boys. "Now listen up. You guys can go, but you're to keep the beach in sight at all times. No wandering off deep into the woods chasing a lizard or anything else. Period. You got that?''

"Yessir," they replied in unison. "We won't. We promise."

"And you have to take Timothy with you. And keep an eye on him so he doesn't get hurt."

"Aw, do we gotta?"

"Sorry, boys. That's the deal. Take it or leave it."

Tyrone rolled his eyes. "O-*kay,* he can tag along."

"So what are you waiting for? Get going." They took off at a run. "And when I call you, you'd better haul your skinny little butts out here, you hear?" he yelled after them.

Maude Ann watched them scamper into the woods, their rubber-soled shoes slapping their heels. When they disappeared from sight, she aimed a bemused look at Matt. "How do you do that?"

"What?"

"Get them to snap to attention that way and obey your orders."

"They're learning to recognize the voice of authority, that's all."

She tipped her head to one side and studied him. "I think it's much more than that. They trust you."

Matt shrugged. "Maybe. I don't know."

"I do. Each of these children has suffered at the hands of an adult. You're gruff and intimidating. Your size alone should frighten them, yet they aren't in the least afraid of you."

"Hell, I hope not. I want to command their respect, not terrorize them. Only a monster would do that."

Wrapping her arms around her drawn-up legs, Maude Ann rested her chin on her knees and gazed out over the water. Sunlight flashed silver on the gentle wavelets, and the houseboat bobbed peacefully in the cove. A flotilla of puffy clouds drifted along as though being pulled by a string. From the woods came the raucous caw of a crow and the angry chatter of a squirrel.

"Believe me, there are plenty of monsters in the world," she said. "I've seen them in court often. As I'm sure you have. Evil has many faces."

Matt turned his head. She could feel his eyes on her, studying her, but she kept her own eyes focused straight ahead.

"Is that why you started Henley Haven?" he asked quietly. "To protect kids from monsters?"

Maude Ann huffed out a mirthless little laugh. "If only I could. No, by the time they come to me, the damage has already been done. All I can do is try to undo it—at least, to the extent that's possible. The nightmarish memories will always be there for these children—there's no escaping that. But with help, they can learn to move on and not let what happened dominate their present and future.

"What I try to do is provide some normalcy, show them that the world doesn't have to be a scary place, that there are people in it who will love them and take care of them."

A sad little grimace twisted her mouth. "Sometimes I succeed—most of the time, actually—but once in a while I don't. Every now and then there's a child who's been so savagely traumatized that I can't penetrate the shell he's built around himself. But I have to try. I have to," she added softly, passionately.

Yes, Matt thought, watching her, she would have no choice. Not Maude Ann. Her nature was too giving, her soul too sensitive, her heart too loving to do otherwise.

Little lost souls with old eyes, the timid, the frightened, hellions and budding delinquents—she welcomed them all with open arms, giving them, some for the first time in their short lives, unqualified love and nurturing, a secure home, freedom from fear and discipline tempered with caring.

He glanced down the beach at the girls, busily building their castle, then at the woods where the boys were exploring. They were not her flesh and blood, but she loved every one of them, and her valiant spirit would always demand that she protect and defend them to her last breath.

Maude Ann Edwards was an extraordinary woman.

As Matt studied her profile, his chest swelled with emotion, a dark swirl of feelings he didn't want to acknowledge, didn't want to think about, but they wouldn't go away. The longer he gazed at her the tighter his chest grew, until it almost hurt to draw breath. The urge to touch her, to put his arms around her and pull her close, to taste her lips, almost overwhelmed him.

He told himself to look away, to change the subject, but he couldn't. "The kids are lucky to have you," he replied in a husky voice.

"No. I'm the lucky one." At that moment the sound of high pitched giggles broke the silence of the cove. She looked at the girls, and her face softened with a gentle smile. "They bring such joy to my life. I would be lost without them."

"You're great with them. You should have a houseful of your own." He waited a beat, then asked, "So why didn't you and Tom start a family right away? Neither of you were exactly children when you married."

Inserting her late husband's name into the conversation had been a deliberate attempt to defuse the situation and banish the desire gnawing at him. It didn't work.

Maude Ann laughed and leaned back on her elbows. Matt had to stifle a groan. Heaven help him. Did she have any idea how sexy and desirable she looked, stretched out like that, wearing nothing but that skimpy bathing suit? All right, as bikinis went, hers was modest, but her womanly curves were delicious enough to tempt a saint.

"My, you're just full of questions today, aren't you? Actually, Tom and I did try to start a family. When we had no luck, we had some testing done and discovered that his sperm count was extremely low. We were about to undergo in vitro, but before we could arrange it, he was killed."

"I'm sorry."

Maude Ann lay down all the way on her back. Knowing he shouldn't, but unable to resist, Matt stretched out on his side next to her and propped his head on his hand. This close he could smell her womanly scent, feel her body heat.

"That's all right. It's been two years now, and I've come to terms with losing him, and with knowing I'll never have babies of my own."

"It's not too late. You should marry again."

She chuckled. "Now you sound like Jane."

"I'm serious, Maude Ann." He reached out and ran a fingertip along her jaw. He felt a tiny jolt of electricity race up his arm from the point of contact, and he knew from her start that she had felt it, too.

Her eyes widened. She lay perfectly still, staring at him. The air between was suddenly heavy, charged with sizzling awareness, with need. Matt could barely breathe, and the rapid rise and fall of her chest revealed that she had the same problem.

"You're a beautiful, desirable and vibrant woman, Maude Ann," he whispered. "It would be criminal for you to spend your life alone."

"W-would it?" She swallowed hard.

Smiling, he slid his finger down her elegant neck and she shivered. The tiny reaction sent his blood racing through his veins to settle in a hot pool in his loins.

He gritted his teeth and cursed himself for a fool. If he

had an ounce of sense he would back off now, pretend he'd felt nothing. It was the prudent thing to do.

His gaze trailed down her face and fixed on her mouth, and his eyes narrowed into slits. Aw, hell. Prudent be damned. If he didn't taste that luscious mouth soon he was going to explode.

His fingers curved around her neck. She stared up at him. At the base of her throat a pulse beat rapidly. He felt her breath feather across his jaw in erratic little puffs.

"Maudie," he whispered, leaning closer, and her eyelids fluttered shut as he lowered his head toward hers.

A bloodcurdling yell rent the air a fraction of a second before his lips touched hers. Matt's head jerked up. "What the hell?"

"Run! Run!" Marshall burst out of the woods first, carrying Timothy over his shoulder like a sack of feed. Hot on his heels, their eyes big as saucers, came Tyrone and Dennis, racing for the water.

"Run! He's right behind us!" Tyrone yelled.

"Who is right—" Matt never got a chance to finish the question, for at that moment, a wild pig came charging out of the woods with blood in his eyes.

"Ah, jeez! They've flushed out a pineywood rooter." Matt sprang to his feet and jerked Maude Ann up. "C'mon! We gotta grab the girls!"

Maude Ann took one look at the snorting animal with the lethal-looking tusks, let out a yelp and did as she was told.

The boys pounded past them, hit the water at full speed and kept going, sending up a tremendous spray. Instantly the pig changed targets and came after Matt and Maude Ann.

Sure he could feel the creature's hot breath on the back

of his legs, Matt turned on more steam, dragging Maude
Ann along with him.

Without breaking stride, they swooped the girls up and
bolted into the lake, Matt with Yolanda under one arm and
Jennifer under the other, Maude Ann clutching Debbie.
They didn't stop until they caught up with the boys, who
had barreled out to the five-foot depth before they realized
that their pursuer hadn't followed.

Treading water, they all stared back at the beach, where
the wild pig trotted up and down along the water's edge,
snorting and pawing and eyeing them with feral hatred.
Unable to reach them, the animal turned and vented his
fury on their belongings.'

Maude Ann, Matt and all the children watched with their
mouths agape as the animal butted the picnic basket and
sent it sailing out into the lake, then savaged the blanket
with his tusks.

As quickly as he had erupted from the woods, the pig
ran back into them and disappeared.

A stunned silence stretched out, the only sounds the gentle lapping of water.

"Man, that was one mad pig," Tyrone finally muttered
in an awestruck voice.

Matt's gaze met Maude Ann's. After a moment his
mouth twitched. So did Maude Ann's. Unable to hold back
any longer, they both burst out laughing.

"What's so funny?" Tyrone demanded, scowling at
them. "We was nearly killed by that pig."

"Yeah, that's not funny," Dennis complained, and several of the others chimed in their agreement.

Matt and Maude Ann laughed so hard they had to lean
on each other for support, and it was minutes before either
could answer.

Still chuckling, Matt shook his head and gripped the

boy's shoulder, but his eyes twinkled at Maude Ann. "You're gonna have to take my word for it, kid. That was funny."

The outing in the cove marked a change in Matt's attitude toward the children and in his relationship with Maude Ann.

After that day, he continued to help with the children, accepting without question his daily participation in their activities, just as though that was his purpose in being there.

If Maude Ann took the kids berry picking or for a walk through the woods, Matt went along. He taught them to play catch with both a softball and a football, took them fishing on the pier, nailed a hoop on the side of the garage and taught them, girls and boys alike, the finer points of basketball. When they played, it was all the kids against Matt, and it usually turned into a squealing, shouting free-for-all.

He helped out in the garden and around the house. In the evening after dinner he began joining them in the living room, and he participated in board games or whatever else was going on.

The children loved having Matt around—having both of them around. Maude Ann knew that she and Matt had somehow become surrogate parents, the kind every last one of these kids had probably always wished for but never had. That was the only thing about Matt's participation in their lives that worried her. How, she wondered, would they would react to his departure?

There was no question that he would be leaving soon, probably in a couple of months, maybe less. His chances of returning to active duty were looking brighter all the time, as daily he grew stronger and his limp had all but disappeared.

In those quiet moments late at night, Maude Ann admitted to herself that she loved having Matt around as much as the children did. Foolish and self-destructive as it was, she knew that day by day she was slowly losing her heart to the man, but there didn't seem to be a thing she could do to stop it.

All she could do was make sure Matt didn't know. If now and then, when they accidentally touched or their eyes met for a few seconds too long and that spark jumped between them, well, so be it. She would keep a tight hold on her wayward emotions and savor their summer of friendship. If there was heartache in her future, she would deal with it when it came.

The call from J. T. Conway came late one afternoon, nine days after their lunch together. Matt and Tyrone were out rowing on the lake somewhere. The weather was unbearably hot, and as a result, the children were cranky and listless, and Maude Ann had spent most of the day breaking up squabbles. She had been about to take the kids to the creek for a swim to cool off when the telephone rang.

She had expected to hear from J.T. sooner, but she suspected he had deliberately made her wait. Maude Ann didn't care. As long as she got what she wanted.

"It went pretty much as I thought it would," J.T. told her. "My boss doesn't like it, but he's willing to accept your first three conditions. However, he won't budge on the prepublication approval. I'm sorry, Maude Ann."

No, you're not, she thought, chuckling to herself. There wasn't a reporter in the entire country who would allow an outsider carte blanche to censor his work. "I see," she said doubtfully, and immediately J.T. rushed on.

"But you have my word, Maude Ann, that I'll write an

upbeat story. One that will have people begging you to take their money, I swear it.''

''Thank you, J.T. Uh...you and your boss *did* sign the contract I gave you, didn't you?''

''Yes. I was hoping I could bring it out today.''

''That would be fine.''

When she'd given him the directions, J.T. went on in a casual tone, ''I was thinking I could come out around five and you could show me around the place, let me get acquainted with the kids, that sort of thing. Then afterward, maybe I could take you out to dinner.''

''Oh, J.T., I'm not sure that's—''

''I thought you could fill me in on some background stuff,'' he went on quickly before she could refuse. ''You could even help me decide what angle to take with the story.''

''I see.'' Maude Ann doubted that was his main reason for wanting to take her to dinner, but the chance to perhaps influence the direction his story would take was too tempting to pass up. Besides, an evening out with an attractive man might help her current predicament. If she was ever going to get over Matt, she might as well start now before her heart was completely lost. And what better person to help her than J. T. Conway? He was an intelligent, charming and witty companion. And he was handsome, to boot.

''All right. If you get here by five that should allow plenty of time for me to introduce you to the children and show you around before we leave for dinner.''

Matt's back and shoulder muscles were screaming as he rowed the last few feet to the pier. When the skiff bumped the piling, he pulled in the oars and secured them, then stood up, rolling his shoulders and flexing his back muscles while Tyrone threw a mooring line around the piling.

"You did real good today. We musta rowed ten miles!" the boy exclaimed, flashing Matt a wide grin. "Man, we was flying across that water like we was a rocket."

"What's this 'we' stuff, punk?" Matt asked. He shot the boy a teasing look and rotated his shoulders one last time. "I didn't see any oars in your hands."

"Hey, man, I was helpin'." Tyrone lifted his chin at a cocky angle and thumbed his chest. "I'm your trainer, remember. Anyway, I was ballast. Without me to balance the boat, you'd'a never made it that fast."

"Izzat so? That's big talk for a pipsqueak."

"A pip what? Whazzat mean?" Tyrone scowled. "Is you bad-mouthing me, pig?"

Matt laughed and put his hand on the boy's shoulder to guide him up the path to the lodge. "Don't get your shorts in a wad, punk. I was just jerking your chain. C'mon, let's get a move on. Jane'll have dinner ready soon and I'm starving."

They kept up a steady stream of teasing insults as they walked along the path. When they emerged from the woods and Matt saw the strange car parked in front of the lodge, he felt a stab of annoyance. Who the devil...?

"Looks like Miz Maudie's got company," Tyrone remarked.

"Yeah." Matt frowned, trying to place where he'd seen that car before.

Just as he and Tyrone approached the front steps, the door opened and Maude Ann stepped out onto the veranda. The first thing Matt noticed was that she was wearing a dress and high heels. Then his gaze fell on the man who followed her.

Matt jerked to a halt, fury turning his face hard as granite. "What the hell are you doing here, Conway?"

Chapter Nine

"Well, well, well. If it isn't our wounded warrior. How's it going, Detective? Long time, no see."

"Not long enough."

"Matt!" Maude Ann exclaimed.

He ignored her. "Who told you I was recuperating here, Conway?"

"You're kidding me. This is where you've been all this time? No wonder I couldn't find you."

"Knock it off, Conway. I don't buy that innocent act. I want the name of the person who told you where I was."

Alert to the discord between the two men, Tyrone stood by Matt's side, avidly taking it all in, his sharp gaze skittering back and forth between them.

Farther down the porch, the girls sat in a circle, playing a game of jacks. They barely glanced the men's way.

J.T. met Matt's hostility with his usual lazy grin. "No, really, no one told me a thing. Not that I didn't ask, mind you. But your buddies down at the precinct either didn't know where you'd disappeared to, or they just weren't telling, and no one else had a clue. I've been beatin' the bushes all around Houston trying to find you. I was beginning to think you'd fallen off the earth.''

"If no one told you, how did you find out I was here?''

J.T. chuckled. "I didn't. This is just pure dumb luck. I'm here to do a story on Henley Haven.''

Matt turned his furious gaze on Maude Ann. "You've agreed to meet with this jerk?''

"Hey! I resent that,'' J.T. protested, but the amused smile still lingered around his mouth.

Before Maude Ann could answer, a look of sudden understanding flashed over Matt's face. His eyes narrowed. "That's where you went a couple of weeks ago, wasn't it? That so-called business you had in Houston was a lunch date with Conway, wasn't it?''

Maude Ann blinked at him, dumbfounded. He made it sound like an accusation. "Yes, it was. Although I don't see why you're so upset about it. Mr. Conway had contacted me about possibly doing a story on Henley Haven for the Sunday supplement. I met him in Houston and we discussed the matter.''

"And I suppose you're going to let him do the article?''

"Yes. Yes, I am. It will be good publicity. The exposure could help raise money for the home.''

"Dammit, you might have had the decency to discuss it with me before you gave him the go ahead.''

"Why should she consult with you?''

Matt stabbed his finger in J.T. direction. "You stay out of this, Conway. I'm talking to Maude Ann.''

The harshness of his voice drew the attention of the girls. Their jacks game forgotten, they stared with wide-eyed apprehension at the three grown-ups.

Not Tyrone. He seemed to find the hostile exchange exciting. His gaze flashed to J.T., eager for the next volley.

Noticing the children's reactions, Maude Ann winced. Learning the reason for the confrontation no longer mattered. She had to put a stop to it before the children became more upset.

J.T.'s good-natured smile vanished. "Listen, Dolan, I've had about enough of your attitude. I don't want to tangle with an injured man, but…"

Bristling, Matt started up the steps. "Don't let that stop you. On my worse day I can handle you, Conway."

"Aw *right!*" Tyrone cheered. "Git 'im, Dolan! Punch his lights out!"

"That's it." J.T. braced as Matt gained the porch, but before either man could take a swing, Maude Ann stepped between them and put a hand flat against each chest to keep them apart.

"Stop it! Just stop it right now!"

"Get out of the way, Maude Ann."

"Listen to the man, Doc. This is between Matt and me."

Over the top of her head the two men's gazes clashed.

"No! I most certainly will not! How dare you behave like this in front of these children," she all but hissed. "Haven't they been through enough without witnessing such a disgraceful exhibition? Look at them. Just *look* at them. You're frightening them."

Instantly Matt and J.T.'s gazes shot down the veranda to the girls' stricken faces. Against her palms, Maude Ann felt a slight easing of tension in both men's bodies.

"Ah, damn," Matt spat. Taking a step back, he stood at the veranda railing with his shoulders taut, his fists clenched at his sides.

J.T. tried to mumble an apology, but Maude Ann cut him off with a sharp look and a curt, "I don't want to hear it.

Not another word out of either of you. Not until the children are inside.''

"Shoot! Whadja go'n stop 'em for?" Tyrone grumbled.

"And that's quite enough out of you, too, young man. You go inside and wash up for dinner."

"Aw, Miz Maudie—"

"Now."

Maude Ann was normally the most easygoing of women, but when she used that tone, not even Tyrone dared to argue. Grumbling, the boy ducked his head and started for the door.

She turned to the girls with as pleasant an expression as she could muster. "Girls, it's time to wash up for dinner."

Unlike Tyrone, they scrambled to obey, gathering up their jacks and ball and scurrying inside.

As soon as Maude Ann was certain they were out of earshot, she turned to the two men.

"It's obvious that you two know each other and there's no love lost between you, but that's no excuse for that childish display you just put on. I want an explanation, and I want it right now, so one of you had better start talking."

"Matt has a problem with reporters," J.T. volunteered. Good humor returning, he aimed a cocky grin Matt's way.

Matt's gaze still burned with anger. "Not all reporters. Just pests like you." He turned to Maude Ann. "Whenever a crime occurs, he barges in, interfering with police investigations, harassing victims for comments at inappropriate times, digging up confidential information any way he can and publishing it with no regard to how he's jeopardizing our case."

"Hey. Ever heard of freedom of the press?"

"Ever heard of the right to privacy?" Matt shot back. His gaze sought Maude Ann again. "When I took a bullet, this guy practically beat me to the hospital. No sooner had

I woken up from surgery than he started trying to worm a story out of me about the drug bust.''

J.T. spread his hands wide. "Hey, I'm just doing my job.''

"Yeah, well, you've got a lousy job, Conway. And I'm warning you, if you so much as mention my name in your article, I'll make you wish you'd never heard of Henley Haven.''

His angry gaze switched to Maude Ann. "I came here for privacy and to get away from people like him. It's bad enough that you've destroyed that by bringing a reporter here, but exploiting these kids for money is low. And to think I believed you when you said you wanted to protect them. Nice going, Dr. Edwards.''

"Matt, you don't under— Matt, wait!'' She stepped forward, reaching out to him, but he ignored her and stalked into the house. Maude Ann flinched as the door slammed behind him.

"Oh, dear.''

"Ah, don't worry. I've known Matt for over ten years. Believe me, his bark is worse than his bite. He didn't mean that stuff about the kids—he's just ticked off. When he cools down he'll probably apologize.'' J.T. paused. "Of course, he'll get angry all over again when the article comes out, but don't worry, he won't kill me.''

Her head snapped around. "What do you mean? You're not going to mention him in the article after what he just said, are you?''

"Sure I am.''

"But why? Do you hate him that much?''

J.T. looked shocked. "I don't hate him at all. To tell the truth, I kinda like the guy. Don't ask me why. He's hard-nosed and crusty as hell, and he sure isn't fond of me or my profession. Still, I can't help but admire him. Go figure.''

"If you feel that way, then why are you going to write about him when you know he'll hate it?"

A wicked twinkle entered J.T.'s eyes. His slow grin was pure devilment. "Partly because I enjoy rattling his cage."

"J. T. Conway, that's terrible."

"Yeah, I know," he replied, not in the least repentant. "Anyway, liking the guy is one thing, business is something else. It'll make a great hook for the piece. You know, a headline like, 'Wounded officer finds healing peace at Henley Haven.'''

"I won't let you do that."

"Now look—"

"You signed a contract, and I'm going to hold you to it."

"C'mon, doc, that agreement was for the kids' protection."

"It states that you will not mention the name of any resident of Henley Haven. Matt lives here. That makes him a resident. So help me, J.T., if you print his name or even allude to his presence here, I'll slap you with a lawsuit."

He gaped at her. "This is crazy. It's not as though I'm going to malign him. Matt's a hero. A fallen member of the thin blue line. That makes him newsworthy. Besides, the readers want to know how he's recovering."

"That doesn't mean he has to satisfy their curiosity—or sell newspapers for your boss. Matt, like everyone else, has a right to privacy. And you will respect that right. Do I make myself clear?"

J.T. shook his head slowly, a look of amazement on his face. "Like crystal. Jeez, lady, you are one tough negotiator."

He glanced at the door through which Matt had stormed

moments before, then looked back at Maude Ann with a speculative gleam in his eye. "Am I missing something here? Do you and Matt have a thing going? Is that why you're protecting him?"

"No, of course not!" she snapped quickly—a bit too quickly, judging from the way J.T.'s eyebrows shot skyward. "I simply think that in this case he's right and you're wrong."

He grinned and gave her face another quick study. "Whatever you say. Now, shall we go?"

"You still want to take me to dinner?"

J.T. grasped her arm and led her down the steps and along the gravel walkway toward his Jeep Cherokee. "You bet. Now more than ever. I like a woman who sticks up for her man."

"*What?* J.T., I just told you, there is nothing going on between Matt and me. We're just friends, that's all."

"Okay. If you say so."

"No, really. It's true."

She continued to protest all the way to the restaurant, which was near the yacht club, several miles down shore from the lodge. She might as well have saved her breath.

Each time J.T. responded with "Uh-huh," but the wicked twinkle in his eyes said he didn't believe her. By the time their dinner arrived Maude Ann was so frustrated she gave up and changed the subject.

After a while, once she had dismissed the matter from her mind and relaxed, she began to enjoy herself. Though J.T. was an outrageous flirt and a tease and didn't seem to take anything seriously, he was also handsome, charming, witty and intelligent, all of which made him a thoroughly delightful companion.

After she had answered his questions about Henley Haven and told him all her plans and hopes for the foster home, their conversation turned to other things. J.T. was a master at wheedling information from people, and before she knew it she was telling him about her college and med school years and what a struggle it had been. She told him about going to work after graduation for the Houston Police Department, and how she had met Tom there and married him, and about the pain of losing him. J.T. listened attentively and sympathetically. It turned out that he had met Tom a few times but hadn't known him well.

"So, you've known Matt for years, then?" he asked.

"Yes. Though, until he came to the haven to recuperate, I never really got to know him well."

"I'll bet." J.T. chuckled and shook his head. "He's as honest as they come and a damned good cop, but he's not exactly the most outgoing guy around."

He tipped his head to one side and studied her. "I can't imagine you working in that environment. You don't seem the type. You're too...too open. Your emotions are too unprotected. My guess is the brutality and senselessness of violent crime would tear you up inside."

"You're right. It did. When my husband was killed, I couldn't take any more. That's when I decided I would put my training and energies to use helping victims of crime. The most vulnerable are innocent children. After investigating the foster system, I realized that I could help abused and abandoned children, not just physically, but emotionally and mentally, as well. So I started Henley Haven."

"Mmm. Lucky for those kids you did. You're really great with them."

"Thanks."

J.T. had a store of fascinating tales and anecdotes, most connected with his work, which kept her laughing. Maude Ann enjoyed the tales, but she noticed that none of them revealed anything personal about him. Whenever she tried to steer the conversation in that direction, he deftly sidestepped and changed the subject. Finally her only recourse was to come right out and ask.

"I've been boring you all evening with my life story. Why don't we talk about you for a change?"

"There's not much to tell." He smiled the same charming smile he'd been giving her all evening, but she noticed the discomfort in his eyes.

"Oh, I'm sure there is. Why don't we start with where you were born?"

"Right here in Houston."

"You've lived here all your life?"

"Yep. Except for four years in Austin when I was going to U.T. But look, Doc, you don't want to hear this. It's really boring stuff."

"Why don't you let me be the judge of that? So, when did you decide you wanted to be a reporter?"

"I didn't." He gave a lame chuckle at her look of surprise. Then, for the first time that evening, his face sobered. "Actually, my dream was to become a novelist. I was sure I was going to write the great American novel. The only reason I took journalism in college was to help me hone my writing skills."

"That sounds reasonable. Did you ever write your book?"

"Naw. I started it, but I didn't get very far."

"Why not?"

"Well, for one thing, when I graduated from U.T., reality set in and I realized that I had to earn a living. I couldn't expect my parents to support me while I wrote. They were middle-aged when they adopted me, and by then they were ready for retirement."

"So after college you got a job with a newspaper."

"Yeah. But I had a plan. I was going to live frugally and save all I could. When I had enough put by to last a couple of years, I was going to quit the paper and work on my book full-time."

"And did you? Save your money, that is?"

"Oh, yeah. I have a tidy nest egg put aside. If I was careful, I could probably live on it for eight or ten years."

"Then why are you still working as a reporter?"

A rueful smile twisted his mouth. "The usual reasons. You get in a rut. The familiar is comfortable and safe. It's difficult to give up a steady paycheck. I've put in twelve years on this job. Made a name for myself, so why throw it away—that sort of thing."

"Mmm."

He frowned. "What does that mean?"

"Nothing. Just mmm."

"Dammit! I'm thirty-four years old. It's too late to make a major life change."

"Is it? People have done it in their forties and fifties. Even their sixties and seventies."

"I have a good job that provides me with a comfortable life style. I would have to be an idiot to give that up for a pipe dream."

Maude Ann spread her hands wide and gave him an innocent look. "Did I suggest that you do so?"

"You were thinking it."

"Not really." She let that soak in, then added softly, "But apparently you were."

He scowled at her across the table for a long time. Then his good humor resurfaced, and he chuckled and shook his head. "Damn, you're good, lady."

It was after ten when J.T. brought her home. When he switched off the engine, he turned partway and laid his arm across the back of her seat. "I'm glad you said yes to dinner. I enjoyed tonight."

"So did I."

The interior of the car was lit only by the yellow glow of the porch light. Above the dark shapes of the trees, lightning lit the night sky in the distance.

"Storm's coming," J.T. murmured as they watched the flickering display. The faint rumble of thunder followed moments later.

"Yes." Maude Ann felt his fingers toying with the ends of her hair. Her nerves skittered. For something to do, she pushed the button and lowered the passenger window.

The wind had kicked up, and the smell of approaching rain hung in the air. Abruptly, the whir of the cicadas ceased, and the only sounds were the whispery soughing of the wind through the pines and the faint slap of waves against the shore. When she turned her head, her gaze met J.T.'s.

"You're pretty special, Maude Ann," he murmured.

Gazing back at him, she didn't move or say a word. J.T. smiled softly and his lips settled over hers.

That he was experienced with women was evident by his easy confidence and expertise, his finesse.

The kiss was exquisitely tender, as though he was taking great care not to rush or frighten her. It was actually quite pleasant, but to her disappointment, it aroused in her none of the heart-pounding, head-spinning passion for which she had hoped. The kind Matt's kiss never failed to produce.

When J.T. sought to deepen the kiss, she leaned in and pressed closer, desperate to light a spark between them, but it was no use.

Maude Ann could have wept.

She had hoped that her reaction to Matt's kisses had been

merely the result of prolonged celibacy. How much easier her life would be if she could fall for a man like J.T.

When he broke off the kiss, he drew back and looked at her with a rueful smile. "It's just not happening for us, is it?"

"Oh, J.T., I'm so sorry, I—"

"Shh. There's no need to apologize. There's nothing anybody can do about chemistry. It's either there or it's not. Although…in this case, I think Matt's the biggest obstacle."

"J.T.," she groaned, "I've told you—"

"I know what you told me, Doc. But take it from me, you can't lie worth spit. Anyway, I've seen how you look at Matt."

"*Whaaat?*" she said on a rising note of horror, staring at him.

"Oh, don't worry. I doubt that Matt's noticed. He's not as observant as I am when it comes to women." He grinned at her stricken expression. "C'mon, Doc. Admit it. You've got the hots for Matt, don't you?"

Maude Ann shot him a quelling look, but his grin merely widened. Finally she gave up and slumped back in the seat, sighing. "Oh, all right, so I'm attracted to Matt. So what. Nothing can ever come of it, so what's the point of this discussion?"

"Why not? I can't imagine that Matt isn't just as attracted to you. He'd have to be stupid not to be."

"For one thing, I don't want to get involved with another law officer."

"Okay. I can understand how you feel, but you must know we don't always get to choose who we fall in love with."

"I know," she replied in a small, dejected voice. "But

even if I could live with his job, Matt just isn't the marrying kind.''

"You sure about that?"

"He's thirty-four years old and never been married."

"So am I, but I haven't ruled it out."

"Back when we worked out of the same precinct, I heard him say many times that he wanted no part of marriage. And his actions bore that out. He dated a lot of women, but none seriously."

"That's what men do, until the right woman comes along. Maybe all he needs is a prod in the right direction. I could—"

She put her fingers over his mouth to hush him. "No. I don't want you to do anything. Matt will go back to Houston soon and I'll get over him. I have the children and my work with them. That'll be enough." She sighed and looked at J.T. wistfully. "I wish it could have been you. I really do."

Grasping her wrist, he pressed a kiss against her fingers, then removed her hand. "So do I."

When his gaze lifted to her eyes again, there was regret and a touch of sadness, but in a blink it was gone, replaced by his usual teasing twinkle.

"But hey, just because it's not in the cards for us to be lovers doesn't mean we can't be friends." He gave her chin a playful cuff, his eyes crinkling at her through the dim light. "I like you, Doc. And I like what you're doing for these kids. If you have no objection to me hanging around, I wouldn't mind dropping by now and then, maybe give you a hand entertaining the little munchkins."

Relief and gratitude filled her. Maude Ann smiled, more sorry than ever that she could not lose her heart to this man. "I'd like that. I'd like that a lot."

"Good." His slow grin was a slash of white in the dim interior of the car. "It'll drive Matt nuts."

"J.T.! That's terrible," she scolded, but she couldn't help but laugh at the devilment dancing in his eyes.

"I know, but it's so darn much fun to rattle his cage now and then. Now c'mon. I'll walk you to the door."

"No, don't get out," she said, stopping him when he reached for the door handle. Before he could insist, she thanked him for the evening, gave him a quick kiss on the cheek and climbed out of the car. At the door she waved as he drove away, then turned back and fitted her key into the lock.

"Did you enjoy your date?"

Maude Ann shrieked and spun around. Her heart nearly leapt right into her throat as a man emerged from the dark shadows at the end of the veranda.

Her relief as he entered the circle of yellow light was so great her knees threatened to give way beneath her.

Sagging back against the door, she put her hand over her booming heart and closed her eyes momentarily.

"Matt, for heaven's sake! You nearly scared me to death! What were you doing, sitting out here in the dark at this time of night?"

"Enjoying the cool of the evening. You see some interesting things at night. You didn't answer me. Did you have a good time?"

"As a matter of fact, I did."

"Yes, I thought so. You sure seemed to enjoy his kiss."

She sucked in her breath. "You were *spying* on me?"

Her outrage didn't touch him. He came to a stop in front of her. His blue eyes glittered like two chips of ice. "Tell me, did you get all hot and bothered and melt against him the way you melt against me when I kiss you?"

"Stop it, Matt. You're being insulting. I know you're

still angry with me for letting J.T. write that article, but I don't deserve this.''

"Don't you? The way you go from one man to another, I'd say you deserve worse.''

She gasped. "That's it. I don't have to stand here and take this.'' She spun around, flung the door opened and hurried inside.

Matt stormed after her. Catching up with her halfway across the foyer, he grabbed her arm and spun her back to face him. "Dammit, answer me.''

"This is ridiculous. You said you wanted us to be friends, but you're acting like a jealous lover. What is *wrong* with you?''

His face was tight and he was breathing hard. She saw his jaw clench, his nostrils flare and quiver. His gaze dropped to her mouth and he ground out, "Dammit, why did you let him kiss you?''

Maude Ann was suddenly as furious as he was. She jerked her arm free and glared right back at him. "Why? I'll tell you why. Because I'm in love with you and I don't want to be. I was hoping J.T.'s kiss would snap me out of it!''

Matt flinched as though she had struck him. Shock drained every vestige of anger from his face. For a full ten seconds, he stared at her with his mouth agape.

The instant the words were out, Maude Ann could have kicked herself, but she couldn't take them back. All she could do was hold her head up and brazen her way through the next few humiliating moments.

Matt's stunned stare never left her. After what seemed like forever he whispered, "Did it?''

Maude Ann's anger evaporated as quickly as it had come. She huffed out a long sigh, her shoulders sagging. She shook her head and looked at him sadly. "No,'' she whispered back.

Chapter Ten

Matt couldn't move. He'd never experienced so many conflicting emotions at one time. They swirled and buzzed inside his chest like a swarm of angry bees.

Maude Ann loved him.

Joy shot through him like a rush of adrenaline.

Fury followed.

Then came fear, longing, confusion, hope—and the most searing happiness he'd ever known.

This last brought fury rushing back.

No! No, dammit! This wasn't right. He hadn't asked for this.

But Maude Ann loved him.

The thought made his heart hammer, his throat tighten. His first instinct was to put his arms around her and never let go, but conflicting emotions and ingrained caution held him back, and in the end he waited too long. He saw the flash of despair and humiliation in her eyes an instant before her chin came up.

"I...that is—"

"No. It's all right, Matt. You don't have to say anything. I know this isn't what you bargained for when you came here. I also know how you feel about serious relationships. You've always been quite open about that."

"Maude Ann—"

"No, please. Don't worry about it. This isn't your problem, it's mine. I'm a grown woman, and I'm responsible for my own actions and emotions, not you. Don't worry, I'll work through this. Life goes on no matter what. Soon you'll go back to Houston, and I'll stay here and continue my work with the kids. I'll be okay. Maybe not right away, but eventually I will be. Really."

"But—"

An ear-piercing scream cut him off.

"What the hell?"

"Debbie!" Maude Ann cried.

She took off before the name left her lips, pounding up the stairs at top speed.

Matt followed as fast as he could. The child's shrill screams continued unabated. By the time he gained the upstairs hall, they had reached a hysterical pitch and ran together into the most chilling sound he had ever heard. At the very least, he thought someone was trying to murder her.

He skidded to a stop at the open door of the bedroom that Debbie and Jennifer shared just as Maude Ann scooped the shrieking child up into her arms.

At first Debbie was as rigid as a post, pushing against the arms that held her, but after a few seconds Maude Ann's gentle voice got through to the child. Debbie's little arms clamped around Maude Ann's neck in a stranglehold, but her cries continued, only fractionally quieter now.

"Shh, sweetie. Shh. It's all right. Maudie's here," she crooned, holding the child close. "I've got you now. You're safe. Nothing's going to hurt you, baby."

Sinking onto the edge of the bed, Maude Ann rocked the child back and forth, murmuring a steady stream of encouragement and endearments. "It's okay, baby. It's okay, little love. Everything is going to be all right."

Matt sat down on the bed beside them. Concern wiped every other thought from his mind. He had never seen a child so upset. Debbie's tear-streaked face was the color of a beet and hideously contorted. She kept her eyes squeezed shut, and her tiny body shook from head to toe. She seemed caught in some terrible hysteria, oblivious to everything and everyone except the safe harbor of Maude Ann's arms. Wailing every breath, the little girl burrowed against her as though trying to climb right inside her skin.

Across the room in the other bed, Jennifer slept on without so much as a twitch. Matt looked at Maude Ann and tipped his head toward the other child. "How does she sleep through this racket?" he mouthed.

"Children can sleep through any noise," Maude Ann mouthed back.

Raising his voice to be heard over the incessant wails, Matt looked at Debbie again and asked, "What's wrong with her?"

"Nightmare. There, there. C'mon, sweetheart. You're okay. Maudie won't let anything hurt you."

Leaning her cheek against the top of Debbie's head, she continued to rock the little girl, stroking her back over and over in a continuous, soothing motion. Maude Ann's gaze met Matt's. "When Debbie first came here, she had night-

mares every night, but as she came to feel safe, they gradually stopped. It's been months since she's had one."

Matt frowned. "I wonder what brought them back."

"I suspect the argument we had earlier. Raised voices
frighten her. It probably caused some horrible, deeply buried memory to resurface."

Stricken, Matt stared at her, then the child. "Ah, hell."
Feeling like the lowest form of life, he reached out and
stroked the little girl's arm. "Hey, Debbie, don't cry,
sweetie. You're gonna make yourself sick, carrying on that
way. C'mon, honey."

Gradually the little girl's wails diminished to choppy
sobs, then little hitching breaths, muffled against Maude
Ann's shoulder, but she didn't move or acknowledge his
presence in any other way.

"Look, sweetie," Maude Ann murmured. "Matt's here.
He's worried about you. Don't you want to talk to him?"

Debbie turned her head just slightly and slanted an accusing peek at him out of one eye. "N-no," she said. "M-
Matt's mean. He y-yelled at you."

"Oh, I don't think he meant it, did you, Matt?"

"No! No, I was just letting off a little steam. That's all.
I swear it. And I'm real sorry about it, too. I shouldn't have
yelled that way."

"See there. What'd I tell you?"

Knuckling her eyes and wet cheeks, Debbie sat up and
eyed Matt with sulky suspicion.

"C'mon, pumpkin, don't you know I'd never hurt Miss
Maudie? Or you? Or any of the kids? Never in a million
years. And I'd throttle anyone else who tried."

"Promith?"

"Cross my heart and hope to die," he said, making an
X sign across his chest. He held out his arms to her. "Now,
how about giving me a hug?"

It was all the invitation Debbie needed. She lunged into Matt's waiting arms and clutched his neck so tightly that he laughed and pretended to choke. "Hey, take it easy, kid. You're strangling me."

Watching them, Maude Ann looked close to tears herself.

The child leaned back and looked him in the eyes, her small blotchy face serious as a judge's. "You're not mad at Mith Maudie anymore?"

"No, I'm not mad at Miss Maudie." His hand looked dark and huge against her face as he tenderly wiped away her tears. When he was done, he placed a soft kiss on her little rosebud mouth, pulled back and smiled.

She beamed. "Good. I don't wants you to be mad at Mith Maudie. I wuv her. An' I wuv you."

Matt's gaze darted to Maude Ann. He could see in her eyes she was remembering, as he was, that she had made the same declaration to him just minutes before.

Matt smiled at Debbie and tucked a blond curl behind her ear. "I love you, too, kiddo."

He was rewarded with another choking hug. When she released him, she said innocently, "Now give Mith Maudie a kith, too."

"Uh…"

"You gots to. So she won't think you ith still mad at her."

"Uh, sweetie, Matt doesn't have to do that. Really. I know he's not mad at me anymore."

Debbie's chin wobbled and her tears threatened to return. "But he gots to," she wailed. "Thath the way you're th'poth to 'pologize."

"Okay, okay. I'll do it. Don't get upset," Matt pleaded. He couldn't take another round of crying.

Mollified, Debbie sniffed and gave him a watery grin,

well pleased with herself, then settled back in his arms to watch.

Matt's gaze met Maude Ann's. In her eyes he saw the same turmoil of doubt and longing that he was feeling. The air between them seemed suddenly thick, making breathing difficult. Outside the storm broke with a clap of thunder that made Debbie jump, and rain began pelting the metal roof like a crazed drummer. The sounds barely registered on the two adults.

As Matt leaned toward Maude Ann, his heart thudded with a slow rhythm that was almost painful. His gaze dropped to her lush mouth. It quivered ever so slightly, and her eyes fluttered shut. His heart picked up speed, chugging like a steam locomotive leaving the station, as he touched his mouth to hers.

It was the most delicate of caresses, the slow, soft press of warm lips, a gossamer exchange of breath, a subtle taste, nothing more, but it brought a rush of sensations so exquisite they were nearly unbearable. His chest ached and his heart pounded so hard it almost suffocated him.

Debbie clapped her hands, giggling, bringing Matt back to reality with a jolt. When he broke off the kiss, she beamed at both of them.

As kisses went, that one had been as pure and chaste as the driven snow, yet it had packed a punch that left Matt shaken.

The confusion in Maude Ann's eyes told him he was not the only one affected.

He watched her blink several times, then straighten her spine and shake off the miasma of feelings, but when she reached for the child, her hands trembled. "Okay, little one, it's time for you to go back to sleep."

Instantly, Debbie's pallor returned and terror filled her eyes. She clutched Maude Ann's neck in a death grip. "I don't wanth to go to thleep. The bad man will hurt me again,'' she whimpered, her chin quivering.

"No, he won't. He's all gone now."

"No. No! He'll come back!"

"I don't think so, but tell you what. If it will make you feel safer, you can sleep with me tonight,'' she said before the child could work herself up into another frenzy. "Hmm? How would you like that?"

"Yeth. I wanth to sleep with you.'' The words came out in a rush, muffled as the terrified child clung tight and burrowed her face into Maude Ann's shoulder.

She stood up with the child in her arms, and after checking to be sure Jennifer was okay, she headed for her own room, which, Matt discovered, was the right across the hall. At the door she paused and turned to him, but her gaze didn't quite meet his.

"Thanks for your help."

"Yeah, sure. No problem.'' He cast a worried look at Debbie, who was already falling asleep on Maude Ann's shoulder. Matt smoothed a lock of baby-fine hair off the child's cheek and tucked it behind her ear. "Is she going to be all right?"

"She'll be fine.'' Maude Ann seemed to grow taller as her chin came up and she met his gaze squarely. "We'll both be fine. There's nothing for you to worry about here. Good night, Matt."

He found himself looking at a closed door. He stared at it for several seconds, not certain he liked being dismissed so summarily. His inclination was to knock on her door until she opened it again, only he had no idea what he would say to her when she did. Left with no choice, he went downstairs.

In his room he merely glanced at the bed as he walked

straight through to the outer door and stepped out onto the veranda.

The rain had settled into a steady downpour. It drummed on the roof and gushed through the gutters and out the downspouts at the corners of the veranda. It peppered the lake in an erratic dance. The air was clammy and warm, redolent with the smells of rain and mud and wet pine trees, mingled with the sweet scent of wild honeysuckle.

Leaning forward from the waist and gripping the veranda railing with both hands, Matt braced himself and stared out through the falling rain, unmindful of the splatters that hit his face and upper body.

Maude Ann loved him.

He closed his eyes and tried to sort through the knotted tangle of feelings in his gut.

Not for an instant did he doubt the veracity of her feelings. Maude Ann was the most down-to-earth, most forthright, honest woman he'd ever known. She didn't play games or exaggerate, nor was she likely to mistake infatuation for the real thing. Maude Ann analyzed, weighed, thought things through and came to a logical and honest conclusion. If she said she loved him, then it was true.

He closed his eyes. Oh, God, she loved him.

Did he love Maude Ann? Never before had he allowed himself to even consider that question in regard to any woman, and it unnerved him to do so now, but he had no choice.

Groaning, he pinched the bridge of his nose between his thumb and forefinger. Ah, hell, he didn't know.

He wasn't even sure he knew what love was. He'd wanted a great many women, and he'd made love to his share. A few he'd even been fond of, but there had been no one he could imagine waking up next to every morning for the rest of his life.

He thought about that and frowned. Oddly, he could imagine that with Maude Ann.

Did that mean he loved her?

He wanted her more than he'd ever wanted any other woman. A helluva lot more. Still...there was more to his feelings than merely wanting her. He couldn't deny that.

He enjoyed just spending time with her. Enjoyed her conversation, her company. He loved the way she looked with all that glorious auburn hair rioting around her face and shoulders. For that matter, he liked it just as much up in that girlish ponytail.

Any man with blood in his veins also had to admire the way Maude Ann filled out a pair of shorts and a tank top, and those long, shapely legs and narrow feet. That husky laugh of hers could drive a man crazy with wanting. And Lord, how he loved to watch her move. Maude Ann had a loose-limbed, unselfconscious grace about her that made even the most mundane action seem sexy.

And there was another thing. Never before had he been possessive of a woman, but he hated the thought of J.T., or any man, so much as touching her.

Was that love? Or was he just being territorial?

Impatient, Matt paced to the far corner of the veranda and back. What did it matter anyway? Even if he did love her, that didn't change anything. He still didn't think police work and marriage mixed. He couldn't offer her a future.

Not unless he failed the reentry physical.

The insidious thought sent a chill rippling through him.

No! No, he wouldn't let himself even think that. He was going to pass that physical. Pass, hell, he was going to ace it. He was a law officer. That was what he did. What he was. It was the only thing he'd ever wanted to be. He couldn't imagine a life not on the force. Didn't want to imagine it.

But, you jerk, Maude Ann loves you.

Too restless and torn to remained confined to the veranda, he muttered an oath and loped down the front steps into the rain-swept night.

Before he'd gone a half-dozen paces, he was soaked to the skin, his dark hair plastered to his head and hanging down in his face in strings. He kept going, oblivious to the storm and the chill of the wet clothes clinging to his body, the soggy squish of his athletic shoes.

He stalked down to the lake and stood on the bank in the rain and stared out across the pockmarked water.

Having the love of a woman like Maude Ann was no small thing. He may have dodged the emotion all his adult life, but he knew that much. Maude Ann was special. Unique. Maude Ann was...Maude Ann.

Intelligent, honest, sexy, fiercely loyal, beautiful, down-to-earth—she was a woman of many virtues, not the least of which was her capacity for love.

In his heart, Matt felt incredibly humbled, incredibly blessed and totally undeserving.

He groaned and tipped back his head, letting the rain slap his face. Lord, he didn't want to hurt her.

Maude Ann dumped more ice over the two dozen watermelons cooling in the galvanized washtubs lined up on the side veranda, but her gaze was fixed on Matt. Early that morning, before it had gotten too hot, he'd used the riding mower to cut the weeds in the meadow that separated the lodge from the woods on the west side. Using a bag of ground chalk to mark off a softball diamond, he poured the white powder in long, straight lines on the fresh stubble.

Marshall, Yolanda and Tyrone were supposed to be helping, but mainly they just trailed behind him as if he were the Pied Piper, carrying the square, sand-filled burlap bags she'd sewn for base markers and dropping them where Matt instructed.

Squealing and laughing, the four younger children streaked around the yard and field in a frenzy of excitement at the prospect of visitors and a cookout. Even Jennifer, who was usually so quiet, was racing around with the others.

Matt's laughter rang out. He ruffled Marshall's hair and gave Tyrone's shoulder a playful cuff. Watching him, Maude Ann's eyes narrowed. Never would she have pegged him as the kind to evade a problem or sticky situation. The hardworking detective she remembered from her days with HPD had always been a "take the bull by the horns" type.

To ignore a problem in the hope it would go away seemed to Maude Ann the coward's way, and Matt Dolan had never struck her as a coward. Yet, for the past two weeks, that was exactly what he had been doing—ignoring the problem.

He acted as though that humiliating scene in the front hall had never taken place, as though nothing had changed. In a temper, she had foolishly blurted out the truth and bared her heart to him, but no one would ever know it, the way he acted.

Not once had he tried to discuss the matter, as she had expected. There had been no awkwardness between them, at least not on his part, no polite brush-off, no pitying looks. Nor did he make the slightest effort to avoid her.

He hadn't even had the decency to try to use her love for him to get her into bed!

It would have been easier for her had he reverted to the bad-tempered recluse he had been when he first arrived at the lodge. But oh, no. Matt was relaxed and friendly as could be, damn him. He continued to help out around the place and involve himself with the children just as he'd been doing.

The only time in the past two weeks that he'd made himself scarce was the day J.T. and the photographer spent at the lodge taking pictures for the newspaper article. That, she knew, had nothing to do with her. He simply did not like or trust J.T.

Maude Ann huffed out a dejected sigh, the brief flare of anger fading. It seemed that friendship *was* all Matt had to offer her.

Well, so be it. As she had told him that night, her emotions were her responsibility, not his. She was hurting right now, but she was a strong woman. She would get past this. Eventually.

If Matt didn't want her love, that was his loss. Someday, somewhere, she would find a good, decent man who would.

In the meantime, she had the children.

For today, though, she was grateful she would have the distraction of guests.

Finished with the softball preparations, Matt snagged Jennifer as she darted by, and the usually quiet child shrieked with delight when he swung her high in the air. Immediately Debbie tugged on the leg of his jeans, demanding he swing her, too, and he laughingly obliged. When he was done, he settled the child on his shoulder and headed for the lodge with the other children trotting along beside him.

His limp was barely noticeable now. In another month it would probably be gone.

And so would he.

The thought brought a fresh wave of pain that nearly doubled her over, but she refused to give in to it.

Telling herself she had things to do, Maude Ann turned away and walked around to the back veranda, plumping the cushions on the chairs and lounges as she went. She had only just returned to the front veranda when the caravan of cars came bumping down the rutted road, horns blaring. As they drew nearer, windows came down and several of the men poked their heads out, waving and shouting raucous greetings.

"Whooie, Maudie! Lookin' *good!*"

"Hey, Doc! How's it going?"

"Long time no see, Doc!"

"Yeah! Did ya miss me?"

Maude grinned and waved, the heavy weight around her heart lightening a bit as she went down the steps to greet Lieutenant John Werner and his men.

At the same moment, Matt and the children came around the corner of the lodge. After swinging Debbie to the ground, Matt hooked his thumbs in the front pockets of his jeans and sauntered over to where the cars were pulling up.

"Hey, Matt! You big ugly son of a bi—" Detective Tony Volturo, the squad's twice-divorced Italian lover, glanced at the wide-eyed kids standing in a close huddle by the porch steps, and grimaced. "Uh…son of a gun. How ya doin', buddy?"

Before Matt could answer, his friend snatched him into a bear hug and thumped him soundly on the back. Behind them, the occupants of the other cars tumbled out, calling greetings.

"Pretty fair, all things considered," Matt replied to Tony. "That is, if you don't crush my ribs."

Laughing, Tony gave him one last thump and stepped back, his dark eyes dancing as they ran over Matt in a quick inspection. "I told all these yahoos not to count you out. Man, you're looking great. Just great. This country air must agree with you."

He winked at Maude Ann, who was standing behind

them, a little to one side, and gave Matt a jab in the ribs. "'Course, if you had a lick of sense in that hard Irish head of yours, you wouldn't be in such a hurry to get back in condition. I know I wouldn't be if the doc was nursemaiding me.''

Matt frowned, but Maude Ann laughed. "Still the same incorrigible flirt, I see.''

A come-hither smile split Tony's handsome face. "Ah, Maude Ann. You wound me. Don't you know you're the love of my life? If you'd just run away with me, I'd never look at another woman.''

"Liar.'' Still laughing, she stepped forward with her hands outstretched. He took them, but only to pull her into his arms and plant a thoroughly lascivious kiss on her mouth.

The other detectives gathering around Matt whistled and hooted and let loose with catcalls.

"Here, now! Unhand that woman, you damn pervert, before I call the cops.''

"Uh-oh. Now you've done it, Volturo.''

"Hey, Lieutenant, where're you going? You haven't even said hello to Matt yet.''

Tony broke off the kiss and winked at Maude Ann's astonished face, then aimed an unrepentant grin over his shoulder at John Werner, who was shoving his way through the crowd around Matt.

All around, the others laughed and hooted, and though red with embarrassment, Maude Ann nevertheless joined in.

"To hell with that. I'm not wasting time on that ugly Mick when there's a beautiful woman standing right here. Now get out of the way, you lot, and let me give my goddaughter a hug.''

John grasped Tony's shoulder and spun him around.

"And as for you, Casanova," he snarled into the younger man's face, only half kidding, "back off. Maude Ann is off-limits to the likes of you."

Planting a beefy hand on Tony's chest, John shoved him away, then turned with a beaming smile for Maude Ann, swept her up into his arms and swung her around.

Laughing, she hung on tightly and returned the hug. When at last he set her on her feet, he held on to her shoulders to steady her, using the opportunity to give her a quick once-over. "Girl, you sure are a sight for these tired old eyes. I swear, you get prettier every time I see you."

"Which isn't nearly often enough, but thanks for the compliment."

He gave her a rueful look. "I'm real sorry I haven't been out to see you before this, Maude Ann, but lately down at the station, we've been busier than a one-armed paper-hanger. Between the heat and the full moon, the bad guys are runnin' amuck. Anyway, Matt was so ticked off at me when I sent him here, I figured I'd better stay away till he cooled off some."

"How wise of you," she drawled. "I don't imagine it helped his temper any that you neglected to tell him about me and the kids being here."

John Werner had the grace to look embarrassed. "Sorry about that, Maudie, but I was desperate. That hardhead never would have come if I had. Speaking of the kids, from what I saw when we drove up, he seems to be getting along with them okay."

"Actually, Matt's wonderful with the children. It took him a while to warm up to them, mind you, but once he did, he waded right in. He's been a huge help."

"And how're the two of you getting along?"

"Oh, just fine." Anxious to change the subject, Maude

Ann slipped her arm through John's and urged him toward the others. "Now then, let me go say hello to everyone and then we'll get this party started."

"I sure hope you don't mind us barging in on you like this, but I thought it was time for Matt to touch base with the guys."

She slanted him a wry smile. What John really meant was, he thought it was time to give Matt a nudge and start him thinking about returning to duty soon, but she let it pass.

"Not at all. I was delighted when you called and suggested it. It'll be good for Matt, and it's also important for the kids to be around other people, particularly ones with children of their own, so they can see what a real family is all about. Plus, two of the children are leaving tomorrow to go live with a relative. The other kids are a bit upset about that. The cookout will give the boys a nice send-off and maybe, for a while at least, take the other kids' minds off tomorrow's parting."

John had brought with him four married officers and their wives and children, plus Gus Jankowski and Tony, the single guys in the group, and Tony's son, Vic, from his first marriage. All together, the children numbered eleven, ranging in age from one to thirteen.

The seventh officer, Gloria Davies, was a twice-divorced, stunning brunette with the face of an angel, a salty tongue that put the guys to shame and, if rumor was to be believed, an appetite for hot, no-strings sex.

At the moment Detective Davies had her arms draped around Matt's neck and her sexy body plastered against his.

Although Matt wasn't exactly encouraging her, he didn't look as though he minded. Experiencing a stab of pain so vicious she had to bite her tongue to keep from crying out, Maude Ann pasted a smile on her face and turned her attention to the women. She greeted them with an almost desperate warmth and enthusiasm, far more than she normally would have done. While she had worked at the precinct she'd met all the women at one time or another, but they were merely acquaintances. Through work, she had developed much closer friendships with their husbands.

Nevertheless, the officers' wives responded to her with open friendliness. Maude Ann chatted with them for several minutes, though she could not have told you what she'd said. She was much too aware of Matt and Gloria Davies. Though it was like probing a sore tooth with your tongue, knowing all the while that it was going to hurt, she could not stop herself from glancing over her shoulder at the pair every few seconds. To her dismay, the woman continued to hang on Matt like wet laundry.

Maude Ann desperately needed a diversion, and she found it by helping to break the ice between her charges and the other four children.

Before long, with Tyrone in the lead, all the children except the two babies took off at a run, laughing and chattering as though they'd known one another for years.

Chuckling, John patted Maude Ann on the back and grinned at the other women. "See? Didn't I tell you she has a way with kids?" Turning to his men, he motioned with a wave of his beefy arm for them to follow and bellowed, "C'mon, you bunch of sorry gold bricks, let's get this show on the road. We've got food to cook."

"My, my," Anna Huttsinger murmured, hoisting her baby higher on her shoulder as they all started around to the side yard. "Isn't it amazing what wonderful cooks men are when all the prep work has already been done?"

They had taken just a few steps when the sound of an approaching vehicle drowned out the women's laughter. Everyone stopped and turned around.

"I don't believe it!" Tony said furiously. "It's that damned reporter."

Suddenly the mood of the party changed as every last man stepped forward, braced for a fight.

The car crunched to a halt on the drive behind the others, and Maude Ann looked around in time to see J.T. climb out. "Hey, Maude Ann, I got something for you," he called, waving a paper in the air, but before he could take a step, Hank, Tony and Gus had him pinned against the side of his car.

"What the—"

"You got some nerve, Conway," Hank snarled in his face.

"Get your hands off me, you ape."

"Watch it, creep. You're just about a half a minute from getting that pretty face of yours bashed in."

"No! Stop it! Stop it right this minute!" Maude Ann rushed in and pulled at the officers' arms. "Let him go."

"Not on your life. Maude Ann, this guy's a reporter with the *Houston Herald.*"

"I know that, Hank. He also happens to be a friend of mine."

"Aw, *jeez,* Maude Ann. Somebody's gonna have to do something about your taste in friends."

"You could be right." Linking her arm firmly through J.T.'s, she gave Tony and the other two men a challenging smile. "After all, I am friends with the lot of you."

Chapter Eleven

"Look, Maude Ann, don't think I don't appreciate your stepping in back there," J.T. muttered as they approached the others. Tony, Gus and Hank trailed after them, thoroughly disgusted and muttering dark insults at J.T.'s back, which he ignored. "But I really wish you hadn't. I could've handled those guys."

"Oh, please," she groaned, "not you, too. I've had just about all the macho nonsense I can take for one day." She heaved a sigh, then relented, giving his arm a squeeze and smiling at him. "But I am glad you came by. I could use a friend right about now."

He raised an eyebrow at that, but they reached the others before he could question her.

"Ladies, I'd like you to meet my friend, J. T. Conway," Maude Ann began brightly before any of the men had a chance to speak up. Ignoring the less-than-friendly male eyes boring into them, she introduced J.T. to all the wives and to the two bouncing infants. "You probably know Lieutenant Werner and the other guys," she said when done.

"Yeah, I think so. How's it going, fellas? Ms. Davies?"

"What're you doing here, Conway?" Matt demanded. Gloria still hung on his arm, but he appeared not to notice.

J.T. grinned and held up a rolled cylinder of paper. "I dropped by to give Maude Ann an advance copy of the Sunday supplement. I thought she might like to see it before it hits the streets tomorrow."

"Oh! Let me see!" Maude Ann snatched the paper out of his hand, unrolled it and gasped. "It's the cover story!"

"Yeah, my boss thought it was a real heart-grabber, so he went with it."

Flush with excitement, Maude Ann held up the magazine to show the others. "J.T. did a story on the haven for tomorrow's paper. We're hoping it will bring in a ton of donations."

A full-page picture of herself with a child cradled in her arms, rocking in one of the porch swings made up the cover of the magazine. The soft-focused photograph had a melancholy look about it that tugged on the heartstrings. So did the title: HENLEY HAVEN. A REFUGE FOR THE INNOCENT.

The women crowded around for a closer look, but the men barely gave the paper a glance.

"I'd read it carefully before I got too excited if I were you," John warned, keeping a suspicious watch on J.T. "This guy has a real flair for twisting things around."

"I tried to warn her, but she wouldn't listen," Matt said.

Too excited to pay attention to the remarks, Maude Ann opened the magazine. The article covered three pages and included four more photographs, each as emotionally evocative as the one on the cover. Quickly, she scanned the text, her gaze flying from column to column. Looking over her shoulder, Patty and Marylou read along, while the other women pressed closer, trying to do the same.

When Maude Ann finished and looked at J.T., her eyes glittered with moisture. "Oh, J.T. This is beautiful."

He shrugged. "No big deal. Actually, it was a piece of cake to write."

Relinquishing the magazine to the other women, Maude Ann surged up on tiptoe and kissed his cheek. "I love it. And trust me, it's a *huge* deal."

Not only had J.T. written a heart-wrenching story, he had honored their agreement to the letter. Not anywhere in the article did he even hint at the location of the Henley Haven or reveal any of the children's names. The pictures were all shot either from the back or from an angle that revealed so little of their faces it would be almost impossible for anyone to recognize them.

Though he tried to act blasé about the praises, Maude Ann saw the bloom of pink beneath his tanned skin. The flush deepened when the other men looked up from the article to shoot him surprised glances.

Laughing, she grasped J.T.'s arm and gave it an affectionate squeeze. She was pleased when he agreed to stay for the cookout.

She urged everyone around to the side yard where lawn chairs were set out under the trees and the brick barbecue pit smoldered in readiness. Out of the corner of her eye, Maude Ann could see Matt and Gloria, walking close together, deep on conversation. Maude Ann grasped J.T.'s arm. "I'm so glad you drove up today and that you're staying."

"Hey, no way I'm going to pass up a chance to spend the day with you and the kids." Then he grinned and, leaning closer, murmured, "Besides, it'll drive Matt nuts."

"I should have known."

* * *

It was a perfect day for a cookout, Maude Ann thought a few hours later. It was scorching hot, but the breeze off the lake made it bearable. Over head the leaves of the giant pecan tree stirred with a swishing sound. The smell of hickory smoke and grilled burgers and hot dogs still hung in the air, mingling with the sweet scent of newly mown grass. Puffball clouds drifted across the blue sky and a squirrel chattered and scolded from the high branches of the pecan tree.

She smiled as the children streaked by again. Everyone seemed to be having a good time—except her.

To Maude Ann the day seemed endless. Never in her life had she worked so hard at enjoying herself, or at least at giving that appearance.

She'd smiled until her face hurt. She'd circulated among her guests and played the gracious hostess. She'd helped Jane and the other women serve the food and clean up afterward, she'd chased after rambunctious toddlers, laughed when the men recounted funny incidents that had occurred while on duty and exchanged girl talk with their wives. She'd joined in a watermelon-seed-spitting contest and pitched horseshoes with gusto and, to the delight of the children, had gotten into a wild water-balloon fight with Tony that had left her looking like a drowned rat.

She tried not to care that Gloria hadn't left Matt's side since she arrived or that he didn't seem to mind. After all, Maude Ann knew she had no claim on the man, and he couldn't have made it plainer that he didn't return her feelings. Matt was a free agent, and if Gloria was what he wanted, it was none of her business.

It was a humiliating and depressing thought that stung her pride. What had she been thinking? It should have occurred to her that Matt might not be unattached. He was a healthy, virile male with the kind of rugged good looks most women found irresistible. Though he shied away from serious relationships, in the time she had worked at his precinct, he had seldom been without a casual lover. If she had remembered that, maybe she wouldn't have made the mistake of falling in love with him.

But then again, maybe not.

Maude Ann sighed and took another mouthful of the ice cream she was eating to console herself. What a foolish, foolish woman she was.

Still, it hurt. Every time she heard Gloria's sexy laugh or saw her touch Matt in that intimate way, she felt her heart break a little more.

"Hey, Doc, great party." Plopping down on the lawn chair next to hers, J.T. shot Maude Ann his relaxed smile. "Even if your friends are trying to make me feel like the bastard at the family reunion."

Maude Ann shook her head. "Well, I'm glad you're having a good time," she said in a dry voice.

"Mmm." Slouching, his head propped on the edge of the chair back, his long legs stretched out and crossed at the ankles, he rested his beer bottle on his flat belly and contemplated it through half closed eyes. "I can see why you thought you needed a friend." He rolled his head on the chair back and looked into her eyes. "Don't let Matt and detective Hot Pants get under your skin, Doc."

Despite her misery, she had to laugh. "You're terrible. Her name is Gloria, as you very well know. And she's a nice person. A little…free spirited, maybe, but nice. Actually, I've always liked her. And I'm okay. Really."

"Good, because he's just trying to make you jealous, you know."

"Oh, I doubt that. I think he and Gloria are lovers."

"Mmm. At one time, maybe. At least, that's what I

heard, but that's been over for a while. I think she's just at loose ends and trying to fan an old flame.''

"Well, it seems to be working." She'd tried for flippancy, but even to her own ears, the comment sounded pathetic.

J.T. reached across and put his hand over hers. "Hey, Doc, there's no game that two can't play. If you want to bring out ol' Matt's green-eyed monster I'm at your service.''

Turning her hand over, she gave his a squeeze and managed a wan smile. "Thanks, J.T., but I don't think so. If Matt prefers Gloria, that's his right. Anyway, it's not as though there was ever really anything between us.''

She had merely laid her heart and soul bare to him and humiliated herself, but that was the price you sometimes paid for honesty.

J.T.'s eyes said he thought she was crazy, but he returned the gentle pressure. "If that's the way you want it. Just remember, if you change your mind, the offer stands.''

As the day wore on, Maude Ann was sorely tempted to take him up on the offer. But she could not bring herself to play games with another person's emotions. That did not mean, however, that she had to let the world see how much she was hurting. She had her pride, after all.

When Gloria gave Matt a sizzling kiss after he'd tossed a ringer in horseshoes, Maude Ann laughed right along with everyone else.

When the woman sat on his good leg and shared her ice cream with him, Maude Ann ignored them and cheerfully set about organizing everyone into two teams for softball. As captain of one team, she picked J.T. first and ignored Matt.

During the top of the second inning, Matt's team had two outs and two players on base when it came his turn at bat. Gloria gave his butt a pat as he stood up and headed for the plate. At second base, Maude Ann punched her glove and chanted vociferous encouragement to Tony to strike him out, as though that was the only thing that mattered to her.

After the first game, which Maude Ann's team won, Gloria didn't want to play anymore and persuaded Matt to quit, as well. They watched a few minutes of the second game, then walked off the field, hand in hand, just as J.T.'s bat cracked against the ball in a line-drive single. Maude Ann jumped up and down and cheered like a maniac.

Her turn at bat came next. She took her place at the plate, held her bat up and wiggled her hips to test her stance.

Immediately, a chorus of wolf whistles and cries of "Shake it, baby, shake it!" came from the bench.

Glancing over her shoulder, Maude Ann grinned at her teammates. She wiggled her hips again, took a couple of practice swings—and out of the corner of her eye saw Matt and Gloria disappear through the veranda door into his room.

"Ah, jeez. How's a guy supposed to concentrate?"

"If you're through, could I please pitch now?" Gus asked in a long-suffering growl.

Gritting her teeth, Maude Ann nodded and braced herself for the pitch. When it came she took a vicious swing and smacked the ball with all her might, sending it sailing high over Anna Huttsinger's head in the outfield.

With a grin fixed on her face and pumping her fists high in the air, Maude Ann took her victory trot around the bases while her teammates cheered and shouted, but her throat ached with the unshed tears she held fiercely in check. When she rounded third and saw the blind in Matt's window close, she could almost hear the crack of her heart breaking in two.

* * *

"Mmm. Alone at last." Gloria closed the blind and turned back to Matt. The seductive smile on her face as she sauntered closer left no doubt of what she wanted from him.

No, he corrected. What *they* wanted from *each other*.

"I've been waiting for this all day," Gloria purred, running her palms over his chest. She looked up at him from beneath her lashes and flicked open the top button of his shirt. "I've missed you, lover."

"Have you now?" Matt watched her with a sardonic smile on his lips, making no effort to hide his amusement. He put his hands on her hips and brought her against him. "Seems to me last I heard before I got shot, you were hot and heavy with some lawyer from the DA's office."

"Oh, that. He was a jerk. But then, he's a lawyer, so I should have known better. Anyway, that's been over for a couple of weeks."

"Ah, I see. Now it's all becoming clear. Knowing you, after two weeks you've got a powerful itch that needs scratching. When the lieutenant mentioned this outing, I bet you figured by now I'd be happy to accommodate you."

She grinned, not in the least insulted. "You'd be damn near climbing the walls is what I figured. I mean, sweetie, it's been more than three months, unless Dr. Edwards has been giving you a little 'physical therapy' on the side."

His teasing smile collapsed into a frown, but before he could object, she twined her arms around his neck and brought his head down for a kiss.

Matt tried. For several seconds he held her tightly against him and returned the devouring kiss with something akin to desperation. But it was no use.

The moment he had seen Gloria that morning, he had convinced himself that the raging desire he felt for Maude Ann was merely the result of propinquity. He had been celibate for months, and since she was the only woman around, naturally he had become obsessed with her. He had figured making love to another woman was all he needed to put things into perspective and rid him of this unrelenting longing for Maude Ann, but he was wrong.

It was true that he wanted—hell, he desperately needed—to make love to a woman, but apparently only one woman would do, and his body knew damned well that woman wasn't Gloria. He wanted Maude Ann. Only Maude Ann.

Regretfully, Matt broke off the kiss and grasped her shoulders to ease her back. "I'm sorry." He shook his head and met her surprised expression with a look of genuine regret that he hoped would take the sting out of the rejection. "I'm really sorry, Gloria. But it's just not going to happen."

"But…I don't get it. What's wrong?" Her face suddenly bore a look of mingled pity and disappointment. "Is it your wound? I mean, is it giving you…you know…trouble in that department?"

It took him a moment to catch her drift, and when he did he gave a bark of ironic laughter. "No, it's nothing like that. I'm not impotent."

Far from it. Although he almost wished he was. Then perhaps he wouldn't be tormented nightly with erotic dreams of making love to Maude Ann, which inevitably resulted in his waking up each morning painfully aroused.

"Then what is the problem?"

"I just don't think we should, that's all." Matt wandered over to the window and opened the blind. Immediately his gaze sought out Maude Ann.

The "bench" for both teams consisted of a line of folding lawn chairs behind and to one side of home plate. She and J.T. sat side by side, talking while they watched the game. A suffocating pressure squeezed Matt's chest.

He watched as J.T. propped his elbow on the back of Maude Ann's chair, picked up her long ponytail and absently toyed with the curly mass.

Matt's eyes narrowed. He gritted his teeth so hard a muscle rippled along his jaw.

Gloria's sharp intake of breath caught his attention, and when he turned his head, he found her staring at him with her mouth agape.

"What?"

Her stunned gaze slid from him to Maude Ann and back. "So *that's* it. I wouldn't have believed it if I hadn't seen it with my own eyes."

"Seen what? What're you talking about?"

"You're in love with Dr. Edwards."

"Don't be ridiculous."

"Sweetie, you don't have to lie to spare my feelings. I think it's great. I just never thought I'd see the day when Matt Dolan fell in love, that's all."

"I tell you, you're imagining things."

"Aw, c'mon. Who're you trying to kid? I saw your face when you were looking at her just now. *And* the way you looked at Conway when he touched her. Sugar, you looked ready to commit murder. This from a man who has never before shown so much as a twinge of jealousy over a woman."

Matt opened his mouth to repeat the denial, then closed it again. "All right. So I love her. No need to make a big deal out of it."

"Does she love you?"

"Gloria," he growled, slanting her a warning scowl. She wasn't fazed.

"Well? Does she?"

Matt sighed and gave up. "She says she does."

Gloria threw up her hands. "Then why did you spend the whole day with me, you big dope? Why aren't you out there right now, jerking Conway off her?"

"What would be the point? Just because I love her doesn't mean I'm going to do anything about it." He glanced over his shoulder at her. "No offense, Gloria, but Maude Ann isn't like you. She couldn't handle a casual affair. She would expect wedding bells and happy-ever-after, and I have no intention of ever getting married. You know how I feel about mixing marriage and police work."

The inning ended, and Maude Ann's team took to the field. Matt watched her slip on her glove and stroll to second base with that easy, sexy saunter, and the pressure in his chest eased fractionally. At least J.T. couldn't cozy up to her for a while, he thought with hard satisfaction, watching the reporter trot past her into centerfield.

"Oh, Matt." Gloria's voice held such infinite sadness he shot her a surprised look. "Love is too precious a gift to throw away. Don't you know that?"

"With two marriages behind you, how can you say that?"

Sitting down on the arm of the easy chair by the window, Gloria smiled at his cynical expression and shrugged. "The first time I married for love. Donny was my high-school sweetheart, and we were head over heels." A smile curved her mouth as her eyes took on a misty faraway look. "He was such a sweet boy, my Donny. He died of leukemia at twenty-six. We only had eight years together, but they were the most wonderful years of my life.

"A year after Donny died, I married Nick. I convinced myself I loved him because I was desperate to recapture what I had lost. Within weeks, I knew I'd made a huge mistake. I stuck it out for a year out of guilt, but without love there was no way to make it work.''

"I'm sorry, Gloria. I didn't know." Matt, like everyone else, had always assumed she was a two-time divorcee just out for a good time.

"It all happened a long time ago." She straightened her shoulders, shaking off the sadness, and gave him a pointed look. "I made a mistake with Nick, but I learned from it. You better believe, if I ever find love again, I'm going to grab hold of it and never let go." She waited a beat to let that sink in, then added, "And if you don't do the same, you're a fool."

Her eyes dared him to contradict her. Matt stared back at her for several tense moments. Then his gaze went to the window again, and beyond to the woman who haunted his dreams. "Maybe you're right."

"I know I am. At the very least, you owe it to yourself and to Maude Ann to explore your feelings. Who knows, maybe things won't work out for you two. But at least you'll have given it a shot."

Outside, the game ended and everyone headed back toward the lodge. J.T. caught up with Maude Ann and fell into step beside her. Matt watched the other man bend his head toward her and say something, watched the way she smiled in response. Pulling her tightly against his side, J.T. gave her a quick hug.

Matt's hard gaze fixed on the arm that remained draped over Maude Ann's shoulders as the pair strolled along.

His jaw clenched. "You're right. I'll do it."

Gloria laughed as he stalked to the outside door and snatched it open. "Go get her, tiger."

The veranda was full of people when he stepped outside, sweaty softball players and kids digging into the coolers for cold drinks or having another go at the ice cream and watermelon.

"Hey, Matt," Hank called, lifting a frosty bottle from the cooler. "You want a beer?"

"No, thanks. I'll catch you later," he replied absently, searching through the crowd.

At first he didn't see Maude Ann. He frowned, wondering how she had disappeared so fast. Then the group by the cooler shifted and he spotted her heading for the back veranda.

Rather than maneuver through the congestion on the veranda, he decided to take the shorter route and went back inside the way he'd come out.

Gloria wasn't in his room when he stalked through, nor was Maude Ann in the kitchen. Matt went outside again through the back door and nearly bumped into her as she came around the corner.

"Oh." For an instant, she looked dismayed, then her expression turned cool. "Sorry. I didn't see you there," she said, and tried to sidle around him.

Matt sidestepped to block her. "Maude Ann, we have to talk."

Surprise and wariness swam in her eyes when they met his. "Talk? About what?"

"About us."

She caught her breath, flinching as though he'd slapped her. "Us? You want to talk about *us?* I don't believe this." Her face tightened and she darted around him.

"Maude Ann, wait! This is important." He caught up with her at the kitchen door and put his hand on her arm to stop her. The look she shot him was glacial.

"I have nothing to say to you." She shook his hand off and opened the door, but when she stepped inside she turned and snapped, "And there *is* no *us!*"

She slammed the door in his face, and for a moment Matt was so astonished he simply stared at it. Then his temper flared. "Dammit, Maude Ann, what is the matter with you? We're going to talk if I have to…" Disbelieving, he stared down at the doorknob. He tried again to turn it, but it wouldn't budge.

"Looks like she's locked you out."

Matt's head snapped around. A few feet away, J.T. stood with one shoulder propped against the veranda post, his arms folded over his chest. His expression held none of its usual cheerfulness, only censure and a touch of what looked like pity. Matt didn't care for either. Especially not from this guy.

"Butt out, Conway. This is none of your business."

He turned his attention back to the door and rattled the knob. "Maude Ann, open this damned door."

"You're wasting your time. She's not going to let you in."

"How would *you* know?" Matt growled, shooting him a look of pure dislike.

J.T. shrugged. "You don't believe me? Wait and see."

Matt banged on the door. Through the window he could see Maude Ann flouncing around the kitchen, her face set as she banged cabinet doors and slammed drawers. She pulled out more paper cups and napkins and slammed them down on a tray, snatched another pitcher of lemonade out of the refrigerator, then filled a bucket with ice and plopped both onto the tray, as well, but not once did she so much as glance his way.

Matt muttered a curse. "Fine. Don't open the door. There are other ways to get in." She wouldn't lock every door, not when she had a yard full of company.

He stormed down the veranda, intent on reaching his room, but when he drew even with J.T., he stopped and jabbed his finger at him. "And you stay away from Maude Ann. You got that?"

"Oh, I got it all right. And I'll be happy to—just as soon as Maude Ann tells me that's what she wants."

"I'm warning you, Conway."

J.T. chuckled and shook his head. "You know, Dolan, for a smart guy, you can really pull some dumb stuff."

Matt's scowl deepened, turned dangerous. "Meaning?"

"Meaning, from the softball field you have a clear view of your room." His eyes, serious for once, bore into Matt's and as the significance of the statement soaked in, Matt felt sick.

"Aw, hell." Cupping the back of his neck, he let his head fall back and squeezed his eyes shut. She had seen him and Gloria go into his room. He groaned, remembering how Gloria had closed the blinds a few seconds later. He could imagine how Maude Ann must have felt.

His anger and frustration drained away, replaced by guilt and gut-wrenching remorse. That nothing had happened didn't matter. He had gone into his room with Gloria, fully intending to make love to her. He'd been so intent on shaking off his obsession with Maude Ann that he'd never given a thought to how his actions might make her feel.

He muttered a scorching expletive. J.T. was right; he was dumber than dirt.

"I must like you, Dolan," J.T. drawled. "That's the only reason I can figure for why I'm standing here trying to help you. But I gotta tell you, man, after a stunt like that, I'm beginning to think you don't deserve Maude Ann. What the hell were you thinking?"

"That's the trouble, I wasn't." Matt opened his eyes and met J.T.'s accusing gaze head-on. "But for the record, nothing happened between Gloria and me."

"Nothing?"

"Nothing."

"Hmm. Well, chum, you're gonna have one helluva time convincing Maude Ann of that. I'd get started if I were you."

It was on the tip of Matt's tongue to tell J.T. once again to mind his own business, but he bit the words back. J. T. Conway might be a pain-in-the-butt, nosy reporter, but he had at least clued him in on what had Maude Ann so upset.

Matt gave J.T. a level look. "I intend to."

Matt found her sitting on the side veranda in the middle of a group that included John, Tony, Hank, Patty, and Ned and Annie Bledsoe. As he approached the group, Maude Ann glanced up and spotted him, but she merely gave him a withering look and turned her attention back to the discussion.

Matt gritted his teeth. Evidently, she felt confident that he wouldn't make a scene in front of other people. Wrong.

He skirted around the semicircle of porch swing, love seats and loungers and stopped behind Maude Ann's chair. He leaned down and put his hand on her shoulder and gritted his teeth when she flinched at his touch.

"Maude Ann, I need to talk to you. In private."

She barely spared him a sidelong glance over her shoulder. "If you don't mind, I'm talking to my friends."

Conversation stopped and the others watched them curiously.

"This is important."

"Sorry. It will have to wait. I just want to sit here and relax right now."

"Too bad. We're going to talk."

"I said not now," she ground out through clenched teeth.

"Now."

Before she could argue further, he grasped her upper arm

and hauled her up out of the chair. She let out a squeak of surprise, and gasps and startled murmurs went up from the others. Tony came off the porch rail, where he'd been perched, like an uncoiling spring.

"Dammit, Matt, what do you think you're doing?"

Hank stood up, as well, his expression worried. "Hey, Matt, take it easy, ol' buddy."

"Matt, stop it! Have you lost your mind!" Maude Ann protested as he pulled her past John. The lieutenant didn't utter a word, merely cocked one bushy eyebrow and watched them with interest, almost as though he found the whole thing amusing.

"Dammit, Matt, I'm not going to just let you drag the doc off that way."

From behind, Matt heard Tony stomping after them, but the sound abruptly halted, and J.T. drawled, "Let 'em go. They've got things to settle."

Chalk up another point for Conway, Matt thought with grudging gratitude as he frog-marched Maude Ann down the veranda steps. As they started across the yard, she recovered her senses and began to struggle.

"Let me go!"

"Not on your life. And if you don't stop that, I'm going to toss you over my shoulder and carry you."

"You wouldn't *dare.*"

"The hell I wouldn't."

Staring at his set profile, she must have decided he meant it. She gave up trying to pry open his fingers and walked in sullen silence beside him.

They crossed the yard, then the softball field. He didn't stop until they stepped beneath an ancient live oak at the edge of the woods.

Maude Ann jerked her arm free and turned to face him.

"I hope you're satisfied," she snapped. "You've made a complete spectacle of us."

He glanced back at the lodge and saw that all their friends were watching them. Matt shrugged. "If you'd come with me in the first place, like I asked, it wouldn't have aroused their curiosity."

"I don't have anything to say to you," she spat.

Her eyes shot fire, and angry color bloomed in her cheeks. Though he found the display of temper almost unbearably arousing, it was also a barometer of how hurt she was, and that he deeply regretted.

"Well, I have plenty to say to you."

"Go tell it to Gloria. I'm not interested."

"I already have." His voice dropped to a gentle pitch. "That's all Gloria and I did in my room, Maude Ann— was talk. About you. About us."

"Oh, please, do I look stupid to you? Do you honestly expect me to believe that you took her in there and closed the blind just so you could talk?"

Matt raked a hand through his hair and sighed. "I won't lie to you. I had every intention of having sex with Gloria."

He saw the pain flicker across her face and felt rotten. She held her hands up in front of her, palms out. "Please. I don't want to hear this. What you do and who you do it with is your business. All I'm saying is, knowing how I feel about you—*felt* about you," she quickly amended, "you could have at least had the decency and the sensitivity not to flaunt your lover under my nose."

"She not my lover—at least, not anymore."

Maude Ann gave an inelegant snort.

"I couldn't have sex with her, Maude Ann," he said quietly. "I wanted to use her to banish you from my thoughts, but I couldn't. Because she wasn't the one I wanted. She wasn't you."

Maude Ann's head snapped up. She was suddenly still as a wary doe. Caution and a hint of distrust filled her eyes. Her expression turned from angry to guarded, but she remained silent, watching him, waiting.

"I'm in love with you, Maude Ann," Matt said softly.

Other than to flinch, she didn't move or speak for several seconds, merely searched his face for the truth. Finally she shook her head. "I don't believe you."

"Nevertheless, it's true."

"This is rather sudden, isn't it? You certainly didn't seem to feel that way two weeks ago when I told you I was in love with you."

He noted her use of the past tense. It sent a little chill down his spine, but he shook off the sensation. He refused to accept that her feelings could have changed. "I was in love with you even then. Hell, I've been in love with you for months, but I didn't want to admit it—not to you or to myself. That's why I behaved like a jerk with Gloria today. I'd convinced myself that what I felt for you was nothing more than normal desire after a prolonged abstinence. That all I needed was a woman. Any woman. I was wrong."

She stared at him, and he could see the struggle going on inside her. She wanted to believe him, but she wasn't quite there. Not yet.

"I've never felt this way about a woman before, Maude Ann. I've never wanted to. I still don't. But where you're concerned, I don't seem to have any choice."

Some of the doubt faded from her eyes, and her guarded expression relaxed into a sad little smile. "So what you're saying is, you love me, but against your will. My, how romantic."

"Dammit, I'm trying to be honest with you. I've never wanted a serious relationship before. I've never made a secret of that. Even feeling as I do about you, I'm still not sure that it's smart.''

She gave a start when he took her hand, but when she made no effort to pull away, he was encouraged. "All I know is that I care for you more than I've ever cared for any woman. I want you in my life, Maude Ann. In my bed. I'm hoping that's what you want, too."

Something flared in her eyes and she opened her mouth to speak, but he silenced her with a shake of his head. "No, don't answer yet. There are some things I have to tell you, because if we do take the next step, I want to be sure that you're going into this relationship with your eyes wide open."

As though bracing herself, Maude Ann pulled her hand from his and crossed her arms over her midriff and nodded. "All right. Go ahead."

"First you have to know that I can't make you any promises. I have no idea where these feelings will lead, or if we'll have a future together." He paused and looked at her with regret, his gaze locking with hers. "I *do* love you, Maude Ann. I've never said those words to any woman before. But I have to be honest with you. I'm not sure I will ever change my mind about mixing police work and marriage. Before we go any further, you need to decide if you can live with that."

"My, my," Maude Ann said with a mirthless little chuckle. "You certainly are a sweet talker, aren't you. You really know how to give a girl hope."

"I'm being open with you, Maude Ann, because I care. I don't want to mislead you. That could only lead to hurt, and that's the last thing I want to do."

Her arms remained folded across her middle. Matt watched her and tried to read which way she was leaning. From her expression, he had the sinking feeling that her

decision would not be in his favor. Panic bubbled up inside
him, and he wanted to snatch her into his arms and kiss
her senseless, sweep her so completely off her feet she had
no choice.

But he couldn't do that. Maude Ann meant too much to
him to coerce or manipulate her.

She glanced at him and attempted a smile, but it wobbled
and didn't quite come off. "I must say, I've had more romantic propositions, but at least you were honest."

"Hey, Maude Ann!"

The call came from the veranda, a jarring reminder that
they had an audience. They both jumped and swung around
to see John standing at the bottom of the steps, waving at
them. Behind him, the others were gathering their children
and belongings.

"We're going to hit the road!" John yelled through his
cupped hands. "It's a long drive back to Houston!"

"I'll be right there," she called back.

She turned to Matt with another wobbly smile. "Looks
like the party is over. We'd better say our goodbyes."

They headed back to the veranda, walking side by side
but not touching. Tension hummed between them like a
high-voltage wire, but they didn't speak. The only sounds
were the crackle of grass stubble beneath their shoes and
the faint murmur of voices in the distance. Several times
Matt glanced at her out of the corner of his eye, but if she
felt his scrutiny, she didn't acknowledge it. She still hugged
her arms tightly and stared straight again.

Halfway across the yard, Matt halted. "Maude Ann."

She stopped a few steps ahead of him and looked back.
"Yes?"

The sadness he saw in her eyes twisted his gut. She was
going to say no.

He was prepared for that, expected it—at least, he

182   *A MAN APART*

thought he was. He'd even told himself it would probably be for the best. So why did he suddenly feel as though he had an anvil sitting on his chest?

''When you make up your mind, you know where to find me,'' he said softly.

She stared at him for the space of several heartbeats, then nodded.

Chapter Twelve

She had to refuse Matt. It was the sensible thing to do.

Maude Ann reached the far side of her bedroom and spun around, and the black silk nightgown swirled around her ankles. She paced back toward the other side, twisting her hands together.

What else could she do? she asked herself for the tenth time in as many minutes. No sane, intelligent woman would deliberately enter into a dead-end relationship with a man she loved. That was a sure formula for heartbreak.

But, dear God, how could she refuse even the little bit of happiness he offered when she loved him so?

She made a frustrated sound somewhere between a growl and a scream. Damn Matt for doing this to her! And damn his brutal frankness! She strove for honesty in all areas of her life and admired that quality in others, but did he have to strip her of every illusion? Every shred of hope?

To tell her in one breath that he loved her and in the

next that he didn't know if they could have a future together was unfair. So he didn't believe in marriage for police officers. Big deal, neither did she—at least, not with her. She hadn't bothered to tell him that because there wasn't any point, since he was so adamant on the subject.

For them to have a life together, one of them would have to give in, and she couldn't see that happening. Matt was a police officer right down to the marrow in his bones—and a darned good one. While she appreciated that, she could not bring herself to marry another cop, she thought with a shudder. Not even loving Matt as she did. She simply could not.

If Matt flunked the reentry physical, they might have a chance.

The wayward thought brought a tiny spark of hope, followed instantly by a wave of guilt.

How could she entertain such an idea? The loss of his job would be a crushing blow for Matt. She wasn't sure it would make a difference, anyway. If it came to that, he would either have to leave the force or take a desk job, and he would hate both alternatives. Knowing Matt, he would be so miserable he probably wouldn't consider making a commitment to her.

Which left her right back where she'd started.

No matter how Maude Ann looked at the situation, it seemed her only choices were to break off things now or settle for a brief affair.

Reaching the other end of the room, she swung around and paced back toward the window again. Matt was no help at all. He had left the decision entirely to her. Damn him! Did he really believe that by spelling everything out for her she would not be hurt when their relationship ended?

The spurt of anger faded as quickly as it had come. Sighing, Maude Ann raked her hand through her hair. Yes, of course he did. No doubt he thought he was shielding her, that forewarned was forearmed and therefore she would be able to ward off the blow when it came—or some such skewed male logic.

She shook her head and squeezed the tight muscles in the back of her neck. Men. When it came to love, they hadn't a clue.

The truth was, they were both going to be hurt, no matter what she decided. It was just a matter of when.

She stopped in front of her cheval mirror. The woman in the glass looked back at her with haunted eyes. Against the black nightgown, her skin appeared paler than usual, almost translucent, the freckles across her nose standing out like tiny splatters of paint. She had washed her hair when she showered, but she'd been too distraught to bother with the blow dryer. Now it rioted around her head and shoulders in a mass of untamed curls, which only seemed to make her appear even more fragile.

She looked brittle, ready to shatter, and she hated that. She was a strong, decisive, resilient woman, dammit. Not some dithering little piece of fluff who went to pieces when life dealt her a low blow. She had survived the loss of her beloved husband, hadn't she? One way or another, she would survive this.

Maude Ann went to the window and gazed pensively out at the moonlit waters of the lake. That she was going to be hurt was a given. She was hurting now, for Pete's sake. The question was, she supposed, would it be any more painful to grab a few weeks or months of happiness before she and Matt parted than to make a clean break now—and perhaps always wonder if they could have somehow worked something out.

Sighing, she closed her eyes and leaned forward until her forehead rested against the cool pane of glass. She was rationalizing, looking for an excuse to do what she wanted. She could analyze and pick at the problem all night, but the truth was, deep in her heart, where it counted, she had already made up her mind....

She was going to turn him down. Matt could feel it. What else could her silence mean? It was after eleven, and not a peep out of her.

His stomach clenched. He went to the window and stared out. He had just showered and was naked beneath his robe. Behind him, warm, moist air, laden with the scents of soap and toothpaste and masculine toiletries drifted from the open door of the bathroom. Except for the light spilling through the same door, his room was in darkness, allowing him to see through the gloom beyond the window. Matt stared past the dark shapes of wicker furniture to the stubbled field beyond the side yard, where the white chalk lines of the softball diamond, almost luminescent in the moonlight, glowed.

He'd handled this all wrong. Of course she was going to turn him down. What did he expect after that miserable little speech he'd given her? "Come be my lover, but don't expect permanence," he mimicked.

Oh, yeah, that was going to sweep her right off her feet, all right. What woman could resist such a sweet deal? You're a real silver-tongued devil, Dolan.

Matt groaned. But what else could he do? He couldn't mislead her. He wouldn't do that to any woman. Especially not Maude Ann. He loved her, dammit!

Oh, yeah, he'd definitely made a tactical mistake in the way he'd handled things. Unfair or not, after laying everything on the line, he should have stuck to her like glue, used the feelings they had for each other to his advantage.

He should have wooed her with gentle persuasion, held and kissed her until she couldn't even think of saying no.

Instead, like a noble idiot, he'd left her alone to think things over and come to a decision. Maude Ann was warm and loving and generous to a fault, and he didn't doubt that she loved him. However, she was also an eminently sensible, pragmatic woman. She had to be to run Henley Haven. She loved every child in her care as though he or she was her own, yet when the courts decided one should go elsewhere, she accepted the order without a lot of fuss. A woman who could do that just might decide the risks of being hurt were too great to take a chance on him. So he had a sinking feeling what her decision would be.

The thought brought a gush of panic to his chest. Anger followed close behind. His mouth folded into a grim line. "We'll just see about that," he muttered. Yanking the belt of his robe tighter, he turned on his heel and stomped toward the door. If she thought he was giving up without a fight, she could think again.

With a face like a thundercloud, he snatched open his bedroom door—and came face-to-face with Maude Ann.

She stood just on the other side of the doorway, her hand raised to knock.

"Oh!"

"Maude Ann."

They spoke at the same time, then fell silent, staring at each other.

Matt's chest was suddenly so tight he had difficulty breathing. From the pulse throbbing at the base of Maude Ann's throat, he knew her emotions were running riot, too.

Time seemed to stand still, and for a moment, he couldn't think, couldn't move. Then his gaze lowered from those wide, whiskey-colored eyes to trail down her body, and his heart gave a thump. She had come to him barefoot, wearing a gossamer-thin black negligee over a sexy black nightgown.

His gaze jumped back to her face, and what he saw there made him catch his breath. The glow of love shining from those expressive eyes told him all he needed to know. Twin bursts of joy and relief exploded inside him, one filling his chest to bursting, the other making his knees weak.

"Maude Ann," he said again, but this time his voice came out low and dark, rough with emotion.

Her soft smile pierced his heart, and he felt his insides tremble. Words were not needed and none were spoken. Never taking his gaze from hers, he reached for her, and she walked into his arms.

Maude Ann's arms went around his waist, and as he pulled her close, she sighed and laid her cheek against his chest. For a time they simply stood there without speaking, holding each other, luxuriating in the moment, savoring the taut, trembling pleasure of anticipation, the sense of home-coming. Then Matt grasped her arms and held her slightly away from him. He searched her face, looked into her eyes, his own serious and intent. "Are you sure, Maude Ann?"

She smiled and cupped his face with her palm. "I'm sure. I love you, Matt."

He sucked in his breath. His heart seemed to swell in his chest, and his throat was suddenly so tight he couldn't swallow. Pulling her farther into the room, he shut the door. They stood mere inches apart, gazing at each other. In the semidarkness she looked almost ethereal, as though she was no more than a misty dream his thoughts had somehow conjured up. But this was no dream. This was real. This was Maude Ann, a strong, passionate woman of substance and heart and earthy sensuality.

The very air around them seemed to pulse with aware-ness. The sweet scent of floral bath talc and perfume drifted from her to tantalize him. Matt lifted his hand to her hair, skimmed his palm over it, glorying in its texture, its thickness. Then he dove his fingers into the vibrant cloud, cupped the back of her head and pulled her closer.

"And I love you," he whispered as he lowered his head to her.

The kiss was hungry, full of pent-up passion too long repressed. Matt's lips devoured her. Maude Ann went up on tiptoe, locked her arms around his neck and kissed him back with unabashed need and eager joyfulness.

His hands roamed her back, her waist, her hips. Beneath his palms the negligee glided over the slippery fabric of her nightgown, impeding his hold on her body in a way that was both erotic and frustrating. Finally he gave a soft growl and partially broke off the kiss, lifting his head just far enough to ask in between soft nibbles, "How do you…take this…thing off?"

He heard and felt her husky chuckle an instant before she took a half step back. Watching him with heavy-lidded eyes and a seductive smile on her lips, she pulled on the ribbon tie at the negligee's neckline.

With excruciating slowness, the satin bow collapsed, and the edges of the garment parted an enticing few inches. Her movements languid and deliberately tantalizing, Maude Ann spread the edges wide and shimmied the garment off her shoulders. The black chiffon floated to the floor without a sound and formed a billowy puddle around her feet.

Matt stared. He had never seen a woman so beautiful, so utterly alluring. She stood before him, tall and proud, the black satin gown lovingly skimming her womanly curves, from her breasts to her ankles, her wild mane of auburn curls billowing around creamy shoulders, bare but for the tiny black satin straps. And that face—that magnificent face—with its wide mouth and delicate, freckled nose, those whiskey-colored eyes, direct and honest and filled with love. He had never seen anything so perfect. Matt knew that he could look at that face for the rest of his days and never grow tired of it.

"You're so lovely," he whispered. With an unsteady hand, he reached out and trailed his forefinger over one smooth shoulder and followed the strap downward to trace the low neckline and the pearly flesh that swelled over it.

He felt her tremble, and the delicate reaction sent heat racing through his body to settle, hot and heavy, in his loins. Desire consumed him, urging him to rush, but he clamped down on the need, forcing himself to go slowly.

He cupped her breasts with both hands, flexed his fingers around the soft mounds, stroked, watched the curves plump and almost spill over as he gently lifted. Unable to resist, Matt kissed and nibbled and tasted, leaving a wet line of fire on her skin as his tongue traced the gown's neckline, just as his finger had done mere seconds before.

Then his mouth trailed lower, to where her nipples thrust against the gown. Maude Ann gripped his shoulders, and her head arched back when he took one hard bud into his mouth and suckled her through the slippery satin.

The pleasure was exquisite, drawing a keening moan from her throat. He drew on her with an evocative rhythm, taking her deep into his mouth, wetting the satin cloth. Everything inside Maude Ann quickened and burned as the slow, sweet suction seemed to tug at her womb.

The sensations were too beautiful, too intense, to bear for long, and she took a step back, breaking contact with that tormenting mouth. Breathing hard, her face flushed with desire, she stared into his eyes and raised her hand to the tiny straps and slid first one, then the other, off her shoulders.

The black satin slithered down her body to join the negligee, and she stood before him with her shoulders back and her head high, wearing only earrings, which winked now and then through her cloud of hair.

Matt couldn't have taken his eyes off her if the world was coming to an end around him. His gaze traveled over every inch of her, from the top of her head to the puddle of black satin and chiffon around her ankles. When his gaze rose and locked with hers he had to grit his teeth to control his raging desire.

"You're perfect," he said in a voice rough with passion. "I wanted to take it slow, but—"

"I don't want you to," she said.

"Good, because I can't. I have to have you. Now."

He reached for the belt of his robe. "No, let me," she said, and stepping forward, she took over the task herself. In seconds his robe hit the floor. Her head tipped to one side, Maude Ann studied his body with the same frank interest that he had hers. When her gaze once more returned to his, she smiled.

"You're perfect, too," she said, and closed her hand around him.

Matt sucked in a sharp breath. Arching his head back, he squeezed his eyes shut and bared his teeth. Pleasure surged through him, but he could tolerate the exquisite torture for only a moment. With a sound very like a growl, he swept her up into his arms and carried her to the bed, and Maude Ann's throaty laugh rang out as he fell with her onto the mattress.

Then his mouth was on hers, and the time for laughter had passed. The kiss was deep and ravenous and demanding, and when he nudged her legs apart, she opened to him willingly, eagerly. Raising himself on his forearms, Matt stared into her eyes and drove into her.

The pleasure was so shattering Maude Ann cried out, her body arching.

Their hunger was too huge, their need too great for a slow loving. Still watching her, Matt thrust deep and hard, setting a demanding rhythm. Maude Ann wrapped her legs around him and met each powerful stroke.

Their bodies moved in unison, fitting together as though they had been made for each other. Urgency drove them. Pleasure grew, reaching such immense proportions they could no longer contain it, and the end, when it came, was explosive.

It left them drained and shaken, and so utterly replete neither could move.

Gradually, the thunderous beat of Maude Ann's heart slowed and her breathing returned to something approaching normal. With her eyes still closed, she smiled and ran her palms in slow circles over Matt's back, luxuriating in her right to touch him so intimately. She loved the feel of him, his warmth, the hardness and strength of the muscles banding his back. She loved his smell—a clean musky maleness overlaid with a hint of soap and herbal shampoo. It filled her senses.

Though Matt's body pressed her into the mattress, she felt deliciously weightless, as though she were floating free.

Her eyes fluttered open, and she gazed over his shoulder at the dimly lit ceiling and waited for the regrets to come, but there were none. This felt right.

She loved this man with all heart, and her soul had hungered for this closeness with him. They had not simply had sex. What they had just shared had been the ultimate expression of love. They'd worshiped each other with their bodies, each giving and receiving a pleasure so profound it can only be achieved by those who truly love. How could she regret that?

Maude Ann trailed one hand up his back and neck and winnowed her fingers through his tousled hair, smiling at its thickness, the silky warmth of the dark strands sliding between her fingers. She had made the right decision; she knew that now with absolutely certainty. If she had his love for only a little while, then so be it. Whatever happened, she knew she would never regret this time with him.

When her fingertips tickled the top of his ear, Matt made a contented sound and stirred.

"Am I crushing you?"

She traced the swirls in his ear and shook her head. "No, this feels wonderful."

She felt him grin against the side of her neck. "I'll say," he murmured, rotating his hips against her. He chuckled when she responded in kind, but when he rose and braced on his forearms on either side of her head, his expression turned serious.

"I love you, Maude Ann," he declared in a raspy whisper.

Even in the dim light spilling from the bathroom, she could see the intensity in his eyes. They glittered down at her like blue diamonds from that darkly handsome face.

His fingertips toyed with the wayward curls at her temples, while his thumbs stroked the tender skin along the underside of her jaw. "Dear, God, how I love you. Why didn't I realize that years ago?"

"Because it wasn't time for us," she replied softly. "And I love you, too. More than life itself." So much emotion clogged her throat she barely got the words out. After that, all she could do was gaze lovingly up at him, her eyes slowly banking with tears.

His gaze ran over her face, studying each feature intently, as though committing them to memory. "I never knew that loving someone would be like this. That I could care so much." He shook his head in wonder. "It's like…like I've found a part of me I didn't know was missing."

"Oh, Matt." Too choked up to say more, she cupped her hand around the back of his neck and brought his head down to hers.

Their lips met tenderly, in a slow, rocking kiss that touched the core of her being. It devoured, it worshiped, it burned, and the intensity of it made Maude Ann tremble.

Their bodies were still joined in the most intimate of embraces, and she felt him growing hard again inside her. As impossible as it seemed, passion and need engulfed her, and her hips moved in invitation, one that Matt accepted with enthusiasm.

As desire claimed them again, Maude Ann's heart soared, and with a sigh, she wrapped her arms around him and gave herself up to the spiraling pleasure.

"No! Come back! Don't leave me! Come back!"

Maude Ann awoke with a start. For an instant, she didn't know what had roused her or where she was. Outside, the black sky had taken on a pearly cast, which signaled that dawn was not far away. She squinted through the dimness at her surroundings, and when she spotted her gown and negligee on the floor, it all came rushing back—the passion, the heated words, the incredible pleasure.

She smiled and snuggled her face into the pillow, feeling smug and content. Matt's stamina amazed her. They had made love three times during the night, and each time had been breathtaking.

"No. No, come back! Don't go!"

At the mumbled words, Maude Ann looked over her shoulder at Matt and realized what had jarred her awake. They were lying spoon-fashion, and though he appeared to still be asleep, he was making restless, jerky movements, his body tense against her back. In the dim light she could see that his face wore an anguished expression.

"Matt? Darling, are you all right?" Maude Ann tried to twist around to face him, but instantly the arm encircling her waist tightened, and he held her clamped to him. Reaching over her shoulder, she gave his cheek several brisk pats. "Matt. Matt, wake up. You're having a dream."

He awoke with a start and shot up into a sitting position. "What? What is—"

He looked around, bewildered, disoriented. I..."

"It's all right." Maude Ann raised herself up on one elbow and stroked his back. "You were just dreaming."

His shoulders slumped. "Yeah. I know."

With a sigh, he flopped back flat on his pillow and draped his forearm over his eyes. Remaining propped above him, Maude Ann put her hand on his chest, stroking her fingers through the silky hair as she watched him try to get his breathing under control. "You've had this dream before, I take it," she said softly, still stroking.

His mouth twisted. "Oh, yeah. Lots of times."

"When did it start?"

"I've had the same dream, off and on, all my life."

She debated for a moment, knowing that with Matt she was on shaky ground when it came to this sort of thing. "Would you like to tell me about it?"

The forearm covering his eyes rolled back a quarter turn. From beneath it he gave her dry look. "Are you asking as a psychiatrist or just out of curiosity?"

"I'm asking as the woman who loves you."

The answer seemed to disarm him, and his eyes softened. He reached out and stroked her cheek. "It's nothing for you to worry about, sweetheart. There's nothing scary or threatening about the dream."

"I'm glad. But why don't you tell me, anyway?"

He gave her an exasperated look, but she merely waited, and finally he sighed and gave in. He told her about the faceless woman in the mist, and how he and other shadowy figures ran after her as she backed away crying.

Maude Ann listened intently, and when he was done she asked, "Do you know who she is?"

"I have a good idea. I'm no psychiatrist, but I'd have to be dense not to have figured out it's probably my birth mother."

"Your *birth mother?*" Maude Ann sat up in the bed. "I didn't know you were adopted!"

Matt grinned at her astonishment and ran his forefinger down her spine, all the way to the shadowy clef at its base. The feathery touch made her shiver. "There's a lot you don't know about me. But you'll learn."

"Matt, stop that." Reaching behind her, she grabbed his wrist. "We're talking about your dream and your being adopted."

"Mmm, I can think of more pleasant things to do."

"You sex maniac. Behave. This is important."

"Spoilsport," he teased, but her look told him she wasn't going to budge,. "Oh, all right. But I warn you, there's not much to tell. For reasons of her own, when I was two years old, my mother put me up for adoption."

"Two? That's unusual. Usually if a woman makes the decision to give up a child, she does so at birth. Do you have any idea why she gave you up?"

"Could be she was bored with motherhood, or she couldn't afford to keep me, or it cramped her style too much to have me around, or she just plain didn't like me. I'll probably never know. Hell, I don't even know her name."

Matt said the words casually, as though the matter was

of no importance to him, but she heard the bitter hurt and anger behind them. "Do you remember her at all?"

"Only in my dreams, and even then, there's no face. But like I said, it doesn't take a genius to figure out who the woman is or why I have the dream. She gave me away, and I didn't understand. Hell, it probably scared the hell out of me."

"Mmm. You may be right. That would be very traumatic for a two-year-old. By then you had bonded with her. And though you say you have no memories of her, they're there, buried somewhere in your subconscious." She thought a moment, then asked, "Do you know anything about her?"

"Not much. She had only two requests of my adoptive parents. First, that I be adopted by an Irish couple, which I assume means I'm of Irish descent, although I don't know that for certain. And she asked that I always wear this medallion piece." The chain that encircled his neck had fallen to one side onto the pillow. He picked it up and held the jagged piece of silver so that she could see it.

"Yes, I remember seeing that before."

Reaching around, Maude Ann turned on the bedside light. Taking the piece of metal from his fingers, she leaned forward to examine it. "There's writing on one side, and it looks like some sort of symbol on the other." She looked at him. "Do you have any idea what they mean?"

"Not a clue. There's not enough there to decipher."

She looked back at the medallion piece again and ran her finger over the uneven edge. "It's looks like it's only a small piece of a disk. Sort of like an uneven wedge out of a pie. I wonder where the rest of it is."

"I assume my birth mother has it, but I don't really know. Or care, for that matter. Hell, I don't know why I even bother to wear the thing."

Maude Ann's heart squeezed and she gazed at him sadly.

Oh, my darling, you wear it because this little piece of silver is your only connection to the woman who gave you life, and whether you want to or not, you do care.

Something of what she was thinking must have shown on her face, because Matt reached out and cupped her cheek. "Hey, sweetheart, don't look so sad."

"I can't help it. It is sad that you never knew her."

"Not really. She probably did me a favor, giving me to the Dolans. I had a great childhood. No kid could have asked for better parents. So don't go wasting all that compassion and motherly concern on me. Save it for the kids upstairs."

A slow smile spread on his face, and his eyes grew heavy-lidded as they zeroed in on her mouth. Maude Ann knew that look, and her body began to tingle. Hooking his hand around her neck, he drew her down to him. "Now that I've satisfied your curiosity about my family," he murmured in a seductive rumble, "it's only fair that you satisfy my curiosity."

Lying half on his chest, she relaxed and luxuriated in the feel of his body against hers. She smiled as his lips nipped and nibbled at hers. "Oh? And just what…could you possibly…still be…curious about?" she asked, between indulging in some nibbling of her own. "After last night…I have no more…secrets."

A wicked chuckle rumbled from Matt's throat. "Sweetheart, I'm just…getting started…exploring your…secrets."

Maude Ann felt as though she were melting from the inside as a languid heat built in the core of her body and spread outward. Responding to the pressure of his hand on her neck, she gave a low moan and surrendered to his kiss, but her lips had barely settled on his when something he'd said jogged her memory.

She jerked back. "The kids!"

"What? Maude Ann, what…" he began, but she was already scrambling off the bed and snatching up her gown and negligee.

He sat up and scowled. "Dammit, Maudie, come back here!"

"I can't. I don't have time. There's too much to do. Oh, how could I have forgotten?" she moaned. She paused just long enough to shoot him a harried look. "Well, don't just lie there. Get up! Get busy!"

"Maude Ann, what the hell is the matter with you?" He glanced at the bedside clock. "It's barely six. The kids won't be downstairs for at least another hour yet. Come back to bed."

She turned with her hand on the doorknob and experienced a flutter of regret. He looked so sexy and so thoroughly male, sitting there in the middle of the rumpled bed glaring at her, hair mussed, jaw shadowed with morning stubble, his naked body bronze and muscled above the white sheet, which lay bunched around the tops of his thighs.

"I can't. Don't you remember? Marshall and Dennis are leaving today. Their cousin is coming for them around ten."

Chapter Thirteen

It was always emotionally devastating when one of the children left the haven, but for the sake of the other kids, Maude Ann tried to present the departure as a joyous event.

She and Jane prepared a special celebration breakfast and did their best to appear happy for the boys. Maude Ann had purchased a small gift for each of the brothers, along with cards, which they all, including Matt, had signed, though some of the smaller kids had needed help printing their names.

To everyone's surprise, Tyrone had a gift of his own for Dennis. The boys had butted heads like two young bulls when Tyrone first came to the haven, but both were scamps, and before long they had been aiding and abetting each other in all kinds of mischief. Now, next to Matt, Dennis was Tyrone's best friend. When he pulled the grubby rabbit's foot, his most prized possession, from the pocket of his jeans and handed it to Dennis, Maude Ann had to look away and blink back tears.

She had been preparing the kids for weeks, ever since she'd received the order from Judge Simpson. She had explained that Marshall and Dennis were going to live with family members who loved and wanted them, and that they were going to have a wonderful life. She had told the other kids that while it was okay to feel sad that their friends were leaving, even to cry if they wanted, they didn't have to worry about them.

She would have given the pep talk, no matter what, simply to allay the children's fears, but after meeting the Hendersons, a pleasant couple in their forties with two apparently well-adjusted and happy boys of their own, she had hopes that this time she was right.

There were tears and a general feeling of gloom as they all said their goodbyes on the front veranda and watched Marshall and Dennis drive away with the Hendersons. That was only to be expected. More troubling was the fear she saw in the children's eyes that they might be the next to be banished from the only safe place they had ever known. Maude Ann wanted more than anything to be able to tell them it would never happen, but she couldn't. And that broke her heart.

She managed to hold on to her composure—just barely—until the car disappeared down the road and the dejected children and Jane and Matt straggled back inside. Maude Ann deliberately dawdled behind the others, and the instant the door closed behind them, she took off at a run.

Before she had taken three steps, she was sobbing and nearly blinded by tears. She would have preferred a private hiding place that no one but her knew about, but there was no such spot. In any case, her grief was too urgent, so the east veranda, which was seldom used this time of day, had to do.

Throwing herself onto the first wicker love seat she encountered, she curled into a ball, buried her face against the blue-and-white canvas cushions and gave in to the wrenching pain.

That was where Matt found her a few minutes later.

He had missed her almost at once. When he'd asked Jane where Maude Ann had disappeared to, she had given him an odd look and muttered a cryptic, "Never you mind. She has to deal with these things in her own way."

He hadn't like the sound of that. Not one bit.

Ignoring Jane's exasperated, "Now, Matt, you come back here!" he had left the kitchen to go look for her.

He had intended to start down at the pier, but the instant he'd stormed out the door, he heard an odd sound from the east veranda and went to investigate.

He came around the corner and stopped in his tracks.

Though Maude Ann's cries were muffled by the loveseat cushions, the sound of her misery and the sight of her shaking shoulders nearly destroyed him.

With an oath, he rushed to her. "Aw, Maudie, come here, baby." Ignoring her weak protest, he scooped her up in his arms and sat down with her in the nearest swing. As she curled against him, he cradled her close and set the swing in motion.

"Sweetheart, what are you doing out here all by yourself," he crooned, nuzzling his jaw against her temple when she burrowed her face into his neck. "No, never mind. Don't answer that. Just let it out, baby. Let it all out. Thatta girl."

It was just as well he retracted the question. He doubted that Maude Ann could have said a word if her life had depended on it. All she could do was huddle in his arms and wail out her grief like a forsaken child.

Her tears soaked his shirt, plastering the cloth to his skin, but he didn't care. As he swung them back and forth, he stroked her back and gazed out at the woods beyond the yard, surprised and bemused. Evidently, she wasn't as stoic as he'd thought.

Normally, crying women sent Matt running for cover, but strangely, with Maude Ann all he wanted to do was give comfort. She was such a strong, self-sufficient woman, that her tears were all the more heartrending, and a measure of how deeply she loved the kids in her charge.

When Maude Ann loved, she loved completely, openly, holding nothing back. He had firsthand experience of that. Her nature was open and giving, and once she accepted the love between them, she welcomed it with a wholehearted joy that both captivated him and scared the wits out of him.

Lord, he didn't ever want to hurt her.

He had no idea how long they sat there, but gradually her sobs subsided.

"Are you all right now?" he asked after a while.

She shook her head. "N-no. But I w-will be." Another little hitching sigh overtook her, and when it was done she sagged against him.

"I—I *hate* to cry," she said with so much vehemence that Matt had to smile.

"I know you do," he agreed solemnly.

"It's just that I h-hate it so much when one of the kids leaves. Today I lost two of them."

"Yeah, that was rough."

She sat up and sniffed, wiping her wet cheek with her fingertips, but she didn't move from his lap.

Stroking her thigh, Matt gave her a curious look. "If it

upsets you so much, sweetheart, why in the name of heaven did you open a foster home?''

Maude Ann looked at him as though she thought that was the most daft question she'd ever heard. ''Because I knew I could help these children. And because they need me.''

And that, Matt thought, said it all.

He knew that her mothering tendencies were part of why he loved her. Each one of these sad-eyed, little lost souls was special to her, and no matter what, she would never voluntarily give any of them away—as his mother had done. Maude Ann's great capacity for love, her unwavering commitment and constancy, were as much a part of her as her auburn curls or the spattering of freckles across her nose, and that made her a woman to prize.

Looking into her eyes, he felt overwhelmed with love for this woman. Her face was streaked with tears, which had all but washed away the small amount of makeup she'd applied that morning to impress the Hendersons. But to Matt she had never been more beautiful. And that beauty went all the way to the bone.

Gazing at her tenderly, he framed her face with both hands and with his thumbs brushed away the lingering moisture. ''You're right, they do need you. So do I.'' Exerting gentle pressure, he slowly brought her face down to his.

He kissed her with all the tenderness he was feeling, savoring her, loving her. She had been through an emotional wringer, and his aim wasn't to arouse, but to comfort and cherish. Nevertheless, the gentle caress packed a wallop, piercing Matt with hot, sweet desire and drawing a last, shuddering sigh from Maude Ann.

''What're you kissin' Miz Maudie for?''

Maude Ann started and would have jumped up, but Matt put his arms around her hips and held her in his lap.

"Tyrone. We, uh…that is…"

"Did you need something, Tyrone?" Matt asked, cutting off Maude Ann's dithering response. To his great amusement, her face turned scarlet and she had trouble meeting the boy's eyes.

"Miz Jane says to tell Miz Maudie she's wanted on the phone."

"Oh, okay. Thank you, Tyrone." Reacting to the statement with the alacrity of a drowning man grabbing a lifeline, she shot off Matt's lap and disappeared around the corner of the porch before the chains on the swing stopped rattling.

Tyrone stayed where he was and eyed Matt with sullen curiosity. "You like that kissin' stuff?"

The disgust in the boy's voice brought a crooked smile to Matt's mouth. "Yeah, I do. You will, too, one day."

"Nuh-uh! I ain't never gonna kiss no yucky girl."

"Yeah, well…" The swing creaked and rocked, rattling the chains again as Matt rose. He put his hand on Tyrone's shoulder and headed for the back door. "The thing is, son, girls don't stay yucky. Round about thirteen or fourteen, they get to be downright tempting."

Tyrone looked up at Matt with an expression that clearly said, "Yeah, right. And pigs fly." A few seconds later, he asked, "Does that mean you gonna kiss Miz Maudie some more?"

Chuckling, Matt gave the boy's shoulder a squeeze. "You got it, pal. Every chance I get."

The following weeks were an eye-opener for Maude Ann. She had not known it was possible to be so happy and so filled with dread, both at the same time, but that was exactly how she felt.

Except for the hours he worked out, Matt spent all his time with her and the kids. He took part in whatever activity she planned for the children, whether work or play, everything from gardening and house-cleaning to doing jigsaw puzzles and playing catch.

After Tyrone caught them kissing, there was no way they could pretend they were not involved, but Maude Ann had not expected Matt to so openly display his affection for her. She had thought, because of the temporary nature of their relationship, that they would behave casually toward each other when they were not alone. Matt, however, was having none of that. He insisted that honesty and loving displays among adults were what the children needed, and she couldn't argue with that.

And loving displays were just what Matt provided. He touched her frequently, putting his arm around her shoulders or her waist, holding her hand, cupping the back of her neck to haul her in for a quick kiss, stroking her hair.

When he felt like kissing her or touching her, he did so, no matter who was watching, whether it was the kids or Jane or J.T. It seemed to Maude Ann that he took special delight in kissing her in front of J.T.

Much to Matt's annoyance, the reporter was a frequent visitor at Henley Haven. He even spent a couple of weekends.

"I just don't see why he keeps hanging around," Matt groused after one such visit. "He knows how we feel about each other." Matt had made sure of that by taking J.T. aside for a talk the very next time he showed up after the picnic.

"Matt! I keep telling you, J.T. and I are just good friends. Friends visit friends. Besides, I'm glad he makes the effort. He's good with the children. He likes them and they like him. These kids need plenty of positive masculine attention.''

"That's another thing. I'm not sure he's a good influence on the kids. Conway tends to be too lenient with them. He's always joking and kidding around, never takes anything seriously. The man's a lightweight.''

Maude Ann's eyes widened. "Why, Matthew Dolan. It's not just me, is it? You're jealous of J.T.'s relationship with the children, too.''

"Me? Jealous of Conway? Don't be ridiculous. I don't have any reason to be jealous of that jerk.''

Delighted, she went to him and looped her arms around his neck, meeting his scowl with a loving smile. "That's right. Absolutely none. The kids like J.T., but you're the one they're really crazy about.''

It was true. Matt would always be gruff and intense and at times impatient, but that was just his personality. The children knew that behind that tough exterior was an old softie. And they adored him.

The change in Maude Ann's relationship with Matt brought a halt to Debbie's nightmares, but to be on the safe side, Maude Ann put a baby monitor in the little girl's room. The receiver sat on the bedside table in Matt's room since Maude Ann now spent her nights in his bed.

Matt's condition improved daily, even faster, it seemed to her, than it had before they had become lovers. While she was happy for him, she knew that time was running out, and her sense of dread increased apace with his recovery.

The day of the picnic, his buddies had brought Matt's Jeep to the haven, and a few days later, for the first time, he drove himself to Houston for his checkup. Being able to drive again was liberating for him, and his mood had been buoyant that morning. Maude Ann had smiled at his obvious pleasure and kissed him goodbye, but she'd watched his Jeep disappear down the road with a fist-size knot in her chest. One day soon, she'd thought, Matt would drive away and not return.

For all that they spent each day together, they had almost no time alone until after the children were in bed at night. Late August marked the beginning of the school year for the four oldest children, but even though they were gone from the aven for most of every weekday, Debbie was still there. Crushed that she couldn't go to school with the others, she dogged Matt's and Maude Ann's steps wherever they went.

The school bus did not come down private roads, so each morning and afternoon one of the adults drove the four miles to and from the bus stop out on the highway. On a Friday morning, almost five weeks after the picnic, Maude Ann had no sooner returned from the bus stop and stepped out of the van when Matt grasped her arm and announced that she was coming with him.

At first she was too startled to protest, but when he started marching her toward his Jeep she managed a surprised "Coming with you where?"

"To Houston. We're going to have some time alone together."

"What? Oh, Matt, darling, I'd love to. Really. But I can't go today. I have too much to do." Her protest hadn't the slightest effect on him. Practically trotting along at his side, she cast a desperate look over her shoulder at her assistant. "Tell him, Jane!"

"Don't look at me. I'm on his side." The older woman stood on the front walk, watching the proceedings with interest. "You ask me, it's about time you took a day off. Now you two have a nice time. And don't do anything I wouldn't do," she added with a chuckle as Matt gently pulled Maude Ann into the front passenger seat of the Jeep.

In no time at all, he was around the vehicle and behind the wheel. Ignoring her sputtering, he started the engine, punched the accelerator and took off down the road, sending gravel and dust flying. Disbelieving, Maude Ann twisted around and saw Jane standing in the drive, cheerfully waving goodbye.

Twisting around again, she flopped back in the seat. "Matt, you have to take me back. I can't do this."

"Sure you can. It's all arranged. I'm having another checkup this afternoon, but we'll have the rest of the time to ourselves. Anyway, you need this. You haven't had a real day off since I came here."

"But just look at me. I can't go to Houston like this."

Matt glanced at her T-shirt and jeans. She certainly didn't bear much resemblance to the dignified professional who testified in court on the children's behalf or twisted the arms of corporate bigwigs and Houston's old guard for money. No, she looked like his sweet Maudie, which was a thousand times better. "You look fine to me. But don't worry, Jane packed you a bag. It's in the back."

With a sigh, Maude Ann accepted defeat. It was a conspiracy, pure and simple. She hadn't stood a chance. "At least tell me we'll be back before the kids get home from school."

"Nope. Sunday afternoon."

"*Sunday!* Are you *crazy?* Jane can't handle the kids alone all weekend."

"Relax. It's all taken care of. J.T. called this morning while you were upstairs with the kids. Wanted to know if it was all right if he came out for the weekend." Matt glanced at her out of the corner of his eye. For all its brevity, the look oozed hard satisfaction. "I told him sure."

"Matt! That's terrible! I'm sure he doesn't expect to be left saddled with the children with only Jane to help."

"The guy claims he wants to help with the kids, so let him."

"Well, it's unfair, and I'm calling him." She snatched up the car phone, only to discover it was dead.

Matt darted her smug look. "Been disconnected ever since I was shot. Relax. J.T. will be fine. He may be a pain in the rear, but like you said, he's good with the kids."

"I'm still calling as soon as we get to a working telephone."

Despite her imperious tone, deep down, Maude Ann was thrilled that Matt had gone to so much trouble to be alone with her. Despite her fierce independence, she had to admit it was kind of exciting to be abducted by the man you loved.

"Fine. You can call from my place," Matt replied, but he didn't seem in the least concerned.

His place turned out to be a charming two-story town house off Dairy Ashford Road in northwest Houston. Along one side at the back, the house was connected to the garage by a utility room, but after parking, they walked through the adjacent small patio and entered through the back door.

Maude Ann was curious to see Matt's home, and as he led her through the surprisingly spacious town house, she was surprised. Not only was the place neat and clean, it was tastefully decorated in a mix of stately antiques and homey modern pieces. The color scheme of subdued pumpkin, rust and silvery gray with touches of navy was masculine without being drab. The overall look was classy. Which, when she thought about it, suited Matt to a T.

The downstairs of the house was made up of a large living/dining-room combination, a kitchen and breakfast nook, a powder room and a den, from which the stairs rose.

Upstairs were three bedrooms, one of which was apparently used as an office/exercise room, and two baths.

It struck her as they were finishing the tour in Matt's bedroom that after being closed up for months, the place should be stuffy and everything covered with a layer of dust, but it wasn't. The air-conditioning hummed, pumping out cool, fresh air, and there wasn't a particle of dust in sight.

"I would have thought you'd have the place closed up while you were at the haven," she said, running her finger along the glossy surface of his Victorian-era chifforobe.

"It was. I called Patty a few days ago. She and Hank have a key to the place. She came over yesterday and gave it a cleaning and brought in some food."

Maude Ann turned and raised an eyebrow at him. "You've been planning this for days, haven't you?"

"That's right." He walked slowly toward her, his gaze never wavering, and her heart began to pound. "I wanted to see you in my home," he said in a low, gravelly voice. "In my bed."

Stopping in front of her, he slipped his arms around her waist and pulled her close, his sizzling gaze searing her. "I wanted to smell you on my sheets."

The words, the intensity with which he uttered them, the dark flush of passion on his face, tugged at her heartstrings, even as something deep in her feminine core quickened and burst into flame. To be desired that much was a glorious thing that no woman could resist. Maude Ann didn't even try.

She wrapped her arms around his neck, and when he lowered his head, she met the kiss with a fiery passion that matched his.

Lips rocked, rubbed, nibbled. Tongues stroked and dueled. Teeth nipped. All the while their hands roamed. Soon, it wasn't enough, and garments dropped to the floor, first Maude Ann's T-shirt and bra, then Matt's shirt.

He bent and kissed and suckled first one nipple, then the other, as Maude Ann moaned and dug her fingernails into his shoulders. He kissed the tender skin between her breasts, drew tiny wet circles there with the tip of his tongue.

Maude Ann retaliated by running her fingers through the hair on his chest until she found his nipples. She toyed with the tiny pebbles, then lightly scraped them with her thumbnail, smiling when Matt shuddered and groaned.

"Dr. Edwards, you're a shameless wanton and a tease," he growled, sweeping her up in his arms and heading for the bed. Maude Ann's husky laugh rang out, then turned to a squeal when he tossed her onto the mattress.

She bounced once, then sank into the softness. Lying there in her faded jeans, bare from the waist up, she stretched luxuriously and gave him a sultry look from beneath half-closed eyelids as he began to peel out of the rest of his clothes. "I know. Aren't you glad?"

Something flared in Matt's eyes, and he paused in the act of unzipping his jeans. Then he flew into action, shucking his clothes and stripping Maude Ann of hers in record time. "Damn right, I am," he growled as he lay down beside her and gathered her close.

"Mmm. How glad?" she murmured, running her hand down his chest, then his flat abdomen, then lower still.

Matt closed his eyes and absorbed the pleasure with a low moan. Slowly he opened them again and glided his hand down her body, mimicking her action. "Why don't I show you…"

Maude Ann's eyes fluttered open, closed, then open again. Finally she focused on the unfamiliar navy-and-rust-striped chair by the window and sat up in bed with a start. Then she remembered.

Matt's side of the bed was rumpled and empty. Hearing no sound from the bathroom, she assumed he had gone downstairs. With a sigh, she lay back on the pillow, put her arms over her head and indulged in a long, sinuous stretch, smiling smugly.

A glance at her watch gave her a shock. It was after one in the afternoon! She couldn't believe she'd slept so long.

Actually, it wasn't like her to fall asleep in the middle of the day at all, even if she *had* just experienced the most beautiful lovemaking of all time. She felt positively decadent. A slow, Cheshire-cat grin curved her mouth, and she stretched again.

Turning her head, she spotted the note propped against the adjacent pillow. She picked it up and read Matt's small, neat handwriting.

Gone for my checkup. Didn't have the heart to wake you. Be back as soon as I can.

Love,
Matt

Smiling, she left the bed and headed for the shower. When she emerged again, wrapped in a towel, she glanced at the small bag Jean had packed for her. Ignoring it, she opted, instead, to wear one of Matt's white dress shirts.

After making the bed, she went downstairs and made herself a sandwich for lunch. When she'd eaten, she spent the next couple of hours wandering from room to room, examining the decor more closely, perusing the framed prints on the walls and the small pieces of Western sculpture scattered throughout the house.

Clouds had begun to roll in shortly after she awoke, and

by midafternoon, when she finished her inspection, the sky had turned so dark the streetlights came on. Lightning flashed almost continuously and thunder rumbled. Then the rains came in typical Gulf-coast fashion, falling fast and heavy. Standing at the patio door in Matt's den looking out was like trying to see through a waterfall.

By four o'clock the storm hadn't abated. Maude Ann was beginning to worry when Matt called.

"This is taking longer than I thought. I probably won't get out of here for another hour. I was going to take you out tonight, but with this storm, that doesn't seem like such a good idea now."

"You're right. This is definitely a night to relax by the fire. I don't mind staying in. I would prefer to, actually."

"Good. I was hoping you'd say that. How about I pick up Chinese food on my way home?"

"Mmm, sounds wonderful."

"Great. I'll be there as soon as I can. But don't worry if it takes me a while. With this storm, there's bound to be some street flooding."

At five after six the lights went out. Matt still hadn't returned, so Maude Ann conducted a groping search in the dark for candles. Knowing Matt's penchant for organization, she knew they had to be either in the kitchen or utility room. She located them in the latter, along with a box of matches.

Thirty minutes later, Matt arrived. "Maude Ann, I'm home. Where are—"

Carrying a rain-spotted sack in each arm, he came to an abrupt halt in the middle of the den and stared. Maude Ann stood at the top of the stairs, wearing only his shirt and a smile. Outside, thunder cracked and rolled. Inside, flickering candlelight cast wavering shadows against the wall and filled the room with a romantic golden glow.

"What are you wearing beneath that shirt?"

Maude's Ann's smile grew sultry, and even in the faint light, she could see his face darken with desire.

Slowly, never taking his eyes from hers, he set the sacks down on the coffee table and started up the stairs.

Later—much later—they ate reheated Chinese food.

The rain continued all weekend, trapping them in the house, but Maude Ann didn't care. As far as she was concerned, the weekend could not have been better, an idyllic three days that she knew would remained etched in her memory forever.

She and Matt made love and talked and made love again. They watched movies, they read the paper together, they shared cooking and cleanup chores. They teased and laughed.

At times, when they told each other about their childhoods, they were nostalgic, even sad when they spoke of their respective deceased parents, whom they had loved dearly.

Matt told her about growing up in a family where police work was a tradition. "I think Dad pinned a badge on my shirt the day they adopted me," he said with a chuckle.

"But what about what *you* wanted? I mean, it seems as though you weren't given a choice, that your career was chosen for you. Didn't you ever have a desire to do something else?" she probed cautiously.

"Not really. When I was about seven, I dreamed of becoming a jet pilot someday, but what kid hasn't? I don't regret making my dad happy. Being a cop is honest work, and it's necessary."

"Yes, but, say, for the sake of argument, you couldn't be a policeman," she said, ignoring his quick frown. "What would you choose to do?" It was touchy territory she was venturing into, but she hoped to open his mind to other possibilities. At the very least, to plant a seed.

"I don't know. Something that would keep me outdoors, I guess."

No matter how she probed, she couldn't get anything more definitive than that out of him, but it was a start. She hoped.

They talked about politics, philosophy, movies, books and religion. They argued good-naturedly over which team would win the Super Bowl and who was the greatest quarterback of all time. They discussed everything—except the future.

As it turned out, Jane could have saved herself the trouble of packing clothes for Maude Ann. The only thing she wore all weekend were Matt's shirts. Or nothing at all.

It was a magical three days, and Maude Ann felt relaxed and happy as they drove home Sunday afternoon in the drizzling rain. When they stopped in the driveway and the children ran out to meet them, her world seemed complete.

Chapter Fourteen

"C'mon, kids. That's enough swimming for one day."

Tyrone surfaced from a dive and wiped his streaming face. "Aw, Matt, do we gotta quit now? We just got here."

"Yeah, we're having fun," Yolanda chimed in.

"We wanna swim some more," Debbie, Jennifer and Timothy all shouted in unison.

"No arguments. Haul your little butts out of there and let's go. It's half a mile to the lodge. I don't know about you bunch, but I don't want to walk through the woods in the dark."

That got them moving. They grumbled and sent him pouting looks and dawdled as much as they dared, but they waded out of the water. Matt tossed each child a towel and prodded them to gather their things and get moving.

Leading the way down the path, he grimaced, imagining the picture they made. Six months ago, he'd been a hard-boiled detective chasing down thieves and murderers. Now here he was playing baby-sitter and swimming instructor and marching through the woods with a troop of bedraggled kids trudging in his wake like a string of baby ducks following their mother. Some tough cop you are, Dolan.

When they emerged from the woods, he wasn't pleased to see J.T.'s car parked in the drive in front of the lodge.

He scowled. He'd thought, after last weekend, they wouldn't see much of Conway in the future, but there he sat on the front veranda with Maude Ann, sipping lemonade like the lord of the manor.

Making no attempt to hide his annoyance, Matt fixed the reporter with a scowl and climbed the front steps. "You again?"

"Ma-att," Maude Ann scolded.

J.T. grinned. "I thought you might need a baby-sitter."

"We'll call you if we do."

"Pay no attention to him, J.T. The kids and I are glad you're here." The look she shot Matt was meant to be reproving, but the effect was ruined by the laughter in her eyes. That was the trouble with Maude Ann. It didn't do one whit of good to let his jealousy show. She merely laughed at him when he did.

He shot a look at the children. "You kids go take a bath before dinner."

"Why?" Tyrone immediately challenged. "We're not dirty. We've been swimming."

There followed a brief debate about the relative merits of creek water versus soap and water from the tap, but Tyrone remained unconvinced, and in the end Matt pulled rank. "All right, that's it. No more arguing. I'm bigger, stronger and meaner, and I say you're taking a bath. So scoot."

"Now there was a masterful bit of child psychology,"

J.T. drawled as the kids stomped inside. "Why didn't you just get out a whip and a chair?"

"It worked, didn't it?"

Switching his attention to Maude Ann, Matt bent over her until they were eye to eye. "Hi, sweetheart. How'd it go?"

She smiled back at him, her eyes lighting with excitement. "Great. I got the grant."

"Good for you." He gave her a kiss, deliberately lingering over it, mainly because it gave him pleasure, but also to needle the other man.

Matt's swim trunks were still damp, so when the kiss ended, rather than join Maude Ann on the love seat, he sat down on the railing and looked at J.T. again. "I suppose you think you can handle the kids better?"

"I don't suppose, I kno—" J.T. froze. He sat forward and stared at Matt's chest. "Where the hell did you get that?"

"What?" Matt hadn't bothered to button up his shirt when he'd put it on after swimming, and he glanced down and saw the medallion piece nestled in his chest hair. "This?"

"Yes. Where'd you get it?"

Narrowing his eyes, Matt closed his fist around the chunk of silver and fired back, "What business is it of yours where I got it?"

"Because I have one similar to it." J.T. reached inside the collar of his shirt and pulled out a chain. Dangling from it was a piece of a silver disk. "This was left to me by my natural mother when she gave me up for adoption."

"So was mine." Stunned, Matt looked down at the medallion piece in his hand, then at the one dangling from J.T.'s.

J.T. did the same. "When's your birthday?"

"February sixth."

"So is mine. How old are you?"

"Thirty-four."

"Me, too. I was born at St. Joseph's Hospital in Houston at ten after seven in the morning. How about you?"

Matt felt the hair on the back of his neck stand on end. "I was born at 6:45 a.m. at St. Joseph's."

For an interminable time he and J.T. stood unmoving, staring at each other. Matt's chest was so tight it felt as though it was being squeezed in a vice.

Maude Ann looked from one man to the other, her mouth agape. Abruptly, J.T. whipped the chain off over his head and walked up to Matt. "Let me see that."

Too stunned to refuse, Matt took off the piece of silver and handed it to him. J.T. glanced at Matt, then at Maude Ann, then held his own jagged medallion piece up to Matt's.

The silver fragments fit together like two pieces of a puzzle, forming two-thirds of a disk.

Maude Ann sucked in an audible breath. They all stared at the joined pieces of silver, and for the space of several heartbeats no one made a sound. Slowly, the men's gazes rose and met. "Well, I'll be damned," J.T. whispered.

Matt could not have agreed more, but the power of speech had deserted him. He felt as though he'd been pole-axed.

Maude Ann sprang to her feet. "For heaven's sake! Somebody say *something!* Don't you two realize what this means?"

"Yeah, we realize." J.T. aimed a wry smile at Matt. "It appears, Detective Dolan, that you and I are brothers."

"It looks that way."

"Now ain't that a kick in the head?"

Maude Ann glared at first one man then the other, her

expression growing more stupefied and outraged by the second. "That's *it?* That's all you have to say to each other? What is the *matter* with you two? If I had just found out that I had a sister I didn't know existed—a *twin* sister, at that—I'd be so excited I'd be turning cartwheels, for heaven's sake! You two just sit there like a couple of lumps!"

"Triplets."

"What?" She blinked at the nonsequitur.

"My guess is we're two of a set of triplets, not twins." Matt nodded toward the pieces of silver that J.T. still held fitted together. "From the looks of that, I think it's safe to assume that we have another sibling somewhere."

"He's right. There's still a third of the medallion missing. Nice work, Detective."

"Triplets?" Maude Ann said in a dazed voice, and sank back down on the love seat.

"Can you make out what's etched on it?"

J.T. studied first one side of the pieces, then the other. "Nope. Just 'Your' followed by a word that begins with 'h-e-r-i.' Under that are three lines that look like an address. The first line is 'The R-o' something. The next is 'P.O. B-o-' something. Under that is 'C-l-e' something." He turned the two pieces over. "The markings on the other side look like some sort of symbol."

Shaking his head, he handed both pieces to Matt so that he could examine them. "Looks to me like the medallion was deliberately cut so that you couldn't make out the message unless all three pieces were together."

"Could be. The question is, why did our mother do that?"

"Maybe she hoped we'd get curious about the message and try to find the rest someday. Which means she wanted us to find one another."

"If that were the case, why did she give us away to three separate families?"

"She probably didn't have any choice," Maude Ann said.

"Thirty-two years ago, that was common practice of adoption agencies. There was rarely, if ever, any attempt made to keep multiples together. I suppose the thinking at the time was, rather than burden one family with three babies, they would make three families happy with one baby each. Nowadays, we understand the close bond between multiples, even fraternals, which you and J.T. obviously are, and every effort is made to keep them together.

"Maybe you're right, J.T. Maybe she split the medallion among the three of you in the hope that you would find one another again someday. That may have been her only chance of reuniting you."

"Maybe," Matt said, but he had his doubts. He thought over what Maude Ann had just said about him and J.T. having a close bond, but he couldn't imagine it, even if they had shared the same womb and the first two years of life together.

Standing at the railing, J.T. stared out across the lawn at the lake, his face for once pensive. "Do you have any memories of before? When we were still with her?"

Matt didn't have to asked who "her" was. "Only in the form of dreams. How about you?"

"Little flashes now and then. A face. The sound of a voice. Nothing really clear. I do remember sharing a bed with other kids, though. Which, of course, I now know was you and our other sib."

The comment jarred Matt. Suddenly the memory surfaced in his mind's eye, sharp and vivid as a photograph. "A big, iron double bed, right? With railings along the sides that she'd added so we wouldn't fall off. And there was a red-white-and-blue quilt with a big star in the middle."

"So you remember it, too?"

"Not until just now when you mentioned it."

They were silent for a bit, then J.T. asked, "Well, where do we go from here?"

"I don't know." Matt had been wondering the same thing, but he didn't have an answer. The revelations of the past few minutes had knocked him for a loop. To find out that he had two siblings was mind-boggling. That one of them was J. T. Conway was almost more than he could take in.

"Isn't it obvious?" Maude Ann sent both men a disbelieving look. "You have to get to know each other."

"Sweetheart, we've known each other for over ten years."

"As acquaintances. You don't know each other as family. You need to talk about your childhoods and other life-shaping experiences. Really get to know each other as brothers."

Matt and J.T. exchanged uncomfortable glances.

"And, of course, you need to find your other sibling, also."

Matt frowned. He hadn't gotten as far as thinking about that yet. "Just how are we supposed to do that?"

"I don't know. You're a detective, and J.T. is a reporter. Between the two of you, you ought to be able to think of a way."

"Matt's right." J.T. said. "We don't have much to go on. Just that there's probably a third party out there with the rest of this medallion. We don't even know if it's a brother or a sister. About the only leads we have are our date and place of birth and that he or she was most likely given to an Irish family the same as we were, but we can't even be certain of that. It would be like trying to find the proverbial needle in a haystack.''

''So what? You're just going to do nothing?''

''For now, I think that's probably best.'' Matt cocked an eyebrow at J.T. ''What's your opinion?''

''I'm inclined to agree.''

''What! How can you—''

''Maude Ann, don't.'' It was the first time in weeks that Matt had used that harsh tone, and it silenced her instantly. ''Look, I know you mean well, but this is something J.T. and I have to work out. Not only am I not sure how we'd go about finding this person, at this point I'm not even sure we should try, or if I even want to try. Hell, it's been enough of a shock to find out that J.T. and I are related. I'm just not ready to further complicate my life.''

''Me, neither,'' J.T. said. ''Maybe at some later date, we'll institute a search, but not now. You've got to give us time to absorb this, Maude Ann.''

She was crushed. To her way of thinking, finding a long-lost brother you never knew you had was nothing short of miraculous. Yet these two hadn't even exchanged a handshake. They just continued to eye each other like a couple of wary male wolves.

However, she had no choice but to accept their decision and allow them to work out their relationship in their own way and in their own time.

''Okay, if that's the way you want it. But I still think you're making a mistake.''

As the days passed, Maude Ann became even more convinced of it. The children and Jane were as excited about the turn of events as Maude Ann was, but after the initial shock wore off, Matt and J.T. seemed to retreat from each other.

They exchanged life stories, as she had suggested, but

they were awkward and distant with each other. As she watched them together, it was painfully obvious to Maude Ann that they felt uncomfortable with the change in their relationship and were unsure how to proceed. When she tried to talk to Matt about it, however, he reacted with impatience.

"Dammit, Maude Ann! You expect too much. J.T. and I may have had the same natural parents, but we've led different lives. Besides, the man's been a thorn in my side for over ten years. Now you want us to start acting like brothers? Forget it, Pollyanna. Life just doesn't work that way."

Matt had never spoken to her with such derision, but she tried not to be upset. She told herself that he'd had a shock, that he simply needed time to assimilate and adjust, and he would be fine.

It didn't happen. As the days passed, Matt grew moodier, more remote. He went off by himself for long periods, and when he was with her and the kids, he was preoccupied and abrupt. The children were hurt and disappointed by his behavior, and Maude Ann grew more worried with every passing day.

She could not understand how something that should have been a joyous discovery could cause him so much turmoil. On more than one occasion, she tried to get him to talk about what was bothering him, but he always cut her off, refusing to discuss the matter. One time he was so curt with her she could not overlook his behavior.

That night, for the first time since they had become lovers, Maude Ann did not go to Matt's room. She told herself that they needed a little distance from each other, a cooling-off time. In her heart, though, she was sure that once he realized she wasn't coming, he would storm up the stairs after her and carry her down to his room.

He didn't—not that night, nor the next one, nor the one after that.

On the third day, she didn't see him until late in the afternoon. Jane had just left with Debbie to pick up the children at the bus stop, and for once Maude Ann was alone in the house, or thought she was. She was sitting at her desk in the living room when Matt suddenly appeared in the doorway.

"I need to talk to you, Maude Ann."

His tone and the harsh set of his features sent a chill down her spine, but she put down her pen and smiled. "All right."

He took three steps into the room, then stopped. He looked at her in silence for an unsettlingly long time. "I'm leaving."

The bald announcement felt like a slap, but Maude Ann willed herself to stay calm. "Leaving?"

"Yeah. I talked to Lieutenant Werner this morning. I start back to work in the morning."

Another wave of shock went through her. "But…but you can't. You haven't taken the physical yet."

"Actually, I took it this morning."

"I…I see. You could have told me."

"It wouldn't have changed anything if I had."

"No. I guess not." A terrible trembling started deep inside her. Tears welled up in her eyes, but she blinked furiously to hold them back. "So…you're just going to leave. Just like that. I thought you loved me."

"I do."

"Then how can you leave? How can you just walk away?"

"I don't want to. This is the most difficult thing I've ever done. But dammit, Maudie, I have to get my life back."

"Excuse me? What does that mean?"

"Everything keeps changing. First I got shot, then I came here. Instead of police work, I'm baby-sitting and playing camp counselor."

"I thought you enjoyed that. I thought you cared for the children."

"I did! I do! They're great." He raked a hand through his hair. "Damn, how do I make you understand?"

"Just…say it."

"I don't resent the kids. I love them, and I enjoy spending time with them. That's the trouble—at least, part of it. I enjoy it too much." Too agitated to remain still, he paced to the other side of the room, then swung back. "When Hank and the other guys were here, they filled me in on the status of the cases I'd been working on and what was going on at the precinct. And you know what? I couldn't summon up any interest. None. Zip. Zero." He thumbed his chest and glared at her with something close to panic in his eyes. "*Me!* A guy who lived and breathed police work his whole life. That scared the hell out of me, I can tell you.

"And that's not all. I swore I'd never get serious about a woman. Then I fell in love with you. Hell, I'm so far gone, lately I've started thinking about the future, about commitment, even about adopting these kids. It's crazy!"

Equal parts joy and astonishment shot through Maude Ann. She wanted to rush over and put her arms around him and tell him they could work things out somehow, but she could see how upset he was and that he wasn't finished.

"Then, out of the blue, I get blindsided with this business with J.T. It's too much. Everything is out of control." His eyes pleaded with her to understand. "I have to get my life back, Maude Ann."

She stared at him, her heart slowly breaking. No matter

what she said or did, she was going to lose him. And the devil of it was, she couldn't even work up much anger, because now she understood a lot of things.

As a child, Matt had had his secure world snatched away from him when his mother had given him up, and though he might not consciously remember the event and he'd had a good life with the Dolans, the event had left its mark on him. It explained why he was so orderly and meticulous—about his work, his personal habits, everything he did. Those were things he could control.

Maude Ann had only one card left, and she played it. "Was the life you had really so wonderful? Better than what you've found here?"

"Maybe not, but it was the life I'd chosen for myself and I was comfortable in it. It worked for me." He paced and raked his hand through his hair again. "Look, I don't know why we're even having this conversation. We both knew this day was coming. I have to go back. I'm a policeman. It's what I am."

She shot out of the chair and stood shaking uncontrollably, her hands fisted at her sides. "No! It's what you *do*. What you *choose* to do. Don't you see? You have other options. Just because you chose one career, one way of life, doesn't mean you can't change your mind. Life is all about change, Matt."

"Please, Maude Ann. Don't make this more difficult than it already is. I've made up my mind."

Her eyes shimmered with reproach. So did her voice. "You're just going to walk away, then? From me, from the children, from what we have?"

"I have to."

Defeat weighed on her shoulders like a lead cape. A sob rose in her tight throat, but she swallowed it down and fought to control her quivering mouth. She would not beg, she vowed. She would not. He had made his choice. "I see. When will you go?"

"I've already loaded my things in the car. I just wanted to tell you goodbye."

"You're leaving *now?*" Panic fluttered in her chest. "But what about the children? Aren't you going to tell them goodbye?"

"I think it's better if I don't." He looked at her somberly, his eyes filled with regret. "Goodbye, Maudie."

"No, wait! Matt, come back," she cried, but he left the room and strode out the front door. Maude Ann rushed after him. By the time she reached the veranda he was opening the door of his Jeep. "Matt, please, wait until the children get here."

He looked at her over the top of his car and started to shake his head, but the matter was taken out of his hands when Jane drove up with the children.

They bailed out of the van, Tyrone in the lead, as usual. And, as usual at the end of a schoolday, he was a mess, his shirttail hanging out, tennis shoes untied, a giant splotch of something red on the front of his shirt, papers sticking out of his unzipped backpack.

He spotted Matt and raced over to him, lugging the backpack by a strap. "Hey, Matt, where you goin'?"

"Uh…" Matt looked at Maude Ann, but she wrapped her arms tightly around her middle and lifted her chin.

If he wanted to be a coward and run away just because he couldn't accept change, then let him. But he'd get no help from her.

"I'm going to Houston."

"Can I go, too?"

"I'm afraid not."

"Ah, shoot."

By this time the other children had reached Matt, and the younger ones began clamoring for his attention.

"I got an A on my spelling test today," Jennifer said shyly.

"Hey, Matt, look at the picture I drawed today," Timothy said, waving a crayon drawing in the air.

Debbie tugged insistently on the leg of Matt's jeans. "If you ith goin' thomwhere, you gots to give me a bye-bye kith first."

Not one to be sidelined Tyrone elbowed the others aside and asked, "When you gonna get back?"

Again, Matt glanced at Maude Ann, but except for the tears streaming down her face, her expression remained the same.

"I'm not coming back. I'm going home. Tomorrow morning I go back to work."

Tyrone looked as if Matt had punched him in the face.

"But you *gots* to come back," Debbie wailed, and burst into tears.

Timothy and Jennifer, the most insecure of the group, hung their heads and began to whimper. Refusing to look at Matt, Yolanda took their hands and led them up the steps. When they reached Maude Ann, all three children buried their faces against her and began to cry.

Debbie wrapped her arms around Matt's leg and clung to him like a monkey, pleading, "Don't go! Don't go! Don't go!"

Matt tried to free himself, but the little girl hung on tenaciously. In the end, Jane had to peel the child off him. After aiming a reproachful look at Matt, she carried the little girl to the veranda to join Maude Ann and the others. Every step of the way, Debbie cried pitifully and strained toward Matt with her arms outstretched.

That left only Tyrone. The boy stared at him with accusing eyes. "I shoulda known you'd run out on us."

Matt grimaced. "Look, Tyrone, I *have* to go. It's my job."

"Go on, then! Get outta here, pig!" he shouted furiously. Anger contorted his face, but he couldn't stop his mouth from quivering or hide the hurt in his eyes or staunch the tears that overflowed. He scrubbed at them furiously, but still they streamed down his cheeks in an unending flood. "I don't need you! I *hate* you, you dirty, rotten pig! I *hate* you!"

The last came out on a choked sob, and he whirled around and ran blindly for the veranda and Maude Ann.

Grim-faced, Matt watched him over the top of the car. Briefly, his gaze met Maude Ann's. Then, with a curse, he slammed into the Jeep and took off.

Through her tears, Maude Ann watched the vehicle disappear around the bend in the road and felt her heart cleave in two. Matt was gone. She had lost him.

The children clung to her, wetting her shirt and the top of her jeans with their tears, but she didn't care. She remained where she was, her arms around the huddled group and let them cry out their grief and hurt and confusion while she cried out hers.

Jane stood beside them, alternately patting shaking shoulders and dabbing her own eyes with a tissue.

It was almost five minutes before the children were calm enough to let go of Maude Ann. Forcing her own hurt aside, she dried their tears, administered hugs and kisses and pitifully inadequate words of reassurance. Then, knowing they had to talk about Matt's desertion and work through the pain, she urged everyone inside and into the living room.

They had barely settled when they heard a car coming down the road.

Tyrone's woebegone expression vanished and his eyes lit up. "Maybe Matt changed his mind."

With the resilience of the very young, the other children let out whoops of joy, bolted to their feet and rushed to the window, only to sag with disappointment when the unfamiliar car came around the bend. It was a shabby-looking older vehicle. One fender was missing entirely, and its faded blue paint was now blotched with rust.

"Who's that?" Tyrone asked in a querulous voice as the old wreck screeched to a halt in the drive. The question had barely left his lips when a man jumped out and headed for the front steps with long, furious strides.

Maude Ann recognized him before he gained the veranda. Her heart lurched when she saw he had a gun in his hand. "Oh, my Lord, no!"

Suddenly Timothy started whimpering and backing away from the window. The terror in the boy's eyes was chilling.

"Jane, go lock the back door! I'll get the front! Hurry!" Maude Ann raced from the room with Jane on her heels, but they had barely taken two steps into the entry when the front door crashed open and the wild-eyed man charged inside.

Spotting Maude Ann, he halted, and his eyes narrowed with murderous hatred. "I knew I'd find you, bitch."

Maude Ann's insides were trembling, but she squared her shoulders and stood her ground. "What are you doing here, Mr. Perkins? Aren't you supposed to be in prison?"

Holding one hand behind her, she motioned for Jane to go back into the living room with the kids.

"Whaddaya think? I busted out and came for my son. I seen that story in the newspaper about this place. You sitting there all smug on the porch, coddling my boy, making a little wuss outta him. Didja think just 'cause the picture didn't show his face I wouldn't recognize 'im? I seen the birthmark on his arm. For weeks now, I been searching every lake around this part of the state, looking for this place. And now I found you.''

''That birthmark, as you call it, is a scar from one of many wounds you inflicted on Timothy. Which is why you and your wife no longer have custody of him.''

He advanced a step, his face twisting in a feral snarl. ''If you hadn't'a testified in court, telling the judge all them lies 'bout me'n my old lady, it never woulda happened.''

Maude Ann smelled his whiskey breath and saw that his pupils were so dilated the irises were merely a thin ring of gray around them. The man was not only drunk, he was stoned out of his mind. And dangerous.

Maude Ann's pulse skittered, but she raised her chin another notch. ''I simply told the truth, and you know it, Mr. Perkins.''

''Don't matter none. Ain't you or no snooty judge or nobody else taking my kid away from me. He's mine to do with as I see fit.'' He looked over her shoulder into the living room. ''I hear sniveling. He must be in there. Timmy!''

Maude Ann sidestepped and tried to block the doorway, but he snapped, ''Get outta my way, bitch!'' and shoved her so hard she stumbled back into the room and nearly fell.

All the kids huddled around Jane, their faces white with terror. Timothy sobbed quietly.

''Timmy, shut up that bawlin' and get over here! You're coming with me.''

''No! You're not taking this child!'' Maude Ann stepped in front of the boy, then cried out when Jim Perkins grabbed her hair and jerked her head back. Needles of pain stung her scalp and tears sprang to her eyes.

''You leave her alone!'' Tyrone cried. He launched himself at Perkins, but Jane intercepted him when the man raised his hand to the child.

Clutching Tyrone tightly, Jane glared at the man. "You sorry no-good piece of trash."

"Shut up, old woman, or you'll be sorry."

He stuck his face close to Maude Ann's, and the foulness of his breath made her stomach roil. "I'm taking my boy. But first I'm gonna make sure you never steal nobody's kid again." He shoved the gun into her stomach and grinned maliciously.

"No! Please, not in front of the children," she begged.

He glanced at the kids clinging to Jane and crying hysterically. "You're right. Too many witnesses. We'll take a little walk."

"Everybody, out on the porch," he ordered, motioning with the gun for Jane and the kids to go first. "And no funny business. Remember, I got a gun in her back."

He swung Maude Ann around by her hair and shoved her toward the door so hard she fell to her knees. "Get up, bitch."

He grabbed her hair again, and she cried out when he used it to haul her to her feet.

On the way to the door he spotted the cell phone on the coffee table. Picking it up, he shot her a taunting grin. "I'll just take this. You won't be needing it. Now move."

"Where are you taking her? What're you going to do?" Jane demanded as he pushed Maude Ann past the group on the veranda and down the steps.

"Shut up! And you bunch stay put right there where I can see you."

Yanking on Maude Ann's hair, he kept her neck arched back at a painful angle and shoved and prodded her to his car. Keeping an wary eye on Jane and the kids, he got a roll of duct tape from the car trunk and used it to bind her wrists behind her back. Then, once again, he tugged her along by her hair over to the van and slashed all four tires with the hunting knife he wore in a scabbard on his belt.

Pausing, he eyed the utility wires going into the lodge. He waved his gun at the terrified group on the porch. "Timmy, go get in the car."

The boy whimpered and clung more tightly to Jane, but when his father shouted, "Now, you snivelin' little brat!" he released her and raced to obey, crying every step of the way.

Maude Ann wanted to object, but she knew doing so would only earn her more pain and wouldn't help Timothy at all.

"The rest of you stay right there. I'm warning you, if I have to hunt you down when I get back, you'll regret it. And don't get any ideas about using another phone to call for help, 'cause I'm cutting the wire." He poked the gun barrel into Maude Ann's back and prodded her around the side of the lodge, stopping at the back to cut the phone wire, then shoved her toward the woods.

Tears streamed down Maude Ann's face as they followed the winding path through the trees. Her knees were so wobbly she stumbled several times, earning herself vicious hair pulls and jabs with the gun barrel. She was so scared she barely felt the pain. This filthy, drug-crazed sadist was going to extract his revenge on her. He'd sworn in court when she'd testified at his trial that someday he would find her and kill her, and now he was going to make good his threat.

"Where does this path go?" Jim Perkins demanded, giving her hair another cruel pull.

Maude Ann gasped at the stinging pain in her scalp, and fresh tears stung her eyes, but she would not let herself cry out. "T-to a small cl-clearing."

"Good. That'll do."

The statement sent a chill down her spine.

The clearing was almost half a mile from the lodge, usually a good ten- to fifteen-minute walk, but they seemed to reach it in a fraction of that time.

"Well, now, ain't this nice," Perkins said, prodding her into the middle of the open area.

"Mr. Perkins, stop and think what you're doing. You'll never get away with this. The police will find you and you'll go to jail for the rest of your life. Is that what you want?"

"Shut up! And get down on your knees."

She had no choice. Her wobbly knees gave way beneath her when he pushed down on her shoulder.

"You're making a terrible mistake."

"I said *shut up!*"

Maude Ann yelped, then gagged, when he jerked her head back and stuffed a filthy rag into her mouth.

Her head fell forward and Perkins laughed, and she felt the cold metal of the gun barrel against the back of her head. "Say your prayers, bitch."

Trembling uncontrollably, Maude Ann squeezed her eyes shut and bowed her head. *Oh, Matt. Where are you?*

Chapter Fifteen

Matt drove the two-mile dirt road to the highway like a bat out of hell, sliding around the curves, ignoring the potholes and trailing a plume of dust that looked like a giant rooster tail. He was so upset he barely noticed the rusty old heap that passed him, heading toward the lodge. It was probably just someone going to rent one of John's skiffs for the day.

He knew he should have left before the kids got back. It was bad enough having to tell Maude Ann goodbye without facing all those hurt little faces.

Remembering, he muttered a curse. He hadn't expected the kids to be so upset. There had been no consoling them. He'd had no choice but to just get in his car and go.

Dammit, he hadn't done anything wrong. He'd been honest with Maude Ann. He'd made it clear from the start that he couldn't make any promises. They had no ties on him—

not Maudie, not Tyrone, not any of them. He had nothing to feel guilty about.

He brought the car to a stop at the highway intersection. There were no cars coming from either direction, but he just sat there, gripping the steering wheel so tightly his knuckles showed white. After a moment he rested his forehead on top of the steering wheel and closed his eyes.

But he did feel guilty. He felt like the lowest kind of louse. No matter how hard he tried, he couldn't erase from his mind the picture of Maude Ann and the kids clinging to one another, staring after him with tears streaming down their cheeks. The scene would stay with him for the rest of his days.

The hell of it was, he was going to miss them as much as they missed him. He missed them already.

Matt thought about his life before he'd been shot, the long hours, the violence and unspeakable horrors he'd seen, coming home to his empty town house. There had been women, but at most those times had amounted to the appeasement of a physical need and a few hours of companionship. So maybe he hadn't been happy, exactly, but he'd been content. Surely he would be again.

Then he thought about Maude Ann and her warmth, her giving spirit, that earthy sexiness she exuded, the love she lavished on him, and on everyone who mattered to her. He thought about the kids who were slowly blossoming under her care, about the laughter and the noisy chaos, about the skinned knees and the tears, the happiness, the affection, the sense of belonging, and the sheer joy of being alive that Maude Ann brought to everything she did, everything she touched. And he thought about how much he loved her, how she filled his heart and all the empty places in his soul.

Matt raised his head. He stared straight ahead at the pine

forest on the other side of the highway and tried to imagine his life without Maude Ann.

After a moment, his mouth folded into a firm line, and he turned the Jeep around and floored the accelerator.

He drove back to the lodge with even more urgency than when he'd left, all the while going over in his mind what he'd say to Maude Ann. He had hurt her deeply. He wouldn't blame her if she refused to take him back, but he intended to do everything he could to convince her. Hell, he'd get down on his knees and beg, if he had to.

When he drove around the last curve, pandemonium greeted him. "What the devil?"

Jane, Jennifer, Yolanda and Debbie stood in the road, jumping up and down and frantically waving their arms at him. He barely had time to screech to a stop before hitting them. When he got a good look at their faces, his gut clenched.

He was out of the Jeep in a flash. "What is it? What's wrong?" His gaze shot past Jane to the piece of junk in the drive. "What's Timothy doing in that car?"

"Matt! Thank God you came back!" Jane cried, grabbing his hands. He could feel her trembling. "Timothy's father burst in on us right after you left. He's going to take the boy," she sobbed.

Matt's gaze darted again to the old car. "Like hell he is. Where is he?"

"He took Maude Ann into the woods. Oh, Lordy, Matt, he has a gun! He means to kill her!"

Icy fear shot through Matt, but the red-hot rage that followed galvanized him into action. "Have you called 911?" he demanded, climbing back into the Jeep.

"We couldn't. He took the cell phone and cut the telephone line to the lodge."

Damn. And his car phone was still out of operation. Matt

quickly unlocked the glove box and removed his service revolver and a pair of handcuffs, hooking the latter on a belt loop of his jeans. "Which trail did he take?"

"The one to the clearing. But wait, Matt, that's not all!" Jane cried, trotting along beside him. The children scrambled after them. "As soon as Perkins disappeared into the woods with Maude Ann, Tyrone took off after them."

Matt halted. *"What?"*

Jane wrung her hands. "I couldn't stop him, Matt. I swear, I don't know what that child thinks he can do. He's going to get himself killed, too. That Perkins is a mean one, and I think he's high on something. He'd just as soon kill a child and a woman as step on an ant."

"All right, listen to me. You and the kids go get on the houseboat. Take it out of the cove as quickly as you can. When you get out into the lake, head for Brown's Marina and call the sheriff."

"The houseboat?" Jane paled. "Y-you want me to go out on the lake in a boat? I...I can't."

"Yes, you can. I know you're afraid of water, but it's up to you to keep these kids safe. A boat is the only way to get away from here, other than my car, but if Perkins hurts Maude Ann or Tyrone before I get to them, I'm going to need it."

"But...I don't know anything about boats."

"I do!" Yolanda said. "I can handle it, Matt. You showed me how."

"Good girl. Now get Timothy and hightail it down to the pier. Hurry!"

Before he'd finished speaking, Matt took off running. He raced around the lodge and across the backyard, skirting around the toolshed and garden, dodging trees and leaping over the kids' toys. Driven by fear, he ran flat-out, straining for all he was worth, his feet pounding the narrow path in rhythm with his thudding heart. Dear God, please let them be all right, he prayed. Don't let that slimeball hurt them. Please.

He was almost to the clearing when he heard the shot.

Matt's heart leapt into his throat. Then he heard Tyrone's shouted taunt and his panic eased fractionally.

It took every ounce of self-discipline he possessed not to charge into the clearing. Instead, he left the trail and crept through the woods to the perimeter. Flattening his back against a tree, Matt held his gun pointed skyward at his right shoulder and cautiously peered around the trunk.

The sight of Maude Ann on her knees in the middle of the clearing filled him with rage. Her hands were taped behind her back, and a cloth of some kind filled her mouth. But what tore at Matt's heart most was her defeated posture. She knelt with her shoulders slumped, her head hung as though all hope was gone. Her glorious hair had fallen forward around her face, leaving her tender nape exposed. That someone had brought this strong, valiant spirit to this was obscene.

Perkins stood a few feet away from her, spinning this way and that and screaming obscenities while trying to get a bead on Tyrone, who, from the shelter of the woods, pelted him with clods and sticks and a few colorful expletives of his own.

"Atta boy, Tyrone," Matt whispered. The kid darted from one tree to another, keeping up the barrage, never giving the gunman an opportunity to turn his attention on Maude Ann. Matt wanted to kiss him.

Tyrone popped out from behind a tree at the two-o'clock position from where Matt crouched. "Hey, stupid!" he hollered at Perkins, and threw a fist-size clod with the accuracy of a major-league pitcher, hitting the creep in the temple as he spun toward him. Perkins cursed and fired, and the bullet splintered a branch just inches above Tyrone's head.

Matt saw red and tore out into the clearing. "Drop the gun, Perkins!"

The man spun and fired, and Matt fell to the ground with a searing pain in his right leg.

"Matt! Matt!" Oblivious to the crazed gunman, Tyrone came screaming out of the woods just as Matt went down.

Perkins turned back and took aim at the boy.

"Go back! Go back!"

In the fall, Matt had dropped his gun, but he hadn't time to find it. He lurched to his feet and threw himself at the man, catching him with a shoulder butt to his kidneys as he fired.

The shot went wild, and Perkins screamed and went down flat on his face. Matt's momentum carried him down with him, and Perkins breath left his lungs in a loud *whoosh* as Matt landed on his back. While the man writhed and wheezed and struggled to suck air into his lungs, Matt pushed up to his knees and cuffed Perkins hands behind his back.

Tyrone skidded to a halt beside Matt. His eyes nearly popped out of his head when he spotted the blood pumping out of Matt's leg. "Oh, *man!* You're hit *bad.*"

"Yeah." Matt rolled off Perkins and pressed his hand to the wound, but blood continued to flow around his fingers. "I need something to tie around this."

"Here, use this!" Without hesitation, Tyrone whipped off the precious Dallas Cowboys T-shirt Matt had given him and handed it over. Tyrone loved that shirt, and his willingness to sacrifice it spoke volumes.

The instant Matt had the shirt tied over his wound he held his arm out to the boy. "Here, help me up. We have to see about Maudie."

Tyrone looked doubtful, but for once he obeyed without arguing. Agony streaked through Matt, but he clenched his jaw and struggled to his feet. Leaning on the boy, he reached down and relieved Perkins of his gun and knife, then hobbled over to Maude Ann.

She had struggled to her feet when Matt went down, but she was so shaken she could barely stand. As soon as he reached her, Matt jerked the filthy rag out of her mouth, hooked his free arm around her and pulled her tightly against his chest. Tyrone held on to both of them.

"Matt, oh, Matt," she sobbed.

"Are you all right?"

Too overcome to speak, she nodded against his chest.

"Thank God. Thank God." With his cheek against the top of her head, he squeezed his eyes shut and repeated the litany over and over.

For a while the three of them stood together in the middle of the clearing, as though isolated in their own world, Matt holding her close with one arm and Tyrone with the other. The boy had his arms wrapped around both adults. After a while, though, Maude Ann stirred and mumbled. "Please. My hands."

"Oh, sweetheart, I'm sorry. Here, Tyrone, take the creep's knife and cut that tape off. And be careful not to cut Miss Maudie."

As soon as she was free, Maude Ann put her arms around Matt's waist. Matt tried to hug her back, but the adrenaline rush that had carried him that far had faded, and loss of blood and shock were catching up with him. He was shaking so hard he could barely stay upright. "S-sorry, love, I…"

"Matt! *Matt!*" Maude Ann screamed and clutched him as he sagged in her arms, but she couldn't support his weight, and she sank to the ground with him.

Tyrone stood over them, his face ashen. "Is he dead?" he asked in a small, frightened voice.

"No!" Maude Ann snapped, but she wasn't sure until she pressed her finger to the side of his neck and felt a faint pulse. "No, he's just passed out."

Across the way, Perkins moaned and tried to sit up. Maude Ann and the boy jumped. She quickly pulled the pistol Matt had taken from him from the waistband of Matt's jeans and aimed it at the man.

"Tyrone, I want you to run as fast as you can to the lodge and tell Jane to take Matt's car and go find a telephone and call 911." She made a mental note to herself to locate Matt's gun when reinforcements arrived.

"Yes ma'am."

J.T. nearly rear-ended the Jeep when he came around the last bend. He slammed on the brakes, cursing. Why on earth was Matt's car sitting in the middle of the road with the driver's door open? He looked beyond the Jeep to the car in the driveway. "Jeez, what a wreck," he murmured. He'd never seen the car at the lodge before, and he wondered who owned it. And why were both driver-side doors standing open on it, too?

J.T. climbed from his car and looked around. Usually the kids came running out whenever he drove up. Where was everybody?

The question had no sooner gone through his mind when Tyrone burst out of the woods near the back corner of the property and came streaking across the side yard toward him, yelling and waving his arms. J.T. ran to meet the boy.

"Mr. Conway! Mr. Conway! M-Matt's been shot!"

"*What!*" J.T. dropped down on one knee before the boy and grasped his shoulders. Winded, Tyrone's chest heaved as he gasped for breath, and he had difficulty speaking. "Matt's been...sh-shot! He's bleedin' real ba-bad."

J.T.'s heart began to club against his ribs. Unconsciously, his hands tightened on the boy's shoulders. "Where is he? Who shot him?"

"T-Timothy's dad. He was gonna...gonna shoot Miz Maudie. They're in...in the c-clearing."

"Timothy's father, too?"

Tyrone nodded. "Matt cuffed 'im 'fore he passed out. Miz Maude, she's h-holding a...gun on him and tryin' to help Matt, too, but that...that Perkins, he's a real bad dude."

J.T. shot to his feet. "Okay, you go in and call 911 and I'll go help Matt and Maude."

"No, wait! We ain't got no phone. Tim's dad cut the wire."

"My cell phone." J.T. plucked the slim phone out of his shirt pocket and flipped it open. "You wait here for the sheriff and the paramedics and take them to the clearing," he instructed, punching in the number as he headed for the woods.

Relaying the information to the 911 operator as he ran down the path, J.T. silently prayed that they would be in time. It seemed to take him forever to reach the clearing, and all the while, a dozen horrifying thoughts ran through his mind. What if he was too late? What if Matt died? What if this Perkins guy somehow slipped out of the cuffs and overpowered Maude Ann? What if he'd already killed them both?

He had almost reached the clearing when he heard the first faint wail of sirens in the distance. Relief poured through him, but it turned to fear again when he heard Maude Ann shout, "Stay down and don't move! I'm warning you, I'll shoot!"

J.T. cursed and turned on more speed. He reached the clearing in time to see the handcuffed man awkwardly climb to his feet. He stood there for a second, sneering at Maude Ann. She was on her knees beside Matt, applying pressure to his wound with one hand and aiming a gun at Perkins with the other.

"You ain't got the guts to shoot me, bitch."

J.T. reached Maude Ann in three long strides and took the gun from her hand.

"Oh, J.T. Thank God you're here," she gasped, before turning all her attention to Matt.

Facing Perkins, J.T. fixed him with a narrow-eyed look and aimed the gun at his chest. "Maudie may be too soft-hearted to shoot you, Perkins, but I'm not. C'mon. Give me an excuse to pull this trigger."

"Who the hell are you?" Perkins blustered.

"I'm the brother of the man you just shot, the guy who is going to blow a hole through your sorry hide if you so much as twitch. Now lie down on your stomach and stay there."

Perkins had sense enough to know he meant business, and obeyed. J.T. dropped to his knees beside Matt, taking a position that kept the prone man in view. "How's he doing?"

"I don't know. He's lost a lot of blood."

He could see that. The cloth she was using to apply pressure was soaked through and blood covered her hands.

Maude Ann's gaze lifted to meet his, and the fear swimming in her eyes made his gut clench. "Oh, J.T., I can't lose him now," she said.

"You won't," he vowed. "We won't. I didn't wait all these years to find out I have brother just to have him die on me. Here, let me do that." J.T. took over from her and applied pressure to the wound in Matt's leg.

The sirens, which had been growing steadily louder, stopped abruptly, and he and Maude Ann exchanged a look of profound relief.

"You hang in there, Matt," J.T. urged in a fierce voice. "Help is on the way."

It was almost nine that evening before Matt was pronounced out of danger. It was later still before all the explanations were made, all the statements were taken and the children reassured and driven back to the lodge by Jane.

After Jane had called the sheriff, the marina owner had given her and the children a ride back to the lodge. They had arrived just as the paramedics emerged from the woods with Matt. Quickly commandeering his Jeep, Jane had loaded the frightened children and followed the ambulance to the hospital.

Now, only Maude Ann and J.T. were left. They stood, one on each side of Matt's bed, waiting for him to wake up. Maude Ann held his hand and stroked it over and over, unable to take her eyes off his beloved face even for an instant.

Finally Matt's eyes fluttered open. His gaze immediately zeroed in on Maude Ann. "Maudie. Are you all right?"

She squeezed his hand and smiled. "I'm fine, thanks to you and Tyrone."

"Perkins?"

"The slimeball's in jail."

At the sound of J.T.'s voice, Matt turned his head and looked at him. "What're you doing here?"

"Where else would I be when my brother has been shot?"

"If it hadn't been for J.T., we might none of us be here. He called for the ambulance, then arrived in the clearing just in time to stop Jim Perkins from getting away,'' Maude Ann informed Matt.

''I was more concerned that he would attack you again,'' J.T. said.

Matt looked at him for a long time, then nodded. ''Thanks. I'm indebted to you.''

''Damned right, you are,'' J.T. said, grinning. ''And I've figured out how you're going to repay me. I've already filed my story about Perkins's rampage, including my firsthand account of what happened during the time I was there, but when you feel up to it, I want an exclusive interview with you, Maudie, and Jane to get the details of the whole story. Plus, this time, I want follow-up interviews to chronicle your recovery.''

''I might have known.'' Matt shot him a disgruntled look, but after a moment he sighed and said grudgingly, ''All right, Conway. I guess I owe you that much.''

Shortly after that, J.T. left, and Maude Ann and Matt were alone for the first time since he had driven away earlier that afternoon. Had it really been only six hours? It seemed to her they had lived a lifetime in those few hours.

They gazed at each other in silence, both profoundly aware of how close they had come to disaster. Maude Ann stroked his hand and said softly, ''You came back.''

''Yeah. I had to.''

''If you hadn't…'' She closed her eyes and shuddered.

''Shh.'' He brought her hand to his mouth and placed a warm kiss against her palm. ''I did come back. That's all that matters.''

She nodded. ''Yes. You're right. Except that you were shot. Matt, I'm so sorry. If you hadn't come to my rescue…''

''I would have lost you, and I couldn't have survived that.'' He looked down at his bandaged leg. ''Can you believe it? Perkins's bullet hit just a inch from the first wound. The doctor told me when I woke up in ICU briefly that I can forget about going back to the street.''

"Don't listen to him. The doctors said that six months ago and you proved them wrong. You will again.''

"Honey, the first bullet did major damage. Sure, I got back enough mobility to pass the physical, but not a hundred percent. There's no way those mangled muscles and tendons are going to come back after a second assault.''

"Oh, Matt. I'm so sorry. I feel terrible.''

"Don't. I doesn't matter.''

"How can you say that after that scene this afternoon? We both know that your job means more to you than anything in the world.''

"Not anymore.'' He smiled at her skeptical expression. "Don't you want to know why I came back?''

"Why?''

"Because when it came down to the wire, I couldn't imagine living without you. I could imagine living without my job, but not you. So you see, I'd already decided to give it up before I took that bullet out in the clearing.''

"Oh, Matt.''

"I'm not much of a bargain, sweetheart. I don't have a job, and I'll probably have a limp for the rest of my life, and if it's possible, I want to adopt all the kids. But if you'll have me, I promise that I'll love you, and them, until the day I die.''

Maude Ann stared at him, not quite able to believe what she was hearing. "Are...are you saying...?''

"I'm asking. Will you marry me, Maude Ann?''

Tears welled up in her eyes and spilled over, one by one. "Oh, Matt,'' she said in a quavering voice. Too choked up to speak, she leaned forward and touched her mouth to his in a soft, lingering kiss, ripe with promise of love everlasting. When at last she raised her head, she looked deep into his eyes, and her lips curved in a misty smile. ''Of course I'll marry you, my darling.''

* * * * *

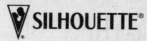

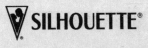

SILHOUETTE®

0806/23b

SPECIAL EDITION™

CABIN FEVER
by Karen Rose Smith

When handsome playboy Brad Vaughn and his beautiful secretary, Emily Stanton, are stranded in a blizzard in a cabin, it seems the inevitable will happen. But Emily plays for keeps and can she convince Brad that they share something really special?

DADDY PATROL
by Sharon De Vita

Sheriff and local coach Joe Marino received a letter from fatherless twin boys wanting to learn how to play baseball. Their mother, Mattie Maguire, warned them from getting too attached to Joe…but would she follow her own advice?

MIDNIGHT CRAVINGS
by Elizabeth Harbison

Sexy Chief of Police Dan Duvall was a man of few words. But then city-girl Josephine Ross strolled into his town and began stirring passions in him…

Don't miss out!
On sale from 18th August 2006

Available at WHSmith, Tesco, ASDA, Borders, Eason,
Sainsbury's and most bookshops

www.silhouette.co.uk

First comes love, then comes marriage...

That was Gracie's plan, anyway, at the ripe old age of fourteen. She loved eighteen-year-old heart throb Riley with a legendary desperation. Even now that she's all grown up, the locals in her sleepy town won't let her forget her youthful crush.

...but it's not as easy as it looks.

And now she's face-to-face with Riley at every turn. The one-time bad boy has come back seeking respectability – but the sparks that fly between them are anything but respectable! Gracie's determined to keep her distance, but when someone sets out to ruin both their reputations, the two discover that first love sometimes is better the second time around.

On sale 1st September 2006

www.millsandboon.co.uk

"I was fifteen when my mother finally told me the truth about my father. She didn't mean to. She meant to keep it a secret forever. If she'd succeeded it might have saved us all."

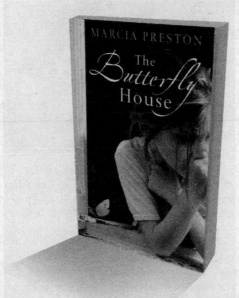

When a hauntingly familiar stranger knocks on Roberta Dutreau's door, she is compelled to begin a journey of self-discovery leading back to her childhood. But is she ready to know the truth about what happened to her, her best friend Cynthia and their mothers that tragic night ten years ago?

16th June 2006

"People look at me and they see this happy face, but inside I'm screaming. It's just that no-one hears me."

While breaking the news of Princess Diana's death to millions, reporter Isabel Murphy unravels on live television. *But Inside I'm Screaming* is the heart-rending tale of her struggle to regain the life that everyone thought she had.

21st July 2006